ROSE POINT

ROSE POINT

HER INSTRUMENTS: BOOK TWO

M. C. A. Hogarth

Rose Point
Her Instruments: Book 2

First edition, copyright 2013 by M.C.A. Hogarth

M. Hogarth
PMB 109
4522 West Village Dr.
Tampa, FL 33624

ISBN-13: 978-1492747871
ISBN-10: 1492747874

Cover art by [Artist]
[URL]

Designed and typeset by Catspaw DTP Services
http://www.catspawdtp.com/

TABLE OF CONTENTS

PART ONE: BLOOD

"And . . . orbit."

"Hi, pretty!" Irine added from her brother's lap.

Hirianthial paused as he stepped off the lift, eyes drawn by the world magnified on the *Earthrise's* old and cranky viewscreen: a tawny ball streaked in aquamarine and cobalt blue and swaddled in sullen gray clouds. He said, finally, "Promising."

"You're kidding, right?" Sascha said, and snorted. "Of course you are." He leaned back, resting a hand on Irine's head. "That is Kerayle."

"And Kerayle . . . ," Hirianthial began, trailing off.

"Is the world Reese asked us to come to," Kis'eh't offered from her station. The *Earthrise's* crowded bridge did not allow for many crew, and Kis'eh't's centauroid body took up more than one person's share; she kept her paws tucked close and eschewed the chair someone else might have used at the sensor station. "It's a colony. She thinks they might have useful things to trade since no other ship comes out here regularly yet."

"They don't even have a Well repeater in system," Sascha said. "Weather satellites, sure, but no station and no repeater. This is honest-to-angels middle of nowhere."

"It's the brave frontier," Kis'eh't said.

"It's something," Sascha said. "I just hope it's not 'too poor to be able to afford shipments.'"

Irine bumped her head against his hand. "Scratch behind my ears!"

Sascha obliged her. As Harat-Shariin activities went, it was one of the less outrageous the twins engaged in; initially Hirianthial had thought Reese's agitation in that regard exaggerated, but he had in fact happened on the twins at least twice while engaged in activities that would probably have made their captain's blood pressure spike. Hirianthial himself had no opinion on the matter. The Pelted had their own history with genetic engineering and reproductive challenges, and what the twins chose to do together was not his business. Unless they asked him to participate, which they did. As they always cheerfully accepted his rejections he did not allow the invitations to perturb him.

"So where is the captain?" he asked.

Sascha and Kis'eh't exchanged looks. Then the latter said, "She's in her cabin, doing accounting for the quarter."

Hirianthial said, "Ah." He glanced at the last chair. "I suppose I might use that?"

Sascha chuckled. "Because you're not volunteering to interrupt her? Be our guest."

Theresa "Reese" Eddings, captain of the registered Terran Merchant Ship *Earthrise*, was sitting in her room at its battered old desk in front of her display. Scowling at numbers was one of her least favorite activities, and yet she always seemed to be doing it. It didn't seem to matter whether she was in the black or the red, she always found a reason. Reese had been frowning at these for so long that her cheeks hurt; she stretched her mouth and rubbed her jaw, wincing as it popped.

An image formed in her head: drooping willows, their melancholic fronds dragged in a leaden gray stream. She looked down at the fuzzy round alien in her lap and said, "All right, all right, it's not *that* bad."

The sun tried to gild the leaves of the tree in her head. "Don't get too optimistic, though," she said. "Fleet gave us a hell of a lot of money, but the upgrades were expensive. And I don't want to dip into our savings." She paused to savor the word. She'd never had savings before. Squaring her shoulders, she said, "I want to protect our reserve, you know?"

The alien's neural fur turned a bright, cheery yellow. She smiled and petted him—it, technically, but she'd never been able to think of Allacazam as an it—and said, "We're going up, slowly. But I don't want to blow it. It would be easy to end up poor again."

The Flitzbe set fire to the tree in her head, added people running around it, screaming, and then threw in a rain of frogs for good measure. Who would have thought something more plant than animal and shaped like a furry ball could have a sense of humor? She hugged him with a grin. "Okay, maybe I'm being a little paranoid. But better that than spendthrift." Lifting her head, she frowned. "Come to think of it . . . the engine noise's changed, hasn't it?" She leaned over and hit the intercom. "Hey, bridge!"

Sascha's voice: "Hey, Boss!"

"Did we make it?" Reese asked.

"We did. Kerayle awaits."

"Great," Reese said. "There should only be one town. Set us down in walking distance. And I mean 'close enough not to give me panic attacks about being able to see the horizon clearly.' "

"Yes, ma'am."

Reese squinted. "Something wrong?"

"The view's a bit underwhelming," Sascha said. "It doesn't look like they get much traffic out here."

"That's fine," Reese said. "It means they'll be happy to see us."

"This is a pretty strange idea of 'happy to see us,'" Sascha opined as he followed her down the deserted lane in the middle of town. The tigraine had his shoulders hunched and his hands in his pockets, and his tail was low and twitchy.

Reese couldn't blame him. They'd been to a few too many worlds with too-quiet towns—well, two, but even one was too many when they'd both turned out to be pirate hang-outs. She said, "We surprised them, I guess."

"Oh, sure," Sascha said. "A merchant ship shooting through the atmosphere and touching down a mile away. Doesn't give them much time to prepare a welcome party."

Reese eyed him and he subsided, or at least, he pretended to.

Hirianthial, at least, was quiet. He was always quiet, though; it made her nervous, not knowing what he was thinking when she knew he could read their minds. Ever since she'd asked him to stay he'd been keeping out of her way. Maybe he knew she hadn't decided yet if she'd forgiven him for reaching into her head and pulling out her carefully unexamined fears.

Or worse, maybe there was no "maybe" about it. Maybe he'd read her mind about that too.

For most of her life, Reese had wondered about the mysterious Eldritch, had read about them, had occasionally dreamed of meeting one. They were tall and beautiful and tragic and courtly and their esper abilities were portrayed in all her romance novels as magical. She'd had no idea, once she'd been saddled with one, just how infuriating the species could be. Tall and beautiful did nothing but make her feel ungainly and inadequate. Tragic and courtly turned out to be a pain in the tail rather than romantic and pitiable. And the magical esper abilities, while fascinating in fiction, were frighteningly invasive in real life; the fact that Hirianthial had never intentionally read her mind only made it more frightening, because if he couldn't control it that was much worse than if he could and chose not to . . . wasn't it?

But for no reason she could really understand, she'd asked him to stay and he had, and the worst part was that he could probably tell *her* why she'd made that decision.

Blood in the soil, it was enough to make anyone crazy.

Still, she didn't object to him tagging along. If she could handle a pair of Harat-Shariin twins, she could handle one Eldritch, no matter how frustrating.

Besides, he was occasionally useful.

"There," he said now. "At the end of the lane."

Reese was about to ask if he'd sensed something but, no, there was someone stepping out of the house there: a Hinichi wolfine in a long shift, the fabric thin enough to show a silhouette of his lanky body. He was padding toward them now, so Reese stopped to let him approach. He was smiling, at least, and his ears were perked.

"Welcome," he said when he was close enough. "We weren't expecting traders." He inclined his head. "I'm Saul, assistant to the Kesh of Kerayle. Won't you come out of the sun, tell us what you've brought to sell?"

"We'd be glad to," Reese said. She glanced at the buildings. "It seems . . . quiet?"

"It's the heat of the day," Saul said. "Most people are napping."

"Oh!" Reese said, relieved. "Right. It is hot, isn't it." She offered her palm. "Reese Eddings, captain of the TMS *Earthrise*."

"Pleased," he said, covering her hand. "Let me show you to our place of business."

The wind in Kerayle did not cool, Hirianthial thought; it blew the heat onto one's cheeks and throat, with stinging spatters of dust as an encore. He found it pleasing after months of the dry cold on the *Earthrise*, but he could only imagine how Sascha was finding it with his dense pelt, and Reese had been born to controlled climates and was already sweating.

There would be water, he thought; no culture that lived in such heat would fail to offer. Nor was he disappointed; it was the first thing Saul presented to them in ritual courtesy, pouring from a sweating pitcher into a bowl by the door and handing it to Reese. He was glad the Hinichi had offered to her first; he suspected she would have balked at drinking from anything he'd sullied with his mouth. It had been several months since she'd asked him to stay, and he couldn't read her—couldn't tell her if her ambivalence was terror, dislike or something more positive but still nascent. And though she refused to believe it, he would never pull it from her mind without her permission. Since she wouldn't talk to him, he remained as confused on the matter as she was, and so he did his best to avoid provoking her.

There were days he wondered why he'd stayed . . . but he had gone through too much alongside the crew of the *Earthrise* to easily turn his back on them now.

Reese handed the bowl back to Saul, who gave it to Sascha. The Harat-Shar drank without reservations, wiping his mouth with the back of one hand, then passed the bowl to Hirianthial. It was shockingly cold to his fingers: when he drank, the water was so frigid it numbed his lips and throat. Even here, he thought, at the most remote corner of the Alliance, there was technology to shame his own species. Cold water from a pitcher left out in the heat . . .

The inside of the building was airy, with large windows and gauzy curtains lining the arches in and out of rooms in lieu of doors. The walls had been plastered and then painted a pale, cool blue and lined near the floor with brown and white tiles. It was beautiful, he thought, and far too comfortable to be natural. Some sort of climate control, most probably. The three of them considered the room while Saul went to see if his lord was awake.

"Quiet town," Sascha said to Reese.

"He said himself they're all sleeping," Reese said. "If I lived in this heat, I would too."

"Harat-Sharii's this hot and we don't all nap during the afternoon," Sascha said. "Most of us, maybe, but not all of us. There are at least a few people on the streets."

"Your hometown's a lot bigger than this one," Reese said.

"Maybe."

Reese eyed him, grew an aura to Hirianthial's sight of irritated sparks in copper and orange. "You might as well get it out before he gets back."

"This looks fishy, boss," Sascha said. "The last time we ended up in a town this sleepy we got harassed. A lot."

"I remember," Reese said, growing more agitated. Before her mood could develop, Hirianthial cleared his throat, drawing both their gazes: Sascha's dark amber, and Reese's startling blue.

"The odds of us earning such harassment three planets in a row are surely astronomical. And a new colony is bound to be smaller and quieter than one of the Alliance's

Core worlds."

"There, see?" Reese said. "Even the resident mind-reader thinks things are fine."

The Hinichi interrupted them, peeking into the room from the hall. "Won't you come with me? The Kesh is awake and eager to meet you."

The Kesh was a human man—not what Hirianthial had expected from a Pelted subordinate. A relatively young one, also, to be charged with the administration of a colony world. Hirianthial was not familiar with the procedure Alliance citizens were required to follow to earn the right to colonize a world, but he couldn't imagine it being a simple matter. Still, the man reclining on the pillows in the room the Hinichi led them to . . . he had an air of confidence entirely suited to someone accustomed to command. And the way he looked at Reese—Hirianthial didn't need to read the sleek red stealing through his aura to know just what he thought of her. The Kesh rose with alacrity, came to her with a long stride that set his robes swaying, and captured her hand to kiss it. Only her astonishment prevented her from jerking it away, he thought, and Sascha apparently agreed; the Harat-Shar was trying not to laugh.

"Captain Eddings of the *Earthrise*," the human said. "How wonderful to see a new face!"

"You know my name," she said, flustered, and glanced at Saul. "Ah . . . your assistant told you?"

"He's very able that way," the Kesh said with a grin. "Please, sit, sit. Saul! Have wine brought, the special vintage, for our guests! And fruit, fine cheeses! Let us entertain our guests!"

"That's . . ." Reese stopped, then said, "Ah . . . fine. Thanks."

Hirianthial found a pillow and had a seat. His last assignment had involved protecting Reese from slavers, a task he'd taken on his own recognizance. She hadn't requested his aid, nor even known he was qualified to give it . . . and had not, he thought, entirely appreciated it; she'd known little of violence before meeting him, and when they'd been acquainted he'd been made known to her as a doctor.

He was a doctor. But it was a profession he'd only lately learned. The bulk of his centuries had been spent with his hands on a sword.

So, while she'd signed him on as supercargo and not as a healer and certainly not as a bodyguard, he still felt responsible for her safety. And the Kesh, from the haze of his aura and the poem it wrote with his body language, was no killer or slaver or pirate. The only thing Reese had to fear from him was his advances . . . God and Lady save them both.

Finding a human in the Alliance struck Reese as strange despite knowing—obviously—that humans did venture out of Terra's solar system. But there were a lot more Pelted than humans. A lot more Pelted worlds than human. More Pelted were well-off enough to travel off-world, or work there; more Pelted worlds had economies sufficient to fielding space-born industry and commerce. It was why she'd left Sol to run cargo in Alliance space: far more lucrative, if you could make it work.

She'd been expecting to find seeing a fellow human more pleasant. Instead, it made her wary. She'd suffered a lot more cruelty and treachery from humans than she ever had from the Pelted. And if she wasn't mistaken, this man . . . liked her.

Liked her.

He didn't even know her yet! She snorted. His inter-est wouldn't live through that process, she was sure.

"So, Kesh—"

"Shamil, please. Do call me that."

"Uh, right. Shamil. I take it we're the first merchant crew to come by?"

"Absolutely," he said. "We've only been established five years! This is a true delight. And we're so far out . . . we were sure it would be at least a decade. Ah, Saul, thank you for bringing the tray. Join us. Captain, do introduce me?"

"My pilot, Sascha . . . and my supercargo, Hirianthial Sarel Jisiensire."

"Charmed," the Kesh said. He glanced at Hirianthial. "An albino?"

Reese's brows lifted. There were people who hadn't heard of the Eldritch? She glanced at Hirianthial, then said, "All of his people are like that."

"Very exotic," the Kesh said. His own skin was olivine, tanned dark but still several shades lighter than Reese's coffee-brown. He took a glass handed him by Saul and offered it to Reese. "Wine, captain?"

"Thanks," she said, wondering if it was what she was looking for. She sipped it and found it very sweet, almost syrupy—she was no connoisseur but she couldn't imagine this was so special a few Fleet officers several sectors away would bother talking about it. "Nice. So, Kesh—"

"Shamil."

"Shamil," she said, trying not to grimace. Did he have to look at her like that? It reminded her uncomfortably of the sort of looks Sascha and Irine exchanged as preludes to activities she didn't want anything to do with. "Maybe you could tell us what sorts of things your colony needs?"

"Straight to business," the Kesh lamented.

"I hate wasting a client's time."

"This is not wasted time!" he exclaimed. And laughed. "But you must forgive me, captain. We get so few visitors.

But very well, on to business." He leaned forward. "Do you have access to leather?"

The choked sound from her right was Sascha trying not to laugh. Reese thought her cheeks were burning and was glad her skin was dark enough to make that difficult to see. "Leather?"

"It sounds ridiculous," Saul said from beside the Kesh, "but we haven't found a native animal yet with a hide we can reliably skin."

"And what do you need leather for?" Reese asked, not really wanting to know the answer.

"Saddles," the Kesh said. "And bridles."

"Okay," Reese said, starting to rise. "Not my department—"

"For horses," Saul said. Both he and the Kesh stared at her as she paused. The Hinichi frowned, puzzled, and said, "What did you think?"

"It certainly wasn't horses," Sascha said for her. "Who in the worlds keeps horses these days?"

"We do," the Kesh said, fervent.

"You have horses?"

Reese glanced to her left. Hirianthial was always composed; he moved so little that she sometimes wondered if he'd spent his childhood pretending to be a statue. And he wasn't moving now. But something in the way he was sitting felt like avid interest: the slight lean, maybe? She could only tell he'd moved because his hair was moving slightly against his throat. For Hirianthial, that was positively broadcasting enthusiasm. But . . . horses?

"We have the best horses in all the known worlds," the Kesh said with relish. "You won't find their equal anywhere else, because we have made ourselves the stewards of all of Earth's most ancient breeds."

"And this you have done how?" Hirianthial asked.

Saul said, "There were gene repositories on Terra." He smiled. "The same sort of technologies that worked on us Pelted when we were trying to expand our gene pool during the Exodus work on animals."

Reese tried not to flinch.

"We started work before we left for Kerayle," the Kesh said. "And decanted on arrival. Our current herd is single breed only, but we intend to turn this world into the Alliance's equine preserve. Every breed we can rescue, we will eventually have here."

"But why?" Sascha asked, ears sagging. "Seriously? Horses? Who would buy them?"

"Do they have to be bought to be worth something?" Saul replied.

Reese cleared her throat. "So, leather. What else are you interested in? Maybe maintenance for your equipment? You must have some machinery that needs parts, if you're doing genetics work. I have general purpose electronics with me, along with perishables and trade goods. And maybe you have some . . . ah . . . horse preserve souvenirs? I could sell those."

"Where are these horses?" Hirianthial asked.

They all looked at him: Reese and Sascha because Hirianthial wasn't known for interrupting people or putting himself forward, and the colonists because they could answer the question.

"Are you interested in buying?" the Kesh asked.

"Are you interested in selling?" Hirianthial smiled. Just a faint smile, framed by that long fall of pale hair. He had a strand of gems on one side, Reese noticed, one in front where it could be seen. Rubies, she wondered? Did the Kesh notice? His next words sounded cautiously intrigued.

"That depends on the buyer."

"Then perhaps I should see the stock," Hirianthial said.

"I am not shipping horses anywhere," Reese interrupted, irritated.

Hirianthial said to her, "Never fear, lady. I am only looking." He glanced at the Kesh. "Yes?"

"Yes," the Kesh said, grinning. "And I am talking to the . . . lady."

Great, he'd passed the term on to this man, and if she hated 'lady' from Hirianthial that didn't cover how she felt about it from strangers.

"I can show him to the pasture," Saul said, rising. "If you will excuse us, Kesh."

"By all means."

"Maybe I should go with you," Sascha said. "I'm kind of curious about this now. You know. Animals being preserved with technology that rescued the rest of us."

"I'd be pleased by your company." Hirianthial stood. "By your leave, lady."

"Yes, fine, go," Reese said. "Don't hit your head on a rock somewhere."

"I shall endeavor to avoid it."

The Kesh watched them go, then lifted his brows. "More wine, lady?"

Reese sighed. "Sure. But don't get any ideas."

He laughed. "I promise I shall guard your honor. Particularly since I don't want to answer to your confederates for slighting it."

"They aren't my chaperones," Reese growled.

The Kesh grinned. "Tell them that."

"So really," Sascha said to Saul. "Horses?"

They were in front of Hirianthial, walking down a dusty lane away from the buildings, toward the sere and rugged landscape that met the horizon in a rumple of low red mountains.

"Sure," the Hinichi said with a grin Hirianthial could hear in his voice. "Why not?"

"Don't they hate the smell of you?" Sascha asked, skeptical. "You're part wolf."

"And part human," Saul said. "They came out of a vat, alet, and the only thing they associate with my smell is food and a curry comb. They trust me. What I really want to know . . ." He looked over his shoulder at Hirianthial, "is why you've got an Eldritch with you."

Sascha snorted. "What, not confused about the albino?"

"The Kesh isn't fond of the Alliance's company," Saul said, tail swishing a little. Agitation, Hirianthial judged, given the sudden cold fog seeping through the wolfine's aura. "He and the others try to stay insulated from it. It's why they decided to leave for such a remote location."

"They could have stayed on Earth," Sascha said. "That's remote."

Saul snorted. "Earth. Earth is the focus of too much Pelted attention to be remote, no matter where it's located." He sighed. "And now you're about to ask what I'm doing here. And the answer is . . . maybe some of us are tired of the Alliance culture too." He looked out over the landscape. "Starting somewhere fresh, somewhere a little less . . . connected . . . to everything else . . . it's nice to deal with local issues. Not to have to worry about intergalactic politics when making decisions that you'd think would only affect yourself. It's nice to just *be* yourself, and not some group." He laughed. "Do you know, these people know as little about the Hinichi as they do about Eldritch?"

"That takes some doing, given that Hinichi are everywhere and Eldritch are just about nowhere," Sascha said, dry.

"Believe it or not," Saul said. "All they cared about was whether I cared about horses, and if I could do something useful." He grinned. "For once, I'm not the token Christian, the token Pelted, the token loyal, honorable and stoic wolfine. I'm just Saul. Who assists the Kesh and helps with the herd."

Sascha eyed him.

"Granted, I'm still all those other things too," Saul said. "But they don't define me here." He glanced over his shoulder at Hirianthial. "You understand, don't you. I'm sure you're tired of being the token mystery, the token esper, the token exotic alien."

Hirianthial cleared his throat. "There have been moments."

Sascha shook his head. "For Hirianthial? Moments, yeah. Probably all of them." He sighed. "Running from your labels doesn't work, though."

"It did here," Saul said. "Come. The path's this way."

The wolfine led them off the road and through the brush, up hills scumbled with dry yellow brush and low, spindly shrubs. Sascha fell back to pace Hirianthial, leaving the Hinichi in the lead, his body silhouetted by the bright sun.

"You believing any of this?" Sascha said after they'd scrambled up part of the trail.

"About why they're here?" Hirianthial answered. He considered. "Why wouldn't I?"

Sascha made a face, tail twitching. "Running doesn't solve anything."

"That depends on which direction you run," Hirianthial said, and waited for the inevitable laugh, which he was pleased to receive.

"You . . . you set me up for that one, didn't you." Sascha held up his hands, grinning. "No, wait. You're about to say 'you set yourself up. I just helped show you the way.'"

"Something like that," Hirianthial allowed, amused.

Against his neck, through the hair dangle the crew had made him, he could feel the laughter of Sascha's twin, and beneath it Sascha's own memories of fixing the *Earthrise's* Well drive, impressions woven into the knotted strand by a very normal magic. For as much as he'd allowed them to know him . . . they knew him very well indeed.

"You really feel like our token exotic alien?" Sascha asked after a moment, his voice low.

Hirianthial glanced at him, at the spotted fur on the mostly humanoid face, and the eyes that could be merry and serious by turns. "Do you really feel like our token Harat-Shariin hedonist?"

Sascha was silent, toiling alongside him in the heat. Then he smiled. "Can't help that. I *am* a Harat-Shariin hedonist."

"Sometimes," Hirianthial said.

"Sometimes," Sascha said.

As they approached the top of the hill, Hirianthial added, "Thank you."

"For . . . ?"

"For not assuming I pulled any of that out of your mind."

Sascha snorted. "Is she getting to you, still?"

He considered his words. "She asked me to stay, but she's avoided me ever since. I must imagine the incident still distresses her."

"Maybe," Sascha said. "She doesn't know how to let a thing go, good or bad. That's one of her endearing qualities." He grinned. "But no. Unlike Reese, I don't care if you go rooting through my thoughts. But if you don't like what you see there, that's your problem, not mine." He stopped alongside Saul, "So how far—oh."

Over the hill was a pasture, and in the pasture were horses.

Hirianthial had grown up with horses. For centuries, in

fact, he had overseen the breeding of horses, had fretted over the crossing of lines, had made expensive and delicate arrangements for stud duties with other Houses who were also jealous of the health and bloodlines of their dwindling herds. On his world, one could walk or ride, either astride or in a horse-drawn carriage: there was no other form of transportation.

But it had not been planned so. They'd brought horses with them from Earth for pleasure, not for need; there had only been a few, not the numbers necessary for a healthy genepool. Not all the most careful husbandry in the worlds had been able to save their animals from the inevitable byproducts of inbreeding. The resulting beasts were all very similar, of delicate health, and had muddy and disappointing conformation. And most of them were some shade of brown.

In all his life, and he had lived almost seven hundred years of it, Hirianthial had never seen creatures as magnificent as the ones grazing on the incongruously lush grass in the field beneath them: dappled gray and sleek black, gorgeous bays with their dark socks, chestnuts so bright a red they shone like fire beneath Kerayle's brassy sun. They were all, to the last individual, beautiful.

Sascha and Saul were both staring at him. The latter was grinning. "Ah . . . a man who understands a horse."

Sascha, more uncertain, asked, "Are you all right?"

"Very much so," Hirianthial said. "Can we come closer?"

Saul grinned. "Even better . . . would you like to ride? If you're interested. I could take you to see our prize."

"Something finer than this?" Hirianthial said, brows lifting.

"Oh yes."

"Count me out!" Sascha exclaimed. "I'm not getting on one of those things. They look smart enough to pitch me off."

The Hinichi laughed. "If you recognize that, you have all the instincts of a budding horseman—"

"—no," Sascha said firmly. "I will stand at the fence and watch."

"They might come over and nibble you," Saul said, grinning.

"As long as they don't bite—wait, how big are their mouths?" Sascha flicked his ears back. "Are you serious about the nibbling? You're teasing, aren't you."

"A little," Saul said, slapping him on the shoulder. "Come on. I'll introduce you to the Lead Mare."

"They have titles," Sascha muttered.

"They have names too," the wolfine said. "Like people."

Hirianthial hid his grin and followed.

"You have a laboratory," Reese said, staring down into the facility from the metal catwalk.

Behind her the Kesh laughed. "Did you think we used magic to make the horses, Captain?"

Reese folded her arms over her ribbed vest and tried not to scowl. At least he'd addressed her correctly. "No, of course not. It's just that . . . you have all of a dozen buildings—"

"More like thirty," he said mildly.

"It's not much of a town," Reese continued, ignoring him. "So finding a state of the art genetics facility in the middle of it is a bit of a surprise."

"It's what we do," the Kesh said, stepping up beside her. Beneath them a handful of people were working. They were mostly human, but she could see at least one Pelted: an Aera, from the length of the ears. Reese frowned. The Aera were nomads by inclination and finding one in a town was strange. Maybe the Aera had chosen the colony life because it was a little like wandering, to be so far from everything. "We are bringing something back to life here, Captain Eddings. Something that was left for dead—" He paused, shook his head. "No. Something that was neglected. Discarded until it came to ruin, but it was only sleeping until we returned for it. And we shall be proper stewards to it now. Do you see?" He rested his hands on the rail. "Some things are left in the past, and should be. Others are left behind, and should be retrieved."

"And . . . you've decided that horses needed retrieval," Reese said, wondering why the conversation was making her uneasy. She had come to distrust passion, maybe. "I guess horses are harmless enough." When he glanced at her, she said, "It's not like you're . . . I don't know. Cloning ancient megalomaniacal human warlords or something."

He snorted. "You have an active imagination, captain."

"Or a paranoid disposition," Reese muttered. She watched the activity below them. "You don't seem to have many people."

"Many of them are with the horses."

Something in the way he said that . . . she glanced at him. "You've got so many already?"

"We do," he said. "Come, let us continue the tour."

Definitely something going on there, she thought, and followed him. "So, these horses . . . I'm guessing you ride them, since you talked about saddles and bridles."

"Of course."

"Is that where your missing people are?" she asked.

He turned. "They're not *missing*."

Holding up her hands, Reese said, "I wasn't implying anything! Just . . . this doesn't seem a big staff for an operation this size. You know. Repopulating the universe's horse . . . ah . . .population."

"You seem skeptical," he said. "Not much of an

animal-lover, captain?"

"I live on a ship," Reese answered. "Fur clogs ducts. I have enough trouble with the crew shedding without adding things that aren't smart enough to help me do maintenance."

"Ah," he said. "Well, you'll have noticed the heat? Most of us sleep through it. We run on reduced numbers during the afternoon."

"Right," Reese said. "So, you were saying about textiles?"

"Ah! Yes."

Reese followed him down the stairs, but she glanced one more time at the lab as they left it. Far be it from her to criticize any person's lifelong dream—God knew her own family had—but she was trying to imagine a planetary pre-serve for a single species. Strange motivation. "I guess you like to ride," she said, more to herself than to him.

"Captain Eddings," the Kesh said. "There is no freedom like the freedom on the back of a horse."

"So, alet," Saul said. "Does it feel good to be back?"

Hirianthial glanced at the wolfine, smiling a little. "Is it so obvious?"

"To me? Absolutely." Saul chuckled. "You don't ride like an amateur. And as little as I know about Eldritch, I still know something. You're probably older than my great-grandparents. For all I know, you've been riding horses longer than I've been alive."

Hirianthial looked up at a sky brittle with glare and broad over the rumpled hills. He'd left his homeworld, gone through the Alliance's medical schools, practiced as a healer, left off that practice to become his Queen's spy and was now tagging along with a merchant captain, and though all of that had been barely a fraction of his life it was still longer than Saul had been alive. He said, "It would perhaps be more accurate to say it's been that long since I've ridden."

Saul's ears flicked back. His chuckle this time was a touch huskier, and his aura fluttered with shadows: rue, perhaps, like a murder of crows passing overhead. "Well. Then you're long past due."

Hirianthial looked between the mare's ears, drew in the familiar smell of leather and horse sweat, the unfamiliar perfume of alien flowers dried on the stem by the pitiless heat. "On that count, you are entirely correct, alet. May I say though—"

"Yes?" Saul looked over at him.

"I have never ridden an animal of this quality," Hirianthial said. "And I am honored to do so." He glanced at the Hinichi. "You will not sell?"

Saul said nothing, riding alongside with his face lifted to the sun and his eyes narrowed nearly to slits. After a moment, he said, "Right now, we're not selling. As far as any askers are concerned. But the right buyer . . ." He glanced at Hirianthial. "You don't want a riding animal. For pleasure."

Had his avarice been that blatant? But then, he had never imagined that Earth would have retained such genetic treasure. "I have perhaps bred horses myself in the past."

"Stud fees—"

"I fear your studs would be wasted on our mares," Hirianthial said.

"Ah." Saul nodded. "I should have known . . . no one who lives as long as an Eldritch can afford to think in the short term, ah?"

Hirianthial said, "Alet—I do not think that anyone can afford to think in the short term. No matter their lifespan."

"Truth." Saul chuckled. "The Kesh might be open to

negotiation. I'll talk to him about it."

"Thank you," Hirianthial said, inclining his head.

"And now . . . come! Our greatest jewel likes the high ground!" With a cluck, Saul urged his mare up a trail, and Hirianthial followed. His neat-footed mare needed little direction; she read his intentions in a way none of the less intelligent animals he'd worked with at home could have duplicated. It was a unity close to pain, to feel so attuned to another creature: he could even sense her aura, something he'd never noticed at home. Was it that these horses were not so burdened by their genetic faults, and so their minds shone clearer?

"There!" Saul exclaimed with an exultant laugh. He rose in the saddle and whistled, his mount side-stepping under him.

Hirianthial drew alongside him, looking out over a small field, and there at its edge was a streak of white, running for the sheer joy of it, like the wind made manifest, poured into flesh.

"Kumiss!" Saul said. "Here he comes . . . in his own sweet time, of course. Just to make sure we know he's coming because he wants to, not at our beck."

And he was, slowing as he approached, calling to the mares, who whuffed their lack of interest.

"Oh, alet," Hirianthial whispered. "A king among stallions, surely."

"We think so," Saul said, grinning.

"Is he gentled?"

The Hinich made a so-so gesture. "He came out of a vat like the rest of them, so he's used to being handled. But he's got a personality of his own. He doesn't tolerate much."

Hirianthial slid off his mare, handing the reins absently to Saul, and cautiously approached the jewel in the grass. Such a proud, clean head, with small ears. And the eyes:

dark, pellucid and very definitely regarding him. His aura trailed off him like an extension of his bright mane: wild and smelling of high fields and sunlight.

The Eldritch was never sure at what point he began touching that sun-warmed skin, but he found his brow resting against the muscled neck and felt the nudge of a curious muzzle.

"Well, look at that," Saul said, hushed. "He likes you."

"And I am honored," Hirianthial murmured, meaning it. And addressed himself to that aura, asking permission and receiving it he knew not how, but he pulled himself on the stallion's back and whispered: *Run!*

Could a horse laugh? Kumiss bolted and took him along, took him on purpose. Hirianthial bent close to his neck, white mane wrapped in white hands, and the wind stung water from his eyes and whipped his hair back from his temples. And for an endless breath, there was nothing for him but the feel of the barrel rising and falling between his legs, the drum of hoofbeats impossibly swift, and the banner of the aura that streamed into his and carried all his careworn memories away.

The stallion slowed to a trot and then a walk, strolling back to Saul with head high. He stopped to allow Hirianthial to dismount and nuzzled the Eldritch, lipping the edge of his tunic.

"I . . . have never seen anything, anything like that," Saul breathed.

"He is a peerless individual," Hirianthial agreed, setting his hand on the stallion's withers and then letting it fall away. "Ah, Saul. What a gift—"

But the Hinichi wasn't looking at him. Was in fact looking past him, and was still doing so when an arrow bit his thigh and his mare shied. The horse Hirianthial had been riding bolted down the trail, and Saul fought to keep his from following. Another arrow smacked the ground in front of his mare's hooves and she reared; this time not all his frantic commands kept her from racing after her herdmate.

Hirianthial reached for a sword and discovered he didn't have one anymore, felt a moment's intense disorientation. A world where people were attacked with arrows was one where he had a sword and a duty to use it. He flung himself around as a group of riders pounded toward them. Eight . . . ten . . . twelve of them, armed. How could a colony this young have criminals already? He could have handled five or six of them on his own, but not double that number. If Saul could bring help. . . .

He asked forgiveness for the insult and leaped onto Kumiss. The stallion spun and then fled . . . in the opposite direction.

Follow me, he commanded the bandits, his outrage and worry blowing into the words, spreading them open like an explosion. He had no idea how badly wounded Saul had been, nor whether he had the training or weaponry to take on twelve opponents. He had to distract them until the Hinichi was out of reach. *Follow me!*

Some of them were trying to separate from the group. Looking over his shoulder, furiously shaking the hair out of his face, he willed them to return. *Look at me*, he urged them. *Look at the stallion I'm on. This is what you want.* His hand curled into a fist as Kumiss raced away. *Come and get us!*

For a heartbeat he thought he'd failed . . .

And then they drew together and gave chase.

"Now," he whispered to Kumiss, letting the wind tear away the words—he knew the stallion could hear them in their commingled auras, feel it as a reckless bravado, as a challenge to their pursuit—"Now, we shall be canny and swift. Show them your heels!"

The one thing he feared did not come to pass: no arrows sang past them. He frowned as he bent close over Kumiss's neck. They had shot at Saul, not at the mare, though crippling the mare would have afforded a better chance at preventing the Hinichi from summoning help. And . . . they had used *arrows*. Who in the Alliance used arrows—other than the Eldritch, with their impoverished technological base? Who were these people?

Their weapons might be poor, but their mounts were not. Hirianthial let Kumiss choose their course; they couldn't outrun the raiders, so their only hope of escape involved the stallion knowing the terrain better than they did. As the horse fled up remote trails over the hills, Hirianthial allowed himself to believe they might have a chance, and this he did until he felt the auras billowing into his consciousness from ahead of them.

"Back!" he cried. "Back—"

But it was too late. More riders poured from the trail above them, and Kumiss caviled, turned . . . and was confronted by their pursuers. Mostly human, but a scattering of Pelted faces—he couldn't tell species with their heads wrapped against the sun. Now that they'd slowed, several of them had raised their short bows again.

Hirianthial slid off Kumiss's back, heard the saw of arrow against bowstring. No one loosed, though.

"Look at this," someone said with a laugh. "We came for one stud and found two."

Laughter. He did not like the way it felt in his mind: like knives, and the minds intent on his too focused by far. Now that they were close he could tell that they wanted Kumiss . . . and he didn't think they'd be inclined to leave him alive to warn the Kesh where his prize stallion had gone.

His hand ached for a sword, and there was no sword.

There was, however, a knife.

Fifteen riders, and just one of him.

"Not a human?" one of them said.

"No," said the first, coming closer. "So he's not one of us, for all he rides like one." He grinned. "A foreigner. The Rekesh will like that."

A second man laughed. "The Rekesh will like him for more than his foreignness."

They spoke Universal. They spoke of 'us.' With instincts honed by centuries of heartbreak and betrayal, Hirianthial knew he had somehow stumbled onto a family quarrel. And there was no quarrel as vicious as the one between family.

His knife was in his boot. He flexed his fingers.

"We'll have to take him with us," the second man said. "A matched pair for the Rekesh. White stallion, white man."

"White stallion, white mare, you mean," the first said, and grinned at Hirianthial. "Come along quietly, prize. You don't make trouble for us, we won't bruise up your pretty hide."

Reese had freed him, God and Lady bless her . . . had taken him on as supercargo when she'd learned that hiring him as a doctor would have entailed swearing the ethical oaths that barred him from harming others. She hadn't liked his admission that he would treat his enemies as well as his friends, given the quality and quantity of the enemies she'd observed him to have thus far.

The raiders came closer, closer . . . one more step. Hirianthial drew the knife and gave himself to the fight, to instincts older than any of the people who sought him. He did not hold back.

"Fine, aren't they?" the Kesh said as Reese studied the blankets in the small outdoor market that had started coming together after the worst of the afternoon heat had passed.

"They are pretty," she said, fingering the tassels. "A little small, though. Are they for babies?"

"For the backs of horses, actually," the Kesh said, much to Reese's lack of surprise. She tried not to be peevish at how horse-crazy these people were. "We weave and dye them ourselves, though. We could do larger ones, if you think them marketable."

Reese frowned at the blanket. It had the inevitable horses running in stylized rows along the edges. "Did you really come out here with no plan?"

"Captain?"

"A plan," she continued. "Most colonies have an idea of what they're hoping to export, and get that up and running as soon as possible on landing so that when merchant traffic starts coming through, they'll have something to sell to finance the expansion of their colony. As far as I can tell, you don't have anything you've thought of selling. You came here to make horses and . . . what? Close off contact entirely with the Alliance?"

"Not precisely." The Kesh leaned forward to stroke the tassel she'd just released. He was a little too close to her for comfort, close enough for his shoulder to brush hers . . . but he didn't seem to notice her at all. "But to minimize contact with it, certainly. We just didn't realize . . ."

"Realize what?" Reese asked, trying for a calmer tone.

He smiled, a slight smile on long lips. "It is hard to pull free from one's family. Have you noticed, Captain?"

"Maybe," she muttered.

"The Pelted know that lesson," the Kesh continued, his eyes distant. They were hazel, she thought: greenish in the light. "They learned it from us, didn't they? We should know better, you and I, Captain. Humanity could write volumes on the difficulties of isolation, and the dangers of turning one's back on society."

This sounded a lot more serious than a lack of an import/export plan. It sounded, in fact, like nothing she wanted to be involved in. Perhaps she should just ask him about the liquor directly and leave—

"REESE!"

Her shoulders tensed and her head flew up, the beads at the end of her braids smacking her jaw. Sascha was running down the street, leading . . . a horse? A horse with a body on it?

"Saul!" the Kesh cried, and rushed toward the Harat-Shar. Reese followed, heart racing. Had they managed to find trouble *here*, in the middle of nowhere?

"Sascha!" she said. "Pirates??"

"Not unless pirates use arrows," he said, panting. He stumbled to a halt as the Kesh went to the horse, put his arms around Saul's slumped body and slowly drew it off. The Hinichi was barely conscious, and his leg was drenched in blood, grown sticky and dusty.

"Sascha," Reese said, her stomach falling. "Where's Hirianthial?"

"I don't know," he said. He looked at the Kesh. "They went riding and he never came back. It was at least two hours ago that they left . . ."

"Kumiss," the Hinichi whispered.

The Kesh froze. "No."

"Kumiss—"

"Raiders!" the Kesh cried. He hauled his man up into his arms and said to Reese, "I need to take him to a healer. Then we can talk."

"Raiders?" Sascha asked, bewildered. "Here? Where'd they come from?"

"We're following you," Reese said. "You can tell us what the bleeding soil this is about on the way. And you can start with where my crewman is."

"If we're lucky, the raiders took him with Kumiss," the Kesh said. "If we're not . . ." He glanced at her. "Then he's dead on the slopes somewhere."

"If he's dead," Reese said. "I'll kill you myself."

"Boss," Sascha began.

"Captain—"

"No," Reese growled. "No excuses. This is your damned colony. It's your responsibility not to have raiders. Raiders with . . . with arrows, for soil's sake! Arrows? Arrows! Who the hell uses arrows anymore?"

The Kesh was striding down the street with Saul over his shoulders. "It's a long story—"

"So start talking!"

"Half the colony defected," he said bluntly.

Reese missed a step, then scurried to catch up with him. "What?"

"We came here to be nomads, to follow the herds," the Kesh said. "The deal was that we'd have one town and we'd take turns living in it, doing the work. But when we got here, there was an . . . argument. About the division of labor."

"So half of you took off for the hills and . . . what? Started killing the other half?" Reese demanded, aghast.

"Not killing. Stealing." The Kesh sighed. "They steal the horses as we make them. Get that door, please, Captain."

Reese waved the door open for him and he disappeared inside. She stopped at the threshold, heart beating wildly. When Sascha joined her, she said, "We did not spring Hirianthial from jail, flee all over the Alliance with pirates on our tail, save him from that crystal mind-sickness and then risk him arresting a drug lord just so he could die on a backwater colony world because the natives are having a fight about who gets to play with the horses and who has to work like normal people."

Sascha rested a hand on her shoulder, and after a moment she set hers on his. She was shaking; she hadn't realized it until he touched her.

"We'll find him, Boss," he said. "He's too tough to die easy."

"You sure of that?" she asked. "He seems pretty frail to me."

He snorted. "Then you haven't been paying attention."

Hirianthial woke when his body hit the ground. It had been centuries since he'd fallen off a horse, so he thought he could be forgiven his disorientation. Unlike his more youthful self, however, he was bound . . . and gagged. The knots were unforgiving, and had been tied so zealously they seemed more an attempt at bondage than detainment.

If he wasn't mistaken, he also had a cracked rib. Maybe two? They had beaten him severely when they'd finally taken him down. That they hadn't slain him outright was a minor miracle, since he'd had no such compunctions. He'd left at least four dead bodies that he was sure of, and with no remorse that he could discern. The fine mores he'd learned in ethics courses in civilized universities had no place among barbarians, and he did not miss them.

His captors were talking now, and not in Universal. Ordinarily he would never have considered reading their minds, but his options were limited and he needed information.

/". . . should just leave him here. If we take him with us, we have to feed him and keep him from killing anyone else."/

/"Are you crazy? If we leave him here, he'll find some way to return to them—"/

/"So kill him and be done with it."/

/"Then they'll find the damn body. Unless you want to

ride back to the herd and leave it there? They're probably already on their way."/

/"Well I don't want to carry him. What if he wakes up and finds some way to kill *me*? You keep carrying him."/

/"My horse is tired."/

Hirianthial tried not to find the situation humorous; while they argued he dared to open his eyes, just enough to look. The bandits were grouped around him, and all the horses were there if he was counting correctly—not something he was entirely sure of, given the distraction of his injuries—and some of them were being led, not ridden. There were bodies slumped in those saddles and, he saw, tied there, if less creatively than he'd been.

Kumiss was also present, with a rope around his neck. His aura blazed like the corona of a sun: bright flares of impatience and indignation, more powerful than any of the humanoids. If there was a way for him to reach the stallion, they could probably make another attempt at escape . . .

But one of his captors was hauling him up onto his horse. He thought about pitching himself over the other side, but didn't think his ribs would appreciate the impact.

"/This is for hell,/" the one gripping Hirianthial's wrists said, and with that hold forced far too much of his mind onto the Eldritch's: anger, disgust, a sweat-streaked miasma of violence and fear. "/We should just push the body over the nearest cliff."/

/"He's for the Rekesh,"/ said the one Hirianthial decided was the leader of this particular party. /"He can make the judgment, and the kill."/

As his newest captor shifted in the saddle, something pressed against Hirianthial's ribcage. He made no noise, but the man holding him down felt the change in tension anyway. /"He's awake!"/

/"Is he?"/ The leader urged his horse closer and balled his fist in Hirianthial's hair, forcing his face up. "So, the butcher awakes. Well, you will lie quiet, mare, or the beating we gave you will be nothing compared to the beating we will. Understood?"

Hirianthial met his eyes and said nothing. When the raider shook his head by the hair, he closed his eyes and suffered it, but held his silence.

"I will assume that's a 'yes,'" the raider said. "Because you don't want to know what 'no' will feel like." He glanced at Hirianthial's captor and said, /"Any wrong move, you say so."/

/"Any wrong move and I might already be dead!"/

The raider was still; then with a movement so abrupt Hirianthial had no chance to defend against it, punched the Eldritch in the ribs. The world swam with black smears that grew despite his urgent attempts to evade them. As he lost consciousness, he felt more than heard the greasy satisfaction of the bandit leader: /"There. Solved your problem. Let's go, before they catch up."/

"You're telling me they've stolen a horse," Reese said over the table.

"Not just 'a horse,' captain," the Kesh said, agitated. "Our prime stud."

"A horse," Reese repeated. "They shot your assistant and stole my crewman over a *horse*?" At his expression, she held out her hands. "Look, never mind why. If the animal's so important, tell me you can find it."

"We do have him chipped," the Kesh said. "And we can follow him. We're assembling a party now."

"All right, good," Reese said. "I'm going with you."

"Boss, are you sure—"

"I'm going with them," she said to Sascha. "I've been

rescuing him for most of a year, dammit, I'm not going to stop now."

"Of course you can come, Captain," the Kesh said. "The party's assembling outside."

Reese jogged after him, expecting dangerous-looking men and women with sparrows and palmers. She'd never seen Alliance riot-gear, but she had seen Fleet in the middle of a fight, so she was familiar with at least some of the high-tech toys. To find the search party throwing saddles onto the backs of horses—"You have got to be joking. You're going to *ride* after them? Don't you people have something that can fly?"

"Not over the kind of terrain the raiders are heading for," the Kesh said. "Do you, Captain?"

"If you could give us the signal we're supposed to look for—" Reese began.

". . . and then what?" Sascha said behind her. "We hover over it and drop out of the cargo hold in our Fleet-issued parachutes?" When she whipped around to look at him, he said, "Boss, we can't park in those hills. The *Earthrise* might be small by cargo-running standards, but she's still big enough to need a proper landing field. And if we follow you, they're going to know we're chasing them. They might run into some cave somewhere. Do you really want to chase Hirianthial into a cave system? With our luck?"

Reese grimaced. "No. But I don't know how to ride a horse—"

"Don't worry, Captain," the Kesh said. "We'll teach you on the way. But there's no time to lose."

"Right," she said, pained. "Fine. Take me to the horse."

The horse in question was brown with black legs and a white nose, and Reese thought it might be as tall as a cargo bin but she could have been underestimating the distance between the ground and the saddle.

"Take hold of the horn," the Aera said—the same one from the lab, Reese thought. "That's the thing at the front of the saddle that's sticking up."

"Right," Reese said, and reached up for it.

"I'm going to grab your waist, all right? Hang on—"

Reese started to agree and then the saddle lunged for her face. She smacked her cheek into the horse's neck, made an inarticulate noise, and felt the Aera manhandling her foot into something, then walking around the front of the horse to do it again with the other leg. "There. Now sit up? Good." The Aera came to her and handed her two leather straps. "These are the reins. They tell the horse which direction to go. Leave them loose and she'll go straight. Pull on the right, she'll go that way. Pull on the left, she'll go that way. Haul them back and she'll stop. Smack her sides with your heels to get her started. That's all you need to get going, the rest is just details. Don't worry about her, she's placid. She'll follow the rest of us as long as you don't do anything strange. And her name is Believer."

"Believer," Reese repeated, trying not to be nervous. The ground was a very long way away, and the thing between her and it was *moving*, was breathing, was unpredictable and alive.

"That's right," the Aera said with a smile. "You'll get used to it. You might even like it." She touched the back of a knuckle to her brow. "Good luck. Howl if you need anything."

"Right," Reese said, clutching the reins. As the rest of the hunting party finished their last-minute preparations, Sascha joined her, standing at her leg.

"Here," he said, handing a telegem up to her. "I took it with me in case we needed it. I've set it to local mode, so you should have enough power for several days. Call the ship regularly, okay? They'll be able to track you with it. Maybe if you end up someplace with a big enough field we can come get you. Cut off all this running around after all."

Reese stared at the telegem. "I had that in a locked panel on the bridge."

Sascha chuckled. "Boss, more things work on the ship than used to, but most of it is still broken. Including the locks."

She eyed him, then sighed and took it, careful not to disturb the animal under her. Fortunately it didn't seem inclined to move much. "Thanks, arii. I'm glad you thought of it. You sure about staying? You could come with us."

"I'll stay," he said, his golden eyes serious. "I'm going to sit down with Saul and get a better read on this situation, then head back to the ship and tell them what's going on."

"Right," Reese said.

"Good luck, Boss," he said, resting a hand on her leg. "And don't worry. He'll be okay."

"He'd better be," Reese said. "Or I'll kill him right after I kill the Kesh."

"Move out!" a voice called from in front of her, and the horse lifted its head.

"Guess that's my cue," Reese said. Sascha backed away to a safe distance, and Reese took a deep breath, then pressed her heels into the horse's side.

Nothing happened.

She checked. The reins were loose in her hands, so that wasn't it. She'd used her heels . . . what was she doing wrong? She tried again . . . nothing. Exasperated, she said to the ears in front of her, "Go, already!"

The Aera rode past, reached over and slapped the horse on the side. With a start it jerked forward and Reese grabbed the horn to keep from falling off.

"You need to be more assertive," the Aera called. "She's

much bigger than you, Captain. A little tap isn't going to impress her."

Clutching the saddle horn, Reese called back, "I'll keep that in mind." As the horse bounced her on its back, she glanced up at the intimidating sky. The sun was already heading toward the horizon. How long would they have before it got too dark to search?

"Don't get down," the Aera said sometime later, before Reese even realized she was contemplating the attempt. When she looked up, the other woman finished, "We're not stopping for a break, we're stopping so they can find the trail again."

"Oh," Reese said weakly.

"Not doing too well, are you," the Aera observed. "Why don't I ride alongside you for a while?"

"Sure. You can catch me when I topple off this thing." She was fairly sure that was a joke. At least, she was hoping it was. "I'm Reese Eddings. I'd shake your hand or cover your palm, but—"

"You'd fall off," the other said, smiling. "I'm Ra'aila. Clan Flait, originally, now Clan Kerayle."

"There are enough of you here for a new clan?" Reese asked.

"About twenty," the Aera said. She shook her hood down to free her long ears and ran a hand along them. "We're thinking in a few years we should be a respectable size."

Reese tried not to shift her weight on the horse. She was pretty sure if she moved at all, either the horse would keep going, which would be punishing, or her legs and hips would fall off, which . . . might be a relief. She'd had no idea riding was so much work, but just staying on the animal as it clambered after the others, hour after hour—when it wasn't running after them, bouncing her on its back—was a strain. "Flait. I've heard of Clan Flait."

"Everyone's heard of Clan Flait," Ra'aila said with a chuckle. "They're one of the most successful clans on Aren. Flait can't lift a finger without making money or hoarding power. But some of us aren't interested in being a junior member of a successful clan." She drew in a breath through her long nose. "To be senior member of something new . . . now that's interesting."

"Even if you might fail?" Reese asked.

Ra'aila laughed. "Especially if you might fail. What else? Risk is interesting." She glanced at Reese. "You should know, yes? Independent merchant captain? Lot of risk in that."

"Tell me about it," Reese muttered.

Ra'aila looked up. "Ah, they have the trail again." She tapped her horse on the sides. "Try to relax into the saddle, alet. You are riding your mare as if she was some sort of machine. She's not. Lean into her, move with her as she moves. Look at the trail ahead and anticipate her next act."

"That advice assumes I know what a horse is going to do when faced with a change in the trail . . . !"

"You'll learn," the Aera said. She grinned, flashing all her sharp teeth. "Be one with the animal."

Reese grumbled as the horse lurched forward, jerking her against the saddle horn. "Be one with the horse. Right. Do I look like I eat hay?" She glanced at the pricked ears in front of her. "You do eat hay, don't you? All the stories say so."

The horse, naturally, didn't answer.

They continued climbing into the hills. Reese was grateful for the unpredictability of the terrain since it kept her from looking up and being unnerved by the size of the sky. But the further they went, the more she fretted over

Hirianthial . . . and herself. If she fell off this animal and broke her neck, what would happen to her? And that was just the most extreme of the things that might happen. Fixating on scenarios kept her from noticing how much she hurt, and how badly she wanted off this thing's back.

"You're doing better," Ra'aila said from behind her.

Startled, Reese looked over her shoulder. "What?"

"Riding. You look distracted, maybe it's what's letting you ride more naturally." The Aera looked curious. "What's got you so flat-eared?"

"How much farther will we have to go?" Reese asked. "I mean, how could they possibly be so far away?"

"They had at least an hour on us," the Aera said, drawing abreast of her now that the path permitted it. "Possibly two. And unlike us, they know where they're going. We're having to track them to find them."

"I thought you knew where the horse was, the one they stole."

Ra'aila snorted. "Sure we do. That way." She pointed. "But maybe you haven't noticed, but we can't exactly go in a straight line around here."

"If you had a Pad," Reese began.

"But we don't." At Reese's mutinous look, the Aera said, "Do you?"

"Well, no," Reese said. "Pads are expensive."

"Ahhh," Ra'aila said with a sage nod. "Of course. Not one of your priorities."

Reese eyed her.

"You should mime your ears," Ra'aila said, amused. "You make them so obvious. Here, that swept-back ear look." The Aera demonstrated by putting her hands at her temples and then swiveling them with the fingers pointing back, and mock-scowled at Reese.

Surprised into a chuckle, Reese said, "Fine, yes. I got

the message. You people came here to do what you wanted, and you didn't have the money to do everything. Right?"

"Right," Ra'aila said.

"I can't help but think, though, that you really didn't have a plan for anything," Reese went on. "The Kesh has nothing to trade yet, despite you people evidently having operating expenses you haven't compensated for. And you planned this division of labor thing so well that half of you gave up on it within five years." She glanced at Ra'aila. "Don't you think maybe you could use a little more thinking ahead, maybe?"

"You can do a lot of thinking ahead, Captain, and still be unprepared when the thing you haven't predicted sideswipes you," Ra'aila said. "Or do you honestly think we were expecting our own friends and family to sudden turn on us?"

Reese fingered the straps—reins—in her hand. "No. I don't think anyone expects that."

The Aera nodded. And added, "I don't mean to be harsh. It's just . . . been very bad here. I'm not making a joke when I say that no one expected this to happen. Had we all been working together as planned, we would have had something worth trading by now. We would have had more of the horses done. We would . . ." She trailed off, shrugged her shoulders. "We would have been different. Things would have been different. But they're not."

"So this happens often," Reese said. "These people stealing from you, shooting you."

"Not often, but . . . enough."

Reese glanced at her. "And you *let* them? I mean, fine, you didn't expect it. But now you know that it's happening. And you're going to let it keep happening?"

"They're *family*," Ra'aila repeated. "What would you have us do? Shoot them?"

"They started it . . . !"

"And we should finish it, is that it?" the Aera said.

"If the choice is between 'let my sister shoot me,' or 'stop her,' I would think the answer's pretty clear," Reese said.

"And do you have a sister, Captain?" Ra'aila asked.

Reese looked away. "No."

"Well, then. Don't be so quick to judge, ah?" When Reese didn't reply, the Aera rode close enough to bump their horses together. Startled, Reese looked at her and found her with her hands at her temples again, flattened back.

She laughed, reluctantly. "All right, fine. Point conceded." She shifted a little in the saddle, wincing. "But please tell me this gets easier."

"I'm afraid it'll get harder first."

To Reese's dismay, they rode until nightfall without finding the raiders or Hirianthial. When the party halted and began dismounting, she said to the person nearest her, "Is that it? We're stopping?"

The Kesh answered her from her knee. "For the night, yes, Captain."

She looked down at him. "Where did you come from?"

"The back of my mare," he said with a smile: a tighter one than the ones he'd been using on her before all this began. "Can I help you down?"

"Ah . . ." Reese looked down the side of her horse, shifted experimentally and tried not to gasp. When she was sure of her voice, she said weakly, "I'm not sure I can. At all."

His smile became a little more natural. "I didn't think you'd be able to." He held out his hands. "Come."

With the Kesh's help, Reese didn't fall off the horse, though it was a near thing. She expected to be grateful to be on her own two feet again, but the moment her heels hit the ground her entire body howled protest. "Let me guess," she said from between gritted teeth. "This is being saddle-sore."

"You know about that?" His voice was surprised.

Her romance digests had been full of saddle-sore heroines, but she declined to mention it. "I've heard about it, yes."

"If it doesn't embarrass you to report," he said, "where exactly does it hurt?"

"My hips," Reese said. "And the insides of my knees. And my ankles." She made a face. "And my back. And . . ."

"All of you," he said, nodding. "We'll see if we can pad your saddle to at least take care of your posterior. That should help with your hips and back." With a smile. "Will you come eat with us? They're digging the firepit now, and there should be coffee and stew soon. I'll take care of your horse for you, if you wish."

"It needs—" Reese stopped, then grimaced. "I guess if I'm a mess from that ride, so is the horse. Thanks."

He inclined his head. "Think nothing of it."

With the Kesh seeing to the animal, Reese walked until she found a likely-looking rock far enough from the group around the firepit for privacy. She sat on it—gingerly—and tapped the telegem Sascha had given her. "*Earthrise*, this is Reese."

Kis'eh't's voice answered. "Reese! We were wondering where you were."

"Who's we?"

"Right now? Me and Allacazam. He's in my forepaws here. Turning blue."

Reese smiled. "What shade of blue?"

A pause, then, bemused: "Light blue. Is that good?"

"Probably," Reese said. Her smile faded. "We're camping for the night. No sign of these people yet."

"Goddess," Kis'eh't said. "Still?"

"Still," Reese said. "Did Sascha find out anything? I assume he got back fine."

"Sure, a while ago. In fact, he was up here with me for a while, entertaining himself by bouncing comm signals off the moon. I'm pretty sure he's sleeping with Irine now . . . should I wake him?"

Given what he and Irine were probably actually doing—"No, it's fine. Have him call me when he's free."

"Right," Kis'eh't said. "I don't think he found out anything useful, or he would have waited for you, or called you directly." She paused, then said, "Have you . . . you know. Heard from Hirianthial?"

Reese frowned at the telegem, even though the connection was audio-only. "I'm sort of on this ride because he's been missing for most of a day, Kis'eh't. Of course I haven't heard from him." Her frown became more pronounced. "Why do you ask?"

"Well, we were talking . . . you know, the twins and Bryer and I. That maybe he could . . . you know. Reach for your mind. Maybe tell you where he was that way."

Reese stared at the telegem.

"I know you don't like the telepathy business, Reese, but this is an extenuating circumstance. Right? So has he?"

"N-no," Reese said. She thought of Ra'aila and her mimed ear-flattening and grimaced. "No. He hasn't." Kis'eh't's pause made her say, "What? I'm not . . . not trying to block him or anything, if that's what you're thinking. I don't even know how I would. I didn't even think of the possibility before you mentioned it—"

"It's not that," Kis'eh't said. "It's just . . . I hope it doesn't mean he's really hurt."

Or dead—Reese shuddered. "Maybe he's just being polite because he knows I wouldn't appreciate it."

"Um, Reese? Extenuating circumstances?"

"I know!" Reese said. "I'm not saying I would ignore it if he was trying, I'm saying maybe he thinks he shouldn't."

"Because you might rip his head off?" Kis'eh't huffed. "Well, yes. All right, I could believe that." She sighed. "Are you okay? Really, I mean. One of us could . . ."

"Come with me?" Reese shook her head. "We're up in these craggy hills right now and I have no idea how we got here, to be honest. Just stay with the ship. I'll break Hirianthial free and we'll get the hell out of here."

"We're all on board with that plan."

"Good," Reese said. "I'll call in tomorrow, all right?"

"All right. Goddess keep."

"Yeah," Reese murmured to the telegem after it closed the connection. "I hope she will." She sighed and looked up at the sky, steeling herself against the sight of it . . . but at night it wasn't as intimidating as it was during the day. It looked too much like the view outside the *Earthrise's* ports. She'd never had any trouble with the vastness of space. Maybe that was her issue: not agoraphobia, like she thought, but claustrophobia. Planets were too finite for her, maybe . . . or she'd learned from Mars's zealously-maintained artificial habitats not to trust them.

"Now that's a look I recognize," Ra'aila said, appearing out of the dark to offer her a bowl. At Reese's quizzical look, she added, "It's dinner."

"Thanks." Reese took it, found it warm to her touch which is how she learned that the air was cooler than she was expecting. "What look is that?"

"Looking out, wanting to go there," Ra'aila said, nodding. "A very wanderer sort of look. You must have a nomadic heart, captain."

"How do you figure that?"

The Aera smiled. "You run a merchant ship. It's an

itinerant life. Who but a nomad could want it?"

"I'm not really a nomad by choice," Reese said, moving the spoon around in the bowl. "It's more like . . . it was a way to get away from home. Maybe find one of my own."

Ra'aila snorted. "I know that look too." At Reese's narrowed-eyed glance, the Aera said, "It's not home you were getting away from, was it? It was the people, the expectations, the roles you didn't fit into and didn't want to fill. What you're looking for isn't a home, it's a chance to find out who you are when you're not being smothered." She leaned forward, eyes luminous in the dark. "Let me share with you some hard-won wisdom from a fellow wanderer, Captain. The moment you set down roots again? You end up with the same old problems. Just look at this place. All fine on the voyage here . . . five years into landing, having fights." The Aera stood and rolled her shoulders. "Better to stay on the move, I think."

"There's got to be a place worth settling for," Reese said, startled.

"There's never a place worth settling for," Ra'aila said. "Not unless you've got the right people, anyway." She smiled wryly. "And it's so easy to fool yourself into thinking you're with the right people. Particularly if they're family." She nodded. "That's why I left Flait." Leaning over, she tapped the edge of the bowl. "Don't just play with it, eat. You might not think you're hungry, but you are . . . and morning will come before you know it."

Reese stared after the woman after she left. Since the bloody, grueling war that had emancipated Mars—and killed most of its men—the women of Mars had been making use of artificial insemination to continue their families. What had begun as necessity had eventually been enshrined as tradition. Seven generations of Reese's family had lacked a father, and the women had been content to keep it that way. Better that than to live with the fear of losing a husband, a fear that had never quite evaporated with the blood from the soil.

But she had never been comfortable with the path that had contented her family; had not wanted to live out her life in that house without ever having seen anything beyond it. The Alliance had beckoned from beyond Sol's doorstep, and the monthly romances that had been Reese's sole escape had filled her heart with the hope that she could maybe find her own way, if only she could summon the courage to leave.

So when she'd hit her majority she'd taken the money set aside for her and left . . . and her family had never forgiven her for it.

No, Reese could not imagine hating her family, though they'd disowned her after her last trip home. Her dream of building a family business hadn't been shared by the elder Eddings women. That she might have wanted to do something for herself, something that she could have used to better their situation, hadn't factored at all into their belief that she'd betrayed them, left them behind. Their belief had created reality.

Reese drew in a long breath of the strange air and licked her lips. The faster they got off this horrible world, the faster they could find some more civilized place to trade. Coming here had been a mistake. She only hoped Hirianthial wasn't paying too much for it.

The next time Hirianthial woke, they offered him the one thing he couldn't reject: a drink. Except it wasn't water, but something sour that burned an already dry throat, and he would have coughed it back up but they shoved the gag back in first. Every time they stopped they dosed him with it; he wondered what the drug was, or did when he could think past the pastiche of phantasmagoric images it inspired.

But the trip did end finally, and he was ushered out of the drugged fugue by the lances of pain that stabbed up the wall of his ribcage with every breath he drew. He was on the ground again, but under a purple shadow; when he rolled his eye upward, he saw the ripple of fabric. A tent? And he was on a rug, it appeared; he could feel it against his skin.

His skin. Which he noted was very exposed. Where had they taken his clothes? And his hands were still tied behind his back. His mouth was so dry he hadn't noticed the gag was still in it.

So then. Bound, gagged, naked and . . . he shifted experimentally, winced. Yes, at least two cracked ribs, and something near the sternum that was either another hairline fracture or a separation from the costal cartilage. No crepitus, though, and no symptoms other than pain . . . not a serious injury, then. Thank God and Lady, as he could only imagine what medical intervention was available to people who were choosing, willfully, to use arrows in defiance of Alliance alternatives.

He couldn't tell what time it was, but the sunlight suggested his captors had ridden through at least one night. Hopefully not more than one.

Reese was going to be furious. He smiled despite the situation. Perhaps he could save her the coronary and rescue himself this time.

The tent flap lifted for a woman with a tray in one hand: human, with a tumble of chestnut-colored curls and hazel eyes rimmed in dark gray, set wide in a strong face with a narrow chin. She paused at the sight of his regard, then said in Universal, "You wake." When he didn't move, she sniffed and set the tray down. "I have water here. No food, you will throw it up." She tilted her head. "So. If I untie the gag, will you spit poison at me? Or bite me? Because I am not interested in coddling my husband's newest toy. If you are going to be difficult, I will happily leave you to rot. Are you going to cooperate? Nod if so."

Slowly he inclined his head, keeping his eyes on her.

"Fine," she said, and walked around behind him. He felt her hands on the sash and with them the brush of her aura: supremely uninterested in him, save as a possession to be maintained.

The gag had to be peeled away from his face. She did it carelessly and tossed it aside. "Now. Sit up."

Hirianthial flexed his wrists and ankles.

"Today," she said, her tone bored. "I have things to do, and ministering to you is the least important."

He hid his grimace beneath a dipped head and rolled himself awkwardly onto his knees, hair spilling into his lap. He would have been glad for that, except that she didn't seem to care that he was nude. Her disregard made him feel like a piece of meat. Like, he thought, a horse. Not the same species. A thing to be owned.

He did not welcome the flicker of red anger that licked up his spine and clouded his vision. After spending months tracking down the people stealing Alliance citizens to sell for slaves, he had become very familiar with rage. It always reminded him too powerfully of the very first time he'd felt its spurs. He remembered the way sweat and blood made his flesh adhere to the hilt of Jisiensire's House sword—

When he opened his eyes, the woman was watching him warily. Could she feel it radiating off him? He wondered.

"The water now," she said, and drew a knife from her sash, showing it to him. "I'll have this in the other hand, so don't try anything." When he didn't say anything, she bared her teeth and said, "Tell me you agree."

"I can hardly kill you with my hands and ankles bound together behind my back," he said, and his raw throat made a ruin of his baritone.

"True," she said, but she'd hesitated. She took the bowl from the tray and brought it warily to his lips. He kept his eyes on hers and drank, slowly, measuring his own queasiness. It was, sadly, some of the best water he'd ever had. Under any other circumstances he would have enjoyed it.

When he'd had the full measure, she backed away and tucked the knife back into her sash. "You are in one of the Rekesh's tents," she said finally. "There are guards outside it. Don't think of running. You belong to him now."

"I thought perhaps he would kill me, for having killed his men," Hirianthial said.

She smiled. "Maybe he will, when he tires of you."

"You are his wife," he observed, ". . . and care not at all that he might spend himself elsewhere?"

That made her laugh, a low, husky laugh. "I chose *him*, pretty prize. I knew his habits. But he is the Rekesh, and marrying him gave me status and opportunities. That he prefers to pass his time elsewhere is a bonus. We both have our separate interests, and dislike interference."

"That does not seem like much of a marriage."

She snorted. "What, you would marry for love?" She picked up the tray. "No matter. Not to you, anymore. Put it out of your mind. You belong to us."

That made him smile. "For now."

She paused. "Don't think of escape—"

"I don't have to," he said. "I will outlive you by several hundred years. And if you think your children can keep me . . ." He trailed off, then looked up at her through his hair. "Then you have no idea how long I can wait for you to make a mistake."

"Hundreds of years," she repeated.

"I only look human," Hirianthial said. "But you don't know what I am or what I'm capable of."

She glanced at his bruised sides, her eyes traveling his naked body, and contempt welled back into her gaze. She lifted her chin and said, "What I see is that ropes can hold you, drugs can weaken you, and your skin bruises just as easily as ours." She stepped through the tent flap, and as it swung shut he saw a glimpse of one of the men standing guard outside it.

With her safely gone, he hung his head, licked his dry lips, sighed. It was not precisely bravado to threaten her—he could outlive the entire tribe, even though he'd lived half his own span already—but he didn't want to stay on Kerayle that long. And Reese would be beside herself with worry, which would undergo the instantaneous alchemy that seemed her specific talent, from fear into anger.

And it mattered to him, that she might become angry. And that the twins and Kis'eh't and Bryer would worry. And that Allacazam would not know what became of him.

He would have to find a way to fight his way free. That he couldn't see a way how yet was of no moment. At some point there would be an opportunity, and he would take it. Closing his eyes, he composed himself to wait. Stripping him, his captors had missed the one thing he hadn't wanted them to steal: the hair dangle the crew had made for him, which they'd braided in at the back of his neck where it might lie hidden. He let the whispered impressions woven into the strands and decorations in it center him. First he would recover from the drug. Then he would explore his options.

"Please tell me you've found your bleeding horse," Reese said, bent over the saddle.

"Soon," the Kesh said, staring at his tablet. He squinted

up the trail until two of his hunters scrabbled down it, pebbles rolling away from the hooves of their mounts. They shook their heads and he growled.

"What?" Reese asked, agitated. "What is it?"

"Our stud is in the mountain," the Kesh said.

Reese eyed him. "Not unless someone Padded him into solid rock."

"Nevertheless," he said, irritated. "The transceiver reports he is in the mountain." He shook himself. "If you don't mind, Captain? I need to have a discussion with my people."

Before she could say anything, his horse moved off and took him along, leaving her with her mouth agape. "Sure," she said to his absence. "Absolutely. Go ahead and discuss your malfunctioning technology—or magical rock-breathing horse—with your peers. I'll just hang out here." She shifted on the saddle and tried not to wince. Getting back up on Believer earlier had been an act of willpower. She'd woken up in actual pain, something she hadn't at all been expecting. Sore, sure, but pain? Ra'aila had been sympathetic and offered an analgesic, which Reese had rejected. She wished she hadn't.

She looked up the scrubby hills and decided she'd had enough. It took several tries, but she managed to fall off her horse; she almost left it behind, but thought it might wander away if she didn't tie it to some bushes . . . wasn't that what they did in books? So she found a likely shrub and looped the reins around it. The horse watched her with soulful eyes and she paused. They really were pretty. A little, anyway. Hesitantly, she reached out and Believer stuck its nose under her fingers.

"Sorry for riding you so badly," she said. "Have a rest, okay?"

The horse made a soft chuffing sound.

Reese turned her back on it and started climbing. Every footfall made her grit her teeth, but she was more comfortable walking than she was riding, and something in her was spurring her on. Some gnawing anxiety . . . what were they doing to her Eldritch? Just because she didn't necessarily want him didn't mean she was ready to give him to the colonial equivalent of pirates. Scowling, she made it over the crest of the hill and lifted her head—

—and fought a surge of panic at the breadth of the sky, its unrelenting, cloudless pallor, and the hills that seemed to loom over her. She sat, abruptly enough that her backside protested, and hugged her knees close enough to set her brow against them. Her skin was clammy; she licked her lips. Who put a sky like that on top of a world? Who lived on worlds anyway? Give her the nice, clean cold of space any day. She concentrated on breathing, slowly, through her mouth. One breath at a time . . .

Her chin dragged off her knees. She hesitantly opened an eye, just enough to see . . . nothing. But she didn't want to look away. Lifting her head, she searched for anything that might have made a noise, cast a shadow, anything that might have distracted her: nothing.

But she kept looking.

Frowning, she pushed herself to her feet, wobbled, waited for her knees to start working again. She started in that direction, cursing the unfamiliar landscape: Mars was nowhere near so unpredictable. At least, her part of it hadn't been: flat as a board and mostly paved, she'd had to climb trees to achieve anything like elevation, and Kerayle's constantly shifting terrain confused her. But she kept moving.

"Reese?"

She paused.

"Reese!" Ra'aila jogged into view, ears swept back, and

joined her. "Winds bless it, we thought you'd gotten lost. What are you doing up here?"

"Going this way," Reese said, and turned, only to find the tiny whisper silenced. As she struggled to pinpoint it again, Ra'aila interrupted her.

"Going which way?"

"Ssh!" Reese hissed. "I lost it. Be quiet!"

Puzzled, Ra'aila subsided. In the silence, Reese closed her eyes and lifted her head. *This is it, isn't it?* she asked, silently. *This is . . . some kind of mental touch. Well, fine. I'd rather have you around to fight about it than have you dead or lost somewhere. So talk!*

No words. Her heart pounded, painfully loud in her ears. And then . . . very faint, her face turned toward the sun. "That way," she said, and started climbing.

His captors did not give him the opportunity to recover from the drug. He was still kneeling, gathering his strength, when the tent flap shot open and four men pushed through it: three in the front, and one strolling behind trailing an aura of power and privilege that crackled off him like a coronal aura. Hirianthial watched them, wary, wishing he could feel his fingers. They returned his regard in silence . . . until their master said, "Do it."

Then they lunged for him, two each for his sides and one for his head. He would have had a chance of fighting the third except one of the others punched his side and the ribs flexed. He lost a few moments, and during them was aware of being force-fed again. He fought it once he caught his wind, but they pressed on his shoulders and sides until the pain made his vision swim.

"Again." More of it.

"Again."

When they finally let go of him he couldn't hold himself

up. He also didn't feel himself fall, though once he'd come to rest on the rug he could sense its fibers against his cheek.

"You may go."

He thought they left, but the world was vague by then, and the Rekesh—for surely it could be no one else—crouched alongside his head. Hirianthial was expecting a fist in his hair again, so to have the man lean over and pull a strand lightly forward was surreal. Was he? The man was, wrapping it slowly around a finger. "I'm told the only way to keep you is to subdue you with drugs and ropes," the Rekesh said, conversationally. "That you are a killer, worse than the stallion we won free of our relatives. That no one who could do to four men what you did in such a short time could be anything less." His aura had gone smoke-dark. "Is that true? Are you a killer?"

This was entirely too much like his incident with the pirates on the *Earthrise*. Was he forever fated to endure his assailants' attempts at conversation while injured or near insensate?

The Rekesh crooked his finger until it tugged gently on the hair. "I asked you a question."

Hirianthial rasped, "Animals don't talk."

His captor yanked so hard Hirianthial's face struck the rug. "Respect when you talk to me."

The Eldritch said nothing, breathing past the white ache in his sides.

"Pain can be very humbling," the Rekesh said. Hirianthial heard his footsteps receding, then the crunch of a pillow as the man sat on it. The scrape of ceramic against wood and then splashing . . . his mouth watered and he closed his eyes. "Water would be good, yes?" When he didn't answer, the Rekesh said, "If you want it, you will have to ask. Politely."

God hear him, but he had tired long ago of such

transparent power plays. He had been born tired of such posturing before he'd been forced to endure six centuries of it from his own people, who were endlessly fascinated with ugly games; he had little patience left to entertain them from the rest of the galaxy. Did they think such ploys arrogated power to them that they otherwise did not have? Let them treasure the illusion, then. He said, in his hoarse croak of a voice, "Please."

"Very nice," the Rekesh said. "I like an animal with manners."

Hirianthial rolled an eye toward him.

Holding up his hands, the Rekesh said, "Your own words."

There was a crawling color around the man that was threatening to drown out his physical form. Hirianthial closed his eyes, fighting vertigo, and only opened them when he felt the hands cupping his chin. He took the Rekesh's hunger and curiosity and greasy self-satisfaction like a spear to the gut and reeled.

"There, there," the other said. "Water, now. Mmm?"

Hirianthial let the bowl be pressed to his lips. Half of it slopped out onto the rug, but half of it didn't, and it was so welcome he shivered.

"Ah," the Rekesh murmured. "Like the stallion. A little flinch of the skin." He was smiling from his voice, but his aura was all sick crimsons and pus yellows. "Much better. How are you liking our kumiss? Relaxing, isn't it. I find it helps, in the beginning." He retreated, leaving Hirianthial puzzled. Why had he withdrawn? The pillow hissed again beneath his captor's weight, and again there was a splash of liquid: wine this time, from the bouquet. The Rekesh did not interrupt the silence, for which Hirianthial was grateful, but the wait made no sense. If he had been drugged, surely the Rekesh would want to act before it wore off?

His captor went through two glasses of the wine, sitting behind Hirianthial where he could not be seen. But his aura—that Hirianthial felt like the radiation of a sun, and it was streaked with grit and red glints sharp as razors. The longer he waited, the more Hirianthial's skin pebbled, as if the edges of the Rekesh's aura were something that could cut him, and was pushing closer.

At last, the man stood, strolled around in front of Hirianthial. Showed him the cup, sloshed it to show that it was full. And then threw its contents at his face.

Hirianthial flinched—or tried to. His body remained slack. He tried struggling against his bonds, and his limbs didn't respond either. Not a sedative, he realized. A paralytic. And one without the hypnotic effects he expected with the sorts of drugs that typically conveyed the effect.

"Very good," the Rekesh said, leaning down and touching the edge of Hirianthial's jaw. He smiled. "You wonder, maybe? That we should have such drugs? Because we live in tents? But most of us are geneticists and doctors. We came to cook horses in petri dishes. Guns we might not have, but medicine . . ." He smiled. "I know what I'm doing. And I know what you are." He leaned forward until his lips were near enough to make his words warm and damp against Hirianthial's ear. "Eldritch."

When he leaned out of sight this time, Hirianthial heard the rustle of clothing. The next thing he was aware of was his captor's body against his back, of the heat of his skin, the visceral weight of the words pressed against his spine. "I wanted the alcohol to burn off so you'd be all here for this." A smile in the words, ugly. "If you can feel my feelings through my touch . . . who knows. You might even enjoy yourself."

Had the alcohol worn off? Because he was having trouble understanding that this was happening to him—that it was his body being handled without his consent, that it was his back being covered . . . that it was a stranger fisting a hand in his hair and using it to pull his head close by. The Rekesh was wrong: his talents did not make him want it, though the Rekesh's own desires were an assault as overwhelming as his body's.

The hair-pulling struck him as a horrendous indignity. It assumed an importance out of proportion to the injury . . . until the Rekesh shifted his grip and found the dangle.

"What's this?" he breathed, voice hoarse. "A trinket someone forgot to strip from you?" He shook it, making the bell on the end of it sing. "Very nice. An animal should have ornaments." He yanked Hirianthial's head back— another chime—and said against his mouth, "I might let you keep it. Or not."

The forced kiss: he wasn't ready for it. Kissing was intimacy. To pretend to it while raping someone—

—and the comment about taking the dangle away, the one that had been given to him in love—

The word erupted from him on the crest of a fury so overwhelming it blanked out the world, faded it to white noise and blood haze.

NO.

No more of this. No more. *NO.*

It ripped him open to roar it, even with his mouth closed. Negation. No more. *NO!*

Silence.

No panting. No scraping of skin against skin. The Rekesh had fallen completely silent. Had in fact fallen on top of him, his fingers slowly going slack. Hirianthial was still, waiting for him to shake himself and continue his assault. But his attacker did not rise. The weight of his body was exquisitely painful, made it difficult to breathe past the ribs, and yet Hirianthial was aware less of that pain than he was of a fear he did not want to name. As time trickled past, he was at last forced to admit it.

His captor was no longer breathing.

How long he remained there he didn't know. The Rekesh never moved. When Hirianthial had the where-withal to look, the silhouettes of the guards outside the tent were gone. It wasn't until much later that he thought to look down at the tent's edge, and found suspicious humps near the ground.

He was still struggling with the implications when the tent flap opened for the Rekesh's wife, whose eyes were rimmed with white and whose aura was a billow of mingled anger and fear. "Are you done yet? There has been an attack—" She stopped and switched languages to something he could not understand by normal means and could not force himself to understand by supernatural ones. He was trembling, he perceived. When had that started?

Her husband did not answer her. She darted to his side and rolled him onto his back, and her aura exploded: panic, grief, rage, fear.

"What . . . did you—*YOU.*" She turned on Hirianthial. "You did this to him, to the guards, to the people beyond them! How? How did you do it?"

It was the question he most didn't want to answer. He cleared his throat and said, "How many?"

She backed away from him. "How many? As if you don't know? No, I won't tell you, if you misjudged. Which you did—you did not reach us all." She drew her knife. "Nor will you."

He'd thought himself beyond adrenaline, but the sight of sun flashing off steel made him roll away from her first thrust. "Stop!" he said as she twisted and lunged for him. As she lifted her arm, he said, "Stop or you will be *next!*"

That halted her so abruptly she stumbled. Panting, she

held her distance, arm still raised.

"Do you think you can kill me before I can kill you?" Hirianthial asked. He barely believed the words himself— he didn't want to believe them, God and Lady—but all he needed was for her to believe them. "I can reach you without touching you."

He was not the only one trembling. The light was jittering on the edge of the knife, and her knuckles were yellow against skin stretched taut.

"Don't do it," he said, softer. "Don't—"

She struck. He didn't flinch back fast enough and took a long bloody slice down the arm. She lifted the knife again to finish him.

NO

She fell on him, her body sprawled on his chest: still breathing, and he shuddered on a prayer of gratitude. But it brought the inevitable realization that he had done it: had knocked her unconscious by thinking her so.

Hirianthial had become accustomed to the strength of his abilities. Eldritch who could read thoughts without touching were rare, but the talent had been accepted as a natural variation on the ability to read thoughts through touch. After all, some Eldritch could only read thoughts skin to skin, while others could read them through clothes . . . surely air was only a step more advanced. To send and receive thoughts without touch . . . that bordered on magic, but acceptable magic.

To be able to turn minds on and off without touch . . .

To *kill* without touch . . .

He had very little to vomit, but he turned to give it to the rug and lay there, exhausted and crushed between two bodies, one warm and one cooling, and thought back to tales of Eldritch mind-mages. Tales, passed on like fictions. But if he could do this, then what were the chances that Corel had been a myth?

Corel, who had killed an entire army with his thoughts.

Corel, who had died only because he turned his power on himself.

Corel—who had been insane. And who had not started out that way.

Reese was still climbing when a wave of nausea swamped her, so strong she staggered and then sat abruptly to put her head between her knees. When the feeling passed, she hesitantly lifted her head and found Ra'aila crouched in front of her, worry in her teal-blue eyes.

"Okay now?" the Aera asked, quiet.

"Yeah," Reese said and swallowed. "Yeah. But something's gone really wrong. We have to hurry." She got up, accepting the Aera's help, and glanced back. "Wait, where are the horses?"

"We left the camp behind a long time ago," Ra'aila said. "Don't worry, I told them where we were going, and I'm marking the trail. They're pursuing their own leads."

"And you're following mine?" Reese asked, touching her stomach in the hopes it would stay calm.

"They can trust technology," Ra'aila said. "I'll trust intuition." She grinned. "It's gotten me this far."

"Onto a world that instantly erupted into civil war," Reese said.

"I'd call it more civil unrest," Ra'aila said, tail swishing once. She offered Reese her canteen; when Reese didn't immediately drink, she mimed her ears flattening.

Reese laughed. "Wait, you *have* ears to flatten at me."

"So don't make me," Ra'aila said, smiling. "Drink, Captain. It's dry out here and we're doing a lot of exercise."

"Fine," Reese said. She was careful with it, though, not sure whether it would stay down; fortunately Ra'aila didn't push. Reese had heard many things about the Aera, but few would have called them a compassionate people; they had other strengths, but their culture didn't breed mercy for weakness. She found Ra'aila's matter-of-fact concern affecting, and a lot easier to deal with than fussing would have been.

"Now . . . ," the Aera said once Reese had finished drinking. "Where do we go next?"

"Right. This way," she said, not knowing how she knew and no longer caring. She heard every pulse of her heart like a drum, urging her on, faster. With Ra'aila following, she headed on, putting one foot in front of the other. Between her aches from the long ride and her lack of conditioning, it had become true labor, but she kept going.

With every heel she wedged into the uncertain orange dirt, she thought about Hirianthial. For most of her life she'd read books with Eldritch in them; they were a common offering in her monthly romances, because it was hard to beat an actual mysterious race to serve as a fictional mysterious love interest. That the Eldritch as a species were commonly held to be attractive by every race in the Alliance was a bonus that made them nearly irresistible to writers. But the qualities that made them wonderful daydream material were infuriating in person. Hirianthial kept his past to himself, along with most of his opinions; discussed his emotions not at all; was frustratingly beautiful, graceful, strong and sounded wise most of the time. It made her want to beat her fists on his chest and demand he be wrong about something. Or get angry in a small-minded, petty, *mortal* way.

And then he'd dipped into her mind and in less than a few minutes put together everything that bothered her and motivated her, and made the mistake of saying so out loud where she could hear him. He'd been half-dead at the time, disoriented by the attacks of slavers, pirates and the slaughter of several hundred unexpectedly sentient crystals, but he'd terrified her. Worse, he'd humiliated her. That all the pain in her life could be so obvious . . . it made her feel small.

She had had a hard time forgiving him for it, and had treated him very badly as a result. Her crew had intervened, and she'd done her best to hold her distance from him while she struggled with her ambivalence.

And he'd stayed, and granted her that distance instead of trying to fix it.

It had all come down to the question: did she trust him with the knowledge he'd taken from her? Did she trust him not to hurt and disappoint her, the way so many people had before?

She didn't know the answer yet. But that he hadn't tried to force the issue had won points with her, and had given her time to calm down about it. And these people had interrupted the process and taken him away from her and her crew, and that made her very, very angry. It was that anger that was putting one foot in front of the other, and her stubbornness propelled her on until she crested a ridge and saw a valley falling away below her, one filled with tents and people and horses. She was still staring when Ra'aila grabbed the back of her vest and jerked her down.

"Are you crazy?" the Aera hissed. "They'll see you."

"Right." Reese scooted away from the edge. "So . . . now what?"

Ra'aila frowned. "Good question. I am suspecting the answer is 'go for back-up.'"

"Did we bring enough back-up to take on all that?" Reese asked.

"No," the Aera said wryly.

"Well, then, we should . . . have another plan. Maybe

wait until dark and sneak in? The sun's already setting."

Ra'aila started laughing. "What, are you a Fleet ranger now?"

"No . . ." Reese trailed off and grimaced. "I guess that was a dumb idea. We don't even know what tent they're keeping him in."

"Oh, it's that purple one over on the edge."

"What?" Reese rolled onto her stomach and inched up to the edge, peering over it. "How do you know?"

"It's too large to belong to anyone but the Rekesh and it's next to the largest tent in the camp. Plus there are guards in front of it. Or were, anyway." Ra'aila squinted. "I can't see them now, but it's the tent design that has a place for them to stand in shade."

"Did they . . . you don't think he's . . ." Reese swallowed. No, she would know if he was dead. Wouldn't she?

"That's strange." Ra'aila inched forward, her shoulders tense. "There are bodies near the tent. Just lying there."

"I wonder if he escaped?" Reese asked.

"Maybe," Ra'aila said, but she sounded doubtful. "There are a lot of horses missing, so maybe they've ridden out after him? No, wait. Someone's going in the tent. Looks like a—"

"Woman?" Reese scowled. "She'd better not have any ideas."

"This is all very strange," Ra'aila said, frowning. Her long ears were slicked back so far their tips touched her shoulders. "What could be going on down there? Where are the guards? If he's escaped, why is she going in the tent?"

"I don't know," Reese said, "but I want to. You go for back-up, have them come as fast as they can." She drew in a deep breath and threw herself over the ledge. Ra'aila squeaked but she ignored the Aera and headed down, trying to keep behind cover. She didn't know what had

happened to Hirianthial and going to look herself was a
stupid idea . . . but she couldn't just sit and wait. The sense
of urgency had only been mounting in her head, and it was
almost unbearable now. If he was alive, he needed her.

Reese scrabbled down off the hill and crouched behind
a bush, waiting to see if she'd been seen. When no one
cried an alarm, she chanced a look past the shrub. Ra'aila
was right: there were bodies scattered around the tent. She
lifted her head and scanned the camp: no movement there
either. Maybe Ra'aila was right and they were chasing
Hirianthial down. But if that was so, why had the woman
gone into the tent? Why hadn't she left yet? And why did
Reese feel like she was supposed to be *here*?

Keeping low she made her way to the back of the
purple tent. She listened and heard nothing, not outside,
not inside. Going around the front seemed a recipe for
trouble, so she felt around the bottom of the wall. It was
too taut to slide under, but Sascha had suggested, a little
too casually, that she start carrying a "utility knife," when
what he'd really meant was "a weapon." She'd brushed off
his concerns and then found herself something she could
keep in her boot. It sliced her an entrance and she slipped
inside . . . and halted abruptly, her breath stopping in
her throat.

"No, no," she said. "No . . ." She dove for the pile of
bodies, shoving the woman off first. "You can't be dead,
you've lived too long to die, you are not allowed to be
dead!" The man on top of him was heavier . . . and stiffer.
She didn't realize until she'd pushed him off the Eldritch's
back that he was almost certainly dead and then she shuddered. No time for collywobbles—shoving her hair out of
her face with her forearm, she bent close. "Hirianthial . . . !
Hirianthial?" No response. She bit her lip, then resolutely
set her palm on his naked shoulder.

He jerked away, eyes opening, and the panic in them—
"No, no, it's me!" she cried, holding out a hand. "Sssh, ssh.
I'm here to get you out of here."

"Theresa . . . Captain . . ." His breathing was disordered,
and it made her heart stumble, that moment of confusion
where he couldn't decide whether what he needed was
intimacy or distance.

"It's all right," she said, willing him to feel her resolve,
to be steadied by her calm. Hopefully this esper business
could be useful that way? It seemed damned inconvenient
otherwise. "We're getting out of here, right now. Can you
get up?"

"I . . . I think," he said, hoarse. "Rib fractures. Can't
move . . ."

"Probably these ropes," Reese said, finding his hands
at his back. She hesitated only a moment at the sight of
his injuries, squared her shoulders and started cutting
through his bonds. "There. Can you feel them?"

"No," he admitted. "They . . . dosed me several times.
One of them . . ." He trailed off and looked at her, his pupils
too small in his wine-colored eyes. "How many dead?"

"How many . . . you mean outside?" Reese sat back,
glanced at the woman. "I don't know. They might be
unconscious, like her. Speaking of which . . ." She plucked
up the ropes and applied herself to securing the prisoner.
She had just finished the feet when Hirianthial said behind
her, "Gag. On the ground . . . at the edge of the rug."

"Thanks." Reese tied it in place, trying not to think too
hard about what she was doing. Sascha would have made
a joke about this; imagining it helped her finish the job.
Then she started hunting through the tent for something
to wrap around the Eldritch, who was going into shock,
she thought. Keep things brisk. Keep them moving. "If it's
all right with you, I can rub your feet and arms until you

can feel them? I can't carry you and we have got to get out of here."

No response. She could hear him breathing, and it was a shaky, strained sound. She let him be and considered the wooden chest. If Irine was here . . . but she wasn't. Frowning, Reese leaned forward and fingered the lock, testing its weight.

It opened. She stared at it for a moment, then bit back an inappropriate laugh and flung the lid up. Clothes mostly too small for the Eldritch, but the robe might work. And there was at least one sash that could be improvised into underwear—that worked in books, so surely it would work in real life? She gathered them into her arms and turned . . . and dropped them, running to him and . . . and hell with the not-touching thing, and with her not being good at comfort, but her crew would say there was a time for hugging and this had to be one of those times. She closed her arms around his head as he shook, set her hand on the back of his head. The twins had once told her his hair was like warm silk. She didn't want this to be the way she found out they were right.

"Hey," she said. "Hey. We're going to get out of this. I promise. And you're going to be okay."

He wasn't crying. That would almost have been easier. The anguish she'd caught in his gaze before she lunged for him . . . surely tears would have helped wash it away. But this silent trembling was worse, somehow, much, much worse. She had wanted him to break down, to be normal, to be fallible and frangible. With every fiber in her, she regretted that desire. She would take his insufferable perfection and thank the bloody soil for every aggravating minute of it if only they could have avoided this moment.

Reese rested her cheek on his hair and closed her eyes, let him lean on her as much as he was willing, and didn't care that her thoughts were in his head. She hoped they hurt less than the ones he'd been thinking himself.

"They do," he whispered. When she raised her head and tried to look down at him, he said without moving, "Hurt less."

Very slowly she felt his hand come to a rest on her back. It was a very broad hand . . . and it was shivering.

"It's not your fault," she said.

"Oh no," he said softly. "The bodies . . . they certainly are."

He expected her to falter, but she did nothing of the sort; in fact, she gripped his shoulders tighter and said, "They kidnapped and tortured you. Good bleeding riddance."

She didn't understand, couldn't possibly. And he needed her to. "I did it with my mind, not my hands."

A pause then, but so brief he almost missed it . . . and the scintillance of her aura, shot through with opalescent rays that had been buoying him up since she found him, remained undimmed. If the shadowed-steel determination beneath it grew more distinct, well, she could hardly be blamed for that. Some distant part of himself could float above his horror and consider the situation, find it untenable on her behalf.

"I know I'm about two heads too short for this," she was saying, "but can you lean on me to get up? For some reason the camp is mostly empty—we thought they were chasing you—and now I don't know why they're gone and I don't want to be here when they get back. Ra'aila was supposed to bring the hunting party but I don't know how long that's going to take."

"Hunting party," he repeated, but he forced himself to try rising. Reese helped, one hand lifting to his chest. "No!" he said, and she froze. He swallowed, eyes closed. Cleared his throat. "Not that side. There's . . . a fracture there, or a tear. Near the sternum."

"Right," she said, resting her small, warm palm on the other side. He staggered, almost taking her down with him; on the second try, he managed to rise completely, though there was not a part of his body that did not protest the effort, from the blinding headache to the angry fire of nerves waking in his feet. "The Kesh sent out a hunting party to find you and some super-valuable horse these people stole. I went with them."

"The ship?" he asked, hoping.

"Not happening," she said. "This valley's too small to set her down, and the terrain between here and there would rip the landing gear off and send her rolling downhill. Can you stand?"

"I think," he said, eyes closed. He swallowed. "Captain. I need to see them. The bodies."

That made her aura contract, a fleeting hesitation. Her voice was guarded when she spoke. "This isn't about you and that oath you took."

He had no idea what she was talking about until a memory skated through her touch into him: sitting in her quarters, reading the medical oath he'd be required to swear again if she took him on as a doctor instead of general crew. She'd been appalled, as the oath he'd chosen had been the most rigorously pacific of the group, and had required that he minister to the wounded in order of severity, friend—or foe.

"No," he said, hoarse. "No, it's nothing to do with that."

"All right," she said, though she was still uncertain, a queasy gloss over her steel-and-opal colors. "Here, hold on to the tent pole here . . ." She left him listing against it and brought back a robe and sash. As he stood, mute, she threw the robe over his shoulders and started arranging its folds. It made him aware that he was naked, and that she had a deep discomfort with nakedness. "It's not long enough, but it's something—"

He touched her shoulder. "Thank you. The sash . . . has to go around the ribs."

"Right," she said. "Just tell me what to do."

Somehow they managed, and somehow he stumbled behind her, waiting until she'd decided it was safe to leave the tent. The sun was too bright for the pain in his head, but he forced himself to open his eyes anyway. It took him a moment to find the bodies, but they were there. He staggered to the first, the guard alongside the tent, and fell to one knee beside it. He didn't bother looking for a pulse. Pushing himself upright he found the next: dead also.

"Hirianthial," Reese began, but she didn't try to stop him.

He made his way outward. It was hard to tell, but it looked as if the dead were limited to a very small radius around the tent—beyond that, the bodies were unconscious, though in one case the man was comatose, not merely fainted. He kneeled beside the farthest body he'd found, leaning back until his heels pressed against the robe. Resting his hands on his thighs, he tilted his head up and closed his eyes.

Past the headache, past the eye-watering pain of his injuries, past the welter of horror and disbelief, he could still feel the sun on his face, like a blessing he was no longer sure he deserved.

She didn't want to watch and couldn't look away: the wind swept the edges of the robe around the kneeling Eldritch, and it was a ludicrous bright purple and it didn't matter . . . nothing could make the tableau less poignant. The look on his face—

—if these people had broken her Eldritch—

Her telegem startled her by squawking. She grabbed it and flicked it on. "Blood and freedom, this is a bit of a bad time!"

"Boss." Sascha sounded focused. She didn't like it when Sascha sounded focused. "Where are you?"

Reese glanced at the tents and the scattering of limp bodies around them. "In the middle of the raider camp, why?"

"There's a receiver down there somewhere."

"A *what*?" She frowned, glancing toward the edges of the valley. Her skin was crawling: how long did they have before someone found them?

"A receiver," Sascha repeated. "One that only lights up when someone's hitting it with a reflected signal at a very specific angle."

Her thoughts snapped back from the reverie. "*What*?" She hugged her arms. "No, no. You are not telling me that there's an offworld link between these criminals and . . ."

"I don't know," Sascha said. "But it sure looks suspicious. I'm hoping you're going to tell me we're leaving soon?"

"The moment we get Hirianthial into and out of their clinic," she said. "I don't think we can handle his injuries onboard."

His pause made her realize she hadn't told him she'd found the Eldritch, and his voice when he spoke this time had gone from focused to that hot stiffness she associated with his anger. "How bad?"

Watching the Eldritch bow over the last of the bodies, Reese said, "Bad in so many ways I can't even describe them yet." She shook herself. "Look, Sascha. I've got some horses to steal so we can get out of here. I'll call once we're back in town."

"Boss . . . make sure you come back in one piece. Both

of you."

"Trust me," Reese said. "There's a knife between me and anyone who wants to argue the point. Reese out." She looked around and muttered, "Now if only I knew where the hell these people were so we could have the argument." With Hirianthial occupied and obviously in need of privacy, she went hunting for transportation. The bandits' horses were corralled near the back of the camp. None of them had rope or reins or anything she could use to catch one, but there had to be a way to attract a horse's attention. Didn't they like food? Maybe she could pull up some grass and offer it? She was just starting to walk that way when Hirianthial called, "Wait."

It hurt to hear how raw his voice was. She stopped so he could join her, his gait a jerky caricature of its usual grace. "Let me come with you," he said. "I can talk them into helping."

"Talk *one* into helping," Reese corrected. "Those things can hold two people, right?" She wished he wouldn't stare at her like that; it made it too clear that his pupils hadn't filled out again. "You don't look like you can make it on your own. And there's no way I'll be able to stay on one of those things without a saddle. This is only day two of my education as a rider. I'm not up to circus tricks."

She thought he would argue. She *wanted* him to argue, wanted some sign of his usual obstinacy. But he just closed his eyes and said, "Very well," and then trudged toward the corral. She scurried after him, packing her fretfulness away. Stay focused. Stay on target.

Joining him at the fence, she said, "So . . . how do we do this?"

"We ask," Hirianthial said. His hands came to rest on the top bar, fluttering as he tried to breathe in and cut the movement off. The lines that framed his eyes spilled shadows, and she hated seeing them, evidence of pain.

But then he lifted his chin and spoke no word, made no movement, did nothing. His eyes remained closed, and his expression . . .

Entreaty was the word she wanted, too intimate to be witnessed. She blushed and looked away.

A horse was trotting toward them. Not just any horse, but a bright white horse, fierce and proud and wild. He came to them not like a pet obeying a master, but like some sort of elemental summoned from thin air. And he walked all the way to the fence and touched his nose to Hirianthial's arm. The Eldritch relaxed, opened his eyes, set a gentle hand on a long, pale nose. Would he? He did. He rested his head against the animal's, and even bruised and exhausted it was a beautiful moment, pale faces, white manes, long milky lashes.

"All right," she managed. "I'll . . . I guess I'll go look for a saddle."

"No," Hirianthial said, quiet. "This horse will take no saddle, nor any bit. But he'll carry us."

Reese eyed the stallion uncertainly. "I've just had a day-long education on what happens to my backside when I ride on a badly adjusted saddle. I can't imagine riding without one is going to be better—"

"Nevertheless," he said. "This horse will bear no saddle." At her expression, he smiled a little, and she was so relieved to see him smile that she didn't care that he found her objection humorous. "We will survive the trip, Captain."

"Better than we'd survive staying," she said and sighed. "Fine. Bareback it is." She glanced at the horse's nearest eye and said to it, "Just go easy on me, all right? What I know about horses I could fit in a Flitzbe's mouth. And Flitzbe don't have mouths."

The horse regarded her for a few moments, then turned

back to Hirianthial and brushed its nose against his arm.

"Right," Reese muttered. "Thanks."

Getting up on the horse was an exercise in itself. She went up first, with Hirianthial's help; then he came up behind her, and she heard the hissed breath he tried to hide when he mounted. She forced herself not to tense her back and shoulders and looked between the horse's small white ears until he settled, his thighs behind hers and his arms reaching past her sides to gather a handful of the mane. Loosely, she noticed. She would have to remember that if he fell unconscious and she was left to guide this boat on her own. Blood and freedom forfend. She was an adequate ship's pilot, but she'd barely managed to make a horse go where she wanted with a pair of reins to steer it and a herd to lend some peer pressure. Managing a tack-less stallion with a body slumped on hers sounded like a recipe for disaster.

"You ready?" she asked, hesitant.

"I was about to ask you such," he answered.

"Let's get out of here."

The stallion walked to the corral gate and stood along-side it as Hirianthial leaned over and undid the latch. As they rode past, Reese steadied herself and reached over, kicking the gate wide open.

"Make it harder for them to catch up with us," she said.

"It's likely those are spare mounts," Hirianthial said.

Reese set her shoulders. "I stand by it. Better free than owned by those people."

No argument. She let out a breath as the horse picked its way through the camp, hooves sounding a hard tattoo against the dry ground. Riding bareback felt a lot more precarious, except that she was enveloped in Hirianthial's body. If she'd been willing to lean back, she could have put her back all along his stomach; as it was, his arms and legs were cradling hers. He was close enough that she could feel how shallow and controlled his breaths were; could smell the acrid sweat and blood, see the dried flakes of it scaling his arm. And all of this while partially nude, in a race that could sense thoughts through skin and had even more of a problem with touch than she did. She frowned at the view past the horse's ears. No doubt he could tell what she was thinking, and while injured and sick—it had to be uncomfortable. She knew that now, having been browbeaten by Kis'eh't into doing at least some basic research on esper abilities.

Well, she could at least do something about that. Think happy thoughts. She had good memories, didn't she?

It seemed strange to realize that . . . she did. A few years ago she would have had to work harder to mine them from the rubble of the life she'd been desperately holding together. Now she could see the value in the smell of hot coffee. Be grateful for naps with Allacazam in her hammock, dreaming alien dreams of burbling brooks and rustling willows. Now she could sense the friendship in her crew, extended to her as well as to one another, and be glad to have them—be glad even of the twins' exuberant hugs, and Kis'eh't's wry comments and Bryer's trenchant if frequently strange advice. She could even, if she was calm enough, think back to Mars and be grateful for the memory of a wind through the eucalyptus she'd loved as a child, for the rich crimson earth and the distant earthrise, pinprick bright in a pink sky.

Reese wrapped herself in memories so deeply that the yelling seemed surreal: another dream, but a negative one, intruding on her disciplined mental state.

"We've found the missing raiders," Hirianthial said behind her, and the stallion vaulted forward and charged through a fight being waged with arrows, swords and palmers. Before she could protest—or scream—they'd broken through the fight and were pounding down the slope.

"Are they chasing us?" she asked, shaking.

"I would prefer not to discover they were by slowing enough to be captured," he said, and something in his voice. . . .

"No," she said. "Me neither."

They rode until Hirianthial began to sag, and then the horse slowed down by itself: magic, or maybe it could read thoughts. For all she knew, there was some mystical horse/ Eldritch bond she didn't know about. But it was walking slowly amid the brush when she felt him lose consciousness. The sudden weight on her back made her grunt, but she reached behind herself until she could feel his side and steadied him as best she could.

The horse eventually stopped. She was trying to decide how to get them both off his back when she heard hooves. A lot of hooves. She grabbed for her knife, startling the horse, which sidestepped. "No, no," she hissed. "Don't do that. Please! Or no, wait. Can you run?" She tried pressing her knees against its side and was ignored. "No, really, we need to get out of here—!"

"Was our company so bad, then, Captain?" the Kesh called.

Reese froze, then said, "Oh, freedom bless. Shamil! Help?"

What would have taken far too long had she done it alone was the work of moments when the group converged on her. She was lifted off the stallion, Hirianthial borne away to a flat patch of ground where the healers that had come along could assess him, and someone else led the very valuable horse away to be brushed and fed and whatever else it was horses needed.

"So you're not being followed," Reese said to the Kesh as she sat by the firepit.

"Not by that group, anyway," he said. "I've left most of our people behind to lead the prisoners back to the town. The rest of us came looking for you."

"Me . . . and the horse," Reese guessed, wry.

"And the horse," he agreed, pouring himself a cup of coffee. He offered her a mug, which she accepted. "He's worth a great deal of money. It would be a little like you abandoning your ship somewhere, not caring where it had gone."

Reese grimaced. "All right, I can see that." She glanced at him. "You have any idea how bad this situation is?"

He pressed the wall of his mug to his brow. "Since the Colony Bureau can revoke our charter if we're found engaged in a civil war . . . yes, Captain. I have some notion of how bad it is." He sighed and returned the mug to his knees, cupping it. "But my counterpart is dead in that camp. I'm hoping that without a leader, things will calm down."

"Just one man?" Reese asked.

"One charismatic man can cause a great deal of trouble," the Kesh said. "Or woman, of course." He tipped his head to her before continuing. "I should have seen it. Jaram was brilliant but impatient, and never forthcoming. He was obviously hiding something, an agenda of his own—"

"I'll say," Reese said. "What with the receiver he smuggled out here." At the Kesh's startled glance, she said, "I'm guessing you didn't know about that. But he's set up to get offworld transmissions. I'm assuming he wasn't setting it up to contact Fleet to ask for help."

"No," the Kesh breathed.

"You have a house to clean," Reese said. "And I don't

really want to stick around for that. If you don't mind, I'll borrow your clinic to get Hirianthial back on his feet and be on my way before any pirates show up in orbit."

He flinched. "Yes, of course. Anything we can do for your man, we will. We are, as I said, quite capable doctors, and our clinic is state of the art."

"Good," Reese said. The Kesh was staring at the fire, his expression so rueful she couldn't leave it alone. "But you know, once you get things settled . . . we might come back."

"For what?" He looked at her, the firelight bright on half his face. "You aren't interested in horses. In fact . . . I don't know why you came at all. What brought you here, Captain Eddings?"

"You'll laugh," Reese said.

"Good. I could use a laugh."

"I heard from some Fleet officers that you made some kind of good alcohol," Reese said. "It was a comment in passing, but you learn to listen for those things when you trade."

"Alcohol?" he said, bemused.

"I know it sounds crazy," she said. "But the alcohol market is pretty intense. People like to collect alcohols specific to different worlds. They claim they taste different." She shrugged. "The stuff you served me, though . . . it didn't seem 'cross several sectors for it' good."

"That was wine from Earth!" he said with a laugh. "I brought it out for you as a way to show respect. We have local alcohols; perhaps while your crewman's in the clinic you can sample them."

A way to turn this trip around? Well, no. There was no turning this trip around. But to at least get something back for the pain and suffering . . . "Deal," Reese said.

"He'll be all right," the Kesh added, gentler. "A few cracked ribs and slices and bruises. A few hours under a halo-arch and he'll be on his feet again."

"I hope you're right," she murmured.

The ride back to town took far too long for Reese's tastes, particularly since the healer overseeing Hirianthial's care kept him sedated. Why, she didn't know; when she asked, she got back an earful of jargon, and the only thing she picked out of it was concern. "But he'll be all right," she asked the woman, who waved a hand.

"Yes, yes. Fine."

Reese wasn't so certain, but there wasn't much she could do except follow, once again mounted on her properly saddled horse. Hirianthial got a travois, which looked suspicious to Reese, but they assured her he would be comfortable in it; it floated a little off the ground, so she guessed these people hadn't eschewed all technology. They'd just used up all their money on medical equipment. Nevertheless, the tension didn't start leaving her shoulders until they'd brought him to the clinic and she'd seen him safely installed beneath a halo-arch. They even treated her for her aches and pains, and they were numerous after her first adventure on horseback. All her romances had made riding horses seem easy. This was not the first time they'd been wrong.

She left the clinic as Sascha was entering it and found herself with an armful of furry. Sascha's embrace was rigorous enough that she was grateful she'd allowed the healers to deal with her friction burns and aching limbs. "I am so glad to see you," she said, and surprised herself by meaning it with her whole heart.

"What happened?" he asked. "Where is he?"

"Not here," Reese said, and pulled him away from the clinic. "Come on, you might as well walk me to my wine tasting."

"Wine tas—all right then, whatever you say, Boss. Hirianthial?"

"They say he'll be ready for release in a few hours," Reese said. "He broke a few ribs, nothing extreme. And had a few cuts and a lot of bruises." She rubbed her arm. "I'm . . . pretty sure there were other injuries." Sascha glanced at her but she kept her eyes straight ahead. "Maybe you have some advice on how to handle those."

"Advice on . . ." His ears slicked back to his skull and he bared his fangs, and all the fur visible on his neck and shoulders bristled. "Don't tell me that. Don't you tell me that."

Reese said, "His mental state is pretty bad." She sighed. "All this and possible pirates too. I know how to pick them, don't I." She handled him the telegem. "Here. We're lifting off the moment he gets out. You're in charge of pre-flight prep."

Sascha closed his fingers around the jewel. "As soon as you two show up, we'll kick the dust of this place off our boots so hard the world'll spin out from under us."

"Sounds good to me," Reese said. Sascha touched her shoulder and started jogging away. She watched him recede, then called, "Sascha!" He paused. "Bring Allacazam to the clinic, okay? He shouldn't be alone when he wakes."

"Good idea."

The alcohol the Kesh poured for her was white. Reese eyed it. "And this is?"

"Kumiss," he said. "What we named the horse after. Try it."

Wary, she took up the cup and sipped, and found it sour and mild. "That's it?"

"Now this," the Kesh said, pouring her a second cup, "is what those officers of yours drank."

She glanced at him, then took a sip from the second cup—and got punched in the sinuses. Sweet and sour and spiced and milky and very, very strong. She coughed and said, "What is this?"

"Arkhi," the Kesh said, smiling. "The distillation of kumiss." At her scowl, he said, "It is fermented mare's milk, captain. What else?"

"That came out of a horse?" Reese asked, staring at the cup.

"Absolutely."

"Maybe they're not so bad after all."

He laughed and began to pour more into her cup. "So you are interested in a few crates? We have some."

She stopped him with a hand on his wrist. "I am, yes. You're going to give them to me, aren't you?"

The Kesh paused.

"Because we've gotten off to a bad start, haven't we?" She took up the cup again but didn't drink. "Wouldn't want to damage a potential business relationship. Particularly when you might need all the friends you can get."

"That presumes you're coming back."

It did. She sipped more carefully of the arkhi, her skin prickling as she swallowed. Running out to Kerayle for alcohol was crazy, particularly if the place was lousy with pirates. But she remembered Hirianthial's intense interest in the horses. Maybe the Eldritch would want some; maybe they'd want a lot more than some. Being powerless to refuse the Queen's requests had gotten Reese into several worlds of trouble; it would be nice to have something material to offer in lieu of her running all over the known universe rescuing helpless Eldritch.

She also thought of Hirianthial's head resting against the horse's, and the soft straggles of white mane falling over long white fingers.

"Well, you know . . . horses. Maybe not so bad after all."

He studied her, then began to smile. Offering his cup, he said, "To possibilities."

"If you clean up your backyard."

"Assuming we survive the rumor of pirates and diffuse our potential civil war," the Kesh said wryly.

"I'll drink to that." Reese tapped her cup against his.

There was water flowing over him: in that way of dreams, it was running over his heart, a musical beck without force or drama. It sang to him of ordinary joys, the contentments that stitched a life together. That sense of quiet healing was so powerful that he knew it to be external; his own heart was nowhere near so clean. When he woke, then, he was not surprised to find Allacazam cradled against his arm. The Flitzbe responded to his attention by streaking warm red over the cool blues and whites of his neural fur.

Before he could answer, a stranger appeared at the halo-arch. "How are we feeling?"

Hirianthial's eyes flicked up toward the readings. "I'm mended."

"So the arch says, anyway," the healer said. "But that's no substitute for patient report." He held out a hand over the arch, waiting.

"I'm mended," Hirianthial said again. "It will do. Let me up, please."

The healer tapped the arch. As it withdrew, he said, "Your captain left clothes here for you. I'll let you dress. You can come out when you're ready."

"Thank you," he said, and rubbed his throat. His voice still felt raw, but it was the only part of him that didn't feel normal again . . . that, and his soul, of course.

God and Lady, had he killed half a dozen men and

knocked another half dozen over without lifting a hand? He looked at his palm and flexed the fingers. It could not be possible, and yet he had seen the evidence.

Allacazam pressed against his hip when he started shaking again. He rested his hand on the Flitzbe's fur and struggled with his composure. All the violence that had been done to him paled in compare with the violence he appeared to be capable of wreaking, and against people who had no defense against his attacks. What was he becoming, that he was able to do such a thing? And as an escalation of the abilities he'd already noticed growing stronger and more varied, it was terrifying. What would he discover he could do next? And would it once again be all out of proportion to the insult done him?

He couldn't decide whether what he needed was a priest . . . or an executioner.

Allacazam turned a lurid shade of purple, and in his mind he heard a howl of protest, like an abandoned dog. He grimaced and said, "I will apologize for distressing you, but not the sentiment." Sliding off the biobed, he pulled the clothing on. When he bent to manage the boots, the dangle slid forward, bouncing against his ribcage with a muffled chime. He froze.

The Rekesh's hand in his hair. That had been the moment: the implication that his captor was prepared to take away the one thing that mattered to him, the memories of the friendship of the *Earthrise's* crew. As an Eldritch, he knew too well that memories would be all he had of them soon enough, and that knowledge invested a significance in the gift that he would have been hard-pressed to describe to one of the shorter-lived races.

And his outrage at that had killed six people.

He would fear for his soul, but he honestly couldn't conceive that it was salvageable after such an act.

One thing was certain: he didn't want to be here. He scooped Allacazam from the bed and left.

Reese was waiting for him outside on a bench, leaning forward with her hands clasping the edge of the seat; with all her braided hair shrouding her face, and the bead-capped ends an eye-watering blue in Kerayle's strong sun. At the sound of his footsteps she looked up. Even without the grayish pall hanging over her aura he could see the worry in her face. She had never been good at hiding her thoughts, which was just as well, given how difficult she found expressing them.

"Ready to go?" she asked.

"Past ready."

"Good," she said. "Kis'eh't and Bryer are loading the ship now, they should be done by the time we get there."

"Did we buy something?" he asked, disoriented. They had come here to trade, hadn't they? He'd forgotten entirely.

"Nothing," Reese said, and her aura crackled with fierce bright sparks. "They gave us goodwill gifts. One of which was some kind of special horse ordering set-up."

"A horse . . . ordering . . . set-up," he repeated.

She nodded. "Solidigraphs that represent different horses they're willing to breed, and then you can order their offspring." She wrinkled her nose. "It seems kind of first century to me. 'Hi, I'd like to reserve the children of your next goat pairing.' But he told me that if I decided I wanted to ship horses, it would be done in vats or something. I'm guessing we could manage that in the cargo hold."

"You? Trade horses?" He smiled a little, which he thought a victory. "I cannot imagine it."

"Me neither," Reese admitted. "But do you know they make amazing alcohol?"

Since she was willing to talk, he let her: about the kumiss and the arkhi and the Kesh's explanation of the distillation process. He mostly felt the sun on his head and the worried brush of her aura, and Allacazam's concern, which warred poorly with the alien's pleasure at the light. Did the Flitzbe perceive different suns to give light of different flavors, he wondered? And who would ever be able to ask in terms the Flitzbe could understand?

Kis'eh't was waiting for them at the airlock, hanging half-out of it. "You're finally here! We're ready to be gone. Sascha's hovering over the board."

"Good, because we're ready to go," Reese said, and waited for him to enter first. He passed through the airlock and into the ship that had been his home for nearly a year: had become his home, when he had been torn loose from his first by circumstance and too many difficult memories. He listened to Kis'eh't and Reese as they traded information with the ease of long acquaintance, left them behind to head for the quarters he'd been assigned. Once in them, he sat on the bunk and took his first deep breath since his injury.

This ship he could leave behind; his attachment to it had nothing to do with it and everything to do with its crew. They had stood by him, had rescued him from villains they would ordinarily have been terrified to face on their own. They were a family he would have been proud to be born to.

And yet, they could not help him now.

He needed to go home.

"Where to this time?" Sascha asked. "And please don't tell me 'another backwater possibly infested with slavers.'"

"There are no slavers in this system," Reese said.

"Yet," Irine murmured.

Reese eyed her, then said, "Nearest starbase. We'll see if we can offload some of this alcohol. And honestly . . ."

She sighed. "I just want to stop moving for a while."

Irine brightened, ears perking. "You mean like a vacation?"

Reese glanced out the viewport. "Maybe like a vacation, yes. But not like the one on Harat-Sharii."

"So . . . where?" Sascha asked, fingers tapping commands on the board.

"If I knew that, we'd be going there." Reese sighed. "Can I be honest with you?" They both looked at her then, and their expressions were compassionate rather than offended, so she finished. "I want to go somewhere safe for a change. Everywhere we've gone lately, there's been a bomb waiting to go off. That dump we dragged Hirianthial out of the first time, it started this whole mess. Then we ended up on Harat-Sharii—no offense, but that was awful—and then Mars, where I got disowned. And then the ice ball where I murdered three loads of aliens, and I'd probably be in jail for that except the crystals keep being completely disinterested in the topic when the first contact teams attempt to bring it up. And the whole mess after that with the Fleet action . . . even space hasn't felt safe, after those pirates chasing us. I just want . . ." She rubbed her forehead. "I want to be able to relax for once."

"It's a big universe," Irine said. "There's got to be somewhere, Reese."

"And a starbase isn't a bad start," Sascha added. "I doubt many pirates are interested on taking a run at a place with active Fleet military bases overseeing things."

She smiled, rueful. "So you don't think I'm crazy?"

"Angels, Boss," Sascha said. "I think we all want a rest. Even those of us who like steady adventure need some downtime."

"Downtime would be good," Irine agreed, and leaned over to pat Reese on the knee. "Maybe we can take one of those starbase cruises I keep hearing about, where they go off to see comet tails or whatever."

"Knowing our luck, it would explode," Reese said.

Sascha coughed and pressed his hand to his nose. Irine glanced at her brother, then said, "He's right. Maybe what we should do is take you to a temple and have you ritually cleansed, see if they find a curse or two."

"You think we could pay the priests in alcohol?"

"I haven't met a priest who didn't drink," Sascha said. He tapped one more glowing square on the console. The deckplates beneath Reese's boots began to quiver. "And . . . we're off. One week and we'll be back in civilization again."

She stood. "Thanks, you two."

"Don't mention it. Getting off this planet was a pleasure," Sascha said. As she headed for the lift, he added, "Boss? Do you want us to talk to him about that issue?"

She glanced at him, then said, "I . . . don't know. Do you have anything useful to tell him about it?"

The twins exchanged glances. Irine said, "Maybe not. But he might just want to talk."

"It's up to you," Reese said after a moment. "Freedom knows I don't know what to say about it."

"I guess we'll improvise," Sascha said. "Go take a nap, ah?"

"Yes sir," Reese said, much to their amusement, and left them the bridge.

The trip from Kerayle was unremarkable, not a given what with the *Earthrise's* recent history. Hirianthial spent the first few days engaged in his normal routine, though he did not speak much to the others when he met them in the mess or on the way to the shared bathroom. Bryer no doubt found his silences unremarkable, being a creature of few words himself, but he knew the others worried.

He had made his decision, and having made it was resolved. But he also didn't want to linger over the reasons he had to leave, and perhaps that was why he waited until they were nearly to the starbase to begin packing. He had few possessions—he could fit them all in one bag and one case—but with the exception of the clothes much of it required careful packing. Once it was done, he put the bag beneath his bunk with the case and surveyed the room. He had never regretted traveling light, but seeing how similar his room looked after having packed made him question his motivations for doing so. He had never expected to find another home, perhaps. Or to be comfortable anywhere for long.

He didn't expect that to change, even when he set foot again on the homeworld.

The door alert sounding didn't surprise him; he'd been awaiting this inevitable visit. But when he called permission, it was not Reese who stepped inside, but the twins. He stood to offer them the bed and took the remaining chair in the room. "Ariisen? What can I do for you?"

They looked at one another, the light gliding off their tawny eyes. Then they sat; Irine slipped her hand into Sascha's and the two of them looked at him, as attentive as children, and somehow as innocent. There was a softness to their auras, as if it could be as furred as their pelts.

"We heard you had a rough time down there," Sascha said without preamble.

"And thought you might want to talk," Irine added. She liked to pick at her tail when nervous, which explained why she was holding her brother's hand instead. He could sense the greasy unease beneath the velvet, a viscosity so palpable he wondered if he could smooth it away.

"That is a kind offer," he said after a long moment. "But I would not be sure what there would be to talk about. I have mended, as you see."

"There's mended, and there's mended." Irine's ears flipped back, though her voice remained calm. "Some things don't mend on the inside without help."

That was a striking bit of wisdom, and applicable, if not to the hurts they thought they were addressing. He inclined his head, trying to decide how to honor their concern and the friendship that had moved them to offer their aid while also preserving his privacy. He very much did not want to share his true fears with them, for he couldn't imagine their feeling for him surviving the knowledge that he was now walking a path that had been opened by a mentally unstable mass murderer. At last, he said, "Do you know what sustained me?" He didn't look up, but he could sense the sharpness of their attention. "The memories you wove into the gift you made me." He lifted his head so they could measure the sincerity in his eyes. "It was truly without price, that gift. Your help was there."

"When you needed it," Irine said.

"Yes."

"If you're sure . . ." She sounded reluctant.

"Without question."

Sascha nodded. "If you ever want to talk, you know where to find us." He grinned. "Just remember to knock."

He smiled at that. "Always."

As they left, he wondered at the colors their auras had shifted: from the greasy gray of fear to something hard and bright as diamonds. It felt like resolve, and one so powerful he wondered what they'd been inspired to do.

"He's going to bolt," Sascha said, ears flat.

Reese was sitting at the desk in her room, studying her data tablet. "I know."

"You know?" Irine said, startled.

"Yes, I know." Reese set the tablet aside and waved them in. "It doesn't take a genius. Are you surprised?"

Sascha didn't answer, so his sister took up the conversation. "He's put everything away," Irine said. "The things on his table are missing. And he talked to us like . . . we were already out of his life."

"Because we are," Sascha said, arms tightly folded. "The moment we dock, he'll be on his way somewhere. But why? Do you think. . . ." When he didn't finish the thought, both Reese and Irine glanced at him. He looked away, grimacing. "Do you think maybe blames us for not rescuing him in time?" Irine inhaled and he rushed on. "We've always managed to get to him before they could really hurt him before. But this time . . . this time we failed."

Reese hadn't considered that possibility, but she discarded it instantly. "No. That's not like him. It's more likely he'd blame himself for anything that happened."

Irine frowned, thinking. "That is more in character. But I don't get it. Why's he leaving, Reese? Did he just get tired all of a sudden of being targeted? Or maybe he wants to settle down somewhere safer than with us?"

But Sascha was staring at Reese, eyes narrowed. "You knew. What are you planning?"

"I did know," she said. She remembered a figure kneeling alongside a corpse, bent with more than physical pain. "And it's not about us, or anything we did or didn't do. He's upset, and maybe he's thinking straight or maybe he's not, but wherever he's going or whatever he's doing, we're not going to make him do it alone."

"I can get behind that," Sascha said, ears flipping forward and spine straightening. "What's the plan?"

"I'm already working on my part." Reese tapped the data tablet. "Your job is to make sure he doesn't vanish into the crowd once we dock."

Irine peered at the tablet. "What's your part?"

"Making sure we can take him where he needs to go," Reese said.

"Which is where?" she asked, tail twitching.

"Home," Reese said. "Back to the Eldritch." She met their eyes. "Talk to the others, all right? The more of you keeping track of him, the better."

"Aye, aye, ma'am," Sascha said, rising. He paused. "Um, Boss?"

Reese sighed. "Let me guess. This is the part where you ask me the impertinent questions."

"She knows us so well," Sascha said to Irine, who managed a weak smile. He turned his attention back to her. "How come?"

"How come what?" She folded her arms.

"You're helping him," Irine said. "A few months ago we had to talk you into just letting him stay. And now you're chasing him? What changed?"

What could she tell them when she didn't even know herself? But her resentment at him for knowing her so intimately hadn't survived seeing him brought so low. Had she been so worried about him hurting him? How could she sustain her anger when she saw what he'd been through? What he kept being put through? That look in his eyes when she'd first touched him in the tent . . .

What had changed? She gave them the only answer that made any sense. "I did."

They looked at one another, then Irine smiled, a bright smile like sunlight and summer. Sascha grinned. "We're on our part of it, Boss. You do yours."

"Get out already, then," she said, but she was smiling.

Once the twins had left, Reese turned back to her tablet. The message she was composing would be sent to an address she'd been given to use in emergencies.

She knew very well that it wasn't a real address, that her message would be received, encrypted, and bounced all over the Alliance before it reached its real recipient. But she'd stumbled into this relationship, and up until now it had been a one-way street. It was time to see whether there was any chance of reciprocation.

She spent a long time going over the note, rewording it, occasionally checking with some of her romance novels to get the right flowery sound. When she replaced one word for the fourth time, she realized she was procrastinating and sent it off.

> *To my patron—*
> *I have rendered my services faithfully and I hope you've been pleased with the results. The person you charged me to aid wants to return home, and I would like to apply for permission to bring him myself. I am also in possession of some trade items that might be of particular interest to you.*
> *I await your response, and hope for it to arrive before my charge makes alternate arrangements.*
> *Yours,*
> *Theresa Eddings*

In two days, the *Earthrise* would reach the starbase. Reese hoped the Queen would get her an answer before then.

Hirianthial was not aware of making any plans to prevent the crew from stopping him. He knew better than to look too closely at his own actions. To explain the reasons for his departure was impossible, and he knew if he told anyone he was leaving, he would not be able to hold fast in the face of their inevitable pleas not to go. But go he must, so as much as he hated to do it, he did not disembark the moment the *Earthrise* settled safely at its assigned docking bay. No, he waited, accepted the disbursed pay along with the rest of the crew, and watched them scatter for the city beyond the port. As he expected, Reese headed back into the ship; she paused at the airlock and said, "Off to enjoy the sights?"

"It would be good to walk a while," he said.

Her gaze was considering; she looked not only at his eyes but his face, as if seeking something . . . or memorizing him? He found it an unusually incisive expression, and yet her aura was liquescent with sorrow over a very steady core.

What was she thinking? And how ironic that she had told him she feared him knowing her thoughts. Without consciously choosing to seek them, he had only the information granted him by her emotional state, and often all that did was intensify the mystery.

"Well," she said, smiling. "Have a good walk, then. Stretch the legs out. You won't have a chance again for a while. . . . I plan to button up and head out again within a few days."

"Of course," he said.

Her eyes lingered on him for another heartbeat, and then she turned her back on him, very deliberately, and walked into the ship.

It disturbed him that this should be his last memory of Theresa Eddings: an enigma he now would never know the answer to, one he sensed was changing in a way he might ordinarily have found intriguing. He fought the urge to follow her and investigate. Instead, he brought his bag and case out from one of the storage lockers lining the corridor and strode away, toward the kaleidoscope of light and activity, the emotional noise of thousands of people intermingling.

He would have to use the trip to decide what to do with himself once he arrived. His instinct was to go to his cousin—no matter the circumstances surrounding their parting—but doing so would involve navigating a court crowded with arrivals for the winter season. Given his notoriety, he wasn't looking forward to it. But his choice was that, or to go back to Jisiensire and the memories waiting in eager ambush there.

There was nothing for it. He needed help.

Somewhere nearby there would be a place he could buy an encrypted comm stream. After that, he should be contacted within an hour or so. He'd have enough time to eat and then he'd be crossing another airlock and on the way.

"Come on," Reese whispered to her tablet. She forced one of her hands to stay on Allacazam's fur, and through it she sensed his attempt to calm her down. It came in the form of a slow glowing field of colors in the back of her head, and all it did was split her concentration and give her the beginnings of a headache. "Come on, I'm running out of time here."

The intercom interrupted her. She smacked it with the side of her hand. "Tell me."

"It's fine, Boss. We're following him."

She pursed her lips. "I hope you're not in plain sight."

"Aw, Angels, Boss . . . we're not complete amateurs. We're doing our best not to be conspicuous."

That sounded ominous. The Harat-Shar were never inconspicuous, Bryer was a Phoenix and easily spotted in the typical crowd of Pelted, and Kis'eh't took up more room than a bipedal.

They were what she had to work with. And abruptly, it was fine. She found herself smiling at the intercom. "Yeah,

yeah. I'll believe it when I don't see you."

"Good try there. You're not getting rid of us so easy—"

Her tablet chirped. "I've got to go. Keep following him!" She switched the intercom off on his promise and spread the message that had just leaped into her queue.

You will be met at the airlock by a representative. God-speed, and we look forward to meeting you at last.

"Yes!" Reese shouted. And then stopped. "Wait, met at the *airlock*?"

Allacazam sent a quizzical buzz and then an alarmed jangle of colors and squeaks when she scooped him up and trotted toward the door. Did the Queen really mean her airlock? Right here? As in—

She stopped at the sight of a Tam-illee foxine waiting expectantly at the threshold, wearing a bright smile, perked ears, and a dark blue uniform piped in silver that looked a lot like livery but from no association Reese recognized. The emblem at her breast was an upside-down U with two ears. Behind her were a pair of Tam-illee in the same uniform, standing in front of two crates.

"Captain Eddings?" the woman said. "I'm Malia Navigatrix. I've been sent to help you prepare your vessel for a trip."

"You have?" Reese said, startled.

"By the Matriarch of the Amacrucian Church," the Tam-illee agreed, serious now.

"You have. You really . . ." Reese trailed off. The logistics of what was happening . . . it suggested a network of communication and people she couldn't even begin to fathom. But then again, her patron was the queen of a planet, and one not a member of the Alliance but an actual allied state. What did Reese know about the resources of queens?

"Please, come in," she said firmly. "Tell me what needs to be done. I'm guessing something has to be, from the crates."

"Nothing you'll object to, I don't think," Malia said. "But yes, let's discuss it."

"Absolutely."

Leading the team of Tam-illee inside, Reese grinned. For once, she'd managed to outflank the Eldritch. She was looking forward to seeing his reaction. In the crook of her arm, Allacazam turned an amused orange and sounded a victorious bugle in her mind.

Hirianthial's needs were far less strenuous than the last time he'd made a comm call; buying the security needed to reach his world directly was far more costly than using the sector drop-code to summon the Queen's couriers. Hirianthial paid for the use of a secure facility, but once he'd been ushered into the room assigned him, it was the work of only a few minutes to set up contact and request a meeting. After that, he shouldered his bag and case and went to the address he'd been given: a park, and a lovely one. He sat on a bench with his luggage at his feet and leaned back to enjoy the light, which while artificial was real enough to fool his skin.

The approaching aura drew his attention long before he heard footsteps in the grass: a brisk sunny yellow, shimmering. He opened his eyes and found a Tam-illee foxine standing before him in his cousin's livery, complete with the horseshoe emblem at the shoulder. It had amused Liolesa to brand her offworld courier service with an obsolete-to-them mode of transport . . . but they themselves had suggested decorating it with stylized fox ears, to imply the generations of Tam-illee who had sworn themselves to her service through another Jisiensire, Lesandural Meriaen.

"Lord Sarel Jisiensire? I am Theodore ChartsStars. I'm here to see you to your vessel. May I take your bag?"

The foxine had known not to offer for the case, of course; they were well-trained, and proud of that training. To deny him the chance to render his services would be uncouth, though Hirianthial was quite capable of carrying both himself. "Please, and thank you."

"My pleasure, Lord. This way, if you will."

Hirianthial took up the case and followed the todfox. The vessels the Queen's Tams employed were very similar in make, private couriers, swift, dangerous and able to dust themselves with the latest in concealment technologies. He anticipated going back to the homeworld in a ship very much like the one he'd left in. It didn't concern him over-much that he recognized the path they were taking: the vessel was no doubt in the civilian dock somewhere, just like the hundreds of others visiting the starbase. It wasn't until he turned into the bay and saw the entire crew of the *Earthrise* awaiting him at the airlock along with two other of the Queen's Tams that he stopped short.

"Hi!" Reese said, arms folded. Her nonchalance didn't fool him at all: she was, undeniably, smug. "We're your ride home."

"I'll bring your bag to your quarters," his guide said, and hopped into the airlock.

The foxine female—the company's senior from the uniform design—inclined her head and said, "My lord. It will be a pleasure," before turning to her subordinate and saying, "See to the final tests, please."

"I didn't think the Tams used private vessels," Hirianthial said to her.

Unfazed, she replied, "My lord, the Queen's Tams use whatever vessels she deems appropriate." She bowed and then followed her subordinate inside.

. . . which left him with his friends, and he didn't know where to begin.

Kis'eh't said, "It's good to have you back. I'm cooking dinner using my fancy new skills, courtesy of Sascha's mother. No toast this time. Don't be late." She smiled and hopped into the ship.

Bryer eyed him but said nothing; he wouldn't. But he expected a remonstrance from the twins, particularly since he could sense their hurt beneath the pleasure of seeing him again. Because he was expecting the remonstrance, Sascha's actual question struck hard and deep. "Was it something we did? Did you think you couldn't trust us to help you?"

"I . . . it was the furthest thing from my mind," Hirianthial said. "Never, arii. It is only that I had a need and did not think the *Earthrise* could fulfill it."

Irine grinned. "I hope that's the last time you underestimate Reese." She tugged at Sascha's hand. "Come on. Let's go keep an eye on the foxes."

As they vanished into the corridor, Reese called after them, "That better mean 'keeping an eye on them' and not 'distract them with sex!'" Irine's giggle trailed after her, a hollow echo.

Reese turned back to him, arms still folded, leaning against the airlock frame. Not anger, he thought. Something more complicated that he couldn't read at all, glossed over with an opalescent glimmer.

"Theresa," he began, and stopped when she held up a hand.

"I'm not upset," she said. "I've done my share of running. But I hope you understand that we're here for you. Sometimes," she paused, then shook her head, rueful. "Sometimes, doing it alone is the wrong way. It's almost always the wrong way, I'm beginning to think."

"You may be right," he said. "But you may not be able to follow where I lead." He thought of the bodies and grew cold. "And I may not be worth following."

She did not immediately protest, which surprised him. He looked at her and found her considering him. At last, she said, "Well, do us the courtesy of letting us make that decision, all right?"

"All right," he said, startled.

"Now come on," she said. "That case has got to be heavy. Go put it back in your room."

He dipped his head to her and walked past her, back into the ship. And as worried as he was about what awaited him . . . he was glad to be back.

PART TWO: STEEL

Taking an Eldritch home was more complicated than Reese had anticipated.

"You mean to tell me you're coming with us?" she asked Malia.

"I fear I must, Captain."

They were in the mess, having some of the leftover apple pie Kis'eh't had made for Hirianthial's 'welcome back' dinner. The foxine had looked at it uncertainly when Reese had set it in front of her, but one taste had convinced the Tam-illee of its merits and she was now scraping the edges of the plate with her spoon, trying to get the last flecks of filling.

Reese watched her, puzzled. She wasn't upset at having to host someone, but she hadn't expected it and she couldn't imagine what would have motivated the request. "I have a good pilot. No, I mean, a great pilot. He can do the job if you tell us where to go."

Malia looked up at her as she stopped, frowning. The foxine's ears perked.

"And you can't tell us where to go," Reese guessed. "Is that it?"

"Yes," Malia said. "I'm sorry, Captain, but these are long-standing orders."

"And when you say 'long-standing,' I somehow bet you mean 'so long standing neither of us were alive when they were originally issued,'" Reese guessed.

Malia nodded, her silver bob swinging around her chin. "I see you've worked out a little of what it's like, dealing with Eldritch."

"A little, maybe," Reese said. "Will I be taking on your other two people as well?"

Malia licked her spoon with a tiny pink tongue. Reese repressed the urge to think her adorable—that was all she needed. The twins would laugh her out the airlock. Noticing Reese's stare, the foxine colored at the ears and said, "Ah, sorry. I've never had pie like this."

"Kis'eh't's baking is something else," Reese agreed.

"But no," Malia said, setting the spoon down and folding her hands around her coffee cup. "I'll be the only one. You won't have to pay me, and any expenses you incur by taking me on—food, air, recycling, medical care, et cetera—would be reimbursed when we reach our destination."

"Wow," Reese said, staring at her. "This is a big production, isn't it? You're part of a company, I guess?"

"Of a sorts," Malia said. "And if you're allowed to go where you're going, you'll probably find out all about us. But in case you don't, you won't mind if I'm quiet about the details?"

"Of course not," Reese said.

"You said that?" Irine asked Reese later, having come for her own slice of pie. Kis'eh't was behind the counter, working on another, having seen how fast the first was going. Allacazam was sitting on the table under his sun lamp, and Sascha was getting mugs from the clatter in the galley.

"Of course I did," Reese said. "What else was I going to say?"

"You could have said 'no.'" Sascha set a tray on the table, then pulled out a chair and reversed it so he could straddle it. He started pouring. "I'm surprised you didn't put up more of a fuss, Boss."

"I think by now we've had enough experience with military matters for me to know when people are keeping quiet for a reason," Reese said.

"Yeah? What's her reason?" Irine asked, setting a plate of pie in front of her brother.

"Oh, I don't know," Reese said. "Maybe slavers constantly trying to steal the people she's taking us to see?" She shuddered. "Can you imagine what would happen if slavers found out where they could get an entire planetful of Eldritch?"

"They'd have to fortify the place like a bank vault," Sascha said.

"Because that's what it would be. The galaxy's biggest bank vault." Reese rubbed her arms, trying to get the gooseflesh to smooth out. "No, I'm not at all concerned about staying quiet. Actually, I'm beginning to wonder if we've set ourselves up for something a little more dangerous than we're up to."

"We did just come from a rather successful military operation," Kis'eh't said from behind the counter, where the smell of cinnamon and dough was wafting. "If we could come out of one pirate den—two if you count the one we brought Hirianthial out of—then surely that counts for something? Practice, at least?"

"It feels more like we're pushing our luck," Reese said.

She shook her head. "No, if that was the last we see of things better left to Fleet, I'll be a very happy woman."

Irine joined them at the table with the coffee pitcher. "Have you seen your cargo bay today?"

"No?" Reese said. "Should I be worried?"

"We have a Pad!" Irine exclaimed.

"We must have a borrowed Pad because I certainly didn't buy one," Reese said.

Kis'eh't joined them, wiping her floury hands on a towel. "It's theirs, all right. Those foxes'. Brand new, too."

"And the modifications to the engines . . . are we keeping them?" Sascha asked.

Reese eyed him. "The modifications to the engines make us harder to track. I'm hoping we don't need to use them ever."

"You have been here for the past year or so, right?" Sascha asked, tail curling. He grinned at her expression, unrepentant.

"I don't know if we're keeping the equipment," Reese admitted. "I'll ask when we get there."

"The Eldritch world," Kis'eh't said. "What do you think it's like?"

Reese tried to imagine a world full of graceful, beautiful people with all of Hirianthial's annoying perfections and none of his humility—because in her experience, people with an Eldritch's supernal qualities were rarely humble—and said, "I'm pretty sure it's going to be insufferable."

Hirianthial waited for the inevitable meeting, the one where Reese would arrive to demand an accounting of his behavior, or the twins would come to him privately to ask what they'd done to discomfit him into leaving, or Kis'eh't to use their shared lab time to ask one of her blunt questions. He was therefore surprised to be stopped by Bryer in the corridor, something the Phoenix accomplished by stretching a hand to rest on the opposite wall and splaying the metallic wing that lined the arm, blocking the way. With his body bent toward Hirianthial, he looked very much like the hunter he'd been modeled on: part avian dinosaur, part bird of prey, all long beak and large, whiteless eyes in a crested head. He extended his face far enough that Hirianthial could sense his aura, usually so tightly contracted it seemed more a second skin. It registered an electric crackle, one the Eldritch interpreted as displeasure.

"You abandoned your charge," the Phoenix said.

Hirianthial paused. "I was not aware I still had one," he said carefully.

"You. And I." The Phoenix pointed to a bare gold breast with one taloned fingertip. "We guard."

"I had matters that needed attention," Hirianthial said. "And did not think this vessel could serve them."

"Did not ask." Bryer pointed at him now. "Next time ask. Ask me, if not Reese. We are bonded in blood. And duty. Do not make this mistake again."

"No," Hirianthial said, startled.

Bryer withdrew his wing and swept past him down the corridor, the grid flooring hissing under the long trailing feathers of his tail.

The *Earthrise* set off from the starbase under the guidance of the Navigatrix, and they'd been several days underway before Malia came to him. He offered her the chair in his room and sat on the bed.

"My lord," she said. "Forgive me, but there is something I would like to discuss with you." Her aura was a muted purple, velvety with deference.

"Go on."

"Your crewmates," the foxine said. "They seem to have

no conception at all of Eldritch customs."

"I have observed the Veil," he answered, wondering where she would take the conversation.

"As we all must, my lord," Malia agreed. "But these people have been invited to the homeworld, and they don't know what to expect or how to behave. Someone must teach them the basics of courteous behavior."

"You assume they'll be going with me on-world."

"I have been told to expect that they will," she said, meeting his eyes.

He had wondered how Reese had secured their passage. A message to his cousin directly, no doubt . . . but what had they said to one another? "I see."

"Shall I teach them, my lord?" Malia asked when he didn't go on.

"No," he said. "No, I would like to discuss the matter with the captain first."

"Of course," she said, rising and bowing. "If you need my services, I am at your disposal."

Very literally, he thought. She was . . . the ninth? Tenth? Generation of Tam-illee to have entered service in the Queen's Tams. Year after year, the progeny of Lesandurel's original mortal friend, Sydnie Unfound, pledged themselves to the Eldritch and died in that service of old age.

"Thank you," he said, and she let herself out.

Did they ever tire of it? Of living so briefly and dying while their Eldritch patron lived on?

Did Lesandurel ever tire of it, of loving them and watching them die?

He did not linger on the matter—could not bear to linger on the matter—but went in search of Reese and found her on the bridge with Allacazam, staring out the viewport. She looked relaxed, but her thoughts were a tangle if the haze of static and colors in her aura was any indication, and in her arms Allacazam was a determined light green. At the sound of his boots, she glanced at the lift and then returned to the view. "It's strange to see the ship flying itself on a course I didn't okay personally."

"That will be the least of the things you will be unable to decide on personally, if you continue on this course," he said. He had her attention, he saw. "What did you ask of the Queen?"

Reese ran a slow hand over Allacazam's fur, leaving a darker green swath behind her fingers. "I said I wanted to bring you home, and that I had some things to trade if she was interested. We both agreed it would be nice to meet in person finally."

"She said that?" Hirianthial asked, hiding his surprise. "That she would meet you?"

Her voice became guarded, and he found he didn't like that he had caused it. "Is that so strange?"

"She is the head of state of an entire world," Hirianthial said, to lighten her mood. "Do you make a habit of personal meetings with such luminaries?"

"I can't say I have," Reese said, and her wariness became asperity, if touched with something pale and bright. Was it humor? "But I did fight a sector full of slavers on her behalf. I'd say I've earned it, with her at least."

"So you have," he said, after a moment, hoping for some clue as to her true mental state and failing to divine it. He sighed. "If you are planning on this, there are things you should know about the maintenance of decorum among my people, so as not to give offense if you are seen by more than the Queen."

She narrowed her eyes. "Is there some reason she'd be hiding me?"

"Foreigners aren't permitted on our soil," Hirianthial said. "Except by royal dispensation, and even then it is a matter not to be undertaken lightly." He thought of the polarization of the court. "It creates . . . issues."

"Issues," Reese repeated, her aura developing a tremor that traveled its length. "What you really mean is 'problems,' don't you."

"That would be a dramatic interpretation," Hirianthial said. "But not incorrect."

He expected a protestation or a demand for more information. Instead, she said, "You really aren't comfortable with any of this, are you. Going back, us going with you, the reason you're going."

Startled, he drew back. Her silence did not require filling, but was so unusual in her that he found himself doing so anyway. "Did you understand what you saw on Kerayle?"

"You explained it, yes," Reese said, petting the Flitzbe. "You killed some people who'd kidnapped you."

"I killed people without the use of weapons. With my thoughts," Hirianthial said. He repeated it to force her to face it. "I killed people by wishing them dead. I would think you'd find that marginally more distressing than my simply reading their minds."

But she ignored his sarcasm. "I'm assuming this isn't a random thought that ran through your head," Reese said instead, the words slow. "Not something that could happen by accident."

"No," he said. Then grimaced. "I don't know. I didn't know I could do it; I'm not sure *how* I did it."

"But you were under duress."

Hand fisted in hair, the muted clap of the bell against his shoulder. "Yes," he said, grim.

She nodded. "So, you're not likely to make Sascha drop over because he said something that upset you."

"No!" Hirianthial exclaimed. "God and Lady. I hope

not." He composed himself, but he felt cold. "I am going home in order to see that I am not capable of such accidents. There are . . . teachers, there. They may be able to instruct me."

She studied him, then said, "Most people would be grateful, you know. To know they could defend themselves without a weapon."

Hirianthial flexed stiff fingers. "Some weapons are never right to use."

"And this one is one of them?" she asked. "Why?"

It seemed appallingly obvious to him. "Because it cannot be defended against."

"You sure?" she asked, surprising him. "You're telling me this talent of yours always works, and you're sure there's no way to fight it?" She shook her head. "Look, I know you're upset about this. But—don't get mad at me for saying this—you are much too quick to think badly of yourself. You're not a monster because you can kill people. Lots of people can kill people. It's how they use—or don't use—that ability that makes them monsters."

"Captain," Hirianthial said, quiet, "You do not know all the things I have done in this life."

"No," she agreed. "You haven't told me. But that doesn't change my opinion. Unless you're going to tell me you're a serial killer? Or a drug lord?" She lifted her brows. "No? Didn't think so."

"It's not so simple," he said.

"Maybe you're just trying to complicate it too much." She tilted her head, her braids crumpling against one shoulder. "So what are you going to tell the crew? You have to tell them something. They like you too much to say it, but they feel abandoned."

And she did not? He couldn't tell from the shimmer of coral and pale gray that flickered through her aura.

Hirianthial looked away. "I had not planned to say any-thing, Lady."

"You want me to tell them instead?"

"No," he said. And thought of Malia's concerns. He sighed. "No. We can have the discussion when I make the attempt to dissuade them from following you on-world."

Reese snorted. "This should be good."

It was exactly as good as Reese expected.

"You're telling us we can't go down ourselves?" Kis'eh't asked, feathered ears flattened. "Why? There's some kind of non-Eldritch quarantine? Is it medical?"

Hirianthial rarely looked flustered and didn't look it now, to Reese's eyes. But she got the feeling he was uncom-fortable and didn't blame him. The entire crew was staring at him from around the table in the mess, and none of them looked happy.

"No," he said at last. "It isn't a medical issue."

"So it's . . . speciesism?" Irine asked, ears sagging. "Is that even a word?"

"Xenophobia is a word." Kis'eh't folded her arms, eyes narrowing.

"Yeah," Sascha said quietly. "It is."

"We're not leaving Reese alone on a world full of xeno-phobes," Irine said, her ears now flat against her golden hair.

"I'll be there," Hirianthial said.

"No offense," Sascha said, voice still low, "but you walked out on us before. How do we know you're not going to do it again, and to her?"

"The Eldritch will not do this again," Bryer said sud-denly. Everyone looked at him, and the Phoenix stared at Hirianthial.

"No," Hirianthial agreed after a moment.

"Maybe you should explain why you left," Reese said

finally. She didn't like forcing the issue, but she also didn't like the hurt she could hear in the room. Even Kis'eh't, blessed with the normally imperturbable Glaseahn disposition, sounded upset. He'd started this, by making the crew his friends . . . had accepted their friendship before Reese forced herself to do the same, admitted that she cared about them as much as they did her. She wasn't going to sit back and let him walk away from the pain he was causing, not without trying to fix it.

Hirianthial looked away, and this time she saw his jaw grow taut, and his fingers . . . they were gripping the edge of his stool so tightly it amazed her that he could carry off the otherwise nonchalant use of it. He didn't speak for so long that she worried she'd pushed too far. So she took a chance and spoke for him. "The esper abilities he's got are acting weird."

"Weird?" Kis'eh't asked, distracted from her distress.

Hirianthial cleared his throat. "I am evincing abilities I was not aware of, and the ones I am aware of are . . . surprising me. I am concerned there may be something wrong."

"So he wanted to get back to the homeworld and see if they knew anything about it," Reese finished.

"When esper abilities go strange it can be very disturbing," Kis'eh't said, studying the Eldritch now thoughtfully. "Do you think the Eldritch healers can help you? If not, we can try my people. The Glaseah have mind-healers."

"I thank you for the suggestion," he said. "And if I find no aid where we go, I will be sure to consult with them next."

"All right," Sascha said. "I get that you had to leave the ship because you thought we wouldn't be able to get dispensation to go. But why did you leave without saying goodbye?"

Reese leaned forward, face cradled in her palms. Since Hirianthial's attempting to sneak away had struck her as cruel, she was not inclined to save him from any more questions. No doubt he knew it too, if he could read her thoughts. Was he? She imagined telling him 'you brought this one on yourself.'

He didn't move his head, but his eyes shot toward her. She straightened in her chair, but he was already looking at Sascha again. "Would it be acceptable for me to admit I didn't think I could bear it?"

That answer surprised them all.

"I think if we could hug you, we would hug you," Irine said. And then, frustrated, "But you're one of us, Hirianthial! You're supposed to lean on us for help! We work together to solve our problems, all right?"

"Irine," he began, and then stopped, looking down until he could compose himself. Drawing in a breath that lifted his shoulders he said finally, husky, "Irine. There are perils in taking on family for someone like me."

"Maybe you should have thought of that before you came aboard and were so charming at us," Irine said. She stood up. "Anyway. I am going to make something hot to drink because it is like a polar ice cap in here, as usual. You—" She pointed at Hirianthial. "—are about to tell us how to behave around Eldritch so we won't get you or anyone else in trouble. Because we're going with Reese. Right?"

"Right," Sascha said.

"Right," Kis'eh't said.

Bryer made a low chirring sound.

"Very well," Hirianthial said. "But there is one rule above all that I must ask of you."

"And that is?" Reese asked.

"When we are on-world," he said, emphatic, "if I command something, it must be done. There are nuances I will not be able to teach you in the time we have, and there will be those eager to find fault. If they do—"

"Then we'll be punished?" Kis'eh't asked.

"Then your hosting family will be punished," Hirianthial said.

"Which will be you?" Sascha asked. "Or . . ." He glanced at Reese.

"Or the Queen?" Reese frowned. "Can they really punish a queen for our behavior just because she's the one who asked us to the world?"

"I think, very much, there are some who would like to try."

"Yeah," Sascha said. "We are very much not letting you go alone into this dragon's lair, Boss."

"Good," Reese said. "Because I very much don't want to go without you."

Irine returned with a pot of steaming kerinne, the scent of cinnamon trailing her. "So, what first? Manners? Forms of address?"

Hirianthial sighed.

For the next few days, Reese attended Hirianthial's sessions on proper behavior among Eldritch, and it was like something out of her worst romance novels, the ones with such stilted and self-important societies they seemed more like caricatures than actual cultures. There was a minimum distance they were supposed to maintain between themselves and strangers—a literal distance, measured in feet— and that distance shrank or grew depending on the level of acquaintanceship one claimed with another person. The rules about eye contact were equally Byzantine. There was, of course, no touching, though in select social occasions the Eldritch worked around that with the use of daggers for men and wands or fans for women. There were rules about when it was polite to speak and when not to, though he didn't bother teaching them the language, saying only that the people likely to want to speak with them would all know Universal.

After one of these lectures, Reese went down the hall to the quarters she'd assigned Malia Navigatrix. The foxine let her in and gave her the room's only chair, sitting on the bed to face her with a posture so like Hirianthial's that Reese paused.

"Captain?" Malia asked, folding her hands in her lap. "What can I do for you?"

"Did they teach you that?" Reese asked. "To sit so still."

Malia did not so much as twitch an ear. "Those of us with direct contact with the Eldritch have had deportment lessons."

"And there are those of you who aren't in direct contact with . . ." Reese stopped, held up a hand. "Never mind. That's not why I'm here. Malia, Hirianthial makes the political situation on his homeworld sound like a warzone. Is it that bad? What exactly am I walking into?"

Malia hesitated, then her ears swept back and she grimaced, a very unplanned expression. It made her look like what she was, a young Pelted woman, and Reese liked her much better that way. "Ah. Mm. You would ask that."

"That sounds bad."

"It's not that, it's just . . . I don't know how much I can tell you. I'm sworn to the Queen's service, which means I get to observe the Veil, just like the rest of the Eldritch. That's their custom of not divulging anything to foreigners, if he hasn't mentioned it yet."

"You're joking?" Reese asked, and when Malia's chagrined expression didn't alter, finished, "You're not. You're telling me that you've committed yourself to a policy of keeping Eldritch secrets from non-Eldritch? You're not an Eldritch, Malia!"

"I know," Malia said. "I know. But this is my job, Captain. It's a job I've trained for all my life. And my family's been involved in it for generations. We've even got a family Eldritch." She smiled, lopsided. "He's been around since my ancestress met him in an apartment on Earth. They went to a party together, dressed in gold and silver."

"Let me guess," Reese said. "He wore silver."

Malia's smile grew fond. "Actually, they mixed and matched, so they were in both colors. You should have seen the pictures. . . ." She shook herself, then nodded. "That's how it's been for us, Captain. He gives a little, we give a little, and we've made a family out of it."

And that explained it, with the suddenness of lightning. *Family.* Malia was Tam-illee, but they'd adopted their ancestress's Eldritch friend. That made sense of her keeping the Veil. She had her own Eldritch to protect. Reese studied her, then said, "All right. Granted that you can't tell me everything. Is there something at all you can share? Even a little?"

Malia looked away, lip between her teeth. She smoothed her hands out on her pants and said, "A little, maybe. At very least you should know if the Queen has taken you on as a potential retainer. She's very forward-looking, the Queen."

"Wait, wait. Retainer?"

"It seemed kinder than saying 'as one of her servants,'" Malia said. "Universal gives connotations to those words that don't necessarily apply in their own."

"Fine. Go on."

"The Queen," Malia said, "looks out for the interests of her people, and thinks that includes us. Us, not-Eldritch" She met Reese's eyes, her gray gaze somber. "She doesn't hold with the xenophobia."

"So that means half the planet disagrees with her and

finds the idea revolting, and probably very much wants to lynch her for the suggestion."

"You're absolutely right," Malia said. "Except it's more than half, I'm afraid."

Reese tapped her knee with her fingers. "What you're telling me, then, is that I'm walking into a situation where more than half the people don't want to have anything to do with me, and the woman who sponsored me is sitting on a bomb."

"More or less," Malia said, ears folding back apologetically.

Reese pulled a hand down her face, stopped with her hand over her mouth. She shook her head. "These people really want that little to do with us? It seems crazy to have this much angst over outworlders. They've solved the problem, haven't they? They don't see outworlders at all. What more do they want?"

"More than that I'll have to let the Queen explain to you," Malia said. "If she chooses to, she'll tell you why it's so important."

"Right," Reese said. She sighed and rose. "Thanks."

"You're welcome, Captain."

"Reese," she corrected automatically. "While you're on this ship, it's Reese." She smiled wryly. "The only people who call me 'captain' are being ironic about it."

Malia chuckled. "All right. Reese."

On her way to the door, Reese paused. "Do you speak Eldritch, Malia?"

The foxine glanced at her. "Ah?"

"You said something about the word servant in Universal not being the same for them. Do you speak the language?"

Malia pleated the edge of her tunic over her thigh. "The treaty between the Alliance and the Eldritch specifies that only a certain number of people can be taught their language, Captain—Reese. I think it's five. Two trainers, and three people in Fleet Intelligence. For anyone else to know the language is a violation of the treaty."

Reese folded her arms and lifted her brows.

"But," Malia said without looking at her, "it's sometimes helpful to know what your enemies are saying about you."

Reese said, "I'll keep that in mind."

When the floor shivered beneath his boots in his room, Hirianthial paused. He had some sense for the distances, having traveled them one way already, but the trip had seemed to last so long—and not long enough—and so he found himself waiting for confirmation. Usually it took only a few moments for Malia Navigatrix to re-orient the ship and send it down its new course, but when the engines re-engaged it wasn't the quick tremor of the Well engines, but the slower pulse of the insystem drives.

They had arrived.

He reached beneath the bed for the case and pulled it out, flipping the catches and pushing the lid open. On the bed of crushed wine-colored velvet rested Jisiensire's swords. His hand traveled the length of the hand-and-a-half, pausing on the opal that rested in the mangled setting beneath the crossguards. He had not worn these swords in over five decades, had renounced the right to carry them when he set aside the seal. In fact, he would not even have them if his House-cousin hadn't insisted that he take them. She hadn't wanted his title, though she'd shouldered the responsibilities of managing the families that looked to them without complaint, but she would absolutely not accept the additional responsibility of the swords. Better Jisiensire be without champion, she had said, than to cut him off from hearth and kin by accepting his complete renunciation, seal and sword.

Hirianthial thought of Bryer's accusation and closed the case without removing any of the weapons inside.

The lift took him to the *Earthrise's* cramped bridge, where Sascha and Irine were using two of the ubiquitous crates shoved into the back of the room as seats. Kis'eh't was at the sensor station, and Reese at comm. Malia was in the pilot's chair.

"Just in time," Sascha said, his aura alive with a crackling anticipation. "We hit the system limit a minute ago."

As if in response, the comm panel chirped, signaling an incoming audio-only transmission. Reese looked down at it, startled, then tapped it open.

"Unidentified vessel, you are entering private space. Give your credentials or be advised we are authorized to turn you back at the border."

Reese's aura bloomed white with incredulity. "Are they serious?"

"Very," Malia said, and leaned over to address the console's pick-up. "Outermost Wing, this is Malia Navigatrix on the TMS *Earthrise*. We have the Queen's authorization to proceed to the planet."

"Malia! Not Ferrell's daughter?"

Malia smiled. "The very same. We're here out of Starbase Psi, carrying home a national."

"Ah?"

Malia glanced at Hirianthial, so he stepped close enough to be heard and said, "That would be me. Hirianthial Sarel Jisiensire."

"My lord! How wonderful! The Queen will be delighted to hear that you've come home."

Reese was staring at him; he could feel the agitation of her attention like an itch. He sifted among all the truths until he found a socially acceptable one. "We have a great deal to discuss."

"All right, Malia . . . you know the way. You're cleared to go. Remember the protocols."

"Always," Malia replied. "*Earthrise* out."

"That was my line," Reese said.

The foxine chuckled. "I'll let you say it next time. Who knows? Maybe you'll be running your own ship out."

Reese huffed. "I'm not ready to swear to an Eldritch Veil."

Malia smiled and said only, "Heading in-system. This may take a while? You all might want to go somewhere more comfortable."

"And miss this?" Irine asked, ears perked. "Not for all the worlds in the Core!"

"All right," Malia said. Then added, ears lopsided, "I felt the same way the first time I came in."

"Well, some of us are here for more prosaic reasons," Kis'eh't said. "Like the fact that I can't find signs of any station anywhere, or any ship. Who hailed us? And where are they?"

Reese frowned, then left the comm board to peer over Kis'eh't's shoulder.

"Don't bother," Malia said. "You won't find them. They're tucked away like that on purpose, and stealthed besides. It keeps the system from looking notable to people cruising past it. Everything in system is locked down that way."

"Even the planet?" Kis'eh't asked. "Planets give off a lot of noise."

Malia glanced at Hirianthial. Turning back to her board, she said, "The planet's not a problem."

He could sense their curiosity and unease, but was not motivated to address it. They would discover soon enough why the Eldritch homeworld was so quiet.

No, he had come to the bridge for a reason, and he had only to wait another ten minutes for fruition. Reese's panel chirped again, and her voice when she spoke was disgruntled. "There's a message here for you, Hirianthial."

He inclined his head and waited for her to move out of the way before sitting. As he expected, it was in text only.

Come at soonest opportunity. Board our guests until I can send for them.

It is good to have you home.

Hirianthial tapped his fingers lightly on the board once. "Malia, what time is it at the capital right now?"

The entire crew was listening; he could feel their straining attention like static electricity. The foxine said, "Just before dawn. We should be there . . . ah . . . say late afternoon local time."

"Thank you." He wrote simply 'Expect me with the evening,' and sent it on before ceding the panel to Reese. "I'll be in my quarters if I'm needed."

If they stared at him on the way out, he did not notice. There was no part of that message he did not find unsettling. The curtness was not unusual—Liolesa was always busy—but the combination of implied urgency and gratitude at his arrival suggested the situation on the world had grown worse, for he couldn't imagine her welcoming him home any other way given how abruptly he'd left. He had told her when she'd been made heir that he had no interest in helping her navigate the difficult political situation, and she had not been surprised; he'd never made any attempt to hide his impatience with the constant maneuvering of the court. But as the head of Jisiensire, he represented one of the most powerful blocs of Liolesa's supporters, and while Araelis was authorized to run the House in his absence she would not make any major decisions on her own. Not because she wasn't capable, but because she was convinced that he would see the wisdom of taking the mantle back up again, and her refusal to wear the seal was her way of forcing his hand.

He was fond of Araelis, so the manipulation he would have found irritating from anyone else merely felt tiresome from her.

What was going on? God and Lady knew they could not bear much more bad news, given the way the world was going. He had come to see to himself. He hoped he would have the chance.

"What was that all about?" Sascha wondered, looking at the closed lift.

"Who knows," Kis'eh't said. "Secret Eldritch business or something."

"Not so secret soon, if we're going downstairs." Irine took her socked tail in hand and started petting it, then gave up on it and reached for her brother's, which was bare. "Do you know, Malia?"

"I don't," the foxine said. "I'm sure it had something to do with preparing for his arrival, though."

"Can you tell us what it's like down there?" Irine asked, and hurried on when she saw the foxine's hesitation, "Not like that. I mean . . . how should we dress? What do the trees look like? Are there trees?"

"There are trees," Malia said, smiling. "They're fond of trees. And as for weather . . . it's early winter, so you can expect it to be cold and gray. If it's been particularly cold, there might be snow or sleet. Or freezing rain, sometimes."

Irine's ears had folded back. "Freezing rain. What fun."

"Maybe we can haul out the cold weather gear Reese made us get for that ice planet," Kis'eh't said, amused.

"I don't think it'll be that cold." Sascha drew Irine into

his arms and she flopped against him with a sigh.

"It would have to be cold, wouldn't it," she said.

"The summers are nice, I hear," Malia said. "But it's no Harat-Sharii."

Reese snorted.

Several hours later, the *Earthrise* achieved orbit around a world with cobalt-blue seas and pale green and sandy brown continents, swirled with glittering clouds. Hirianthial did not have to see it to remember it, but the sight of it when he stepped onto the bridge to find Reese arrested him. Sascha was the only one on watch, sitting once again in the pilot's seat with Allacazam on his lap.

"They're all in the cargo bay," the Harat-Shar said before he could ask. "Malia's setting the Pad up for you. Apparently they have limited coordinate sets for it, and they haven't said why." He lifted his brows, aura simmering with barely contained sparks.

They were all insatiably curious, and while Hirianthial couldn't blame them he could not feed them either. He had no idea what his cousin intended, bringing them here; he would have to know her mind before he could share his. "I'm not familiar with her protocols in regards to the Pad."

"Mmm," Sascha said. "Nice dodge." He shook his head. "And no, I'm not going to push you about it. But you know, if ever we needed information, arii, now would be the time. Before we walk into a completely foreign situation—"

"You'll have some time to become accustomed to it," Hirianthial said, "as I'll be hosting you initially."

"You—what?"

"You will be staying with me," he repeated. "And there will be few people there to see you, or react to your initial attempts at orientation."

Sascha's eyes narrowed. Then he said, "You have a

minute? They won't be sending anything down for a bit, not until Malia's done configuring the thing."

"Of course?" Hirianthial said. He took the seat across from Sascha's and waited.

Sascha ran a hand over Allacazam's fur, a pale beige frosted with white. "You listened to me when I told you about the problems I had with my own home. That conversation . . . it was the first time anyone had really heard what I was saying, really understood it." He smiled, self-conscious, showing a touch of his fanged eye teeth. "So you know if you ever need anyone to listen to your problems, you have more than one person who'll pay attention."

"Thank you—"

"But," Sascha said, and the earnest warmth in his aura stiffened into an abrupt ferocity. "You need to promise you'll never abandon us like that again, without warning. You want to leave? Fine. Go. But not like that, with us wondering if you've been kidnapped or killed or if you hate us or what have you."

"Sascha," Hirianthial began, startled at the anger he could sense just beneath that drum-taut surface.

"You think I'm kidding? You should know better. You know how many people are on your tail," Sascha said. "And that's you personally. You, generically, an Eldritch? Quadruple that number, because every slaver in the galaxy wants one of you people." His ears flattened. "Maybe you don't believe it, but we've got your back here, all right? But we can't do our part if you don't do yours."

In some other universe, one where his Butterfly had lived and he'd remained the true head of Jisiensire, he would have taken a man like Sascha to squire and brought him up to guard captain one day . . . had Sascha been Eldritch, of course. But Sascha was Pelted, and Hirianthial was no longer the head of Jisiensire no matter what

Araelis might hope, and his Butterfly was long gone. Still, the blazing brightness of Sascha's anger had led him to the source of the flame, and it was loyalty. He felt it anew in the dangle he still wore woven into the hair at his neck, with its echoes of the Harat-Shar's feelings as he assembled it. Hirianthial could not turn his back on such a thing without dishonor. So he did what he so rarely allowed himself—and made a vow, hoping he would not be forced to break it—or worse, keep it, when the keeping of vows so often led to heartache and bloodshed. "I promise."

Sascha searched his face. His ears slowly eased from his skull and perked up again. "Thanks," he said, finally.

Hirianthial inclined his head. "Unless there's anything else?"

"No," Sascha said. "Have a safe trip down."

Hirianthial stopped for his case on the way to the cargo bay. He also unpacked the coat and scarf he'd bought off-world and a pair of gloves he'd brought with him from home: pale tan leather, soft still despite the years. He smoothed the fingers out, running a short nail along the raised embroidery stitched between thumb and forefinger: a curling vine, complete with pale silver flower. As the culmination of a culture such flourishes had power . . . but as a symbol of all they'd lost, it was merely pitiable. And as beautiful as the gloves were, the Alliance's coat was as comfortable and had been far more affordable. He wondered what he had become, to have such thoughts, and to wear such a hybridization of cultures without fanfare.

Whatever the case, he was glad of the clothes when he reached the cargo bay, having forgotten how cold Reese kept them. His breath was leaving his lips in wisps.

Malia was the first to look up as he advanced on them. She said, "My lord. The Pad is ready for you."

Bryer was examining some reading on the Pad's base, but Reese straightened when she saw him. When he was close enough, she held out a data tablet, careful to keep her fingers on the edge.

"What's this?"

"Malia says you need to send up coordinates for any place indoors you might want us to be able to go to. That'll let you get them to her."

"Ah," Hirianthial said, tucking it under his arm. "Thank you."

"Which leads me to ask," Reese said, eyeing Malia, "Just how will people be able to get back up here once they're down there?"

"There's a Pad on-world," Malia said, which both surprised and did not surprise Hirianthial. He'd had no idea Liolesa had one, but knowing Liolesa it was also an inevitability. She kept secrets well; in many ways, she was the most Eldritch Eldritch Hirianthial knew. Would that her detractors understood that. Malia continued. "Barring that, there's a landing field large enough for the *Earthrise* within a day's riding distance from the palace."

"Blood and freedom." Reese rubbed her forehead. "More horses."

Bryer stood, chuffed. "Is ready from our end. You?"

Malia tapped in the coordinates and the Pad light flicked blue, registering an open tunnel. "My lord. You may step through when ready."

"Call us," Reese added.

"I shall," he said. "Thank you." And he stepped over the Pad and into a wall of visceral memories. The smell of the sea, of autumn leaves gone long since to mold, of the dampness of a recent rain—the color of twilight, that pale gray purple sky seen beyond the silhouettes of the distant buildings—the utter silence that wrapped around him on this world absent modern technology. He had become so accustomed to the boom and bustle of the Alliance, of the sound of passing transport, of people living elbow to elbow. . . .

He stood in that silence until the cold wind lifted just enough to break it, soughing around his shoulders and hips, ruffling his hair away until it exposed the dangle. He twitched as if it had nicked a nerve. In the distance, a night loon crooned, raising the hair on the back of his neck.

He was home.

He was also standing in a field not far from his destination, and he was already too aware of the chill; winters often seemed mild on the coast, but the damp winds off the ocean could be cruel. Flexing his fingers against the case's handle, he set off for the capital. He was approaching it from the wilderness near the sea cliffs, where no one dwelt; it was as discreet a route as he could have chosen without the ability to Pad directly into his own townhouse, something he couldn't do without coordinates . . . and also without warning the caretakers. It would have been cruel to surprise them by appearing in their midst.

So he walked, and in time found himself on the edge of Noble's Row. Jisiensire's townhouse was the last in the road, nearest the cliff; it was not difficult to skirt the drop and become another pedestrian on his way home. The calling hours had concluded much earlier and he hadn't expected much traffic this early in the month; it struck him as strange that so many of the townhouses were lit in a manner suggesting occupation. The winter court technically convened at the season's opening, but in practice most people didn't make the journey until several weeks later. Their houses should have been boarded still, or lit to reflect a minimal occupation, by servants or staff.

Allied to the royal family through family ties as old

as the Settlement, Jisiensire always left a presence in the capital to support the Queen. When Hirianthial stepped up the stone stairs, the lamp leading to the door was lit and there were candles burning in the windows. He glanced at the bell-pull and steeled himself. Once he passed over this threshold, there would be no returning. All that he had done, all that he was capable of, and all that had happened to him would be addressed, for weal or woe.

The bell sounded. His hand fell from the chain and he waited, resigned. God and Lady succor him, for he knew not what the weeks to come would hold—

The door opened on the saturnine countenance of one of Jisiensire's oldest senior servants, and even among Eldritch who held strong displays of emotion in contempt there was no mistaking the joy that leapt into the man's eyes, one that lit his aura on fire.

"Neren," Hirianthial said, remembering in time to trade tongues for the baroque flourish of the language he'd grown up speaking, so different from the more utilitarian Universal he'd been using now for decades. He shaded the words silver for gentleness and pleasure. "As you can see, I have come home."

"Oh my lord!" Neren said, hushed. "Please. Let me take your case."

Hirianthial set it down for the servant to carry, reserving the data tablet, and let the man precede him into the central hall. The townhouses on the Noble's Row had been designed to receive guests and allow the family to conduct their business during the seasonal courts, and the door opened directly onto a vast space, with a tall desk overseeing the bottom floor and the two groupings of furniture arranged around the front windows, and two sets of stairs leading to a balcony overseeing the interior. The private rooms were on the second floor. All of it had been meticulously maintained, but Hirianthial expected no less. The smell of the place, of wood polish and candle wax, was like an incense, and made him abruptly aware that he no longer worshipped the gods it pertained to.

Several more servants had appeared at the bell, and Neren gave the case to one of them to carry upstairs before shooing the rest back to their dormitory. Hirianthial waited until he'd finished before speaking, and all the mood modifiers and intricacies of their grammar returned to him as if he'd never left, colors to shade the words with nuance, silver, gold, white and gray. Not for his house the shadowed and black and carnal modes, not here, among kin and retainers. "Neren. You look well, and it is good to see it."

"You are kind to say so," Neren said, aura flushing with the pleasure he kept off his face. "My lord! I scarcely believe your presence. When I received the message from the Queen's Tams, I was afraid to hope they were correct. How greatly you have been missed! The lady Araelis will be gratified to have you home."

"That may be," Hirianthial said. "But tonight I am the Queen's, and I must go to Ontine forthwith."

"Of course," the man said. "I have set out your court coat in the master suite, sire. I would be delighted to attend you."

Somehow the man still had clothing to fit him. How long had someone been maintaining it here in the hopes of his return? "Thank you," Hirianthial said.

Upstairs, Neren set to the duties of a valet with his usual aplomb. He'd been in service to Sarel Jisiensire for so long he'd overseen the outfitting of Hirianthial's nursery, and there was little he could be taught about the staff roles in a noble House; it was why he'd been made castellan of the principle estate. To have him here was a puzzlement, and as Neren stood waiting with the coat over an arm, Hirianthial asked, "Have you retired then?"

"Ah? Oh, that I am here, you mean, my lord?" Neren approached with the coat once Hirianthial had finished buttoning the vest. "Lady Araelis requested it not long after your departure, sire. She wanted someone here to listen for news."

News had been spoken in the shadowed mode, hinting at uncertainties and unease. Hirianthial held out his arms as Neren straightened the coat, gloved hands carefully never touching skin. "Has it been so dire, then?"

"Dire is perhaps a poeticism, sire," Neren said, stepping back and offering him a sword belt. "But the unrest has only been mounting, and rumors have been thick on the ground."

Such old and familiar movements, leather tongue through the buckle, moving the frog over his flank. Hirianthial opened the case, bringing out the sword. "Anything true?"

"No one knows," Neren said. "But the heir has been little seen of late, and there is concern there. Also, there was a rather significant event with the heir to the Seni involving the induction of a mortal into their family. That was some years ago, but it is still much discussed."

Hirianthial froze. "For sooth?" he asked.

"Verily, sire," Neren said. "And a strange beast it was, from all accounts. Four feet and wings and a tail and another half a body at that, and black and white all over."

"A Glaseah!" Hirianthial exclaimed. Who was the current heir to the Seni? A man, he thought, Jeasa's eldest son, but he couldn't remember the name. What courage, though, to do such a thing; he would have to ask Liolesa for the full story, if she was disposed to talk to him. Taking the peace cords from Neren, he bound the sword and sat on the padded bench, acting now on habits so old he no longer remembered their formation; after dressing, one sat to have gemstones braided into one's hair. A nobleman's hair should be as long as his years, the saw went, an expression of the family's wealth and the luxury of displaying it. "I assume that went over poorly."

"Fortunately, most people gave little credence to the story," Neren said. "It being so outrageous as to seem unbelievable. Even I had some trouble with it, particularly given the description of the creature."

"You shall not find it so unbelievable soon," Hirianthial said. "While I am gone, I would be pleased if you would prepare the house for the receipt of my guests: six, possibly seven, though you will need five bedrooms at most. I am not certain if we will be hosting the Queen's woman, but if we are, then five."

"Six guests, sire," Neren said, opening a small wooden box and sorting through the selection of jewels there. "Very good."

"They are all aliens," Hirianthial said. "And one of them . . . is human."

Neren's fingers paused. "Human."

"Yes, I know," Hirianthial said. "But the Queen herself has asked for the human, so as a courtesy we are hosting her until Liolesa decides what is to be done with her."

"I see," Neren murmured. More distinctly, "It will be done. When shall I expect them, sire?"

"I'll call before I leave and see," Hirianthial said. "But within an hour. Best to have them here at night, when people are less likely to notice the activity. Unlike me, they will be arriving by Pad, probably in the main hall."

"Of course," Neren said, and then, diffident, "Very unusual times, these, sire."

"And about to become more so," Hirianthial said. He

dipped his head as Neren lifted a chain of rubies and opals. The lamplight flashed off the metal fittings, and he saw— felt—the hand reaching toward his hair. The flood of panic was so abrupt he inhaled sharply.

Neren paused. "My lord?"

Hirianthial held up a hand, hoping its tremor was not as obvious to the servant as it was to himself. "I shall forgo the ornamentation. It is a private meeting, and my cousin knows how I feel about such displays."

"Of course."

Hirianthial struggled with his composure as Neren turned from him to put the chain away. If the man had touched him, would he have lashed out, without thought, without the chance to quell himself? Could he have killed his family's oldest servant . . . by accident? Even now his heart was racing and there was sweat chilling his palms, though he hadn't moved.

Neren was speaking. ". . . horse brought 'round the front for you, sire."

"Ah? Thank you, Neren. That will do nicely." Hirianthial rose. "Tell my guests I'll be with them shortly, if they arrive before I do."

"I shall do so, sire."

Without allowing himself to look back, Hirianthial left for his meeting with Liolesa. If anything, his errand had become more urgent.

"You all have everything you'll need for a few days?" Reese asked. "Remember, we're not going to be able to come back up here until we're sent back by the Queen, and it's hard to know when that will be. Plus, this world doesn't have Pelted, so none of the clothes are going to fit and who knows what they'd use to groom a sapient's fur."

"Probably one of those brushes they use on their

horses," Kis'eh't said, pursing her lips.

"Ugh!" Irine wrinkled her nose. "No thank you."

"We're good, Boss," Sascha said. "Honest. We thought of everything. Did you?"

Reese checked herself. Duffle bag filled with clothes and horse sales materials. Telegem and tablet. Round fuzzy alien, who murmured a sleepy chime in her head in response to her itemization. "No, I'm good." She glanced at Malia. "Everything arranged on this end?"

"Looks like it," Malia said, double-checking the coordinates between Pad and tablet. "You should show up in the lobby, and the people there are expecting you." She looked up, ears perked. "And I'll take good care of the *Earthrise* for you while you're gone. Anything starts making you nervous, just tell me and I'll set her down at the royal landing field."

"Thanks," Reese said.

"You sure you want to stay here babysitting by yourself?" Irine asked, ears sagging.

Malia smiled. "I'll be fine . . . it's not like there's not company in-system if I get lonely. To be honest, it'll be nice to be by myself for a while. And I like the view. It never gets old."

Reese drew in a deep breath. The prospect of leaving the ship with a stranger made her anxious, but the Queen of the Eldritch had sent Malia as her representative, and the foxine had guided them here as promised; no one on her crew could have set that course, or rescued the ship had Malia failed them. For better or worse, Reese had committed to this network of contacts and trust. And besides—she was about to see the Eldritch homeworld with her own eyes! How many people could say that? How could she miss it!

"All right," she said. "Let's do this thing."

"You first, Boss," Sascha said. "And remember to move out of the way or it won't let us pass."

"Right," Reese said. She resettled her bag's strap and hugged Allacazam against her midriff. "Here we go," she murmured, and stepped over the Pad into a dim space that seemed to go on forever into shadows and the suggestion of ornate railings and furniture. She stumbled a little further to give the Pad room to emit its next passenger and found herself staring at an Eldritch, and he was not Hirianthial.

"Oh, no," she blurted. "I don't speak the language!"

"Never fear, madam," the man said. "I speak yours." He touched a palm to his breast and bowed. "I am Neren Fasith, castellan of the Jisiensire estate, in service to the Sarel family. My lord asked me to make you welcome."

It was such a smooth delivery that she almost didn't notice the shiver of his wrist . . . but his skin—gloves? Were white and his livery was wine-red, and that made the tremor visible. "Ah . . . thank you. I'm Reese—Theresa Eddings, captain of the TMS *Earthrise* . . ."

Sascha appeared with the silhouette-limning flash of a Pad transfer, and behind him almost on his tail, Irine. Kis'eh't and Bryer followed in short order. "And . . . ah, these are my crew. Irine and Sascha, those are the cats. Kis'eh't is over there and the tall one is Bryer."

The man's pause was brief but Reese saw it anyway; she'd gotten too used to scrutinizing Hirianthial for similar minimalist cues. "Welcome to the Jisiensire townhouse. I have rooms prepared for you all, and there are refreshments upstairs in the solar. If you will follow me?"

Her people didn't say anything, but the look Sascha flashed her was just visible in the low light, and she could tell his brows were lifted. She shrugged and shifted Allacazam to the other arm before starting after the man. The

dark was strange: she'd never been in a place where nightfall meant the insides of buildings were dark too. Was there
some custom against using artificial lights? Or . . . did they
not have any? Crazy idea. Who didn't have artificial lights?
And the smell . . . the smell was overwhelming and alien.
Not bad, but she was accustomed to the odorlessness of
enclosed environments. When the *Earthrise's* air started
to smell, good or bad, it was because some filter somewhere needed changing.

The man leading them picked up a lamp at the top of
the stairs. It had glass panes set in some sort of metal, and
there was a candle in it. A *candle*. Reese had only enough
time to give it a look of utter incredulity before their guide
brought them to a tall and ornately painted door, which
he pushed open for them onto a parlor lit by several more
candles, and a fire in a fireplace. The furniture looked like
museum pieces, with carved wooden finials and upholstery with embroidered scenes of people riding on horses
or sitting on picnic blankets in the countryside. There were
tapestries and paintings on the wall, rugs on the wooden
floors, and in the corner, an honest-to-bleeding-soil harp
as tall as Reese, its strings glittering in the flickering light:
firelight really did flicker. Who knew? She hadn't.

As they stared into the room, the man said, "The lord
should return within an hour. If you will permit me to have
your bags taken to your rooms? You need only set them
here against the outside wall. Just so, thank you. If you
need anything, use the bell-pull."

And with that, he was gone, leaving them in the
chamber with each other. For a long moment, no one said
anything. Then Sascha said, "Uh, Boss . . . I'm afraid to sit."

"I bet they don't like animals on their furniture," Irine
muttered, which made them all glance at her. "What?
Don't you get a feel about this?"

"From that man?" Kis'eh't said, surprised. "Absolutely nothing. Did you?"

"Not from him," Irine said. She waved a hand at the room. "From this. I mean, it's beautiful and I really want to enjoy it but we know they're xenophobes. We know Hirianthial never talks about his past. What more do we need to get the picture? We're not wanted here."

"I was maybe less worried about them hating us and more worried about putting my posterior down on a chair we could sell for a year's worth of fuel," Sascha admitted.

"That's the other thing," Irine muttered. "He didn't tell us he was rich!"

"We could have guessed that part, though." Kis'eh't padded toward the fireplace and stopped short of the raised flagstones of the hearth. "That feels really nice to be so dangerous and inconvenient."

"Don't set yourself on fire, please," Reese said, nervous.

"I won't. It smells good though, doesn't it?"

"Is that what that is?" Reese asked, and stepped a little closer herself. She hugged Allacazam tighter as sadly inadequate protection against his neural fur catching on fire, a possibility he found unworthy of worry from the soothing green colors he kept painting in the back of her mind. With him working on her she allowed herself to inhale the rich scent of hot sap and burning wood. And it was warm, which made her notice that it had been cold in the hall, very cold. "It is nice, isn't it."

"You're ignoring me!" Irine said, exasperated.

"I think maybe you're reading too much into one room," Reese replied, but she felt a hint of unease herself. She had assumed Hirianthial had good reasons not to discuss his home. She'd also assumed he hadn't wanted for money either, but the size of this place, even disguised by the dark, implied a level of wealth she wasn't prepared to accept. She glanced up at the ceiling and found instead a peaked roof formed of glass panels, and beyond their silhouetted panes, the high vault of a night sky with alien constellations. What would this place look like during the day? And would she be ready for it?

"I guess these are our refreshments," Sascha said from the side of the room. He gingerly took the pitcher from the candle-warmed cradle and sniffed the inside. "Wine, maybe? With cinnamon?"

"Food," Bryer observed, and took one of the fruit slices, popping it in his mouth. "Apples."

"Apples?" Kis'eh't looked up sharply, then went to the sideboard to investigate. She frowned at the tray, then tried one. "Aksivaht'h. Apples!"

"They're particularly good?" Reese asked, puzzled at the Glaseah's fixation.

"They have apples," Kis'eh't said to her. "Why? Do they grow them here?"

"Maybe they're imports," Sascha said.

"On a xenophobic world?" Kis'eh't shook her head. "So they don't talk to outworlders, they only trade with them? That doesn't make sense."

Reese sat on the edge of the hearth, holding Allacazam against her stomach. "Why are we so upset about this? We should be happy, right? Someone we like has invited us home with him, offered to let us stay at his place, and we see that it's a nice place and it's very comfortable. Why are we picking at it?"

"First of all, he didn't invite us," Sascha said, ears flipping back. "We pushed him into letting us do this."

"And he ran away from this place. If it's so nice, why?" Irine asked. "I mean, really. He's got a nice house, it's gorgeous and he's even got servants. So what made him leave it behind?"

"And why do they have Terran apples when they hate outworlders?" Kis'eh't said.

Reese stared at them, wide-eyed, then looked up at Bryer. "What about you?"

The Phoenix swept the room with his strange white-less eyes, then shrugged, a motion that rippled through his metallic wings. "Here now. Deal with what is, when it becomes necessary."

"Of course," Reese said and sighed. She petted Allacazam, who sent a query through her mind, like the rising flight of a bird. "I don't know," she said to him. "But I guess for now . . . we wait."

Sascha poured a glass of the wine and brought it to her. "You don't have any questions of your own?"

Reese took the glass, fingers stinging from the unexpected heat. Who warmed wine? She glanced at it, then up again at the ceiling. Finally she said, "All I want to know is . . . why are there no lights?"

Painfully inbred and weak in both constitution and temperament, Eldritch horses were already prone to skittishness, and Hirianthial's unease made his mount painfully fractious. By the time he was waved through Ontine's gates he was ready to be quit of both the ride and his own thoughts, tense and cruel with the fear of what might have been, and what might yet be if he did not learn to control a talent for which there was no curriculum. A groom took his mount and left him to mount the palace's stone steps to the entrance, a cold wind off the nearby ocean stinging his cheeks and working on his joints. His court coat and cloak were little protection, and his gloves even less so; the stiffness of his fingers was new, though. When he'd been younger, the season hadn't seemed so cruel.

Entering the front hall cut off the wind, but Ontine was

cold in winter, something no number of tapestries or rugs could mitigate. He straightened his clothes and allowed the inevitable guards to examine his bona fides, and then he was striding behind one down the halls to his cousin's quarters. He surrendered his sword to a man in the white uniform he'd once worn and was escorted into Liolesa's office, and there he was left, in the quiet. The suite was exactly as he recalled it—he could have been gone only a few days, rather than over fifty years—with the chairs and coffee table arranged on the rug before the hearth, and her desk and cabinet of books on the raised and carpeted dais, in the corner between two windows. Her office faced the city; her bedroom, the sea. That was Liolesa: pragmatic and visionary by turns.

She was also habitually overextended, and it didn't surprise him that she wasn't awaiting him. He sat on one of the chairs by the fire, grateful for the warmth, and composed himself to wait. He was in fact drowsing when the door whispered on its hinges, but the sound brought him to his feet, and he would have bowed save that her expression quelled him. She was standing by the door, arrayed in taupe and cream and citrines braided in hair coiled to hold her abbreviated crown in place, and she was glad to see him for no reason he could fathom but exhausted in every other way.

"Hirianthial," she said at last. Her heels clicked on the stone floor and then the rug muffled them as she joined him. "It is good to see you, cousin. Welcome home."

So simple. So easy. He had not expected it, and that was why he said, "I did not think you would be so forgiving."

"Because you fled without so much as saying goodbye?" She rested her eyes on his, and it was rest; they had known each other that long. "Did you suppose I would hate you for it?"

"I abandoned my duty," he said. "My House. My Queen."
He paused, finished. "My cousin."

"I would hardly be worthy of your regard, did I blame
you for leaving in the face of all your losses," she said, and
her sincerity glowed in her aura, warm as hearth-fire.
"Hirianthial . . . it is in the past. You are here now, and I
am glad of it."

"My lady," he said, and put all his gratitude in it, for
he had not realized until now how painful he'd found the
possibility of losing their long friendship.

She offered him her turned cheek as she used to, and
because they were both people who permitted very few
intimacies, even with those they trusted, he kissed it as he
used to. Her tension was almost imperceptible, would have
been had he not been able to sense her sudden concern; he
withdrew just enough to see her face and her gaze, always
too insightful, was studying him now. He could see the
green flecks in their tawny irises, and on them, his own
reflection, too grave.

"Something has happened," she said. "Tell me."

"Corel was no story," he said. "You so intimated once."

"I did," she agreed. "And it was true. He was no story."

"I have his worst power."

She was silent for several heartbeats, her aura tight,
too close for him to read. Then she said, "Sit."

He obeyed and allowed himself the luxury of putting
his head in his hands. Liolesa's gown rustled as she strode
from him, and he heard her pouring something. When she
brought it back, he could smell the sweet almond of the
cordial they'd shared when they were younger. "Drink," she
said more gently, and again he obeyed. Once he'd had a
long sip, she said, "Now, tell me."

Where to begin when he wanted to talk about it not
at all? "I had been kidnapped on a colony world and was

under duress in my captor's keeping when . . . I could no longer bear his company. In a spasm of negation, I killed him and some six other people, and struck several more unconscious outside that radius." He looked at the liqueur. "Having discovered this ability, I immediately applied to return home. If Corel was real, there must have been . . . training for such talents, real training. Protocols. Something I might learn to prevent myself from accidentally hurting anyone."

"Was it so easy to do that you fear such accidents?" Liolesa asked, in a voice thankfully devoid of horror. It was always thus with her: practical matters first. Emotional reactions, if any, later.

"No," he answered. "At least . . . I don't think so. But I have had it demonstrated to me that I can be triggered unexpectedly." He thought of Neren and flinched. "No, I need help. Tell me there is help here to be found, cousin."

When she didn't answer, he looked up at her sharply. "Liolesa. Tell me there is help to be found for my condition."

She said, "I don't know." She lifted her fingers at his expression. "Soft, cousin. I don't say this to fret you, but because the history of it is tangled and you know none of it; I knew none of it myself until Maraesa passed me the crown. Indeed, if I tell you any of it, technically I am committing treason—"

"Treason!" he exclaimed.

She laughed, rueful and low. "But I think I will write myself a pardon if I am ever discovered." Rising, she went to the sideboard and poured her own glass. "I shall put it curtly for you. The Church was founded to seek and cull talents as powerful as Corel's, not to foster brotherly love, no matter that they developed that mission later. So while it's true that they probably have some understanding of how to train your abilities, we would have to ensure they didn't kill you first."

Hirianthial stared at her, stunned.

"And for the choicest of ironies," she concluded, "I am the titular head of the arm of the Church devoted to slaying these rogue talents—as one might expect, given the permissions they would need to stage rampant executions—but both Jerisa and Maraesa gave them their heads for so long they no longer report their activities to the crown." She sipped from her glass. "I have been putting pressure on them, but I suspect they lie to me. Cleaning house would require a near-dismantling of the entire priesthood of the God and I don't need them throwing in their lot against me when the rest of the court is about to explode . . . a court, I add, that you have timed yourself perfectly to disrupt with your presence, given that we are convening in two days."

His cousin had never been prone to hyperbole. Hirianthial set the cordial down with fingers grown suddenly numb and said, "What's happened?"

"Decades I've spent slowly moving us toward the point where our enemies can no longer fight the inevitability of my plans," Liolesa said. "More than that. Centuries. You know, cousin." She sighed. "And it has come all undone. I no longer have an heir, Hirianthial."

"That rumor's truth?" Hirianthial said, startled. "But what has happened to Bethsaida?"

She set her glass down and rested her hands on the sideboard, her shoulders hard. Then she drew in a deep breath and returned to the chair opposite his. As she sat, she said, "Bethsaida had been making noises about proving herself to me, and it appears she decided to go off-world to demonstrate that she was capable of the same exceptionally stupid acts as I was when I was her age. While she was gone, the Chatcaava took her."

"No," Hirianthial whispered.

"She was rescued from their throneworld by the last scion of Imthereli at great cost to himself," Liolesa continued. "But she has returned completely unsuitable for anything but religious orders, preferably someplace far from people, particularly men. Aliens too she will no longer countenance without terror. I have sent her to the Abbey of Saint Avilana, which is as remote a location as I could manage while still placing her on allied lands, and I have done my best since to make people think she is on retreat there. But that story hasn't held. Few people who knew Bethsaida would have imagined her on retreat."

"My God, cousin," Hirianthial said. "What will you do?"

"That is exactly what I have been trying to decide," Liolesa said. "But I am without issue and consort. So are you, and your brother, of course, is no longer an option—more on that matter later. I could go outside the royal bloodline and choose someone from a minor family within Galare, but such a move will incite people to demand I consider their children since I am already looking outside Jerisa's line. But most importantly, my enemies see that I have no one to carry on the work, and they no longer wish to stand for my policies. They think it might be easier to find some way to pressure me into accepting their choice of successor . . . or worse, take the throne themselves."

"No doubt because you have made their lives more difficult for them," Hirianthial murmured.

She snorted. "They make their lives difficult for themselves, cousin. Most of them have been incapable of fulfilling a responsibility as basic as feeding their tenants. So I have fined them for it. Every time I have to pay for food, shelter, clothing, any of the necessities they are duty-bound to provide, I charge them for it." At his expression, she said, "It is my right. They fail in their vows to me as vassals."

"God and Lady," he breathed. "How much money have you taken from them?"

"Enough that most of them are now in debt to the crown," Liolesa said. She smiled faintly. "It was my plan at this point to allow them to pay off that debt by lending me their men-at-arms, so that I might begin to win their loyalty from their lords in preparation for the inevitable conflict. Now, though, my enemies are more like to withhold those men, and the war I was hoping to win over a parley table will probably escalate to actual fighting. That, I fear, is where we are."

"And into this, you have brought a foreigner, and a human?" Hirianthial asked, astonished. "Why? So you could accelerate their plans to usurp the throne by giving them unforgivable insult?"

"The war is coming either way," Liolesa said, tired. "I must consolidate my allies and see where I might use their talents to curtail the conflict." She looked up at him. "We have been shrinking too fast. If I allow a drawn-out war, cousin, I might doom us to extinction. Since it's clear that my enemies care not at all about insignificant long-term plans such as species survival, I must continue to shoulder that burden. And if that means I call the Alliance in, then I will."

"You do that," he said, soft, "and you will lose them forever."

"But we'll survive," she said. "And maybe, if we live long enough, we'll evolve out of this lunatic xenophobia that's killing us. Because it is killing us, Hirianthial. We can no longer maintain our civilization without external aid. In fact, we don't. My off-world fortune—one I built in anticipation of this crisis, and I am not happy to have been proven prophetic—is paying for imported food. We eat from the Pelted table, a bounty brought on ships staffed by the descendants of Lesandurel's first friendship. One that Maraesa tried to forbid." She rubbed her brow, just beneath the gleaming crown. "Bringing food may in fact be the most useful thing your Theresa Eddings can do for us—or running it from another continent, which is how far away I would have to put any sign of technology in order to prevent its sabotage. But before I put her to work, I would like to meet her for myself. Perhaps there is some other way she can be of use."

"And you will put her to use," Hirianthial murmured.

"I'll put anyone to use for this cause," Liolesa said sharply. And then reined herself in visibly. "I apologize, cousin. It has been a difficult few months. When I set you to the task that saw you immured in a slaver's jail, I did not anticipate being so stunningly vindicated by the results."

"Yes," he said. "I imagine so. And I apologize for my part in your difficulties—"

"Stop," she said, shaking her head. "I am glad you're home, Hirianthial. I mean that." Her smile was faint, but real. "I have missed the benefit of your counsel. I know it has been several centuries since I was an impetuous heir and you my trusted White Sword, but I have never forgotten how much easier things were when I had you at my back." She drew in a breath. "And this is just the beginning."

He looked up at her.

"This conflict here is as nothing, and you know it," Liolesa said softly. "We have a far greater enemy outside this world." When he straightened, she said, "Do you care to imagine what will happen when the Chatcaava finally find us? Us, as we are now? Without so much as a ship to our name, a fortification to defend us? God and Lady bless the Tams, but they are couriers, not warriors, and they have neither the firepower nor the training to prevent a determined assault force from reaching us. And then we are dead for truth, cousin: enslaved and then killed, because we never last long in their hands." She squared her shoulders. "This thing with Asaniefa's supporters must be put paid to as swiftly as possible, or we are done."

"The Alliance," Hirianthial began. "They would never stand for such a thing, surely. We are their allies."

"They have their own concerns," she said. "Oh, they'd come if we called for help. But they would be too late. We are remote, and the queens of the past have done nothing to cement that friendship. I am certain the Alliance would seek us once the dragons had raided us, but like Bethsaida, we would return from that experience broken as a culture. Some few of us would survive, but . . . enough to begin again?" She sighed and sipped from her cordial. "I need all the allies I can draw to my breast, cousin. And all the weapons I can take to hand. I won't apologize for doing what I must to see us through this crisis."

"I am here now," he said into the silence that followed, and shaded it in the white of pure intention and vow.

"I'm glad," she said. "Perhaps we can begin to mend what we set in motion when we destroyed Corel . . . Corel and every other person with even a hint of his talents. I have to believe that's when it began. Too many died in those purges, and left us vulnerable to gaps in our knowledge and skills, to faults in our biology. We have to stop killing ourselves, and we can start with you." Her smile was sardonic. "Which will be its own task because the brother that—might I remind you I advised you to kill—is at Ontine now—"

"Now? Here? How—"

"—and he is the head of the order of priests charged with the culling of talents," Liolesa said, and at the expression on his face said, "Yes, indeed, he has found work to suit his proclivities. And I assure you, cousin, he has not forgiven you for sparing his life."

"He was the last of my family, Lia."

"Not yet he isn't," she said. "But he is dying for the chance to make sure that he is. Mark me: he wants your blood. See to it that he has no reason to call for it."

"Other than my being the reincarnation of Corel," Hirianthial said dryly.

She sniffed. "Let me take care of that. I will send you to my chosen priests first. That should tie them up in factional battles."

"Things really haven't changed a whit, have they," he murmured.

"Oh, Hiran," she said with a sigh. "Most certainly they have. They've gotten much, much worse." She held up her cordial glass. "To the task ahead of us."

He had never wanted to come home to stay, not after Laiselin's death and Baniel's betrayal. But he raised his glass and touched it to hers anyway.

Hirianthial rode home against a bitterly cold wind, smelling strongly of the ceaseless air long over sea. By the time he dismounted his limbs were graceless with it and his cloak clung damply to his sides. His discomfort was acute, and yet none of it proved distraction from the meeting with his cousin—whom he had called Lia, falling back on habits as old as their childhood friendship, and who had called him Hiran, as she had not since they set Maraesa's crown on her head. How long had it been since he'd heard his milk name from anyone's lips? The familiarity of it should have been comforting, and instead had revealed how very dire their respective situations had become. He, a killer and heir to powers unmentionable, the abused become the abuser, without family save for a murderer he'd left alive in a fit of mercy and weakness . . .

and she, a trapped lioness beset from all sides, with her cub to protect and no time for scruples.

It was surprising to discover that he still cared about the world. Because of her, he thought: through her passion, he saw what was worth preserving in their people. But he did not welcome that knowledge.

One of the servants let him in, took his cloak and brushed his boots. From there he went upstairs in search of the crew. The solar door was cracked enough to cast a ray of light across the carpeted balcony. He paused; through it, he could see Reese sitting on the hearth with the twins by her side and Allacazam on her lap. She looked—it struck him suddenly—much as his cousin had: tired but determined. There was something of the same steel in them both. And the warmth in the room was palpable to him, not just from the fire and light, but from the weave of their auras, separate and yet harmonious. They had become familiar to him. And they would claim him as theirs, if they could.

How could he explain that there were prior claims he could not cast from him? He touched his coat; against his breast, the parchment envelope in the pocket crinkled. With a sigh, he pushed open the door.

"You're home!" Irine exclaimed, jumping to her feet. The others were turning too, and Reese looked up. Her heart tightened. He was like something out of a painted storybook in bronze and burgundy, the coat all elegant sweeps glittering with embroidery. All he needed was some sort of crown, and she could be the grubby commoner, come to beg for a piece of bread.

Which in a way was what had happened, with the Queen paying off the *Earthrise's* debt.

The whole thing would have been disheartening if

Reese hadn't had the very strong impression that . . . Hirianthial didn't want to be here either. She petted Allacazam
and let the twins make much of his arrival, while Kis'eh't
asked him impatiently about the apples and received the
expected enigmatic reply. At last, Reese called, "Hey, hey,
can we calm down a little? He's barely stepped in the door.
Let him sit."

"Thank you," Hirianthial said. "And I shall, in a moment."
He walked to her and withdrew from inside his coat an
envelope. "For you, Lady."

"Me?" Reese took it, startled. The texture of it beneath
her thumb . . . she shivered. "It's real, isn't it?"

"Paper?" Hirianthial said. "Yes, I suppose it is." He sat
on one of the chairs near the fire, turning his attention to
it. Either he wasn't interested in what it said, or he was
granting her the courtesy of not hovering, something the
twins wouldn't if she didn't open it quickly. She turned it
over and found it sealed in blue wax, like something out of
one of her books: a unicorn on its hind legs. And she would
have to break it? She tried wedging her thumb under the
flap and working it gently open, but it split in half.

That bothered her. She stared at the seal a moment,
then took the card on the inside out. Fortunately, it was
written in Universal, in ink that glimmered silver when she
tilted the paper.

> *Captain Eddings,*
> *Do you come for breakfast, for I have been greatly antic-*
> *ipating our meeting. Hirianthial can show you the way.*
> *—L. G.*

"I guess I get to dine with royalty," Reese said, proud
that her voice didn't shake. She handed the card to Kis'eh't,
who shared it with the twins. Glancing at Hirianthial, she

added, "You're supposed to bring me?"

"I have my own appointment there in the morning," Hirianthial said. "We'll be leaving while it's still dark; the Queen wakes early."

"And goes to sleep late, I'm guessing," Reese said. Allacazam turned an amused sunny yellow beneath her palm. "Any protocol I should know? Other than what you taught us on the way here."

He twitched his chin in faint negation. "You'll find her the most cosmopolitan of our people. You are not likely to offend her. Be polite as you would to anyone else, that is all."

"And don't touch her," Reese said.

"And don't touch her," he agreed.

"Do you think she'll want to meet us?" Irine asked, looking up from the card.

Hirianthial smiled. "You are here, Irine. You would not be, if there were not plans for you."

Reese didn't like the sound of that, but she didn't say anything. She couldn't tell what it was about the Eldritch's body language that was bothering her, but she wasn't going to ignore her instincts. "It's been an exciting day. Why don't you all check the bedrooms? Get some rest, maybe."

She expected protestations, but the twins glanced at one another and at Bryer and Kis'eh't, and then Sascha held out a hand to his sister. "I bet the beds are big enough to sleep six."

"I'll be fine with a bed that sleeps two, but let's go look anyhow," Irine said cheerily.

As they chorused their good-nights, Reese called, "Wait, do you even know where you're going?"

Hirianthial said, "Head back toward the stairs. First door after the solar should lead to a hall, and the rooms will be off that corridor."

"Problem solved," Sascha said. "See you in the morning, Boss."

Bryer closed the door on all of them, meeting Reese's eye with one of his inscrutable expressions. And then she was alone with her Eldritch who was, she thought suddenly, not quite as much hers as she'd assumed. He'd claimed not to belong anywhere until he'd started belonging to the *Earthrise*. Now . . . she wasn't so sure.

"Did she have an answer for you?" Reese asked, knowing the question dared much. But he answered.

"Perhaps. There are historical precedents, but no modern role models."

Which was a strange reply. He was staring into the fire, close enough for her to touch, but he might as well have been a sector away. "You have a nice house here," she said, to distract him.

"This?" he roused himself, shook off his reverie. "It is not mine. It belongs to the family."

"Is that . . . Sarel? Or Jisiensire?" she asked, careful of the names.

Startled, he looked at her.

"I wasn't sure what the extra names meant," Reese said. "But the man who showed us in, he said he served Sarel."

"Ah, yes, Neren." Hirianthial threaded his fingers together. Was that a touch of a smile? She thought so. "Our oldest retainer, and very exact with words." He stopped for so long Reese almost thought he wouldn't continue. "It is Jisiensire's townhouse. Maintained for visits to the palace for the seasonal courts. Jisiensire has lands elsewhere. The family seat is there."

She'd been barely able to wrap her mind around how wealthy he must be to have a house like this with servants. To learn that it was just a nicety, and his real home was somewhere else? On land with a capital "L"? Reese tried to imagine being a land-owner, a real land-owner, with acres of it, not just the soil directly under the house you were paying a mortgage on. The skin on the back of her neck prickled.

She hadn't expected him to notice, but he did, glancing at her sharply enough to make the hair framing his chin sway. "I have affrighted you?" he asked. "How? What did I say?"

Reese stared at him. "Excuse me?"

"Tell me."

"Are you really asking me a direct question?" she managed, and his expression made her chuckle, dispelled the unease.

He didn't quite scowl, but she could tell he wanted to. "Captain—"

"Reese," she said. "What is it with all you excessively formal people? It's just Reese, Hirianthial. For the billionth time. And you didn't scare me. It's just that . . . you're . . . in a completely different league from someone like me, and I never knew it. You could have bought and sold my ship with spare change. I can't imagine you getting dirty with common people." She thought back to old epithets. "Slumming it. That's what it is."

"Is that all?" he asked, surprised.

"Is that all?" Reese repeated. "Bleeding soil, Hirianthial. Yes? It's a little like discovering you're some long-lost prince." Her skin ran cold at the thought. "Wait, you're not a long-lost prince, are you?"

"I . . . am not in the succession, no."

She didn't like that pause, but she also didn't want to know what was behind it. She rubbed her forehead.

"Lady—" Better than 'captain', but still not what she'd asked him to use. "—I fear there are many such shocks in your future."

"Maybe you should tell me about them so I hear them from someone I trust, and not from your enemies," Reese said dryly. At his pause, she said, "Did you really expect me to think this would be some kind of fairy tale world, with princes and princesses and unicorns and magic and everything was beautiful and clean and perfect?"

"I . . . perhaps expected you to have no experience with which to make such judgments either way," he admitted.

"I don't," Reese said. "Not with fairy tales, except in books. But you know, that's the only place you find fairy tales, Hirianthial. In books. In the real world, there's always someone who has to clean the kitchen and take out the trash. There's always politics. There's always someone who wants to get ahead and doesn't care who they squash on their way up." She studied him. "You're rich, you seem to know the Queen—personally, maybe—and you're smart, talented, and not bad to look at. People probably love you when they don't hate you. So, no. I'm not going into this completely naïve."

She waited, wondering what he would say. Hoped he wouldn't call her impertinent, lecture her on how little she knew that she thought she did, or assay some cryptic response she'd spend all night fretting at when she should be sleeping.

Instead, he said, with a hint of amusement, "'Not bad to look at?'"

"Well, you know how it is," she said. "I wouldn't want you to get a puffed head about it." She eyed him, hand resting on Allacazam. "Though knowing you, it would probably be more you blaming yourself for inflicting your looks on other people."

"Ah!" He rested his fingers over his mouth, but she could just see between them to the twitch of his lips he was trying to hide. Nice lips. Not as full as hers, but still nice. "I am not entirely so self-effacing, lady."

"See? You're even modest about how modest you are." Reese snorted and stood up. "So, next door over, yes?"

"Yes," he said. "I'll have someone knock in the morning."

"All right," Reese said. She stopped at the door and said, "Whatever you're worried about . . . you know we're here to help."

"You hardly know what you are committing to," he murmured.

"Since you won't tell us, you're right. We don't. But that doesn't change that we're with you, no matter what."

Slowly he looked over his shoulder at her, and that expression she couldn't read at all.

"I mean it," she said. "See you in the morning."

"Good night, Lady."

The bed in the room was not just large enough for six. It was also tall enough to merit a tiny set of wooden steps, elaborately painted with columns of purple hyacinths and intertwined jasmine flowers. Reese stopped at the threshold of the room and remarked to Allacazam, "You'd think they were tall enough without having to make their furniture high too."

Allacazam had no opinion on this, save a faint drowsiness. She set him on the mattress and let herself stroke the fabric of the coverlet: flowers and arabesques embroidered with gleaming floss on a purple fabric that was too soft to the touch to also be so glossy. The rest of the room gave the same impression of opulence, from the densely woven rug to the gilded and elaborately carved furniture.

Someone had laid in a fire for her, and she changed near it because it was too cold in any other part of the room. Why didn't they heat this place? What good was such a beautiful residence if it was uncomfortable? It made no sense. After rushing across the chilled floor, Reese climbed into her bed and found it warm. Puzzled, she crawled all over it, hanging over its edge, until she spied the hint of a handle protruding from beneath the mattress. And then she sat back, holding the covers up to her chest. She looked from the fireplace to the pitcher and bowl she'd dismissed as ornamental on the side table. When Allacazam rolled into her lap and muzzily sent a curl of a query into her mind, she said, "They don't have lights. They don't have heat. They don't have sinks. Freedom, they probably don't have indoor plumbing." Her skin prickled. "And apparently those Tam-illee are their only way off-world."

The Flitzbe wondered why this was important, an impression she derived from birds he populated a tree with, all of them cocking their heads at her.

"It would be one thing if they chose to live like this," she told him, reluctantly lying down. It was a very soft bed, but even the softest bed was unlike her swinging hammock. "But what if it's not a choice?"

To that, Allacazam had no wisdom to offer. She sighed and murmured, "Just don't get lost on this thing. It's the size of a cargo hold."

A tinkle of chimes in her head. She smiled and drowsed off.

She was not quite so sanguine when she met Hirianthial downstairs the following day, just before dawn.

"It doesn't matter how expensive your sheets are," she said, "or even how palatial your bathtub is, if what you use for a water closet can still be called a water closet."

He remained composed but she thought she saw a twitch at the corner of his mouth. "I regret the facilities did not meet with your approval, Captain." Before she could speak again, he handed her a spill of dark brown cloth. "I assume you have no coat? It's cold out. You'll want something."

"And *this* is 'something'?" Reese breathed. It was a cloak, but like no cloak she'd ever seen, lined on the inside in fur the same deep brown as the fabric. "Oh no. It's too beautiful to wear. It'll get dirty!"

"Then someone will clean it," he said gently. At her wide-eyed look, he said, "As you said yourself, ah? Someone does the laundry."

"Right," Reese said, flushing. She drew the cloak around her shoulders. The clasp in the front was a lozenge of bronze metal with a hippogriff relief and she stroked it with her fingers once. "It really is warm." She looked all the way down at her feet and added ruefully, "If a little too long."

"No doubt if you stay you can have one made to your measure," Hirianthial said. "Shall we? It is not a long ride, but we don't want to be late for our appointments."

"Right," she said. "I . . . don't guess this thing has a pocket for my data tablet."

"No," he said, and the amusement was more obvious now. "But there should be one on the inside for envelopes that might suffice."

Reese checked, and he was right. "You people must write a lot."

He said nothing to that, which didn't surprise her.

Outside, there were—inevitably—horses. Reese could barely make them out against the dimness. As Hirianthial talked with the men holding the animals for them, she looked up and inhaled. When had she ever been out this early on a planet? The sky was a deep shade of gray tinged with lavender, and there was a smell . . . not like flowers, or water, or anything she could name, except to call it newness. And it was so still, after living with the noise of a ship for so long, so still that the noise of the horses lifting their hooves was muffled and distant, as if silence could have a weight.

"Shall I help you up?" Hirianthial asked in a low voice as the first horse was led to her. Did he notice it, too, the quiet? Of course he must.

Reese shook herself and eyed the animal. "No, I think I got this." She grasped the saddle horn, put her foot in the stirrup, and shoved the cloak out of the way when it fouled her first try. Her second was successful, if utterly without grace. "There. I got it." She patted the animal's neck. "Not so bad once you're used to it."

He threw her cloak over the back of the horse and arranged it around her. "Put your hood up, Lady."

"The hood?" Reese glanced over her shoulder at it. "Is it going to be that cold?"

"It is," he said. "And also, some discretion is to be advised."

"Right," she muttered, and couldn't tell if she resented the idea or found it unsettling. As she pulled the hood up the wind flattened its fur-lined interior against her cheek, convincing her that she cared a lot less about tender Eldritch sensibilities than she did about not feeling the cold.

The ride felt long; her placid horse was easy to handle but not very quick, and while the cloak shielded most of her body, somehow the wind found its way to every unprotected cranny: her wrists, her hands, her chin, her shins and feet. By the time Hirianthial reined his horse to a halt, Reese didn't need to be told to keep her head down. Tucking her entire body into the smallest space possible was her first priority. She heard murmured conversation in a language she couldn't understand, and then they were riding past great stone walls, through a fretwork gate tall enough to drive a cargo loader through. That was just enough preparation for the palace, which even in the uncertain gray dark of the time before dawn was . . . huge. Reese had the impression of endless flanks of ghostly pale stone worked with statues and reliefs.

"How many people live here?" Reese asked, stunned.

"Enough to maintain it and the royal family," Hirianthial said. "But it is mostly function and guest space. And much guest space is needed."

He held her horse while she dismounted beneath the watchful eyes of several guards. Reese wondered if they needed to be protected from the sight of her too, but Hirianthial seemed unconcerned about their reactions. He led her up a set of stairs to doors sized for giants, and then they were inside a warmly lit hall, a severe palette change from the dim gray outdoors. Here it was brilliant creamy stone and warm golden light, high distant ceilings spangled with ochre shadows.

"Here we part," Hirianthial said. "But I will come for you when I am done with my engagement."

"How do I know where to go?" Reese asked. There were guards stationed at intervals, but not one of them was looking at her. "Is there really no one to announce people? We just walk in?"

"It is too early, Lady. Visitation is not permitted before select hours save by invitation . . . and we are expected. You see, here are the pages."

Down the hall came slim Eldritch youths in blue and silver livery, elegant and light on their feet. They separated in a maneuver that seemed choreographed, one stopping before Hirianthial and the other before her. She sought any sign of alarm in his face and saw none: only a smooth mask.

"If you will, Lady," said the youth.

Reese hesitated, and Hirianthial said, "Go on, Captain.

It's safe."

"All right," she said. "I guess I'll see you later." She nodded to the page. "Let's go."

"This way, Lady."

Obscured by the dim glow of the lamps, the wide halls Reese passed through were something out of a book. There were patterns inlaid in the stone floor, and the high ceilings were coffered and painted in deep blues and gold and white. The tapestries that hung from the walls, if they were handmade, were probably worth more than Reese could have earned in a year—or five—and there were recesses with statues, and paintings that glistened in the low light with their linseed oil finishes, and alcoves with more of the delicate painted furniture with embroidered upholstery. The implied wealth was so dizzying she almost ran into the page when he stopped before a set of double doors. She looked up and found two guards studying her, and she froze. Unlike the guards at the palace's entrance, they were dressed heel to crown in white, with a single red strip lining the neck of their shirts. Memory intruded, brought her the image of Hirianthial awaiting her in the *Earthrise's* bay with Bryer: exact same outfit, if without the blood-colored trim.

They scrutinized her and then without uttering a word opened one of the doors. The page continued; so did she. But she glanced back at the closing door and wondered what the hell that had meant.

"Here, Lady," the page said, interrupting her thoughts. He had brought her to an open door through which spilled the flickering illumination of a fire.

"Thanks," Reese said, and cleared her throat before stepping inside.

The woman sitting by the fire was everything Reese had expected from a painting of a queen of a fairy tale race, with the weight of the beige gown, embroidered with pearls that had probably been caught, not cultured, to the elaborately braided hair and the slim band of a crown that ran over her brow. It wasn't until the woman looked up that Reese saw what a painting would have left out: the incisive gaze, the perfect posture and the controlled elegance of her movements as she set her teacup down, and the steel implied by the whole.

None of that mattered quite as much as the shock of recognizing her face. She looked like Hirianthial. A lot like Hirianthial. She also spoke flawless Universal.

"Captain Eddings! Please, join me."

Reese hastened to bow. "Ah, Your Majesty, thank you—"

"None of that now. I have been looking forward to this since I sent you that first message years ago. You needn't bow, alet . . . you are not one of my subjects to be scraping the floor for me. Come by the fire, you must be cold."

Reese tentatively sat across from her and unclasped the cloak, letting it fall back. She found the Queen studying her with interest, and with no hint of xenophobia at all. They regarded for one another for several moments, and then . . . they both grinned at the same time.

"Do you approve of what you see?" the Queen asked, amused.

"You look like I imagined," Reese admitted. And then asked, a little shy, "Do I?"

"Exactly as I hoped," the Queen said, reaching for the pot.

"Are you really going to pour for me?" Reese asked, appalled. When the woman paused, she said, "You're a queen!"

"And I was a hoyden before I was an heir, and a rebellious maiden when I was, and I fear I have not changed overmuch," the Queen said with a laugh. "Please, relax,

Captain. There's no reason for us to stand on formalities. In fact, call me Liolesa if you like. And I shall call you—"

"Reese," Reese said. "If you're sure—"

"Completely," Liolesa said, filling their cups. "I hope you like a varied morning meal. I have ordered one prepared, not knowing what you eat to break your fast."

"Chalk tablets, for most of my adult life," Reese said ruefully. "Or protein bars."

Liolesa chuckled softly. "So much trouble, then?"

"With money?" Reese said. She shook her head. "Always."

"I know the feeling." Liolesa took up her cup. When Reese didn't, she raised her perfect brows. "You think otherwise?"

Saying 'yes' seemed rude, so Reese said, "I hope your revenue problems aren't so dire they won't mean you're interested in what I've brought to sell you. . . ."

"Ah, yes," Liolesa said. "Do tell? We have some time before they bring the food if you prefer to do business beforehand. You mentioned it would be of particular interest."

Reese drew in a breath. She was surprised at how anxious she was to find out if all the suffering Hirianthial had undergone because she'd decided to lay over at Kerayle could be redeemed, even a little. She brought her tablet out, set it on the table between them and activated the advertising materials the Kesh had sent with her. The tablet's emitter built a miniature horse for them, jogging in place, pausing, shaking its forelock from its face. It had a glossy white hide and mane of waving silver, like something out of a romance.

The Queen had frozen in place. Then she reached forward and turned the tablet slowly. "Is this what I think it is?"

"There's this colony . . . they're breeding back all the

Terran purebred horses," Reese said. "They said they could sell some to the right buyers. I thought maybe you would be the right buyers."

"And would they have, say, draft horses?"

"Probably," Reese said, though she hadn't the faintest notion what differentiated a draft horse from a normal one. "They said they had everything, though they were starting with these."

The other woman stared at the trotting horse for long enough that Reese offered, "I could set the emitter to life-size? Or if you have a gem grid I could sync the tablet to, it could even do solidigraphic data." She glanced at the floor and said, "Ah . . . if you have a gem grid."

"We are a society that needs horses," Liolesa said. "Not wants, Theresa. *Needs*. It would be a startling thing to find a gem grid anywhere on this world."

"Except maybe in the Queen's rooms?" Reese said. "Given that she keeps company with an entire clan of Tam-illee somehow. . . ."

"Ah?" The other woman looked up, drawn from whatever thoughts she'd been contemplating. She laughed. "You have me there, yes. Though there is no gem grid here—we have no infrastructure to support it. We have to fall back on older-fashioned means." She glanced at the horse dancing on the table. "Yes, I would be interested in horses. Shall we discuss it in depth now?"

"Sure," Reese said, wondering what a bargaining session with a queen would be like. Glancing at the stern lines of Liolesa's face and quickness of the humor in her eyes, she got the feeling it was going to be . . . interesting.

There were two men in the room to which the page brought Hirianthial, one standing and the other seated by the fire. The former was a youth in the robes of an acolyte of the God, his aura a darting brightness of blue and green thoughts, wholesome but charged with the nervous energy of a adolescent forced to stand still for too long. The latter was an elder priest, nearly lost in the weight of his robes, with an aura so tranquil it evoked deep waters.

"The Lord Hirianthial," the page announced, and withdrew, the door shutting softly behind him.

"Elder," Hirianthial said, inclining his head to the priest. "Novice."

The priest studied him with interested eyes. "So, here you are, then. Do you know why you are here?"

The question was so like the ones his tutors had offered him as a child that Hirianthial couldn't help a smile. "To serve life?"

"Directly from scripture," the priest said with a grin. "But you're not here to please me with your recall, my son."

"Very well, Elder," Hirianthial said, sobering. "I am here because I have developed powers that may make me unfit for that service."

"That is what the Queen has asked me to evaluate," the priest said. "We shall do that now."

"Now?" Hirianthial asked, startled.

"Now," the priest agreed, and tucked his hidden hands further into his sleeves. "I would like to take a nap. Please demonstrate your powers by assisting me."

Hirianthial stared at him, despite the impropriety. "You . . . would like me to cause you to lose consciousness?"

"I am prepared," the priest said, unflustered. "As you can see, I am seated, so not likely to knock my head by falling. And I have young Belinor over there to aid me if you turn out to be a ravening monster."

Hirianthial looked at the boy, incredulous. "You? What special talent fits you for the task of helping a man being attacked by a mind-mage?"

Solemnly, the youth said, "I can run very fast."

He laughed then, unwillingly perhaps, but still. To the priest: "I'm not sure I can safely do what you ask. You may be hurt. Or even die."

"Then I die," the priest said. "And we have all learned something. But I do not think I shall die today." He shifted on the cushion, closed his eyes. "Proceed."

Faced with such trust, Hirianthial could do nothing but obey despite his dismay at the command. He considered the tranquility of that aura and then reached toward it until he could feel it against his palms, as tangibly as if he held a glass ornament. He suggested to it that it might part, and it peeled away beneath his attention; closing his eyes, he focused on what he might find beneath. Thoughts, yes, peaceful and slow and unconcerned. Under the thoughts, something else, something truer, a source of light, strong as a flame. To dim it without extinguishing it . . . he cupped it and exhaled, a sigh born of his own exhaustion and resignation, and knew when he'd succeeded.

There was more there, though, a distracting distant sparkle, like the sun shining off caltrops. That he followed to its source in the body: arthritis, born of an auto-immune response, something he'd realized while studying off-world was the source of many afflictions suffered by his kind. He swept the offending glints away as he withdrew, and found himself again in his body with the priest sleeping peacefully across from him.

And then he fell, and would have struck the unforgiving ground had not a chair appeared beneath him with a scraping squeal against the floor. As he looked up, disoriented, the novice said, "You were falling, Lord."

"I suppose I was," Hirianthial said. His hands were shaking, and he felt weak with . . . hunger? And fatigue. "You are as quick as you promised."

The youth smiled. "Shall I send for something to drink and eat, sir?"

"Yes," Hirianthial said. "That . . . that would be well."

The novice left him with the priest and his own ambivalence. That the execution of his talent could be gentle did not change that what he'd done was possible at all, possible and easy; or at least, it had felt easy while he'd been acting. If he ended up this exhausted after every attempt, perhaps the ease was illusory. Why he hadn't felt it in the tent? Perhaps adrenaline-fueled attempts cost less, or perhaps he'd been so injured already it hadn't mattered. The back of his neck prickled at the memory, which he packed away before it could fully rise.

Belinor returned with a meal and hot mulled cider, and Hirianthial ate with an appetite he couldn't recollect having for a very long time. Afterward, he drowsed by the fire himself until the priest roused, saying, "Ah, now that was a fine deed."

"Elder?" Hirianthial said.

"The fingers," the priest said, leaning forward. He brought his hands from his sleeves, displaying their inflamed joints. "They are not so bad right now. Your doing, I assume?"

"I made the attempt," Hirianthial admitted. "I do not know that I was successful."

"Mmm. Healing can come with the greater talents, or so the stories go." The priest stood. "I have everything I need to know. Tomorrow you will come to me in the library and we will begin your training."

"Just thus?" Hirianthial asked, startled. "No further question? You know all that you need to know?"

The man smiled. "You are no Corel, my son. Have no fear on that account. But practice you do need, to learn to control what you now command. So . . . tomorrow."

"Whom shall I ask for, if I do not find you?"

"Ah. My name is Urise," the elder said. "I was the palace chaplain during Maraesa's reign, now retired. Such as any priest retires. I suppose God and Lady decided I needed special enticement to rouse these bones from the fire in the common room." He paused at the door and said, "The library, tomorrow. Come before breakfast. Be prompt."

"Tomorrow, Elder," Hirianthial said.

How long would Liolesa keep Reese? Come to that, how long had it been since he'd entered the room? Hirianthial rose and glanced out the window, saw the sun on the lake's surface. Long enough, surely. He rested his hands on the sill and centered himself. Despite the food, he still felt uncertain on his feet. It would be good to be back at the townhouse where he could rest. Depending on the frequency of his lessons, he might be forced to request quarters in the palace, but if at all possible he would prefer to avoid it. The apartments allotted the Jisiensire were Araelis's now, and she was no doubt already in residence with the court opening tomorrow. He set off for the royal wing, on the opposite side of Ontine. If Liolesa was not done with Reese he could find one of the alcoves and rest.

It was pure bad luck that he reached the main hall at the same time as the party in Asaniefa's colors—worse luck that the woman leading them was Surela. They stopped at the sight of him, much as he did at them, and together they formed their own tableau, another thing he remembered despising about court life: the endless dramatics.

"Why, my Lord Hirianthial!" Surela exclaimed. "What an unexpected delight! You've returned!"

"From the out-world," her lady-in-waiting added, wide-eyed. Hirianthial also remembered Thaniet, who while less offensive than her lady was nevertheless too meek to disagree with her on any topic of importance.

"From the out-world," Surela agreed. "How relieved you must be to have come back to more civilized lands." She came closer, drawing her entourage after her; Athanesin was still dancing attendance on her, which meant—God and Lady help him—she was still looking for a spouse. He'd always found her interest in him appalling, particularly given their opposing political leanings.

"And just in time for winter court!" Thaniet agreed, smiling at him. "How pleased everyone will be to see you here."

He doubted the unanimity of feeling she implied with that comment, but said, "Thank you. It will be good to see the Lady Araelis again."

"And take back the reins from her?" Surela asked. "Jisiensire has been long without its head."

"The Lady Araelis is the head of Jisiensire," Hirianthial said. "And well-suited to it, being wed."

"You have no plans to marry then?" Thaniet asked, guileless.

"Nonsense," Surela said. "A man of Hirianthial Sarel's poise and power? Of course he must." She smiled at him. "Besides, everyone loves a man already broken to saddle."

The tastelessness of it was typical of her, yet it had been so long since he'd heard anything like it in reference to his previous marriage that it caught him off guard. When he was certain of himself, he said, "Some horses will bear only one rider. If you will excuse me, ladies? I have a previous engagement."

"Do you?" Surela asked, canting her head.

It was purer bad luck to have the page bring Reese into the hall at that moment.

By the end of breakfast, Reese had decided that Liolesa was one of "her" people, if a rather terrifying specimen of that class. The Queen was easier than Hirianthial in company, more talkative, and far more forthright: when she couldn't discuss something she told Reese so, which made the Eldritch mania for mystery far more bearable. Their bargaining session had sounded like something out of a street fair, and that more than anything had convinced Reese of the Queen's character . . . and of the truth of her claims about money. No one with uncountable wealth haggled with that much aggression.

As she was putting her borrowed cloak back on, Liolesa said, "I would be honored if you would accept my hospitality, by the by."

"You mean . . . stay in the palace?" Reese asked, startled. Then added, "What about my crew?"

"They may come as well, of course," she said. "But I'd be pleased to have you introduced to the court once it's in session."

Reese paused. "Are you sure about that? I've heard so much about Eldritch hating non-Eldritch—"

"Hatred and ignorance cannot be addressed without confrontation," Liolesa said. She lifted her brows. "How else? But I will not ask you to be the head of that spear, if the notion discomfits you."

Reese petted the inside lining of her cloak. The notion did "discomfit" her. "I don't like to make trouble for anyone."

"Anyone—by which you mean Hirianthial," Liolesa said, with rather too fine an insight for Reese's taste. "I can understand that, Theresa. But Hirianthial won't be able to leave for some time . . . and if you stay, it will be increasingly burdensome to keep you hidden."

She looked at the Queen, torn. "You think we could stay? He's . . . he's been through a lot. I don't know if he told you."

"A little, yes."

"He needs to not be alone. And he never made it sound like there was much here by way of support." Did she imagine the shadow that crossed those eyes? Probably. "I don't want to abandon him."

"Then move into my guest suite with all your people, and in two days I shall have you presented to the court as good servants to the Eldritch crown." Liolesa rose, pulling at a chain around her neck until she drew free a medallion. She held it out to Reese. "Take this as proof of my intent."

Reese eyed it, her skin stippled to gooseflesh. "I'd have to touch you."

"We began our association over six years ago now, Theresa Eddings," Liolesa said. "Consider it the continued fostering of our relationship."

The medallion gleamed in the woman's palm: a brilliant cloisonné unicorn in shining white on a lapis backdrop. She could have let it swing from her fingers so Reese could catch it without touching her. Because she didn't, Reese reached and took it from her, holding her breath and struggling with her sense of gratitude and humility. The Queen's eyes never wavered from hers as Reese took her hand back, and when it was done Liolesa smiled. "That was well-begun. Or shall I say well-continued?"

"Thank you, Your Majesty. I'm honored," Reese said, quiet.

"Hush, hush," Liolesa said. "None of that. Go on, then, and see to your man."

Reese stopped abruptly.

"Did I say aught amiss?" Liolesa asked, for once surprised.

"He's not my man," Reese said, flushing.

"Not your—oh!" The Queen smiled, a wry twist of her mouth. "I did not mean it thus. We say 'your man' and mean . . . your vassal, your person, your retainer. Someone you take care of. I would not suggest otherwise with him."

Pulling the medallion over her head, Reese hesitated. She looked at the Queen.

Surprised, Liolesa said, "He has not told you?"

"Told me what?" Reese asked, and was rewarded by the sight of a woman with more temporal power than any person she'd ever met—and most she hadn't—putting a hand to her brow as if to still a nascent headache.

"For once," Liolesa said after a moment, "I can honestly say I cannot say more, not because of an Eldritch Veil, but because it is a personal matter. Though if you remain at court long enough you will inevitably hear about it."

"Something that could cause trouble?" Reese asked, uneasy.

The Queen laughed. "What doesn't, here? Go on, Captain Eddings. Collect your people and come back." Her eyes sparkled. "It will be . . . an adventure."

Given how her last adventure had ended up, Reese wasn't sure that was the best way to entice her. Then again, her last adventure had brought her here, to a place she'd never anticipated seeing even in her wildest fantasies. And if it had its issues, what world didn't? "All right," she said. "I will see you later, ma'am."

"Liolesa."

"Liolesa," Reese said, and let herself out. In the corridor, she reflected that she finally knew how it felt to want to call someone by something more formal than they preferred. She would have to be gentler with Hirianthial and Malia next time they tried it on her.

Her worries that she wouldn't know where to go next were assuaged by the arrival of a page, who seemed to appear out of nowhere. She started and said, "Where did you come from?" And then a heartbeat later, "That was probably a horrible question to ask. I'm sorry, I didn't mean to be rude."

The page's smooth mask twitched, but he composed himself quickly and said in accented but fluent Universal, "No offense was taken, ma'am. This way, please?"

Reese followed him, glancing once more at the white-robed guards. As they passed out of their field of view, she said, "Since you can talk . . . can I ask why the guards are differently dressed in here? Is it because of the Queen?"

"Just so, ma'am. Ontine's guards wear the Galare colors. The Queen's personal guard wears white. Also—" He glanced back at her. "They do not speak while on duty, save to their captain or to their liege-lady, so it is not productive to attempt to engage them."

"Wow," Reese murmured. "Serious."

"It is a high honor to be so selected," the page agreed. "Few are worthy."

She nodded. "Thanks for explaining it to me. And not being . . . ah . . . surprised by me."

"Ma'am, our Queen has been a friend to the out-world for all her reign. As she goes, so do I."

They passed the remainder of their walk in silence. As Reese walked, she studied her medallion, turning it in her hands, brushing her thumb over the enamel. A Queen who was comfortable with out-worlders though her world hated them, who knew Hirianthial well enough to have at least one of his personal secrets in her keeping. And he had one of these guard's uniforms . . . was that it? Had he once been one of her personal guards? No wonder he'd been so good with a knife. When the guards in white opened the doors that led out of the Queen's wing of the palace, Reese stole a glance at them in passing. Their stern faces were unreadable, but they looked dangerous to her.

Hirianthial's baritone murmur reached her from the entrance hall, familiar enough that it took her a moment to realize she couldn't understand what he was saying. Then she spotted the clot of people blocking the path between them. It took her all of a glance to tell that he wanted no part of them—that in fact he had an antipathy for them— and she had no idea how she knew but she'd been living with the man for nearly a year.

"Back," she hissed to the page, and turned with a hiss of her shrouding cloak.

The page didn't miss a step, but back-pedaled and took the lead again, heading the way they'd come.

How had she known? Hirianthial waited long enough to allow Reese to retreat before saying, "I do, and I would not do the discourtesy of being late." He inclined his head. "Ladies."

He left them fluttering behind him, heading the way Reese had gone . . . but he stopped just around the corner and waited, extending his senses until he could perceive their agitation at his abrupt departure. They were talking amongst themselves, from the shifting colors in their auras and the emotions they were passing one another with their words; one of those emotions he liked not at all, a salacious coral-colored speculation they shared until they'd tinged each other with streaks of it. Gossip, God and Lady help him, and Surela no doubt in the middle of it. She'd not for-given him for choosing Laiselin over her, but he suspected she'd marry him anyway if she could force him to the altar . . . her and every other eligible woman at court. He had forgotten that he was something worth chasing.

At last Surela's party moved on toward the lakeside apartments, and he judged it safe to follow Reese. He found her loitering near the door to the Queen's wing beneath the watchful eyes of the Swords. When he approached, she said, "I could tell you hated them, so I thought it would be a good idea not to let them get a better look at me."

"You could see that?" he asked, startled.

"Oh yes," Reese said. "There was just something about the way you held yourself. Like you were revolted." She looked up at him. "I'm guessing I was right?"

"Yes, and it was well done. There are other ways out of the palace." He said to the page, "You may go, and thank you."

"Lord," the page said. And added a dip of his head to Reese. "Ma'am."

Reese smiled. "See you later."

Did he imagine the return smile? He saw it in the adolescent's aura, if not on his face. He tilted his head. "Befriending the natives, then?"

"He was nice to me first," Reese said, pulling the cloak more tightly around herself. "How'd your appointment go?"

"Well enough," Hirianthial said, feeling anew the fatigue. "Though I may be forced to remain at Ontine for some time."

"The Queen said that might be the case," Reese said. "So they found someone to help you?"

"I believe so." The Swords opened the doors for them and he led her back into the Queen's wing. He would take her out through the servants' corridors; it would land them closer to the postern gate near Jisiensire's town-house anyway.

"Good," Reese said. "Just remember, if you need any help, you tell us."

"I shall," he said, moved by her matter-of-fact offer. Such a different conversation than the one he'd just had, from the frank phrasing of the language to the ease of speaking with people who wouldn't push him or, God forfend, suggest that it was high time to replace his dead wife. He felt a flush of some emotion: gratitude, perhaps.

Looking down at Reese as she paced him, he said, "And how was your first conversation with royalty?"

Reese snorted. "Other than it not being my first conversation, technically?" A touch of amusement then, bright sparks dancing. "It was good. I liked her."

"Except?" he said, sensing something else.

"Except there's so much going on here that I don't know," Reese said, the words slow to leave her as if she considered each before release. "I like her and I want to trust her, but when you're in charge of things you don't always get to make the choices you want to make. I get the feeling that happens to her a lot."

The perspicacity of that statement caught him by surprise. "I suspect you're correct."

"Yeah." Reese sighed and glanced at one of the paintings as they passed. "Anyway. I'm supposed to collect the crew and come back here to stay. I'm guessing I'll have to bring them at night? So no one will spot them. I could probably disguise the twins, but Bryer's feathers are going to stick out of everything but a boat and Kis'eh't is never going to look bipedal. Though I guess we could make her look like a small horse. Are there small horses? Ponies maybe? Ponies are real, aren't they?"

"The Queen has asked you to stay here?" Hirianthial said, cutting through the words to the one thing that mattered.

"Yes," Reese said. "And she wants to introduce us at some court session in a couple of days."

He stopped. So did she.

"The Queen wants to introduce you formally," Hirianthial repeated.

"I know it sounds crazy," Reese said, her unease palpable. "I told her so myself. Even I know that you don't shove a bunch of out-worlders in front of a culture of xenophobes like that, but she says that things can't change unless you have some confrontation."

God and Lady. He said, "And you said you would?"

"Yes," Reese said, far more seriously than he expected.

"You understand what you've agreed to?"

"Not completely, no," Reese said. "But you'd have to be stupid not to know she's trying to start a fight." She looked up at him. "Isn't she?"

"Yes," he said, the word profound as the toll of a bell. It colored her aura, his, a somber gray hinting at the black of tombs and shadows.

And yet, she did not shiver, and something in her solidified. The shadows became steel and she let out a breath and nodded. "Then I have only one question," Reese said. "Is she going to take care of us when the fight starts? Because I'm okay with taking risks for someone who's going to treat us like her people, but not if we're just the wood she's going to use up to torch the planet."

Turning to face him had put her in the light of the lamps, and the glint he saw at her breast . . . "Is that a medallion?" he asked.

Reese glanced down, then brought it out for him to see. "She gave it to me as proof of her intent."

"Can you turn it over?" he asked.

Her puzzlement streaked her aura bronze and purple. He ignored it, waiting for the inevitability . . . and when Reese showed him the back of the pendant he sighed out. He should have known she would work quickly; Liolesa was nothing if not a master of thinking on her feet. Hirianthial had presented her with an opportunity to catalyze the war she knew she could no longer avoid and so did not want to put off. If she could start it on her terms, she would do that rather than allow her enemies to choose the time and the ground. And they both knew time was running thin.

"Yes," he said. "She will protect you. That is her personal emblem, and she would not give it to anyone she planned to discard."

"All right," Reese said. "That's what I thought from meeting with her, but you can't be sure with politicians." She grinned at him, then faltered. "What?"

"Just like that," he said. "You have thrown in your lot with us."

Reese sighed. "Blood and freedom, Hirianthial. Haven't you figured it out yet?" She met his eyes, fierce. "We threw our lot in with you the moment we went after you in a slaver's prison. That it took me most of a year to stop denying it doesn't make it less true. You're here. This is your fight. That makes it our fight."

"You're so sure you speak for the others?" he asked. "They may have signed up for adventure, but not for . . . this."

She snorted. "Oh, hell, Hirianthial. They knew it before I did. They spent months trying to beat it through my head. And you know what? They were right. Maybe I'm too stubborn for my own good, or maybe I'm just stubborn enough to get us through things and they're the ones who remind me to act like a normal human being, but however that works, it did, and I got it." She shook her head. "You come back to the townhouse with me, Hirianthial, and tell them the story. I'll bet you a horse they're going to agree with me."

"A horse," he said, amused despite his dismay.

"I've just found out how important the things are to you people," Reese said. "So, yes. A horse."

"Does that mean if you win I must buy you one?" Hirianthial asked.

She huffed. "Of course it does. You're the one with the money anyway. I'll have to take out a loan to pay for yours if I lose."

Was he really so surprised by her reaction to the Queen's plan? Maybe he'd forgotten she'd grown up with stories of revolution. The descendants of Mars still reared their children on the bloody history of their emancipation from Earth, and as one of the more traditionalist families the Eddings had been particularly proud of their world's struggle for independence. Reese didn't need the whole picture to sense the tensions that were poised to rip this world apart. All she needed to know was that Liolesa had no gem grid and went through the trouble of maintaining out-world connections anyhow. That meant the people here wanted no part of the technology the Alliance offered, and that suggested technology might make it harder for them to keep whatever power they were used to wielding.

And that story she was familiar with, from bones to skin, cell-deep where stories are born. It might be dressed in silk and jewels, but she recognized it all the same.

As Hirianthial led her through the palace, she surreptitiously examined the back of her medallion and found a tiny design: a white flower twining around a sword. Obviously that meant something, but he hadn't told her what and it was unlikely he would if she asked. As usual. She sighed and smiled a little. As irritating as he was, he was part of the *Earthrise* family. That meant she had to find his foibles at least a little endearing, even when they frustrated her.

"Here," Hirianthial said, pushing on a wall which was, in fact, a door—that seemed normal for Eldritch design, these doors painted to look like the rest of the corridor. "We will exit through the servants' halls, but we should be swift. It's impolite to importune them."

"Right," Reese said, and followed him. The decor here

was somewhat plainer, but the walls still had moldings and paint, and the floors were nicer, she thought: wood rather than stone. They detoured past what looked like storerooms without seeing a soul and ended up outside the palace near a gate sized for a person, rather than an army. There were guards there too, though they recognized Hirianthial on sight and let them pass.

The walk back to the townhouse took them near the cliffs. Reese looked out over the horizon, over endless waves that glittered pale gray and pewter under the morning sun. She waited for the agoraphobia and felt instead a mute wonder at the sight. What did she know about oceans? Mars had none, and she'd gone straight from there to a ship. She'd seen mountains since, and Harat-Sharii's plains, but the sea . . . the sea was new.

"You find it compelling?" Hirianthial asked, quiet. When had he come so close? And why did she find it steadying?

"What? Oh." Reese pulled the hood closer over her head and answered, "I've never seen the ocean. It's . . . big."

"Jisiensire's lands include the coast in the south," Hirianthial said. "I had missed it."

"It's a little like space," Reese said, glancing toward it again. When she could pull her gaze away she found him looking at her with interest. "It has a presence. And it's bigger than you can wrap your arms around. There are things in it you'll never know or reach or understand."

"That bothers you not at all?" His voice remained quiet.

"I think it bothers me less than feeling it's finite and might fall on top of me," Reese said, though that wasn't quite it either and she didn't know what the difference was. But she took a few deep breaths of the brine-scented breeze before going up into the townhouse, and the taste on her tongue felt as old as blood, but cleaner.

They found the crew at breakfast in a room Reese hadn't seen yet, a long hall sized for its gleaming wooden table, with high windows casting slanted light across what remained of a very large meal. Even Allacazam was somnolent from the slow yellow flow of colors across his neural fur; they'd set him in a sunbeam. The twins and Kis'eh't stood when they arrived, and Bryer looked up, the light flowing down his face.

"So?" Irine asked, bouncing a little. "Are we staying?"

Reese was deeply gratified to hear the confusion in Hirianthial's voice when he said, "I beg your pardon?"

"We're staying," Reese said. "There are rooms in the palace waiting for us. And it looks like the Eldritch Queen wants to use us to upset her enemies into making a stupid move."

Sascha pursed his lips. "Wow, sounds dangerous. I'm in."

"What?" Hirianthial asked, now sounding ever so slightly bewildered.

Reese said, grinning, "I think he means 'are you sure.'"

Kis'eh't snorted. "How's this world going to be worse than being chased by slavers? If their bathrooms are any indication, they certainly can't manufacture a working firearm."

"Can we go see the ocean?" Irine asked.

Bryer said, "The sea is good."

Reese pulled out a chair. "You should move Allacazam, he's going to get fat if you keep stuffing him."

Irine scooped up the Flitzbe as Sascha brought her a cup of cider. "Here you go, Boss. No coffee, I'm afraid. It's tea or alcohol. We're going to have to import coffee along with the horses."

"Sounds like a plan," Reese murmured, hiding her amusement.

"You want to stay?" Hirianthial asked Sascha. "You understand the Queen is trying to start a war."

"Are you staying?" Sascha asked, and the others grew quiet to listen to the answer.

Hirianthial looked at them, very still, very contained. "I must."

"Then we're staying," Sascha said.

Reese said to Hirianthial, "You owe me a horse."

INTERLUDE

"Your brother is home."

The man turned from the bookcase to face his subordinate, who unlike him was dressed in the plain blue and white robes of Ontine Cathedral's clergy. "Since that would be a very poor jest, I must assume you aren't making one."

"I wouldn't," the priest said. "Not about that, anyway. No, we have reports he was seen in the Queen's wing. The following morning he met with Urise."

"Urise!" The man closed the book he'd been considering. "Is that so."

"For over an hour," the priest said. "God knows why he wanted to talk to that old relic. He hasn't done anything more useful than teach children their catechisms in decades."

"Indeed," the man murmured.

Watching him, the priest said, "I assume you want him followed? Should we suborn Urise's novice? We know someone in the dormitory, a boy the same age."

"What? No." The man put the book away. "Urise's chosen pupils never defect. The boy would report the attempt and they'd know we were prying. No . . . just keep a watch on him. I want to know how often they're meeting."

"And your brother? We could bribe the servants for information."

The man snorted. "Liolesa's servants? Not likely. Nor will you get much gossip out of them if you ask. They'll only chatter to each other. A stranger, even a trusted one, will probably not inspire their confidences. Put Surela's coterie to work. They already have a reason to be interested in him, and he knows it. He won't find their behavior out of character."

"Consider it done, sir."

"Good," the man said, and sat, arranging his dark red robes. "Now, tell me the latest weapon shipment has reached the cache."

The recitation took some time: there were weapons moving across several borders, and thanks to the Queen's meddling there were now random patrols riding the length of settled territory. Their activities had not yet been discovered, but the detours they'd been forced to take to avoid detection had stretched their timeline, particularly since he insisted on their assuming aerial reconnaissance. His co-conspirators had argued that the likelihood of one of the Queen's foxes being overhead at just the right time to see their movements was astronomical, but he knew Alliance technology better than they did. There might be stealthed satellites in place. It was better not to assume.

The man dismissed his servant at the conclusion of his report and considered, fingers steepled. Many things he had anticipated, but not that his brother would remain free for so long. Had events not conspired so magnificently against it, Hirianthial would have been some Chatcaavan's slave long ago, a possibility that had pleased him enough to go through the lengths required to arrange it. But not only was his brother free, he'd come home.

It was somewhat of a pain, but an opportunity nonetheless.

Sometime later, he left his office and made the long walk to the catacombs where his order used to serve its mission. The cold stone rooms were empty now, their rotted leather restraints swept away. He'd made cleaning the maze a penance for brothers in need of it, which kept the place free of dust that might betray the passage of any people who might be using it. It took him some time to reach the chamber he sought and no one saw him enter it . . . which was well, for he wanted no one touching the equipment he'd been at such pains to procure.

Sitting at his desk, the man tapped the emitter awake and waited for his signal to traverse the labyrinth of obscuring protocols that hid it in the Queen's own out-bound signal. The royal House aggregated the outgoing traffic from all the people on-world who used a Well feed, a group that included not only Galare but Jisiensire and several of their allied minor Houses as well. It was a surpris-ingly dense flow; while it hadn't been easy to disguise his own requests, it hadn't been as hard as he'd feared either.

His call connected. "I have news," he said.

"Yes?"

"Your target's here."

A pause. "Here. Where you are."

"Yes. Can you get here? Soon."

"Yes. But I don't see how him being there helps me. Unless he's out in the country somewhere we can pluck him up."

"Just get here, and mind the system guards," Baniel said. "Leave the rest of it to me."

"Fine. Two days."

The call closed. The man leaned back in his chair, folded his arms on his torso and half-closed his eyes. This thing between them had been a long time coming. The ending of it would be rather more dramatic than he preferred, but there could be a satisfaction in that. He stood, brushed off his robes and settled his stole, and left for his office. Not long now.

PART THREE: SNOW

Left to their own devices, her crew scattered to investigate the Jisiensire townhouse while they had the opportunity, leaving Reese some welcome time in front of the fire with Allacazam. She'd been feeling the need to assimilate her day and something about the Eldritch lack of technology made it easy to slow down, stop fretting so much about where she was supposed to go next, or how she was going to make ends meet. The *Earthrise* was safe in orbit, there was no perishable cargo to worry about, and for now their room and board was being paid by someone else. Absurdly, even with her nebulous grasp of the political situation she was about to be embroiled in, she found the Eldritch world relaxing in the way she'd been hoping Harat-Sharii would be, and hadn't been. Had anyone asked her if she'd thought herself capable of spending hours curled up in a fur watching a fire slowly wear through a few logs, she would have laughed. And yet, she did just that, and found it deeply soothing . . . enough so that Sascha's arrival didn't bother her. It was novel not to feel that little flinch of irritation when someone wanted her attention.

The Harat-Shar sat at her foot, one leg stretched in front of him, the other propped up. His tail was curled over his shin, the tip flicking. The sun had set, and the fire was now the room's sole source of illumination; they considered it together a while before he spoke.

"Tell me the truth, Boss," Sascha said. "How's he doing?"

She looked up from petting Allacazam, then glanced out the door. "I don't know," she admitted. "Except that he's tense."

Sascha nodded. "Irine and I were talking about it. He's been pretty tightly wired since we got him out of Kerayle, and coming here has made it a thousand times worse. We were hoping maybe they'd be able to help him and that would relieve it. Did he talk about it at all?"

"All he said was that they'd found someone to help, and that he'd have to stay awhile." Reese made a face. "Oh, and that it went 'well enough.'"

"That sounds like him." Sascha sighed. "I guess we'll have to wait and see how it goes."

"How what goes?" Kis'eh't asked, peeking inside. When Sascha waved her over she joined them and settled sphinx-like with her paws pointing toward the fire.

"Hirianthial," Reese said.

"Whether he'll be less tense when he gets the help here," Sascha added.

"Ah." Kis'eh't mantled her wings, then tucked them more securely against her second back. "The real question is 'what if he doesn't.'"

"We leave?" Sascha said.

Kis'eh't glanced at him. "That presupposes—interestingly—that we're not going to."

They both looked at her. Reese held up her hands. "You know as much as I do. We're here at the Queen's invitation until it looks like it's time to leave." She rested her fingers on Allacazam again, who murmured a drowsy sound in her head, like rain falling. She wondered if he could eat firelight as well as sunlight, or if he was just sensitive to warmth. "We are going to have to leave at some point to get the horses the Queen wants to buy."

"We're going back to Kerayle?" Sascha asked, aghast. "Are you kidding?"

"At the price tag that woman's willing to pay per horse?" Reese said. "Hell, yes."

Sascha's ears were flat to his head. "Even with pirates."

"We'll be careful. And besides, we never saw any pirates."

"Probably because they hadn't arrived yet," Kis'eh't said dryly.

"What she said, Boss."

Reese chuckled despite herself. "We'll take some of the Queen's foxes. Will that make you feel better?"

Sascha grimaced. "Only if they're better armed than we are."

"Since someone buttering a slice of bread is better armed than we are," Kis'eh't said, "I think we are in good shape. Speaking of which . . . have you had the bread here, Reese?"

"A little, at the Queen's table," Reese said. "Why?" And let the Glaseah fill her ears with enthusiastic praises about the food quality. She and Sascha were debating the flavor of the sparkling juice they'd been given with breakfast when Hirianthial arrived.

"Finally! Someone who can end this debate," Sascha said. "What did they serve us at breakfast, Hirianthial? Kis'eh't says it was some kind of mild citrus. I think it was a grape varietal."

"It was most probably elderflower cordial," he said.

Kis'eh't threw up her hands. "Of course it was something

neither of us have heard of."

Ignoring them, Hirianthial said to her, "Lady? It is time."

As they all stood, Reese said, "Are you coming?"

"To escort you? Of course—"

"I mean are you staying at the palace," Reese said. "Or are you going to stay here?"

Did he wince? It was startling to see him do anything so obvious. "I probably should stay there, but doing so would be . . . problematic. I will have to consult with my teacher."

"I'm assuming there's enough space," Reese said.

"The space is not the issue," Hirianthial said. "But rather the placement. Come, Lady. We have an escort."

Outside was none other than the page who'd been so forthcoming with Reese, shrouded in a dark blue cloak that smeared him into the dark—and it was very, very dark. The sky overhead, untroubled by the brash lighting of a modern city, looked like a jeweled scarf: she could even see the haze of the galaxy. The shudder that took her then was joy, and joy had a taste and a smell and definitely a countenance, and it was the shimmering wink of those uncountable eyes as seen through a sea-softened atmosphere.

She alone had fallen still amid the bustle until Hirianthial joined her and followed her gaze.

"It's nothing like Kerayle," she said, hushed. "Or Mars. Or Harat-Sharii."

"Those places have towns with artificial lighting." He kept his voice low, matching hers.

Her neck ached from the angle she was holding it at, but she couldn't look away. Her eyes were damp. She had never seen anything like it, couldn't understand why it affected her so powerfully, except that she had named her ship for a distant star because stars meant something—

"We call it io gevaerea."

The last thing she'd expected was a comment from him, much less one that revealed . . . well, anything. She glanced at him, holding her cloak closed and hoping he didn't notice her shaking.

"Gevaerea," he said, stepping up alongside her. "It means 'caul'. We shade our words with modes named after colors, and when we speak of the caul of the sky, we use the white mode, for holy things."

Because they'd all been born from stars? She shivered, but it was happiness, not cold, not discomfort. Yes . . . she could see that. More, she could understand a people who did, could envy them a world that let them nourish that perspective.

Was this the sort of thing that had made the man standing next to her? She was suddenly as aware of him as she was of the sky, a good awareness, a vibrating, open-hearted awe. On a whim, she held out her hand to him. She didn't expect him to respond, but if he was willing . . . then she was too, to share what she was feeling. How long had it been since the sight of his own stars had been new to him, after all? He'd been through so much lately. It seemed the least she could do was to trust him.

She hadn't expected, really believed, that he would take her up on it. But a moment later, his cool fingers cupped her smaller hand.

Kis'eh't called, "We're ready over here, Reese."

"Coming," Reese said, and drew her hand back. She glanced at the Eldritch, caught only the hissing fall of his hair over his shoulder as he started toward the others. Just when she thought it was for the best to leave him the privacy of his thoughts, he glanced over his shoulder at her, and she saw a reflection of her own cautious vulnerability in his eyes.

"Theresa," he said. "Will you come?"

"Sure." And she ambled after, keeping her head down and wondering at how her chest could hurt without leaving her feeling bad.

The page's name was Thevenel and he apologized for having to lead them through the back gate as if they were unwanted guests, something overwhelmingly disproven by the second-floor suite he led them to.

"This is for us?" Irine asked, wide-eyed, tail so limp it had fallen on the floor.

"We apologize for putting you in a single suite, but we had only the one in this location, where you are likely to be undisturbed—"

"This is fine," Reese said before he could fluster any worse. "Please tell the Queen she has our thanks."

Once the youth left, Sascha said dryly to Hirianthial, "So this is the worst you've got to offer here?"

"I would say rather that Ontine is the best you will find on this world," Hirianthial said. "The guest quarters are designed for long periods of occupancy. It should be comfortable."

"But it's so big!" Irine called the next room.

"The entourages using them may include up to fifty people." Hirianthial had remained by the door, as if unwilling to commit to entering the room. "That would include the principals of the family and their servants. The front room is for entertaining guests; the rooms to the sides are private."

"Fancy," Sascha said. He flicked an ear back and added, "So, you part of our entourage?"

"Yeah, should we save you a bed?" Irine asked, peeking out of the adjacent room.

Reese waited with interest for this answer and wasn't surprised to see Hirianthial hesitate.

"Let me guess." Sascha folded his arms. "It's complicated."

"It is," Hirianthial said. "And if you will excuse me, I will see if I can unravel those complications. Should you need anything, you can use the bell-pulls."

"Good luck," Reese said, and let him go. When she turned to pick up her bag, she found Kis'eh't and Sascha staring at her. "What?"

"Just like that? 'Good luck'?" Kis'eh't asked.

"You expect me to pry?" Reese snorted. "We've been living with him how long? I think I've figured out how much that accomplishes. Exactly nothing." She looked around. "Besides, I want to check out the new place. Don't you?"

They did. As a group they trailed from room to room, exploring every corner, and every corner rewarded them with some new delight, from tiny jeweled pomanders on an elaborately carved dresser to a tub lit by stained glass windows and deep enough to need steps. The paintings were real, and smelled of exotic pigments; the tapestries, now that Reese was at liberty to examine them, showed signs of being hand-tied, and were inevitably pastoral scenes, or depictions of Eldritch wandering with unicorns through forests and over fields. It truly was a vast set of rooms, and the riches in it so opulent Reese's head swam at the thought of itemizing the costs. She was studying a painted miniature on the mantle of the fireplace in one of the bedrooms when Bryer stuck his head in the door. "Have guest."

"Someone we know?" Reese asked.

"Have guest."

"Right," she said, and threaded her way back to the front room, where she found an Eldritch woman in a slim brown gown edged in gold, and with a simple long braid crowning her head. At her arrival, the woman curtseyed.

"Milady," she said in accented Universal, "does it please you, the Queen has assigned me to your service."

Taken aback, Reese blurted, "Permanently?"

The woman stared at her, then touched her finger-tips to her mouth to hide her smile. "Ah . . . no! I say this wrongly, perhaps? Temporary service, to help you while you are here. She guessed you have no servants."

Reese snorted. "I have employees, and mouthy ones."

"We heard that!" Irine called.

"Like I said." Reese smiled at the Eldritch, puzzled. The Queen must know she didn't need servants, so why had she sent her one? "I'm Reese Eddings. What's your name?"

"Felith," she said. "I was previously in service to the heir as a lady-in-waiting, so I hope you will find my credentials acceptable. . . ."

"Previously?" Reese wondered.

"The heir is considering a religious order and is at a monastery now," Felith said, flushing pale peach. Reese wondered what about that situation was blushworthy, though she guessed that taking vows conflicted with the whole being-an-heir business.

"I didn't meant to imply anything," Reese said. "Come on in. Are you supposed to stay here with us or do you just visit?"

"My pardon, Lady," Felith said, "but I stay here with you. Otherwise, who can help you dress and prepare for the day?" She hesitated, glancing at Reese's apparel, and added, "The Queen also thought you might appreciate a . . . native guide. And someone who speaks the language."

Implying that Hirianthial wouldn't be around? Or maybe assuming he wouldn't be forthcoming? Reese wondered. But what she said was, "That sounds very useful, yes. Let me introduce you around . . . though be warned, most of the crew's even more alien than I am."

"I assure you, Lady," Felith said with all evidence of candor, "none of them can be as startling as you."

This was a meeting he'd been putting off—had in fact hoped he wouldn't have to have at all—but it could no longer be helped, so Hirianthial took himself down the hall to the apartments that would once have been assigned to him and were now Araelis's. A man he didn't recognize let him in and made him comfortable in the parlor with a cup of hot cider; he was surprised she was out, given the lateness of the hour, and waited with some perplexity for her return. When she did at last arrive, she stopped at the door at the sight of him. There was a moment of mutual astonishment, and then everything fell away from him—every concern, all the tangled and tiresome politics, everything he'd been intending to say—and he rose and went to her. "How long before you're due? You look second trimester. Maybe four months?"

"Y-yes," she said, startled. "How did you . . ."

"Have you had any issues?" he asked, evaluating her aura and that of the sleeping child. He hadn't done an obstetric round since school but his recent experience on Harat-Sharii had given him cause to refresh himself on the topic. And right now, nothing was as important as making sure that this baby didn't die, the way his had, the way too many Eldritch children did. "Spotting, cramping, dizzy spells?"

"No," Araelis said, her voice now thoughtful rather than surprised. "Nothing like that. Though I'm tired and irritable."

"Tired and irritable is normal," he said. "Have you a midwife yet?"

"I have one engaged, yes," she said. "Hirianthial?"

He looked up, found her considering him, her aura

gone iridescent with wonder.

"I did not expect you to be interested," she said at last. "Particularly given your history."

He smiled, as much at himself as at her confusion. "I know something about these matters now, having spent my time away profitably."

"To become a midwife?" she asked, incredulous.

"A doctor," he said. "And I have some tools with me—" On the *Earthrise*, which he had not packed. Perhaps he could ask Malia to send them down. "—but not all I would wish to support a pregnancy. You and Ceredan have been trying for a long time, I know."

"Yes," she said, resting her arms over her belly. She canted her head. "Is that why you're home, then? Have you come to be our first modern doctor?"

The idea stunned him. It had been the furthest thing from his mind, plying his new profession on his own world, mostly because he'd never planned to come back. There was no question that the Eldritch needed modern medicine, needed facilities as well as people to staff them. But such an infrastructure implied a world that welcomed it, and for that Liolesa had to succeed in her aims. Hirianthial backed toward a chair and paused at it, realizing he couldn't sit until his cousin had.

"So that's not why you're here," she said, frowning. And then, "Oh, take the chair, Hirianthial. Please. I will too, my feet hurt."

Nevertheless, he waited for her to settle before seating himself, composing himself as he did so. He had become so accustomed to being clouded by anxiety when confronted with the concept of pregnancy that it was gratifying to discover his training could overcome it. Here was a task, a case, someone he could manage in a way he could not the fretful girl on Harat-Sharii whose miscarriage had most probably been induced by her senior wife. Here was someone who welcomed her pregnancy and would be eager to work with him to support its successful conclusion. He could never bring back Laiselin or the child they would have had together . . . but he could ensure his cousin never suffered the heartbreak he had. He breathed out and folded his hands together in his lap while she spread her skirts and accepted a cup of tea from her servant.

"I am glad to have you home," Araelis said once she'd had a sip. "You have been missed. Not just by me, but by everyone in the family . . . Liolesa as well. Particularly, even."

The memory of Liolesa's forgiveness was still tender. "I am sorry to have grieved you and the others," he said. "But it was necessary."

She met his eyes. "Was it truly? Really? You deprived us of a great deal, Hirianthial."

He watched the fire, feeling her gaze on his profile. "Did I? Of what? The sight of me in extremis?"

"The opportunity to *help you* in extremis," she said. "The chance to demonstrate that we loved you, and we were there for you. The ability to support you when you needed it, after so many years of you sustaining us through your generosity and your leadership of the household. You allowed us ample opportunities to take from you, Hirianthial . . . but you never permitted us to reciprocate."

The accusation felt like a dart shot painfully true, all the more deeply because of the months he had spent on the *Earthrise* watching Reese struggle with the very same issue. Had he truly committed the same sin? And he had blamed her for it, and thought himself the superior for noting it. God and Lady. He cleared his throat and said, "I would not have been able to accept it then."

"And have things changed?"

He thought of Urise and his swift-footed novice . . . of

Reese's stubborn offers of aid and Liolesa's happiness at his return. "I hope I am becoming more capable of receiving."

Her sigh brought his attention back to her. "I suppose that's better than nothing. Having put that to rest—for now—perhaps you can tell me why I had to have news of your arrival from Surela of all people, rather than from you."

He hid a grimace. "So she has been bruiting it about."

"Very enthusiastically," Araelis said with asperity. "I doubt there's a soul in Ontine who doesn't know that the wayward Jisiensire has returned." She eyed him. "So? Why did I hear it from Surela first? Is there something you'd rather I not know?"

"I'm not here to take Jisiensire back," Hirianthial said. "I will not have you raise your hopes."

"I didn't assume you were, given that you snuck in like a thief," she said tartly. "I'm not stupid, cousin. So what is it?"

"I had need of a priest," Hirianthial said. "For this, I shall be staying here until he declares I am fit to go. Which brings me to the matter of lodgings."

"Surely you aren't here to ask if you can stay with us?" Araelis said. "You *are* Jisiensire, Hirianthial. It is we who should be asking your permission—"

"God, Araelis," he said, touching his hand to his brow. "Don't be ridiculous. I gave you the seal—"

"—which I tried to give back—"

"—and I don't mean to have it, not now, not ever. Jisiensire needs a fecund head, someone to continue the line. You and Ceredan are far more suited to the task. And I won't hear any argument about it!" She stopped, mutinous. When he was sure she wouldn't interrupt again, he finished, "The issue is political, not pragmatic."

"Oh?" she asked, frowning. "Are you wooing someone who would take it amiss if you were to be housed with your own family?"

"You," he said, "have not grown more tactful, cousin."

She grinned. "Unlike Liolesa, I don't have to be mindful of such things. What then is the issue that so concerns you?"

"I have brought some compatriots with me," Hirianthial said. "I had thought to lodge them in our townhouse, but Liolesa has asked them to be her guests and intends to introduce them formally. Most probably she wishes to separate us so that any opprobrium is solely leveled at her."

Araelis stared at him, then sat up, one hand on her belly. "You have brought aliens here!"

"I have," he said. And smiled at the firework patterns shimmering on her aura. "Two of them are even Harat-Shar, though tigraine, not pardine."

"There are more?" she asked. "How many? What races?"

"A Phoenix, a Glaseah, one of the Flitzbe . . . and a human."

Araelis sat back. "Oh, cousin." She laughed. "Oh, cousin! Ha! We will take back the torch from Galare! They were far too smug having scored that coup with the Glaseah the scion of the Seni brought home and made kin. They thought that more than made up for Fasianyl's friendship with Sellelvi, despite our also having supplied the Tams—nine generations of them!—through Meriaen. But now we will be responsible for the arrival of no less than six aliens! Six! The flag will be restored to our House—"

"—save that Liolesa has claimed them," he reminded her, unsure whether to be amused at her eagerness or appalled at the collection of aliens being turned into a game.

"Lady bless it!" Araelis scowled. "Those were our aliens! She should get her own."

"She did, in the main," Hirianthial said. "She reached

out to Captain Eddings first. I met them through their association with her. Araelis . . . please, this is a serious matter. She is introducing them at court. You have some notion what that means."

"Yes," Araelis said, and sighed. "Yes, I do." She grinned. "If I'd known this year's winter court was going to be so exciting I would have brought Ceredan with me. He loves a fight."

Her aura was a warm, bright gold, shimmering with health and ease. He studied it and said, quieter, "You look well, Araelis. The family is well too, isn't it?"

"You heard?" she asked, head canted. Another smile, proud this time. "We've been growing. Nessiena had another child—another!—and Foreia had her first, successfully. We haven't lost anyone to duels or hunts for almost three decades now, and the crops have been good for years running. The House is prosperous, even the junior lines. We've even been talking about endowing a few new families."

"Ah," he said, smiling. "Good."

"It is, isn't it?" She shared a fond look with him. "Not quite as good as under your tenure, but we've had some fair fortune, and things are improving. And if Liolesa can win her fight and we can open the world . . ."

"It would be amazing," he murmured.

"Well," Araelis said, "Far be it from me to interrupt her plans for moving us toward that end. I will kick you out of our apartments myself if it serves her purpose. Where shall you stay, if not with the aliens or not with us?"

"I have an idea," Hirianthial said.

Six aliens sat in a semi-circle, spread across floor, hearth and chairs. Their focal point was the single Eldritch in the room, who had resorted to embroidery to keep from fidgeting at their fixed attention. She was speaking in an even voice despite her nervousness, however. "The Queen entertains the nobility twice a year at the summer and winter courts. In summer, because on the coast it is cooler than it is on many of the country estates, so she hosts as a courtesy; summer is a time for arranging marriages and alliances, particularly, and for the introduction of debutantes to society. Summer is a time for the young." She trailed off and sighed. "Ah, a good time for the young." She pushed her needle through the fabric and continued. "Ontine rarely gets snow in winter, again because of the sea. But the weather becomes so inclement on the roads that most parties stay for several months. Because of that, winter is the time for politics. Nobles bring their tithes for the year and evidence of their commitments to the Queen, and she reaffirms her own duties to them, including the dispensation of funds, supplies or arms. Any major changes in policy are announced in winter, and any discussions that the Queen is willing to hear on those changes are held then also."

"So our arrival in winter is good timing," Sascha said. "What with the major changes in policy part."

"Yes, we're a major change in policy, aren't we?" Irine added, ears perked.

"That would be somewhat of an understatement," Felith admitted, but she was smiling.

"So what do we have to know about this?" Reese asked, petting Allacazam's fur. "There's got to be some kind of ritual or protocol. I don't want to embarrass anyone."

"It is a rather irregular event," Felith said, setting her embroidery hoop on her lap. "The last time an alien was presented so was when Fasianyl Mina Jisiensire brought Sellelvi the Harat-Shar to the summer court. That was some almost two centuries ago now."

"Two . . . *centuries*?" Kis'eh't said carefully.

"Just so," Felith said. "We have not had notable contact with mortals here on the homeworld until very recently, a few years ago, when the Seni Galare heir made a male of your species kin."

"Wait, what did you call us?" Reese asked.

"Ah—" Felith paused, blushed so brightly her pale skin turned rose-petal peach. "My pardon, it is the translation. I should have said aliens."

"Mortals?" Sascha said. "Really? That's what you people call us when we're not around?"

"Wow," Irine murmured.

Reese ignored them, tugging at a memory until it spilled: the smell of parchment and ink, the low lighting of a Harat-Shariin room, the rustle of pages . . . and paintings. "Sellelvi . . . a Harat-Shar? Was she one of the leopard intraraces?"

"She was indeed," Felith said, touching her bright cheek with some embarrassment.

"Blood and freedom," Reese breathed. Allacazam sent a querulous tone rising through her mind. "Did anyone ever paint pictures of her?"

"You know that story?" the Eldritch asked, surprised. "One of the lady Fasianyl's suitors was a portrait painter and did many paintings of the two of them together."

"Boss?" Sascha asked.

"I think I've seen them! On Harat-Sharii . . . blood in the soil." Reese hugged Allacazam, who soothed her with the soft burble of a brook. "So our last known precedent was two centuries ago? What about this Glaseah?"

"That was done at the Seni estate," Felith said. "Not formally here at the court. And Sellelvi's introduction was irregular as well, since Fasianyl debuted that year with Sellelvi as her sole companion." At their blank looks, she added, "Debutants are introduced to society with their chosen ladies-in-waiting. The women who serve that role have chosen to attach their fortunes to their lady's, and become a part of a society themselves as a tier of support beneath the significant players of a House but above the class of household servants."

"That was you," Reese said suddenly. "You said you were the Heir's lady-in-waiting."

Felith brushed her fingers over her embroidery. "Yes, Lady."

"And she cut you loose?" Irine asked. "That seems callous."

"She was not well," Felith said. Squaring her shoulders she said to Reese, "I assume the Queen wishes to use the same rite she would use to introduce a new House retainer. During it, she will make clear her duties to you as your liege-lady, and will ask you to commit to her service. If you would like, in the morning I can instruct you on the format of the rite."

"Yes," Reese said. "I think you'd better."

There was a soft knock at the door. Felith, Reese and Sascha all rose to answer it and were looking at one another when Hirianthial let himself in.

"My lord Hirianthial!" Felith exclaimed, startled.

"Felith?" he said, surprised. "How come you here?"

"The Queen has sent me to serve the out-worlder captain." This said with another blush, but at least she didn't call her the 'mortal' captain. Blood in the soil, did they really think themselves so far above everyone else? Especially when a palmer killed them just as dead as the rest of them?

"A kindness," Hirianthial said. "If you will excuse me? I must speak with the captain."

"Of course," Felith said, curtseying. To Reese, "If I may?

I will settle into my quarters."

"Sure," Reese said. "Um, you'd better talk to everyone else about who's sleeping where."

Felith frowned, a touch of a furrow between her brows. "They should by no means be sleeping in the rooms allotted to the service—"

"Maybe you should tell us which is which, then," Sascha said, tail curling. He pulled Irine up. "Night, Boss."

"Good night, ariisen," Reese said.

It surprised her how large the room felt once it had emptied of her crew. The fire had burned down to low flames, shrouding the room in sepia shadows, and the rugs and tapestries muffled the sound of the conversations going on in the other rooms to vague murmurs.

"Do you ever get used to the quiet?" she asked him.

He drew closer. "I became accustomed to the noise. One presumes the process works in reverse."

She glanced up at him. He looked drawn to her, too pale where the wan firelight touched his skin and too severe where its shadows pooled.

"Go on," she said, quiet. "Tell me the bad news."

"I cannot stay here with you," he said. "The Queen has gone through a great deal of work to divorce you from Jisiensire—to protect it, and to protect you—and my being found among you would confuse the issue."

"So where will you go?" Reese asked.

"I will stay with the priests. They have a set of rooms here adjacent to the palace chapel."

Reese nodded. "All right. If we have to give you up to anyone, priests seem a good choice."

He smiled. "I am glad you approve. Captain . . . I trust I need not say you should be careful leaving these rooms?"

"Not born yesterday," Reese said. "Not even by your standards. Don't worry, we'll all be careful." She thought of the deteriorations she'd failed to notice on Harat-Sharii because she'd been willing to push him out of sight. "But you . . . I want to see you regularly, all right? We all do, to make sure you're doing okay."

That curved his mouth, just enough that she could tell he was glad. "After my lessons, then. Which brings me to another matter. Lady, are you armed?"

"Not unless you count the rinky-dink laser mounted on the *Earthrise*," Reese said, concealing her alarm. "Somehow I doubt it would penetrate atmosphere if I asked Malia to aim it down here." She made a face. "Well, that's not entirely accurate. I *used* to be armed, but my knife's somewhere in the middle of Kerayle-nowhere, and I'm not going back for it any time soon."

"A knife, ah?"

"Sascha's suggestion," Reese said. "And Bryer's." She grimaced. "I should have taken better care of it, but I was a little distracted at the time."

"You'll learn the awareness," Hirianthial said, as if it was a given she'd be handling weapons for the rest of her life . . . maybe it would be. Maybe it was time she stopped pawning off her own defense on other people. He distracted her from her thoughts by saying, "But you should not go unarmed here." He unbuttoned his coat, and the light streamed down the length of bronze filigree as he offered her a dagger, hilt first and draped in wine-colored silk cord. She recognized the opal on it, and the tooling: this was not the plain weapon she'd washed for him after their adventure with Surapinet, but part of the antique set she wasn't supposed to have seen. Was it her imagination that it gave off a sense of purpose and age, or was that just her reaction to the patina on the metal and the weathering on the scabbard?

"Should I really have that?" she asked. "I might

break it—"

"Not likely," he said, with another twitch of his mouth.

"Or lose it like I did my first—"

"Really?"

"Well, no," she admitted. "I can't imagine ever losing this one. I just don't want to . . ."

"To what?" he asked, canting his head just enough for his hair to shift against his throat.

"To dishonor it," she blurted, before she could restrain herself for sounding ridiculous.

His chin rising was subtle enough that in anyone else she would have dismissed it. In him, though . . . what was it? That look on his face. Maybe it was pride? Satisfaction? She didn't want to think there was something tender in his smile, or that she could read it so easily.

"Theresa," he said. "Reese. You are the least likely person on this planet to accomplish such a thing, I assure you." He turned it and offered it on his palms as if it were a sword being pledged in some fealty ritual. "Please. It will ease me to know you have some recourse if you are given insult, physical or otherwise. A woman here always has protection, and should even if she undertakes it herself."

"All right," she said. "But . . . well. All right." She took it, gingerly. How many hands had held this thing? It was probably older than her entire family line on Mars. Flushing, she added, "Thanks. For trusting me with it."

"Good," he said. He tapped the cords, making the tassels sway. "These should be wrapped hilt-to-sheath if you plan to go into the Queen's presence. Otherwise, leave them unbound. Unless I am sore mistaken, your rank permits that."

"I have a rank here?" Reese asked, bemused.

"Anyone destined for a court presentation has a rank," Hirianthial said. "Now, I should away. You have what you need? Felith will be a good aid to you; don't let her genteel demeanor fool you on that count. The ladies-in-waiting chosen by the Heir must be approved by the Queen, and she is Liolesa's, heart and hand. Use her."

"I'll do my best," Reese said. "We'll be fine. All of us."

"Do you so promise?" he asked, seeming to find that funny. And then, abruptly grave: "Be wary of committing to vows on behalf of your people, lady. The breaking of vows is a serious matter."

"I really do promise," she said. "And it won't matter if I break it, because I'll die trying to keep it."

That made him go still, very very still. Fine by her. Let him feel how serious she was. When he didn't speak, she added, "I didn't dodge three planets' worth of pirates just to get in trouble on a world full of xenophobes armed with swords, Hirianthial."

"Swords kill full as well as any palmer, lady."

"They'll have to catch us first," Reese said. She rested the dagger against her chest, fist clenched around the scabbard. "Good night, Healer."

He paused, then stepped back, inclined his head. "Good night, Captain."

His leaving made the parlor feel unbearably empty. Reese sighed and sat on the chair in front of the fire, working her boots off. The dagger on her lap felt far heavier than it should, and she was far too aware of its weight; once she'd tossed both boots to one side, she sat up in the chair and loosened the cords so she could draw it, just enough to watch the dim red flames flicker over bright steel. She didn't need to touch it to know it was sharp; something in the way the light bled toward the edges suggested the perfection of it.

"Hey, Reese?"

Startled, Reese looked up and found Irine peeking in

from the door. "Blood and freedom, Irine. Make a little more noise next time?"

"Sorry," Irine said, padding in. "We've set aside the big bedroom for you. I thought you might want to be introduced to it."

Reese sheathed the dagger and rose. "Everyone else asleep?"

"Or at least in bed," Irine said. "It's a nice world, gravity-wise, reminds us of how you keep the *Earthrise*. But I think maybe the days are longer? It's a little disorienting. We're going to need a week or two to get used to it." As Reese joined her, Irine added, "Are we going to have a week or two?"

"I don't know," Reese said. "I guess we'll see."

The bed was once again a towering edifice requiring stairs to reach. Someone had left Allacazam next to her pillow, and she pulled him close under her chin. It wasn't as comfortable as a hammock, but she could get used to it.

The dagger she put beneath the pillow, an act that caused Allacazam to form a picture of it in her head along with a rising tone of curiosity.

"A gift," she told him, quiet. When the image persisted, and included the pillow, she finished, "It's his, one of his important ones. It feels wrong to leave it out of reach." She stared past his neural fur at the distant wall. "Besides . . . this place feels like something out of a fairy tale. There are always dragons in fairy tales."

A cold wind blew through her mind. She shivered and said, "Exactly," and wrapped an arm around him.

There was an austerity to the clerical quarters that suited Hirianthial after years of living off-world, for while he could have afforded luxurious housing he never chose to spend the money. He had his own funds, but for most of his adulthood he'd held the reins for Jisiensire and he had never lost the habit of treating the money available to him as wealth held in trust for his steaders. Thus, the simple narrow bed troubled him not at all, and he slept far better than he'd expected.

In the morning, he bathed, dressed, and went to the library to await Urise.

The library remained one of the more beautiful rooms in Ontine, tall-ceilinged with lancet windows, clear-paned to allow light for reading. The shelves were dark, fragrant wood and lined with leather-bound tomes, some as old as Settlement, and here and there were narrow wooden tables for setting out the larger books and paging through them. There was still a short step up to a dais under a half-cupola, lined in lancet windows topped with cinque-foils. He sat there to enjoy the thin, pale gold of the winter sun while he waited, and it was there the priest found him.

"Good morning, my son," Urise said. "You look rested. Are you ready then to work?"

"Straight to the task, then?" he asked.

"We may live long, but that is no reason to waste the time we're given." Urise joined Hirianthial on the dais and folded his small, thin frame into a chair, robes pud-dling around him. "We shall begin with the most import-ant teaching."

"Very good," Hirianthial said. "What might that be?"

"Breakfast," Urise said, grinning. At Hirianthial's expression, he said, "Everything is less dire on a properly fed stomach."

Hirianthial laughed. "Very well. But I shall not answer for the trouble we'll endure if the Queen discovers we have been eating in her library."

"That will be the second most important teaching," Urise said. "There are rules that protect us from grave harm . . . and rules that exist to save us from inconvenience. Most of the rules we are taught as children, in regards to our talents, are of the latter type. They served your teachers, but as you have noticed, they did not serve you—did in fact, do you harm."

Hirianthial looked away. "I object to the characterization. It was I who did harm to others."

Urise leaned back. "Do tell." When Hirianthial glanced at him, he said, "I presume there is a story there, most likely relating to the discovery of your powers. I also assume it is a dark one. Yes?"

"I fear so—"

"And you want to know how I guess, when you and I both know that we discover our own depths when we are pushed to our limits. So go on. Unburden yourself of it, my son. I am a priest, your confession will not surprise me. At this age, there is little I haven't heard."

It surprised him how much he craved the prospect of absolution, that it might prove more powerful than his reticence to discuss the events on Kerayle. But it did. He told Urise everything. Nor did he limit himself to his doings on the colony world; he spoke of his original mission for Liolesa and the acts he had committed to buy, steal or force the information she needed out of people, and while most of those acts had not involved the terrifying powers he'd exhibited in the Rekesh's tent, there were things in retrospect he now questioned: had it been Reese's performance that had convinced the jailor to release them from the slaver prison? Or had he been showing signs of his nascent abilities? What about the time they'd been fleeing Surapinet, and he had been able to tell where their enemies were? When they'd nearly been accosted, and he had tasked the crew to silence lest they be discovered, and he had been praying—demanding—that they not be noticed . . . had he been forcing the issue?

He paused only when swift-footed Belinor arrived with two servants and the breakfast trays; once the acolyte withdrew he continued until they had eaten and set the plates aside. Once they had finished, he folded his hands and waited for the priest's response, carefully ignoring his own anxiety. But Urise only sighed.

"You see what I have become," Hirianthial said, low.

"I see what you think you have become because you have been poorly prepared for what you faced," Urise said. "And I cannot lay all the fault on the shoulders of your teachers, for what teacher thinks to prepare his charges for slavers, murderers and rapists? Yet that is our duty, and we shirk it in order to shutter our eyes from a world we would rather not have congress with, though inevitably it will have congress with us. No, my son, you have acquitted yourself well. Better than I would have expected, given how little you knew."

"Elder," Hirianthial said, stunned. "I am soiled!"

"Child, so are we all who walk on this earth, and make no mistake. Not even a saint is without blemish. We strive, in despite of our sins." He canted his head. "Or is it the other matter that concerns you? That others have touched you?"

"No," Hirianthial said, the words slow. He tried to sort the thoughts from his antipathy. "What soils me is that I have been hurt in a way many others have been hurt, and yet they did not destroy their abusers. To survive violence is one matter. To inflict it in revenge—"

"Was that what it was?" Urise interrupted. "Revenge?"

"I fear it may have been." He cleared his throat and looked at the remains of the scone on his plate. "I fear I may have been avenging my insulted pride."

"So," Urise said. "This is not about the assault at all. It is about your brother."

Hirianthial looked up at him sharply.

Urise leaned over and refilled his cider, using the cup to warm his hands. "You question your rectitude because you acted in hot blood when your parents were killed."

"They died," Hirianthial said, because it was what he had been telling himself for so long that the words spoke themselves. "They were not killed."

"They were encouraged in their excesses by a son who should have been warding their health when they became distressed and melancholic," Urise said. "Let us not mince words, Hirianthial Jisiensire. Your brother abetted their unlawful experimentation with mind poisons. If he did not administer the dose to them directly, he did not stop them either."

"There was never any proof—"

Urise stared at him until he subsided. Then, deliberately, the priest set his cup down and said, "You knew him. Was proof necessary?"

It hurt to say it, but pain did not change the truth. "No."

"So is your guilt on account of your leaving him alive when you should have executed him?" Urise asked. "Or is it that you feel you undertook the entire process while still angry and grieving?"

Hirianthial pressed a hand to his brow.

"You will have to cease to blame yourself for both things, my son. For your anger . . . and for finding mercy at the end."

"You think I blame myself for the mercy I showed Baniel?" Hirianthial asked, head still lowered.

"I don't know," Urise said. "Do you?"

Hirianthial said, quiet, "I have to believe in the possibility of redemption."

"A man must seek God to find him," Urise said. "Speaking of which . . . we must begin your training. Are you prepared?"

"Adequately so."

Urise nodded. "Then, relax, close your eyes . . . and tell me all that you perceive with your finer senses."

"Tell you . . . all? All of it?"

"Start with me," Urise said. "What do you sense?"

Hirianthial did not have to reach for the priest to feel the coolth of his serenity. "You are relaxed."

"Which looks like what to you?"

"Like blue waters enshrouding you."

"And is that all?"

Hirianthial studied. "There are streaks of gold—"

"Don't pause," the priest said, eyes closed. "Talk. Don't stop. Dig deep and when you run out of observations, keep moving."

"The gold streaks are interest, perhaps. Fondness—"

"Be more definitive."

"You are exhibiting signs of fondness and relaxation. There is a hint of lightning crackle . . . pain?"

"Don't pause," Urise said. "Keep going."

Hirianthial drew in a breath. "Pain, physical pain, and your thoughts are composed and move at a stately pace, and your heart rate is low and your blood pressure and . . ." He spread outward, "and your acolyte is outside the door, and he is vigilant and streaked in gray worry and steel determination and he has eaten recently and is content with his lot but has the physical agitation of the young and beyond him is . . . beyond him there is a servant in the corridor—in a hurry—very focused—and further on a guard . . . ."

He kept going. The words fell from his lips until they came in a rhythm as he flowed outward, seeking, and the more he sought the more he sensed, and the more he spoke the faster the words came until he found a pattern in them, a metronomic beat. The moment he became aware of it, he heard his heart—what had come first? The beat of his heart or the beat of the words?—but one or the other, he felt its artificiality, its busyness, its lack of peace and true understanding.

He sank below that rhythm and found a stillness so profound his eyes spilled over in shock. Here there was an emptiness that was full . . . because it implied, somehow, a listening.

Hirianthial broke from his trance, shaken and still hearing the echoes of that silence. He looked at the priest, mouth open.

"Immanence," Urise said, without surprise, as if he had been waiting. As if he knew.

"Yes," Hirianthial whispered.

The priest nodded. "Very good. We are done for the day. But bide a moment. You will be more tired than you think."

So he did, resting in the chair, grappling with the vastness. "How does that help? With my training?" he asked finally.

"Mmm. You tell me."

Hirianthial paused, then managed a laugh. "Turning the question."

"Permit me my pedagogical idiosyncrasies," the priest said, smiling. "And answer the question."

"That it helps to know where you begin and end?" Hirianthial guessed. He moved through the answers as he had moved through his impressions. "That it helps to be able to know the difference between yourself and others. That it helps to leave yourself behind."

"All good answers," Urise said. "I might have said to build a solid structure one must have a foundation."

Hirianthial inhaled, let the breath out slowly, eyes closing. "And I am exhausted, and know not why."

"So it goes, when one touches the truth," Urise said. "But you did well. You found it faster than any of the priests I've trained. I suppose that is one of the gifts of Jerisa's Veil. It teaches those who leave this world to stop talking, and that gives them the chance to practice listening. One learns much from listening."

"Like that the palace is seething with discontent," Hirianthial said, reaching for a glass. And then he stopped, hand hanging mid-air.

Urise chuckled. "Didn't realize you'd brought that back with you, did you?"

"No," Hirianthial said. "Though I suppose it is not surprising, given the situation."

"No," Urise agreed. "So I will give you your first assignment outside the classroom. Go piece out your impressions and examine them, see if you can remember anything more granular. To be able to sense is only part of the talent. To be able to interpret it, to grasp it wholly without needing time to consider it . . . that needs practice."

"Very well, Elder," Hirianthial said. "And thank you."

"It is my pleasure, my son," Urise said, and pushed himself upright. "If you take to all your lessons with such alacrity, I will have the rare pleasure of teaching a brilliant student before I die."

A woman's shrill scream yanked Reese awake and out of bed—unfortunately, for she'd forgotten she was sleeping in one tall enough to fall out of. Cursing under her breath, she felt her face and arms to make sure they hadn't broken while hurrying toward the commotion in the next room. Halfway there she realized she was unarmed and sprinted back to the bedroom for the dagger.

Despite her tardiness, the woman responsible for the screaming was still screaming when she burst into the room, surprising everyone. "What is going on here?" she asked into the sudden silence.

"Ah . . . we were sleeping," Irine said, ears flat. She was holding a sheet flush to her body in an uncharacteristic show of modesty. "And this woman sneaked in like a ghost!"

"Which surprised me," Sascha said, still bristled. "So I jumped."

"And then she started howling," Irine said. "And we tried to calm her down and that just made it worse."

"And then Felith showed up—" Sascha paused.

Felith, shrouded in a dressing gown so ornate it looked more like clothing than something from a woman's boudoir, said with resignation, "And I have been trying to calm her down with little success."

"You seem to have done the trick, though, Boss," Sascha observed.

The woman, who'd backed away until her spine was flush to the wall, was staring at Reese in fascination. Reese looked down at herself. She guessed showing up barefoot in a nightgown with a dagger in hand was enough to distract anyone.

"At least she's not screaming anymore," Irine muttered.

"Why was she screaming?" Reese asked Felith. Then she held up a hand. "No, wait." She turned to the twins and gave them a significant look. "Why was she screaming? You weren't doing anything shocking?"

"We were sleeping!" Irine squeaked. "Honestly! Look, we're even covering ourselves!"

Reese faced Felith. "All right. Back to you, then. Why is she screaming?"

"There were giant tigers in the bed," Felith replied, flushing. At Reese's expression, she hastened to add, "You must realize, my Lady, almost no one here will have ever come face to face with an alien . . ."

"At least we're not 'mortals' anymore," Irine muttered.

"What was she doing in the room?" Reese asked, ignoring Irine to eye the stranger.

"She came to rebuild the fire and refresh the water," Felith said. "All the suites have a servants' door to permit the tending of the linens, the fire, the water, and to clean."

"You let people just walk in? All the time?" Irine's ear sagged, leaving the other propped upright. "No warning?"

"They come while the occupants are out, or asleep," Felith said. "Usually."

Reese rubbed her head with the back of the hand holding the dagger. "Ask her to leave, please."

Felith stared. "What . . . are you holding?"

"A weapon," Reese said wearily.

"Nice one, too." Sascha peered at it. "What happened to the last one?"

"It's baking under Kerayle's sun somewhere."

"May I . . . ?" Felith said, stepping closer, eyes fixed on the blade.

"Yes, but tell her to leave first, please." Reese studied the servant warily. "I think we've had enough screaming for one morning."

The door, like all the others in this place, was painted to blend into the wall, in this case in a corner in the main room. Reese watched the servant vanish into it with deep misgivings before she turned back to Felith. "We're going to have to do something about that. Either find some people who aren't going to be frightened of us, or bar servants from coming into the suite at all."

"Oh!" Felith said. "I don't recommend the latter, lady. The upkeep on apartments is time-consuming and you will be very busy. . . ."

"Doing what?" Irine asked. "It's not like we can leave, is it? We'd be seen." She glanced at Reese. "We're supposed to stay invisible, right?"

"Right," Reese said. "Though honestly I'm not sure how doable that's going to be." She sighed and pressed her thumb against one of her brows. "I guess we'll take it as it comes."

"Lady?" Felith said, hesitant. "May I now?"

"What? Oh, yes." Reese sheathed the dagger and showed it to the other woman. She felt a curious reluctance to let someone else hold it, though, so she didn't extend it, but Felith surprised her by making no move to take it. The Eldritch's wide eyes were as obvious a sign of shock as she'd ever seen on one of their faces. "What?"

"That is the dagger from a House set," Felith said, hushed. "From Jisiensire's House set."

"I gathered that," Reese said.

"And the lord gave it to you?" she asked. "You didn't . . . perhaps . . . take it by accident?"

Reese eyed her.

"She wouldn't take any of Hirianthial's things," Irine assured Felith.

"And that's not the dagger Hirianthial carries around anyway," Sascha said, studying it. "He uses plain ones. That we've seen, anyway."

"He gave it to me," Reese told Felith. "Is that a problem?"

"No," Felith said, and breathed, "But oh, Captain Eddings! Hirianthial Sarel is a single-dagger man!"

In the confused silence that followed her exclamation, Reese muttered, "I think I need a chair for this."

"Let's all have chairs," Irine said. She took Reese by the wrist and pulled her toward the hearth in her own room. Reese let the Harat-Shar push her down; the stones were still warm, though the fire had died. She set the dagger in her lap and hugged her knees, looking up at Felith.

"So?"

"Ah . . . you know we dance?"

Wondering what this had to do with anything, Reese said, "Yes—oh wait, does this have to do with the wands and the fans and things?"

"Yes," Felith said. "We don't touch when we dance, so women have fans in summer and wands in winter, and men have—"

"Daggers!" Irine said, remembering. "He said that on the way here. You're supposed to touch wands and daggers instead of hands."

"Just so," Felith said. "Most men will use a plain dagger for this purpose, to make it clear they are not courting entanglements. If such a man uses his family weapons, it is a statement of interest. But there are men who only ever use their family weapons, because they seek commitment and will have no truck with dalliances or casual alliances. Your lord was one such. He only ever danced with his wife."

"His . . . what?" Reese said, her extremities going cold so quickly her fingers started trembling.

"His wife," Felith repeated, her expression puzzled. "The lord Hirianthial is a widower. You did not know?"

"That's . . . something he never told us, no," Sascha said.

"How . . . was . . . when . . ." Reese trailed off, unable to phrase a question, unable to choose one. A wife?

Hirianthial had had a wife?

Irine's voice seemed to come from a distance. "How long ago was this?"

"And are there any kids we should know about?" Sascha asked. "You know, as long as we're talking about things everyone seems to know except us."

"Oh no, no children," Felith said. "The lady Laiselin died in childbed, attempting to bring forth the first, a daughter who would have been the new heir to Sarel Jisiensire. That was some sixty years ago, seventy perhaps." She sighed.

"They were very happy, and had so little time. Not even forty years together and she was gone."

"'So little time,'" Irine repeated, one ear sagging.

"I guess forty years is 'so little' when you live a thousand or two," Sascha said, quiet.

"I'm sorry," Felith said. "I thought he would have mentioned it. He was very devoted to her . . . it was a rare thing to see among us, two who loved each other so and were unafraid to have it known."

"We never asked," Reese said. She set her hand on the dagger, tried to flex her stiff fingers around it. "Maybe I should give this back."

"Oh, no, no," Felith said. "Keep it, my Lady. Unless you wish to repudiate him . . . ?"

Shocked, she said, "No, never."

"Then keep it," Felith said. A distant knock floated to them and she looked up. "I shall see to that. Are you receiving visitors?"

"Sure," Reese said, forcing herself to leave the dagger in her lap. She set her hands back on her knees. "Or . . . maybe. I don't know. Use your discretion."

Felith hesitated, then curtseyed and said, "As you wish, my Lady." And vanished into the foyer.

"I'll go with her," Sascha said. "Just in case her discretion needs a second opinion."

Once he'd left, Irine bent and pried Reese's clammy hands up, warming them with her own. "Come on, I'll help you dress for whoever's out there."

"I guess it was inevitable, right?" Reese said. She should stand, shouldn't she? If she was going to dress? Why weren't her legs moving? "You don't live a million years and not have a wife."

"I wouldn't," Irine said, sitting next to her and sliding an arm around Reese's shoulders. "I'd have a husband too."

Reese glanced at her, then managed a weak laugh. "All right, that was a good one."

Irine grinned and touched her nose to Reese's shoulder. "What can I say, girls are cuddly." She flipped her ears back. "Can I ask you something?"

"You probably will anyway."

"Probably," Irine admitted. "But still."

"Sure."

"Why'd it bother you to learn?" Irine said. "It bothered us too, but I'm guessing not for the same reasons."

"I guess . . ." Reese tried to examine her feelings, found them slippery and nameless. "I never thought I really knew him, but it's still a shock to know just how little I knew."

Irine glanced at her, yellow eyes close enough that Reese could see the bright golden lashes framing them. "Are you worried that there might be things about him you won't like?"

"No," Reese said. "No, nothing like that. Just . . . maybe . . . I wish he'd trusted us more."

Irine's eyes flicked down to the dagger. "Maybe he's starting to." She reached over and wrapped her golden hand over Reese's on the hilt. "He's been alone a long time, Reese. When you're used to being alone, it takes a while to remember how to act around people you like."

Reese snorted. "Let me guess. You might have noticed this recently in someone else."

Irine grinned. "This someone else is a lot less prickly lately, and she started out a whole lot less trusting than Hirianthial."

"Ow! I was not less trusting than an Eldritch!"

"Maybe not all Eldritch," Irine said sagely. "We seem to have gotten one of the few good ones."

"Isn't that the truth," Reese muttered.

Sascha glanced in. "Hey, Boss. You'll want to come out

here for this."

Reese grimaced. "Don't tell me something exploded."

"Uh-uh. But Hirianthial's got a cousin and she's come to meet us."

The woman awaiting them in the parlor was, like all the Eldritch Reese had met so far, tall and fair and elegant. Pregnant—that was new, and knowing how Hirianthial's wife had died made her suddenly far more aware of it—and animated by an eager interest that made her seem almost human. But for all that, what unnerved Reese was the realization that this woman, who was supposedly Hirianthial's cousin, looked less like him than the Queen.

Felith said, "Captain Eddings, the Lady Araelis Mina Jisiensire, Shield-bearer and current holder of the seal for Jisiensire, and kin to the train Roshka."

"Wait," Irine said. "That's a Harat-Shariin name!"

"So it is," Araelis said, eyes dancing. "Sellelvi was made sister to Fasianyl Mina years ago, and so I can claim the relation. She was pard, though, not tigris. May I sit?" she added to Reese. "My feet never cease with the aching."

"Oh, yes, please," Reese said, startled. "I'm sorry, I'm not used to hosting in a place like this. Felith, can we get something to drink, maybe? Please?"

Felith smiled. "I shall have it fetched."

"Don't feel you have to stand on formality," Araelis said, an invitation Reese felt a lot more comfortable accepting from her than she had from the Queen. "I have been waiting these many years for out-worlders to come here. We have had a long association with them, through Sellelvi and then the Tams—you know the Tams, of course?—yes, they are friends to us through Lesandurel Meriaen Jisiensire. Outside the Galares, you will find no firmer friend on this world than through us, as I'm sure you know, having traveled with Hirianthial."

"Your cousin," Reese said.

"Just so," Araelis said. "I imagine he has not told you, nor that he used to be the seal-holder for Jisiensire."

"Does that mean what I think it means?" Irine asked.

Araelis linked her fingers together over her belly and said, "I think we have a great deal to talk about, you and I. We could begin with my cousin's relation to the throne, something that should be of particular interest to you." This she directed at Reese.

"I'm almost afraid to ask."

"I'm not!" Irine said, ears perked. "Tell us! Wait, let me guess. He's the heir to the throne!"

"Not quite . . ."

"Not *quite*?" Reese repeated.

Araelis smiled. "He and Liolesa are cousins, and have been close since childhood. Queen Maraesa's sister Rylan-iel remained a Galare when she married, of course, being a woman, and had Liolesa . . . and Maraesa's brother Theval married into Sarel Jisiensire, and became Hirianthial's father. So you must understand, Captain . . . Hirianthial is quite the eligible man. Particularly since he was once, and might be again, a seal-holder. That is to say, a decision maker for all the families that live beneath the banner of a House, and their tenants. He may need your help, thus."

"My help!" Reese said. "Doing what?"

"Beating all the interested ladies off him, I'm guessing," Sascha said.

"Look," Reese said, holding up her hands. "Let's start from the beginning, all right?" She looked at Araelis. "You seem willing to actually explain all this stuff that no one else wants to talk to us about. I'm not going to ask why in case that gives you a reason to talk yourself into not doing it." She paused as Araelis hid a grin, poorly. "So . . . how's this. I'll keep pouring the . . . whatever this is. Tea? Cider? Whatever it is. And you keep going."

"I can think of no finer way to spend the morning," Araelis said.

"Even if it breaks the Eldritch veil?" Reese asked.

Araelis snorted. "Once a man's gotten under it and started kissing, it's a little late to pull it back down again, Captain."

Irine pressed her face into Sascha's shoulder, snickering.

"Oh hush," Reese told them. To Araelis, "Fine. I'm used to being the knight in dented armor by now. Let's get on with it."

The immensity of the morning's training kept Hirianthial in the library long after Urise had gone, sitting alone in the light with the revelations of the world's receptive stillness and feeling it implied in the quiet of the room. By the time he found the wherewithal to rise, he had grown stiff enough to need to stretch to settle his joints.

There were people outside the library.

He had not labeled them as threats, had not even realized he was assessing the surrounding area for company. Curious, he let himself out and waited, sensing they were seeking him in particular. When they came into view, he understood some of why: the man leading was in the white-on-white uniform of the Queen's Sword, and the man at his side in the red-piped white of his second.

They halted before him and saluted. He held up a hand. "Gently," he said. "I no longer wear the uniform."

"No," said the Queen's White Sword. "But you filled it once and with honor. My predecessor spoke well of you, my lord."

"Your predecessor," Hirianthial said. "Was that Suleven?"

"Suleven's protege was my predecessor," this man said. "Thelerenan, out of Nuera."

Two terms since he'd stepped down—not surprising, given the rigors of the work. Protecting the Queen was a job for the young. "And you are, then?"

"Olthemiel Nase, if you please, my Lord. This is my second, Beronaeth."

"Very good," he said. "I perceive you were seeking me?"

"You perceive rightly," Olthemiel said. "Though I fear what I ask might be construed as impertinence."

The sheen of his aura was fiercely hopeful, touched with a delightful aggression; in the people assigned to his cousin's safety, he approved. "Let me have the judgment of that. What is it?"

"We have heard a great deal of your prowess, sire," Olthemiel said. "And thought you might not take it amiss to be invited to use the Swords' salle, rather than resorting to any lesser facility."

Hirianthial couldn't help a chuckle. "And you hope to see me at work. A spar is what you're asking, is it?"

"Only tangentially," Olthemiel said with commendable candor. "But yes, that also."

"You will be disappointed," Hirianthial said. "It has been six decades since I've regularly carried a sword. It is rarely done in the Alliance."

"Perhaps," the White Sword said, eyes sparkling, "you might let us have the judgment of that."

In keeping with the theme of his return to the world, the Sword salle was just as he remembered it: a round room floored in wood with clerestory windows investing everything with a cool, diffuse light. The changing rooms and armory were next to one another at one end of the salle, and the corridor leading to the palace on the other.

The Swords' barracks fed off that corridor as well as their mess. The arrangement led to a close community, one Hirianthial was surprised to learn he'd missed.

He was saluted as he walked behind the White Sword and his second as if he was still one of them. It was always thus: one doffed the uniform, but the brotherhood never forgot one of their own. He'd done it himself, when he'd served his tenure, but to receive it was a very different thing than to offer it.

He stripped down in the changing room among them, aware of their curious glances. He no longer looked entirely like them after his sojourn off-world; like most natives of light gravity worlds, he'd taken poorly to the typical environment in the Alliance and had been offered a medical regimen to acclimate his body. After a year of attempting to make do on his own, he'd finally accepted the treatment. He remained tall and lighter-framed than most of the Alliance's members, but among Eldritch he was far more solid. Heavy gravity built denser muscle. By the time he'd donned a spare uniform, he'd acquired an audience that followed him onto the salle floor, where Olthemiel offered him his choice of practice weapons; he would not draw a House sword save to blood it. He selected one carved to evoke the standard broadsword issued the Swords and said, "I suppose we shall see how poorly in practice I have kept. Shall we begin with the exercises?"

"As long as we can all join you, sire," Olthemiel said, grinning. Sobering, he said, "Will you lead them?"

Hirianthial canted his head, smiled. "You are the Queen's White Sword now, Olthemiel. I will follow your lead."

The approval that washed over him from the soldiers watching was as tangible as a wind off the ocean, bracing and bright as salt. He could taste it, wear it like a cloak; it

was lined in the peach-pale shimmer of Olthemiel's gratitude to be honored, and to have his authority bolstered
when it would have been so easy to tear him down. So it
went, among the Eldritch, even here among this confeder-
acy so different from the rest of society. But he had never
subscribed to such pettiness, and would surely not begin
now. Hirianthial issued him the short bow all Swords made
their captain before training and took his place among the
ranks that assembled to join them.

The drills done by the Swords were as old as Settlement. Running them made Hirianthial realize they were
another form of meditation; he was not long into the
forms before he felt the heartbeat throb of his own power
fade away, granting him access again to the great calm of
the universe. He breathed through the joy of it and seeped
into that deep quiet. It was the only thing that saved him
when they paired off to begin the paired drills. His feet had
moved him into position, and memory had bowed him in
the traditional salute to his partner before beginning. It
did not occur to him until his opponent attacked him that
he had put himself in a position to duplicate the circumstances on Kerayle.

That calm gave him the heartbeat pause he needed to
stay his reflexive response. The shattering strength of the
blow he pulled—its physical expression but a thin shadow
cast by the mental attack he had to fight to arrest in full—
felled him, and the entire room halted. Olthemiel sprinted
for him. "My Lord!"

"A passing spell," Hirianthial said, panting. The dizziness was overwhelming; he had not expected it, and it
had been a very long time since he'd battled nausea like
a stripling new to training. "Being off-world has changed
me. I should perhaps sit on the bench for a time."

"Of course!" Olthemiel said, solicitous, and nothing

would do but that he escort Hirianthial there.

He did not mark the time. He spent it exhausted from the effort of having not lashed out, dismayed at the raw sensitivity of his skin and nerves, and acutely aware that he was crippled. Men among the Eldritch carried the weapons and fought on behalf of their families, for it could be no other way with mortality rates so high for women in child-bed. One answered insult on the dueling field; patrolled the family land for wild things that needed slaying; meted out justice to those who'd earned it and did battle with those who would take what they wanted in violation of laws both tacit and formal. The eldest male member of the family who was still hale bore the family swords, holding them between violence and the almost inevitably female holder of the seal and all the wealth it implied.

He had trained since before he'd left dresses to bear swords. Even having left the seal to Araelis, he still carried Jisiensire's weapons, and everyone would expect him to be the defender of Jisiensire's honor. With Liolesa conniving to start a fight, it was folly to think he'd be able to avoid drawing them.

And the first time someone lunged for him. . . .

Hirianthial ran his hand up the back of his neck until he found the dangle's ties at his scalp. The bell Irine had braided into it shivered, and he flinched.

The practice ended and the company disbanded. It was Beronaeth who approached him then, with Olthemiel following at his shoulder a few respectful paces behind. Hirianthial looked up at them, eyes narrowed, still resting his hand on the back of his neck.

"My lord," Beronaeth said, hesitated. "If I speak out of turn, prithee tell me. But I am the man charged with coun-seling the injured, and you have the reactions of a man who has been in a terrible battle. If there is anything I might do to aid you, I am at your disposal."

Surprised, Hirianthial said, "Thank you. I will consider your offer."

Beronaeth bowed and withdrew. Olthemiel stayed long enough to say, "You are welcome here at any time, sire."

How good it would be to belong again—and yet he was no longer one of them. Because it would have been rude to say so, Hirianthial answered, "I am honored by the invitation, Captain. Thank you."

Nevertheless, he waited until the rest of the company was done before using the changing room himself. He left the barracks out of sorts and thought to seek Reese, to keep his promise to her that he appear daily. But when he arrived, he was not greeted by her, nor did Felith open the door and announce him. Irine let him in instead, and her aura was a complexity that disarmed him. Then she spoke and disordered his mind entirely. "If you're looking for Reese, she's gone to the library."

"She's done *what*?"

"Gone to the library," Irine repeated. "Felith needed a book and she insisted on going along. Araelis gave her a map and told her it should be safe enough since the library is next to the Queen's wing and all your enemies are over on the other side of the palace—"

"Araelis?" Hirianthial said, fighting dismay. "Has been *here*?"

Irine folded her arms, and something in her aura was as powerful a warning as any he'd ever received. "Yes . . . yes, she has."

"The Captain . . ."

"Isn't exactly upset at you," Irine said. "But I wouldn't waste any time doing damage control. If you take my meaning, Lord-cousin-to-the-Queen."

"Araelis," he growled.

"I liked her," Irine said. "But don't take it wrong if I say she reminds me of some of my mothers."

"The characterization is apt," Hirianthial said. "If you'll pardon me?"

"Please, get going," Irine said with a lopsided grin. "Before she talks herself into a temper."

Reese was not in fact angry. There was no earthly way she could be angry when confronted with Liolesa's library.

"Oh, my," she whispered, staring up the shelves. The smell alone gave her shivers. She wandered from one side to the other, stepped onto the dais and paused, feeling the unexpected give of the raised floor beneath the carpet—was it wood? Then drifted off it again and back among the stacks, through shafts of sunlight too weak to be responsible for the warmth rushing through her at the sight of such treasure. "How many books do you have?"

"I would not know, my Lady," Felith said, nervous and disguising it poorly as she sought the etiquette book she'd said she needed to coach Reese through the presentation. "I have not known anyone to undertake a count, though I presume there is one somewhere." She picked a slim volume down and turned to face Reese. "Lady? This is the book. We should go, you should not be seen. . . ."

"But we just got here!" Reese said. "Who's going to come all the way over here for anything? You've seen the size of this place, Felith. Blood, you should know it in your bones, you've lived here long enough! Besides, if anyone shows up I can hide behind a shelf or something."

Felith sighed. "As you will." A little more kindly, "It is a magnificent collection. Not as large perhaps as the Cathedral's, but quite respectable."

"If a library this big is 'respectable' for Eldritch, you've gone a long way toward redeeming your annoying habits,"

Reese said, drifting through the long slanted columns of sunlight. She stopped in front of one shelf and reached for a book, paused. "Can I. . . ."

"Of course," Felith said. "A library is hardly useful if not used."

Reese took the book down and balanced it in the crook of her arm while she leafed through it: creamy parchment pages, inscribed with glossy ink that was ever so slightly raised on the paper, ink that smelled like a memory of something more pungent. The chapters started with beautifully illuminated capitals, leafed in silver that shone when she tilted the book toward the sun. She swallowed, fought tears and tried not to feel ridiculous. "Blood, it's beautiful. Are they all like this? I bet they are. But they can't be. Handmade? Hand-painted?"

"It is how it is done here," Felith said.

Reese looked up at the shelves, over her shoulder at the rest of the library. She tried to calculate the amount of work it must have taken to create all these books by hand and failed. The Eldritch lived hundreds of years, but even so. . . . "Wait. These are all unique? Do you make copies?"

"There may be one or two of each book," Felith said. "But it's rare to make more than a handful. The creation of a book is a laborious process."

Which made everything in this library so expensive that most people couldn't afford to keep one. "You mean . . . almost no one has books."

"No," Felith said, and amended, "The nobility typically keeps them. Among the good families, the libraries are made available to the tenants for borrowing. Some families hoard theirs, however, and do not permit them to be lent."

Reese looked down at the work of art in her arms and tried to imagine a world where books were a luxury only the very rich could afford—and only the very generous would share. How poor her life would have been had she not been able to read! Her monthly romance subscription was almost twenty years old now. She'd never skipped a month in all that time. Was there some Eldritch peasant somewhere, wishing her life was better, without even the meager escape she could derive from an afternoon reading?

The lack of good plumbing was bad enough. The lack of lights and heat. But no books?

How did these people live like this?

The creak of the door opening caused Felith to gasp. Reese stepped behind the shelf and peeked out, then sighed as Hirianthial entered, shutting the door behind him. Walking back around the shelf she said, "Is it true? Books are for the rich?"

"In most parts of the world," he said after a hesitation. "Lady—"

"They're so beautiful," Reese said, pained. "How can I love them for being beautiful when I know almost no one can appreciate them?"

His hesitation became more pronounced, and his voice gentler. "Should we cease to make beautiful things because not everyone can have them?"

"No," Reese said, looking up at him. "But this is different. Books are like people. They can be beautiful on the outside and it's wonderful when they are, but what counts is the inside. And the inside of a book can be communicated in a dozen different ways, and cheaply enough that everyone can have access. And everyone should. They're books!"

"I know," Hirianthial said. "And God and Lady willing, one day soon it will be so, even here. But it is not yet, and there is much to do between now and then—"

"And I want to be part of it," Reese said. The moment she said it, she felt the truth of it, so large it was too big for her skin. "I want to help. I can, can't I? That's why I'm here."

Hirianthial's pause this time. . . .

"Unless," Reese said, backing down, "you don't want us here."

"No," he said. "No, that's not it at all. But I would not expose you to—"

"To what?" Reese said. "What could possibly be worse than what we've already been through? Slavers, pirates, drug lords . . . they shattered Sascha's arm, they assaulted you, they broke my ship." She drew in a breath because she was trembling and said, "They used me to commit murder."

"And you wish to continue?" Hirianthial asked. "I cannot guarantee matters here will not devolve into such darknesses."

"I don't know," Reese said. She closed the book and gently set it back on the shelf. "Maybe it's time to take a stand somewhere." He was looking at her, she could feel it. Self-consciously she ran her thumb down the rust-colored leather spine.

"Captain . . . about Araelis and anything she might have told you—"

Reese turned and set her back to the shelves. "It was a lot, and I'm betting she didn't ask you about it first. I'm sorry about that. I should have told her to stop." Another pause in his breathing. She wondered how often she would surprise him. "Not what you expected me to say, I guess."

"No," he admitted. "I expected that you might be cross."

"Because you keep secrets?" She shook her head. "Who doesn't? Besides, we never asked."

"You never asked because you sensed it would discomfit me," he pointed out.

"Yes. It was still a good reason not to ask. Our curiosity isn't more important than you being ready to talk about something." She looked up at him. "Can we agree to just . . . move on from here? I won't bring it up. You can assume

I know things."

"I . . . if you wish," he said. "It would probably be easiest."

"I figured," Reese said. "I can't speak for the twins or Kis'eh't, though. Bryer hardly talks, but the other three might have questions. Or might not. Araelis was . . . forthcoming."

"I feared she might be," he said, rueful.

"Look, just . . . forget about it, and I'll do my best to do the same." Reese glanced at Felith, who was standing by the door trying not to fidget and failing. "I should get back before I give the Queen's maid an attack."

"For good cause," Hirianthial said. "To be seen together without a chaperone would be. . . ." He paused, then laughed.

"What?" Reese asked, trying not to notice how much she liked seeing him laugh.

"I was beginning to say 'entirely inappropriate for a man and a woman,' but I am rather hoping I'll be considered too ungentlemanly to be sought by a woman who cares more for the opinions of the court than for the truth . . . and you would probably find the entire concept ridiculous. You do, do you not?"

Reese snorted. "You can just tell the idiots that if we'd wanted to fornicate we could have had a six-month orgy with or without three other people."

"Only three?"

Was he teasing her? He was! She grinned. "Well, Kis'eh't's never shown any interest and Allacazam doesn't have any parts. I can't figure out Bryer so I thought it would probably be a dice roll whether he'd want in."

"The idea is appalling," Hirianthial said.

"Probably to him too." Reese laughed. "Come on, before we scandalize Felith any more. Look, her cheeks are pink."

"No fear, Lady," Hirianthial said. "A properly reared lady's maid does not eavesdrop. Is that not right, Felith?"

"Pardon me, my Lord?" Felith said, curtseying hastily with the book tucked under her arm.

"You're horrible," Reese muttered to him and said, "All right, Felith, I'm ready to go. Do you think I could bring a book too?"

"If you wish?" Felith asked, perplexed. "You cannot read them, though, can you?"

"No, but they're beautiful," Reese said. "I'm sure the crew would like to see it."

"Take this one," Hirianthial said, reaching above her head and bringing down a tall book bound in blue leather and debossed in copper.

"Just like that, you pick one?" Reese asked, bemused.

"I *can* read the spines," he said, amused. He presented it to her. "An atlas, with illustrations of common flora."

"Perfect!" She took it, careful of his hands—though what did that matter anymore, when he could read her thoughts without them? Still it seemed polite. "Thank you."

"And now," Felith said, firm, "we shall leave first, and then the lord Hirianthial will follow some moments later."

"If you say so. It still seems a lot of trouble for someone who has no honor to compromise," Reese said. "Me, I mean, being an alien. Ladies here probably have problems with compromising."

Felith stared at her. "Of course they do. To become pregnant is a very serious matter. Women die of it. One does not undertake it without a formal liaison to support it!"

Reese hesitated. "Right. Sorry. I . . . ah . . . forgot. No birth control here or anything."

"No what?" Felith asked.

Reese glanced at Hirianthial helplessly. The lift of his shoulders was almost imperceptible, but she read it anyway; he had no idea how to begin to explain it either. She sighed. "Let's get going."

"Yes, Lady."

Felith peeked into the hall, looking in both directions before opening the door fully for them to use. Reese followed her, holding her borrowed book, far too aware of the texture of the leather beneath her fingertips: real leather, that clung to her fingertips because—she realized—she was sweating despite the cold. But they made it to the safety of the suite upstairs without being discovered, and Reese sat with the atlas hugged in her arms.

She had yet to meet any of these enemies of the Queen's; she didn't count the glimpse she'd caught of them before retreating as a real meeting. She had no idea if they were as bad as they'd been painted. But she was starting to grasp the world finally, in the same way she might have grasped one of the worlds in her monthly downloads. She could almost get her arms around the idea of a place where having children killed women regularly, where there was no modern medicine, where people who didn't look like you were evil. Her problem was that it felt just as fictional as one of her stories.

She hoped that wouldn't get her in trouble, but she knew better. Lately all she'd been doing was falling face-first into trouble. She sighed.

Irine showed up with Kis'eh't a few moments after she'd settled. "Did Hirianthial find you?"

"Yes," Reese said, then squinted up at her. "Did you tell him where I was? Is that how he knew where to go?"

"Yeah." Irine dropped onto the floor and rested her hands on her knees. "Was that the wrong thing to do?"

"No," Reese said as Kis'eh't padded up and sat next to Irine, curling her tail over her haunches. "No, it was okay. And no one saw us. Plus, I brought back riches!" She handed the book to Kis'eh't, who took it with interest. "You should see their library."

"Is this hand-painted? Who hand-paints maps anymore?" Kis'eh't asked, one feathered ear sagging.

"Sounds just something they'd do to me," Irine said. "If they can be stubborn about doing things the hard way, just to be fancy and superior about it, that would be Eldritch. I can't believe Hirianthial came out of these people."

Reese thought of Mars and said, "I can."

Hirianthial waited until he was sure the two were away and then rested his brow against the door. How had it come to pass that he found himself more comfortable in the company of an off-worlder than among his own people? And with Reese, with whom he'd never seemed to find the key to any rapport? When had that begun to change?

God and Lady help him, but he thought she actually liked it here . . . this place that he wanted only to escape and was bound to until he completed his lessons, and perhaps not even then, if he failed them. He sighed out and straightened, opened the door and stepped through it, and halted at the sight of Thaniet at the end of the hall. Urise, he thought, would find his lack of awareness appalling.

"Lady Thaniet," he said. "If you have come to use the library you will find it quiet."

She drifted closer, her aura a maze of colors he couldn't begin to decipher. He thought wariness and speculation played some role in them, though, and liked neither. "Thank you, my Lord. It is easier to read in the quiet." Shyly, almost ashamedly, "I like to come here. It helps settle my mind."

"Alone?" he asked, surprised.

"It is better that way," she said, looking down. "It's easier to have my own thoughts, when I'm not around people."

"The Lady Surela can be somewhat overwhelming," he suggested.

Thaniet smiled hesitantly. "She is a strong woman. It's

a good thing, to be strong."

. . . and a bad thing to be weak in compare. He felt a surge of pity for her. "You might consider leaving her."

"Leaving her!" Thaniet exclaimed. "Oh no, my Lord. I could never. She has been so kind to me. To be born noble but poor . . . she raised me from regrettable circumstance. I am grateful."

What could he say to such a thing? "Your loyalty is commendable."

She flushed. "Thank you. I hope I was not interrupting anything?"

That seemed a strange comment given that he'd been leaving when she saw him. "Not at all. Enjoy your visit."

"Thank you, my Lord." She curtseyed and stepped into the library, leaving him to puzzle at the density of her aura, and at the more abstract mystery of how someone as spiteful as Surela could have kept someone as good-hearted as Thaniet, no matter how weak her will.

He let it lie and returned to his quarters. In the morning, he was Urise's . . . and in the afternoon, the court would convene.

"I need to do what?" Reese asked.

"Wear formal dress," Felith replied, wide-eyed. "You have formal clothes, do you not?"

Reese looked down at her jumpsuit and vest. "This is my newest outfit."

Sascha, sitting cross-legged in one of the brocaded chairs by the fire, said, "Don't ask, Felith. Her closet's all jumpsuits and vests." The Eldritch glanced at him and he added, "Hell, us too."

"I have a formal sari," Kis'eh't called from the table where she was poring over the book of maps.

"And Bryer has that red thing he wore when he was

being your bodyguard, Reese," Irine said. She frowned. "Come to think of it, that was a vest too, wasn't it."

"What's wrong with vests?" Reese asked.

"You must not wear a vest to see the Queen!" Felith said, horrified.

"I hate to tell you this, but I already have."

Felith covered her face, drew in a shuddery breath, and let her hands drop. "Very well. But the Queen is a different matter from the court. You cannot appear. . . ."

"Alien?" Irine offered.

"Practical?" Kis'eh't said without looking up.

"Poor," Reese said dryly. She glanced at Felith. "That's my guess. Yes?"

Felith cleared her throat. "Allow me to see if I can gather some resources on your behalf, my Lady."

"You're talking about putting me in a dress?" Reese said. "Me? In a dress like you people wear?" She grimaced. "I don't even look good in the same colors."

Gravely, Felith replied, "Let me handle that issue."

"It would be dishonest," Reese said. "I'm not an Eldritch—"

"Actually, I think it would be nice," Irine interrupted.

Surprised, Reese looked at her. "Excuse me?"

"You wear nightgowns to sleep and read romance novels," Irine said. "Why shouldn't you wear a dress sometimes?"

"Because . . . because I don't have time for dresses," Reese said. "Or money for them. They're not me. I'm Reese Eddings, captain of a trading ship. A *poor* trading ship."

"You're also Reese Eddings, the merchant with the patronage of an alien queen," Sascha said. "Doesn't that entitle you to some fancy clothes now and then? She's already given you a necklace."

Reese hesitated, and into that pause, Felith struck. "I

can also find appropriate livery for your crew members, for later court appearances."

"You want to dress them up too?" Reese said, and grinned at the resulting mental image. "Great! If I have to wear the ridiculous clothes, they can too."

Unperturbed, Sascha said, "As long as it's not gold. I look horrible in gold."

"I go, then, with your permission," Felith said, curtseying. "I know just where to look."

"Sure," Reese said. After the door closed, she folded her arms. "Did you really have to tell her all about my bad habits?"

Irine sniffed. "If nightgowns and romance novels are a bad habit, I'm in worse trouble than you."

"No you're not. You don't wear clothes to bed."

"True," Irine said, ears perking. "All right, I'm better off than you." She grinned. "Come on, Reese. Haven't you ever wanted to try it? Just once? After reading about these fancy costumes?"

"Maybe a little," Reese said. "But it still feels. . . ." She trailed off. She wanted to say dishonest because it was true, and it was. But the tiny part of her that loved her romances and her nightgowns complained. Was it any less real than the rest of her just because she had never lived a life that made those things practical? And she'd already met something out of a fairy tale when she'd rescued Hirianthial.

Of course, if her experiences with him were any indication, she'd find the costumes far more trouble than they'd seemed in books.

"You know, this place is so pristine they could use it as a planetary park," Kis'eh't said from her table.

"What?"

The Glaseah sat back from the maps and rubbed her eyes. "I mean it's a huge world and they've barely put down any settlements on it. The entire population's concentrated on a single stretch of coastline, and not a very big one."

They all converged to examine the maps. Kis'eh't pointed out a long patch of land divided into parcels, each shaded and overset with a small heraldic mark. One of them was the white unicorn on blue of the Queen's pendant, the other a bronze hippogriff on red, like the one Reese had seen on Hirianthial's sword case. "I'm guessing from the heraldry this is a political map. I've looked through the whole book, but these seem to be the only territories marked this way, so I'm guessing they represent the entire political structure for the world. But if you look on the next page . . ." She turned it and tapped an area. "See this bit you could fit under my finger? That's the size of the area on the previous page. That's all they've got marked as belonging to people with family crests. Look at the size of the continent! And this is only one of the land masses."

"That's a lot of guesses," Irine said, ears flipping back.

"But reasonable ones, I think," Kis'eh't said. "Unless there are large numbers of people on the world who don't have family crests?" She glanced at Reese. "What do you think?"

"I . . . think . . . no," Reese said. Most of what she'd read in books about the Eldritch had been wrong, but one woman hadn't been: the Harat-Shar Natalya, who'd had the paintings of Sellelvi and Fasianyl. Nothing in any of her novels had suggested vast numbers of people without important family names; in fact, most of the Eldritch in those book had spoken of the people under them with the same feudal concern Reese had noticed in Liolesa and Araelis and Hirianthial. "No, I'm betting that everyone works land for someone with a crest. It seems that sort of system."

"How old is the book, though?" Sascha asked. "Maybe they've expanded since then?"

"Maybe," Kis'eh't said. "But how likely do you think that is, really? If we take for granted that they've always eschewed high technology, they would have had to colonize the planet the old-fashioned way, and by old-fashioned I mean with machetes and animal power. I don't see it. They just don't seem the type."

Reese frowned at the map. "I guess most of the population lives in the country. We haven't seen much of the city but it didn't look too big from orbit."

"What if they're not?" Irine said suddenly. Her ears had flattened. "What if the reason we don't see many Eldritch offworld is because . . . there just aren't that many Eldritch?"

None of them answered.

"Think about it," Irine continued. "Say that either the population's equally split between the Eldritch who like the Alliance and the ones who want us to stay away . . . or assume that the side that likes us has fewer people but enough power to keep their enemies in check. Wouldn't we see a far bigger percentage of them off-world if there were more of them? Half of the population of Harat-Sharii is huge, and even if only five percent of them decided to emigrate that would still be a noticeable number. But there's all of . . . what, one? Two? Eldritch off-world?"

Reese murmured, "They die giving birth."

Irine snorted. "I'll say they do. And without real medicine, they probably die of scratches and bad falls and stupid curable diseases too."

"You're telling me," Reese said slowly, "that the population of this whole world—of all the Eldritch in the entire universe—might be less than my town on Mars."

Irine said nothing.

"That's a lot to build on a few suppositions," Reese said.

"So let us find out if they're true," Sascha said. He pricked his ears forward. "Don't give me that look, Boss.

In two days, we're not going to be a secret anymore, and if nothing else we know we have an ally in Araelis. Assuming we can't get it out of Felith, Araelis will tell us anything we ask, I bet. You can hobnob with the important people, and we can go do some investigating."

"All right," Reese said with a sigh. "Though honestly I don't know why you're doing this. It's not like this is your problem."

"It's not," Kis'eh't said, quiet. "It's your problem, Reese. That makes it our problem, because we care about you." Her feathered ears sagged. "Besides, we've all gotten fond of Hirianthial."

"What she said." Irine looked hopeful.

"Fine, fine. Just don't break any dishes," Reese said.

"I think we should start with the heraldry," Kis'eh't said to Sascha. "Have you got your tablet with you? Let's start associating them with names, if we can."

Reese left them to it and went back to her bedroom to climb onto the monument and sit on its edge. As she contemplated the very distant floor, Allacazam rolled up to her side and bumped her. He formed a question in her mind, a sound like a very distant song she couldn't make out.

"I'm okay," Reese told him, petting him. "Confused, but when is that not normal?"

The swath of sudden black was disagreement.

"All right, maybe I'm not always confused," Reese said. "But when I'm not, it's because I'm in denial about all the things I don't understand."

A peep of light at the edge of the fading black, and the surprise of a sunrise in her mind.

She chuckled. "Well, I can learn." She pulled him into her lap and hugged him. "Maybe it's being around people who are even more into denial than I am. I can see how stupid it is. No, worse. How dangerous. And ridiculous, too." She made a face into his fur. "I don't want to be ridiculous."

The strands tickled her nose until she wrinkled it. In her mind a picture formed of Hirianthial with a lute, serenading her on a grassy sward. She hid her grin, shook her head a little. "Don't be silly."

One of the lute strings broke with a twang. Tiny Hirianthial looked astonished.

Reese snickered, then quieted. "No, I mean it. It's not like that."

The scene was washed with twilight blue, faded into that mist. She sighed at the sense of reproach, even as gentle as it was. But she didn't say anything. She didn't feel ready to say anything . . . maybe she never would be. Clearing her throat, she called, "Hey, Irine! Wake me up when the dinner tray shows up!"

"Will do!"

Reese kicked off her boots and curled up on the mound of blankets. Two more days, and then . . . who knew.

The following morning Urise saw him and said, "You have had an unfortunate event."

Hirianthial replied, "Would it be presumptuous for me to ask how you derived that knowledge?"

The priest huffed softly and sat across from him in the dull light seeping in through the library windows. "You think I took it from your aura?" He smiled, shook his head. "I am an old man, and have had many, many students. You have a look to your shoulders and face, my son. I could no more describe it than I could fly. So. What disordered you?"

"I still react to attack with too extreme a response," Hirianthial said. "Even against people I know to be safe."

"You are living in the past," Urise said. "We shall have to remedy that."

Hirianthial glanced at him. "Is that my problem?"

"It's everyone's problem," the priest said with that blend of humor and resignation common to the elderly. "Why should it not be yours?" More gently, "You relive your experience on the colony world. You relive the cruel sorrows of your life before that. You live by those lessons. But you no longer have that luxury. Your power makes it too perilous for those around you. You must learn to live in the present, truly be here, now. So, let us go."

"Go where?" Hirianthial asked.

"Out," the priest said firmly, and rose.

Bemused, Hirianthial followed. They walked to the opposite end of the palace, where the priests quartered, and out the door beside the chapel to the lakeside. The weather was grim and the sky wan, and the chill in the air stiff enough to make his wrists hurt. The ever-present breeze off the sea only exacerbated the ache; he could only wonder how Urise bore it.

"And now?" he asked his teacher.

"Yonder woods," Urise said. "Go there. Do not come back until you touch a deer."

"Touch . . . a deer," Hirianthial repeated.

"Go on," the priest said, folding his arms into his sleeves. "I'll wait for you here."

Hirianthial started off, paused. He said over his shoulder, "Deer are shy of people."

Urise's brows lifted, but he answered not at all save to smile.

Resigned, Hirianthial headed for the woods on the opposite end of the lake. It was not a short walk, and while one dressed for the cold of the palace, he was still several layers short of what he would have preferred had he known he would be exposing himself to the wind. The trees, once he gained their shelter, protected him from that . . . but also cut him off from what little sun could be felt through the cloud cover. The gloom that enshrouded him was moist and cold, and his breath plumed white in it as he wandered, wondering how he would manage to find a deer much less touch one. He supposed he could compel them to come, but the idea was distasteful.

If the object of this lesson was to force him to leave his cares behind, he was failing already. He found a fallen tree grown over with a lace of frost-pale mold and sat. He didn't remember the cold plaguing him this much, but he was no longer three hundred years old and immune to the consequences of physical punishment. There was a time he could have spent all day in these woods in a thin court coat and come back to stand a night shift at Liolesa's door—

—but that was the past again. And yet the past had made him who he was. How could he let go of it? He reached back under his hair and drew the dangle over his shoulder. The memories associated with it now were unfortunate, and yet he would not hurt the *Earthrise* crew by cutting it off. To cauterize the traumas of his past seemed to require the sacrifice of the beauties and joys he'd also lived through. His grief over Laiselin—and the memories of their too-short life together. His pleasure at being a good steward for Jisiensire—and the pain of his brother's betrayal. The relationship he'd relied on for so long in his cousin, the Queen—and the knowledge that to have it back, he would have to stay here.

The fist in his hair, living close by the touch of Irine's fingers as she braided in the ornaments.

He didn't think he could let it go. Any of it.

He didn't know how long he spent there, bent over his knees, head down, breathing in the cold damp air and feeling the shadows of the trees on his back like a pressure that bore him into the earth. In his heart, the joy of living fought with the hurt of it until he could no longer separate them, and the effort made him understand that they were not him. That he was apart from them, evaluating them.

The sudden sense of choice was so dizzying he lost a breath to it, and the world seemed to also. The hush in the glade was so intense his ears rang and he shuddered.

He looked up and found a gray-coated doe studying him, her sides dappled in trails of icy moss. It seemed the most natural thing in the world to touch her nose as she extended it toward him, feel the heart's-blood warmth of her. She was living now, and so was he.

He left the woods carrying that sense of timelessness with him, a trailing cloak of otherworldliness that made him feel the cold less. When he joined Urise, the priest nodded. "Very good. Now, the lesson."

Surprise made the world move at a normal pace, and the change was jarring. "That was not the lesson?"

"No, no," Urise said, shaking his head. "That, my son, was the lecture. The lesson is maintaining some of that epiphany this afternoon, when you go to court." He grinned. "You will tell me tomorrow how it goes."

Hirianthial considered the horizon, then said, "You are good at this, Elder."

The priest snorted, aura shot through with sparkles of humor. "Flattery won't improve your grade."

"What do you think?" Felith asked.

Reese and Irine were bent over the offerings, their shadows falling on the fabric.

"They're pretty?" Reese said, touching the sleeve. "I guess? What do I know about dresses?"

"You must try them," Felith said, decisive. "For they will need to be adjusted. You first, my Lady, as your tigraine's dress will not be needed for a few days." As Sascha, Kis'eh't and Bryer entered the greeting chamber, she added, "I have something for you, sir Sascha, but I fear nothing for you, miss Kis'eh't. Nor you." She looked up warily at Bryer, who said nothing.

"I didn't expect you to," Kis'eh't said. She joined Reese and Irine.

"What do you think?" Irine asked, amused.

Kis'eh't said, "Why is Reese getting the same sort of dress as Irine?"

"I beg your pardon?" Felith asked.

Kis'eh't pointed. "There are only two female bipedals, and there are two dresses, so these should be for Irine and Reese. But Reese is our captain. She should be in something fancier."

Taken aback, Reese said, "I'm sure this is fancy enough for me."

Kis'eh't shook her head. "Reese, this is a feudal culture, or something similar enough to look like it. That means that you having people under you makes you important. If you walk in there signaling that you're our equal, then you're losing out on the status you'd have by claiming us as your people, to be protected."

Reese eyed Felith. "Is she right?"

The Eldritch wrung her hands. "It does grant you more prestige, to have vassals of your own."

"I'm guessing that reflects well on the Queen too," Reese said, fingering the sleeve of one of the gowns. "To be taking on a retainer with employees?"

"The Queen cannot take on a retainer with employees," Felith said. "If you are a lady with your own people to care-take, you can only serve her as a vassal, a true vassal. It is the only way to preserve the lines of duty . . ." She trailed off. "That is one word for us, draevilth. I don't know how to say it in Universal. From the Queen comes the authority that protects the lady, and that authority is passed through the lady to the people. Too from the Queen comes the power and gifts of that authority, which the lady is to pass down to her people. From the people come the gifts and duties that are due the lady, and those she passes up to the Queen. A retainer is always at the end point of that relationship. Not in the middle." She made a face. "Does that make sense when I explain it thus?"

"Yes," Reese said. "And it means I need a fancier dress."

"Oh, but you must not!" Felith exclaims. "If the Queen wishes you for a retainer—"

"She knew I had crew," Reese said. "And hell if I'm not going to protect them. I found out the hard way that they're mine—" She eyed the twins, who grinned, and even Kis'eh't smiled and gestured encouragement. "—so absolutely, I'm not going to pretend otherwise."

"The Queen cannot take on a human vassal!" Felith exclaimed, aghast.

"She should have thought of that before she offered," Reese said. "And she did offer. She gave me the jewelry and everything."

Felith passed a hand over her eyes and sighed. "I am not certain where to find anything more ornate than this in less than a day."

"The answer to that is obviously Araelis," Kis'eh't said.

"But the court convenes in four hours! She will be engaged!"

"That gives you plenty of time, then," Sascha said.

Felith pressed her lips together. "Very well," she said finally. "I will go and ask. But be aware, Captain . . . a lady being taken on as a vassal must bring some sort of gift, something that makes her worth to her liege-lady clear."

Thinking of the horses—and even the *Earthrise*, which, while no prize in the Alliance, represented more carrying capacity than this world had—Reese said, "I think I can come up with something or other."

Felith considered her warily, then sighed and said, "I will return."

After the door closed, Reese said to Kis'eh't, "That was a good catch."

"Thanks. It makes sense in the context of the society," Kis'eh't said. She sat, folded her tail over her feet. "And the last thing we want is for you to be considered someone unimportant. If the Queen gets in trouble, her servants are fair game. But someone with enough power to be one of the Queen's vassals might get wooed by the other side before they decide she's more likely to be loyal than bought and kill her."

"Just a little bit violent there, don't you think?" Irine asked, ears flattening.

"Better to assume the worst," Kis'eh't said. "Violence figures largely into cultures that don't have formally codified laws."

"These aren't feudal kings from Earth's past, though," Sascha said. "They're aliens."

"Are they?" Kis'eh't said.

A very, very long pause.

"You're suggesting they're colonists?" Reese asked, when she could trust her voice.

"They look awfully human," Kis'eh't said.

"So do we!" Irine said.

"That's exactly her point." Sascha's ears had flattened to his skull. "We were made by humans. That's why we look human."

"Isn't there a theory that intelligent life will tend to evolve in similar ways?" Reese asked.

"Reese," Kis'eh't said. "You hug a Flitzbe every night."

"They're more like plants than animals. . . ."

"I'd argue that," Kis'eh't said. "But fine. What about the Platies? They're true-alien. And the Akubi? Not very humanoid, are they? Giant flying dinosaur bird things . . . they don't even look like the Phoenix, who were designed." She added to Bryer, "Pardon me for saying so."

Bryer ruffled his wings. "Truth is not offensive."

"I tend to agree, myself," Kis'eh't said. "And the Chatcaava? Really? Dragons that can fly and shift their shape?"

"That doesn't mean that two sets of human-looking people can't co-evolve," Reese said.

"All right," Kis'eh't said. "I'd consider that myself since we have no direct evidence. Except for one thing." She leaned forward. "They know about horses."

"Oh, my," Irine said, eyes wide.

"Maybe they traded Earth for some a few thousand years ago," Reese said, frowning.

"A few thousand years ago, Earth hadn't made alien contact with anyone," Kis'eh't said. "And not long after that, you were a little occupied with some wars, remember? So where did the horses come from? This place has horses. What's more, they have bad horses. You all had to ride them, so you maybe didn't have a chance to look at them the way I did, walking next to them. They've got signs of inbreeding."

"Maybe it's just that batch that's bad," Sascha said, thinking.

Kis'eh't snorted. "You are telling me that Hirianthial— who is apparently a rich relation to the Queen of the planet—can't afford good horses? Or the Queen?"

Reese covered her face. "You are implying they brought horses with them from Earth."

"I think they're colonists, yes," Kis'eh't said. "And I have absolutely no solid evidence to back that guess up, but Aksivaht'h tells us to trust our instincts and I trust this one. These people came here on ships. And they don't have that technology anymore. They chose this barbarism. So yes, I expect violence from them. They embraced a world that concentrates most of the power in the hands of the very few and sentences the rest to Goddess-knows-what sort of lives, but probably involving back-breaking labor. Why? I don't understand it. It sounds sociopathic to me." She shrugged. "But I come from a scientist culture with a Goddess who reveres life. We don't think going backwards is progress."

"Unless you think you've gotten something wrong and need to backtrack," Sascha murmured, frowning.

"So what is it the Eldritch are trying to correct for?" Irine wondered.

"I don't know," Reese said. "But whatever it is, they're failing."

It was unsurprising to find clothing had appeared in his temporary quarters; no doubt Neren had seen to it, as he would have felt obliged. The retainer had not arrived with the clothing, however, and while court dress did not require the aid of a servant, it was designed with the assumption that one would be dressed by a valet or lady's maid. Hirianthial bathed and began the laborious process of doing without help. White gloves of thin leather, white stockings of thin silk, white blouse, edged with thin, soft lace; vest and coat and pants the dark red of a claret, embroidered in bronze thread and sewn with topazes, citrines, garnets; he fingered them, wondering what they would fetch at market, and what Reese would have done with the money. They were beautiful, but on this world the only purpose they served was ornament, like the people they decorated.

Gentlemen wore pointed shoes with heels . . . or boots,

and he had always favored the latter. Hair for men, always long and loose, required either braids sewn with precious stones or fillets to keep it back; Hirianthial wore the one piece of hair jewelry he needed at the back of his neck, and chose to go unadorned. Surely there was some value in being outrageous.

The swords came with him, both of them, and the dagger as well. He remained Jisiensire's sword-bearer until Araelis awarded that duty to someone else, and he was entitled and required to wear them to court, one on each side. The dagger, of course, was with Theresa, but his Alliance purchase served him well enough. Few people would look at his feet carefully enough to notice its foreign issue, and having something there was better than not: it would keep the curious from wondering, given his reputation as a man who only ever gave a dagger once.

That he had done it twice now, he did not contemplate closely. Theresa needed a weapon; it was that simple.

He maintained his forest-won calm throughout the process; it stayed with him even as he regarded himself in the mirror and saw the man who'd loved and lived here before everything had fallen apart. His face had changed, had grown more lined, and his eyes . . . he'd seen things, leaving this world. They had pushed the horizon from the rim of a world to the edge of a galaxy emblazoned with stars finer than any gems a tailor could sew onto a coat. He surprised himself by wanting that for all his people . . . that sense that the universe was vaster and more astonishing than anything they could conceive. Of all the races in the Alliance, surely they needed that perspective the most, for they had so many more years to fill and so little to fill them with.

He turned from himself and the revelation that he cared, squared his shoulders, and went to the great hall.

Ontine had a throne room: a narrow gallery that ended in the Queen's seat, a room small enough for thirty people perhaps, meant for petitioners and envoys and the business of governance. The palace also had a great hall for times when the entirety of the ruling class of the world needed to meet one another before their Queen, and it was there that the winter court session was opened. Hirianthial had begun attending the twin courts of the year when his mother had designated him the heir to the Sarel family, and he had continued to attend them after he'd succeeded his parents. He was familiar with the routine. And if the overpowering glitter of the courtiers in their multitudes was no longer quite so familiar, he could also call upon his new out-world experiences to understand just how small a gathering it was. Some two hundred and fifty people? Maybe three hundred at most?

Their numbers were fewer than he remembered, as well. They were dwindling. It was something he not only saw, but sensed, suddenly, shockingly: a taint in too many auras. Ennui? Sickness? Genetic disorder?

Araelis headed for him the moment she spotted him, hooking him around the arm with her wand and drawing him discreetly aside. "Cousin, thank God and Lady. Come bring the swords over and look intractable for me."

"You and I should talk," he said, pushing the tip of the wand down and away.

Annoyingly, her aura changed not at all, not even for the faintest hint of remorse. "Is this about that appealing young woman of yours? Yes, I think we should talk about her."

Then again, perhaps broaching the topic had not been wise. "You spoke overmuch on things I would have kept private—"

"That woman is very attached to you," Araelis said.

"And all her people too. How can you not have told them anything about your life, Hirianthial?" She tsked. "You owed them something of yourself."

His brows lifted. "You are discussing out-worlders, do you recall, cousin."

"Yes, I know," Araelis said. "Have you forgotten we are Jisiensire, Hirianthial? Or has your father-come-lately from Galare clouded your eyes to your mother's legacy? We are the House that welcomed the first alien as kin. We are the House who supplies the Queen's couriers, generation after generation. It is for us to cultivate the alien. That is done by mutual trust," the latter two words punctuated with taps of her wand on his forearm, "and mutual trust is grown by confidences."

"If the alien is so much your concern," Hirianthial said, "do you go into the Alliance and seek your own. But don't tell me how to manage my companions."

"Ah," Araelis said, cold pallor spilling into her aura as she stopped. "Ah? Ah. Your . . . companions?"

"Yes," he said, irritated. "What else?"

She held up her hands, wand held horizontal to the ground in one of them, the symbol for yielding an argument. "Pardon me, my cousin. I see I did amiss."

"You did," he said, not trusting her withdrawal, for he didn't understand what had occasioned it. Why had her aura washed so shocked so suddenly? As if she had made some mistake and did not want his attention drawn to it.

"I had thought you were closer to them than you were," Araelis said. "Forgive me! I shall make no mention of you again."

Before he could answer her, the fanfare played, announcing the arrival of the Queen. The rustle of the crowd turning to face the long blue carpet that led to the end of the hall prefaced the silence as Liolesa strode to the seat awaiting her, a less formal throne than the one in her throne room, but on an elevated dais. As always, she moved with purpose, climbing the dais and settling herself on her cushioned bench. She rested the scepter against her shoulder and said in a carrying voice, "The Winter Court is now convened. The Houses may now present to their liege."

A herald called, "House Sovenil. Families Kiviel, Juran, Thani, Brel and Shin in attendance," and began the long process. It was not the formal exchange that would take place in the days to come in the more intimate throne room, where each courtier would bring a tally of the duties he owed Liolesa for her examination, but it involved the presentation of newer members of the family and the explication of their lineage and credentials. Hirianthial found it harder to focus on the people than it was to sense their emotions: their feelings toward Liolesa as they spoke to her, their general state, their health. That more than anything distracted him; as each House was called forth, he was shown their true allegiances, felt their connection to others in the court like a web dewed with water drop-lets, a spangled light that had him looking into corners at places where no person stood but some line extended as tangibly as any silk thread. It was so involving he almost missed Jisiensire's cue.

Following Araelis, he went to a knee as was proper for a sword-bearer, and one who'd personally served the Queen. And here, rather than sense his own party's dis-position, he felt the pressure of the court's attention, their spikes of curiosity, their sudden interest, the fencing of their loyalties as they shifted to accommodate him as a possible player. There were many women willing to make allowances for his politics if they could capture him as a husband.

Liolesa's aura surprised him not at all: a thing of steel,

like armor, completely in control of herself.

There were only two Houses after Jisiensire to be called, and the last of them was Asaniefa, Surela's House and their enemy. He expected something in her people to hint at their anger and frustration, but what he sensed instead was a smug anticipation that made his skin prickle. They were planning something—of course they were, they always were—but this plan they thought assured them success. Was this what Liolesa was determined to flush into the open?

Were they so convinced Liolesa wouldn't use the technology of the Alliance against them, that they could scheme against her in relative security?

Araelis whispered, "You have your hand on your sword, cousin."

He let it drop, folded his hands behind his back, felt the creak of the leather gloves as he flexed his fingers.

After the introductions, the courtiers were free to mingle or to leave as they preferred. In practice, the first session lasted until supper, and everyone would use it to see whether their alliances had lasted the year or if they needed reevaluation, if they had gained allies or lost them, who they should plan to invite to more private soirees. Hirianthial followed Araelis as if he was still a part of Jisiensire, mostly to prevent too many eligible ladies from descending on him. He hoped between his cousin's known allegiance to Liolesa and his forbidding look he would not attract too many.

It was a vain hope. He found himself deflecting far too many women, some of them so young they'd probably only had their introductions to society earlier in the summer; the thought of marrying any of them was risible.

"Oh come now," Araelis murmured when he'd shooed the latest away. "They're not all that bad."

"Anyone young enough to be my daughter should know better," Hirianthial said. "It's in appalling taste."

"Perhaps," Araelis said. "But you know you're likely to attract such hopefuls until you settle down."

He glanced at her, eyes narrowed, and was rewarded with her faint shrug.

"You might consider marrying just to take yourself out of the pool, you know."

"I'm not interested," he said. "I had Laiselin. One love in a lifetime is blessing enough."

She sighed. "Yes. Exactly. One in a lifetime is blessing and rarity. One doesn't marry for love, cousin, or why would all these children be after you? They want the prestige, and your proven virility, and the money you'd be endowed with by Jisiensire when you leave it. Marriage is an economic arrangement. If you are lucky, as I was, you marry a good friend. And you, Hirianthial, have a good friend."

"I cannot imagine who you might mean—"

"I mean the Queen," Araelis said.

He stopped entirely.

"She needs an heir. You need peace. And the two of you are well-suited."

"God and Lady!" he exclaimed.

"You of all people should not fear our strictures against marrying a cousin," Araelis continued. "If indeed you are a doctor trained off-world as you so said, then you know the Alliance has methods. It may be a touch scandalous, but people would accept it. And then both of you would be safer."

Incredulous, Hirianthial said, "Enough! No more, Araelis, do you understand? Bad enough to overturn our own customs—and you have been soaked in the stories of Sellelvi too long to have even had the thought—but completely aside from that, it would be as if to marry my own sister!" He grimaced. "And God hear me, I have no desire to be king-consort."

"You would be a good one—"

"Araelis!"

She sighed. "Fine. But don't come to me later complaining of all these women throwing themselves at you. I have offered you a solution."

"An entirely untenable one!"

"Only because you insist on being difficult," she said. "If you did not have all these romantic notions you would find your life far easier, cousin."

"Where are you going?"

"Away," she said firmly. "I am off to speak female business with other women. Since you are so confident in your rectitude, I will leave you to the swarm. No doubt you can manage them."

This he found himself forced to do, for he could either confine himself to the discourse of Eldritch men, which was limited in scope for someone who'd been touring alien worlds for six decades, or he could expose himself to the attentions of women, who wanted only to flutter at him and express their admiration of his astonishing courage in braving the terrifying worlds beyond the skies!

Liolesa found him with his second glass of wine near one of the tables, where he'd hoped the shadow of one of the stone columns would hide him.

"Ready to flee yet?"

"God and Lady," he said, fervent.

"A very typical start to winter," she said, taking up a glass from a passing tray and sipping it. "Though far more pleasing with you here. I notice you can't seem to move without the pack snapping at your heels."

"I feel like a particularly fat quail," he said, wry.

She smirked. "Pity them, cousin. They've had no

fresh meat lately. Certainly nothing as fine as a former seal-bearer."

"I had hoped my out-world adventures would taint me in their eyes."

"It would take a great deal more than that to make someone with your dower a poor choice," Liolesa said. "And for my enemies, the temptation to win you from my side is overwhelming. I'm surprised Surela hasn't made it clear to all and sundry that you are hers first, and anyone else must wait on her suit before attempting you."

"It is enough to make me beg Reese for passage off-world tonight."

"Ah, no," she said with a laugh. "Don't abandon me yet, cousin. Not with the game afoot! You sense it, don't you?"

"Yes," he said, though he was unwilling to say more around so many.

"We might discuss it later," she said. "Perhaps you'll be fortunate and people will assume you're paying court to me."

He stared at her, appalled, found the wicked humor wreathing her aura in silver sparks utterly preposterous. "You're not serious! Has Araelis been filling your ears with wild ideas?"

She grinned. "Of course she has. It's one of her charms, that she fears nothing, least of all my position." Observing his expression, she snorted. "Please, cousin. Me, marry? When have you known me to have that sort of patience?"

He exhaled. "Pray you, don't frighten me thus."

She tapped his glass lightly with a finger. "Drink, cousin. You are too tightly wired, if you are ready to take such things for truth. Did Araelis approach you already?" At his pained expression, she said, "Oh, don't fear. She has been at me as well, and she should know better. As should you. But do come later, and carry me your impressions."

"As you will, cousin."

"Mmm, yes. As it should be." The merriment that pierced her aura was as good as a wink, and she was away, back to mingling among the crowd. He fortified himself with another sip of the wine and followed her example, steering well clear of Surela and reflecting that he would have a humbling experience to relate to Urise on the morning. His hard-won calm had lasted perhaps half an hour.

He did find it odd that he had not seen Thaniet in attendance on her lady. She had been presented, but was now missing. Perhaps at last she'd found the moral fiber to part herself from Surela. Would that it be so.

"That must be Felith," Irine said at the sound of the knock.

The Harat-Shar began to rise, but Reese waved her back to the table. "I'm closer."

"Thanks, I'm kind of comfortable here."

"Kind of," Reese said, wryly; the twins were intertwined, going through the book Felith had brought back from the library and comparing unintelligible Eldritch words in it to the text in the atlas. They were hoping to find some basis for understanding the written language, but Reese thought it more likely they'd uncover the lost archeological temple of Mars. None of them were linguists. Amused, she went to the door and opened it on an unfamiliar Eldritch woman who shrieked at the sight of her.

Reese leaped back, startled, then lunged forward. "Wait!"

The woman was already in flight down the corridor. Reese gave chase because she hadn't yet pursued a woman in a fluffy gown and that was no doubt a necessary part of her role in this farce. Fortunately, fluffy gowns and tiny heels were a lot more trouble to run in than pants and boots. Reese drew abreast of the woman and then ahead of her and stopped, throwing her arms wide. "Stop!"

The woman came to a halt, gasping for breath, her hand pressed to her throat. "A human!" she cried in accented Universal.

"Not a poisonous snake or a rampaging bear," Reese pointed out. "So you can stop looking like I'm going to drink your blood, all right? Who were you looking for?"

"I was not!"

"You knocked on our door," Reese said. "Why'd you do that if you weren't looking for someone?"

"I must have made a mistake," the woman said, breathless. "If you will excuse me?"

Reese stood aside to let her pass, but not before noting the little pin on the square-cut neck of her bodice: a silvery-gold creature on green, like a lion but with hooves. She frowned and headed back.

"I'm guessing that wasn't Felith," Sascha said. "What with the screaming and all."

"Are there any hooved lions on green fields on that map?" Reese asked.

Kis'eh't flipped back to the right page and scanned it. "Sure, here. This big parcel."

Reese frowned at it. "Well, all right. I know she's associated with someone with a lot of land. The question is . . . who?"

"Felith would know," Sascha said.

"Felith's not here." Irine put her chin in her palm.

"I have an idea," Reese said. She went into her room and returned with Allacazam under her arm and the telegem in her hand.

"I'm pretty sure Allacazam won't know," Irine said.

Reese snorted and handed him to the tigraine. "Here, put him in the sun, he hasn't been getting enough to eat."

She sat next to Sascha at the table and tapped the telegem. "Reese to *Earthrise*. Malia, come in please."

"This is *Earthrise* . . . sorry, Captain Eddings, Malia's asleep. Should I wake her?"

Reese stared at the gem. "Um, who are you?"

"Taylor Goodfix. I'm another of the endless Tam-illee the Queen's got tucked up her sleeve. I help maintain her fleet."

"Her fleet?" Sascha said, leaning in. "How many ships are we talking about here?"

"Oh, don't get any notions about a navy or anything. There are only three, and the clan keeps them out in Alliance space, doing normal courier routes. We are an incorporated messenger service, it helps with the bills."

"And the cover," Sascha murmured.

"And the cover," Taylor agreed.

"How did you get on my ship? How . . . what . . ."

"Malia asked me to keep her company, Captain, so I Padded over from the observation post. I figured while I was here I'd do a little fixing? Nothing serious, your engineering compartment is ship-shape, my compliments to your crew there. But little things, like leaky vents and blinky lights that aren't blinking."

"That's . . . nice of you," Reese said. "But I have no budget for repairs—"

"Don't worry about it, ma'am. I like to have something to do and everything else in the area's fine." A hint of frustration crept into the woman's mezzosoprano. "There's so much I could be doing and can't that it's nice to have some kind of project, no matter how small."

"If you're sure . . ."

"Absolutely, please. Think nothing of it. Or if you must, consider it a gift from the Queen. Now, what can I do for you? Should I wake up Malia?"

"No," Reese said. "Let her rest. We just wanted to ask her about a heraldic device."

"Oh, I can tell you about those. We all learn when we join the Tams. What have you got?"

"It's a silvery-goldish lion with hooves on a dark green field," Reese said, and they all leaned in to hear the answer.

"Oh. OH. Asaniefa, that is. The Queen's mortal enemies."

"Figures," Irine said with a sigh.

"Do you know all the rest?" Kis'eh't put in. "It would be nice to have the full list."

"Oh sure. You have something to take notes?"

Kis'eh't tapped her tablet. "Whenever you're ready."

As Taylor ran down the list, Reese leaned back with her arms crossed over her chest, frowning.

"Upset about Hirianthial's enemies finding out about us?" Sascha said. "Or about someone inviting a stranger onto your ship without asking you first?"

"It's kind of hard to be offended at someone who decides to do repairs for you for free," Reese said.

"I'm surprised that part didn't upset you, actually," Sascha said. "That she's not letting you pay for it."

"Yeah, well, there are better things to be upset about than someone being nice to you," Reese said, massaging her forehead. When she looked up she found both the twins staring at her and managed a weak smile. "What can I say, I'm learning. Trying, anyway."

Irine blinked, then reached across the table and rested her hand on Reese's arm. "You're doing great."

Reese patted the furry hand. "Thanks." She sighed. "Besides, I know a little of how she must feel. Looking down at this world and thinking of everything she could do to help and not being allowed."

"I can't imagine what a clan of Tam-illee could do to this place," Sascha said, bemused. "Between their talent for engineering and their fanatical focus on reproductive medicine . . ."

Irine said, "I'm surprised the Queen hasn't brought them in anyway . . . !"

"Reese?" Kis'eh't interrupted. "Can you think of anything else you want to know from Taylor?"

"Sure," Reese said. "Hey, Taylor-alet . . . why hasn't the Queen turned you loose on this world? You set down far away enough, no one would know. It's not like they have satellites or anything that could possibly find you."

"I don't know." Taylor's frustration returned. "I haven't ever been told a reason. The Lord—that's Lesandurel Meriaen Jisiensire, our Eldritch—says the time isn't right, and that to start an endeavor wrongly is to doom it. But they're superstitious that way."

"It sounds like something they'd say," Reese said. "All right. Are you sure you and Malia are fine up there?"

"Now that we have someone to play cards with, sure. Call us anytime, Captain. She's lovely, your *Earthrise*, we're both delighted to be ship-sitting."

"Thanks for taking good care of her," Reese said. "Reese out." She tapped the telegem, then drummed her fingers on the table.

"What are you thinking?" Sascha asked, tilting his head.

"That maybe the Queen thinks now is the right time," Reese said. "And also that there are two foxes on my ship, and I'm not up there, and that's weird. And finally that I've scared some woman beholden to Hirianthial's enemies straight back down the stairs. Maybe I should tell the Queen her surprise has been spoiled."

"It'll have to wait, won't it?" Irine said. "Isn't there some big event going on right now? She'll be busy."

"This evening then," Reese said. "I can ask Hirianthial to take me to see her." She glanced at Kis'eh't. "Did you get what you needed from Taylor?"

"More than that," Kis'eh't said. "She's also told me the political disposition of all these Houses." She tapped the map. "Here, look. You got the Galare in the center here, around the palace. To the north and south, she's got enemies. But in the south she's got Jisiensire squeezing them in the middle, so they can't expand any further. In the west she's got a lot of neutral parties, but they're hemmed in by this mountain range."

"What's up here, then, above Asaniefa?" Reese asked.

"Nothing," Kis'eh't said. "Apparently these areas here are all the property of noble families that have petered out. So Asaniefa's expanding into Imthereli's old territory, for instance. Jisiensire could move south too, into some of these abandoned areas."

"Still, if the Queen wants to hem in Asaniefa, she should have an ally up here in the north," Reese said. "What's this area? It looks like it was someone's once."

"Taylor didn't know," Kis'eh't said.

Reese frowned. "And this really is all there is?"

"Yes."

"Blood in the soil," Reese said, soft. "We might be too late to save them."

The function proceeded much as he remembered such things going: slowly, and involving a great deal of talk that revealed nothing more substantive than the latest opinion on the newest divertissement. Given Eldritch constitutions, 'newest' meant at least a decade old. He drank a great deal of wine, discreetly watered, smiled politely at far too many young faces and wore more guarded expressions before old ones. The families that counted themselves Galare allies had little by way of news to share; sixty years was not long enough for more than one or two babies to have been successfully conceived, and deaths, while less rare, were also infrequent. Liolesa's partisans remained much the same in strength and conviction since last he attended a winter court; her neutrals remained unmoved, and her enemies, of course, were stalwart.

How did they breathe through so much stasis?

He tarried there for several hours, though he quit the gathering before it began dispersing near supper. He had never had much patience for the courts, and being among the out-worlders had not improved it. His boot-steps echoed in the large, empty corridors as he left the hall behind, and the murmured conversations faded as he passed onward, toward the nearest stairwell and up it, to the second floor. Did his stride quicken as he approached the *Earthrise* crew's suite? And if it did, who could blame him? It would be good to speak with people who used speech to exchange meaningful information, rather than to manipulate the emotions of their auditors.

It was Irine who opened the door, and upon seeing him her pupils dilated. She called over her shoulder, "He's here!" Before adding to him, "Have we got a lot of questions for you, arii."

"I shall endeavor to answer," Hirianthial said, startled by her gravity. He entered and halted at the sight of the group clustered around the atlas, data tablets scattered amid the anachronism of Eldritch porcelain cups. "Ariisen? You have a look of consternation?"

Kis'eh't looked up at him and said, "You people are dying, aren't you?"

He stopped, felt the noise in his head rising. Cautiously, he said, "Perhaps you might elaborate."

"We're thinking there's only about a hundred thousand of you left at most," Kis'eh't said. "That's our generous estimate. Mine is closer to half that. Maybe less."

Reese said, "Is it true?"

Sascha, studying him, said, "Maybe you should sit. By the fire, it's gotten cold. Maybe we can all sit by the fire."

"And drink something," Irine added. "Why is it cold, anyway? Isn't it afternoon?"

"Sun's on the other side of the palace," Kis'eh't said, collecting her tablet and cup and heading for the hearth. "It's not like the buildings we're used to, Irine. There's no climate control."

Irine grimaced. "I should have brought more socks."

Sascha pulled her over. "Come on, I'll keep you warm."

They resettled by the fire and nearly as one looked at him, waiting. How much had they derived from a solitary atlas? God and Lady. And yet, if they had, how much grief would it save them all for him to simply explain it to them? He sat in one of the unoccupied chairs, stretching one leg out to work the ache out of the joint. "Your suppositions are correct," he said finally. "Though I could not give you an exact number. I doubt anyone knows, save perhaps the Queen and her minister. There is an imperfect census, she would have the data."

"So this little finger's width of land along the coast is really all that's settled of this world," Reese said.

"You have the right of that."

The silence then was filled only by the hiss of sap burning in the logs. Irine was hugging her knees, staring at him with wide eyes; her brother's gaze was harder to read, but his aura was somber as winter soil. Kis'eh't and Reese were no better. Bryer, resting with his back to the wall, only opened his eyes enough to meet his, then closed them again.

"So is the reason the Queen hasn't picked up and moved to the opposite side of the continent and left all her enemies to die that . . . she's afraid there won't be enough of you to keep from inbreeding?" Sascha said finally.

"That doesn't make sense." Kis'eh't folded her arms. "If she wants to use the technology to lift half a town of people elsewhere, she can very well use the technology to gene-correct. That's some of the oldest technology the Alliance has."

"Still, twenty-five thousand people . . . that's not much," Sascha said.

"That's plenty if you try to sleep with them all," Irine said.

"Ariisen," Hirianthial said, stilling them instantly. "I believe the Queen has done no such thing because matters are not so simple."

"How is it not simple? Either 'yes, I want to go with you' or 'no, I don't want any part of you,'" Irine said.

"She has a point," Sascha said. "How hard can it be to decide to live in a century with indoor plumbing and heaters in winter? And why did you people give it up anyway?"

"Give it up?" Hirianthial repeated.

"We've decided you were human once," Sascha said. "Yes? No?"

The vertigo that assailed him was so extreme he lost sight of the room. Was it horror that made the room spin . . . or relief? To be quit of all the secrets—and yet, if they knew. . . .

"Hirianthial?" Kis'eh't said.

Reese lifted a hand before he could find the words. "Wait." She drew the pendant from around her neck and said, "Is it enough to swear on this that what we're discussing stays in this room?"

"Only if you understand what it means to swear that vow," Hirianthial said. He sought some way to make them understand—ah—"Malia Navigatrix is bound by the vow that her ancestress swore to Lesandural Meriaen Jisiensire nine generations ago. Do you understand? If I tell you these things, your children and your children's children may still be bound by your promise. We live different spans, but the secrets must remain until the day the Veil is forever lifted."

"Do you think that will happen?" Kis'eh't wondered, more curious than distressed.

"Maybe when the right suitor comes along," Reese murmured, surprising him. She glanced at him. "Nine generations is a long time."

"I like that he assumes we'll be having children," Irine said.

"We should probably get busy with that." Sascha grinned. "Once we find someplace to settle down."

Reese cleared her throat. "Stay focused." She set the medallion down and put her hand on it before saying to the others. "If you want to."

Kis'eh't rested a furred hand on Reese's. The twins joined fingers and set theirs over hers. They all looked at Bryer, who slitted open an eye and then reached forth and covered the mound with golden talons, flashing in firelight.

"We swear," Reese said, firmly, meeting his eyes. "To keep the Eldritch Veil until such time as it is declared no longer needful."

Their resolution melded their auras into something bright as steel. It wanted more than speech. He drew the glove off his sword hand and rested it on theirs. "I accept your vow in the name of the Unicorn's seal-bearer, and swear to carry your oath to her if you do not do so first."

"So," Kis'eh't said. "Are you human?"

"No," Hirianthial said. "But we were, once."

The medallion's edges cut into Reese's palm in that new silence. She was grateful that her crew was willing to fill it, because she felt as if someone had smacked her head against a wall.

It was true. All those things she'd thought on meeting Hirianthial about feeling not good enough, not beautiful enough, not delicate or strong or graceful enough, just . . . *not enough* . . . that feeling had been leading her in the right direction. She'd been comparing herself to the Eldritch because they'd shared roots somewhere in the distant past, and in that distant past the Eldritch had decided that humanity was not enough. They'd been family once, and they had been abandoned.

"So wait, did you leave before us or after us?" Sascha was asking.

"Before," Hirianthial said. "By some three, four hundred years? I am not entirely certain of it due to the calendars being different."

Kis'eh't frowned. "Earth still keeps a different calendar from the Alliance. If you have your own . . ."

"Still the Alliance isn't all that old," Sascha said. "If the Eldritch live as long as they seem to, there can't have been many generations of them?"

"Each generation lives longer than the one before," Hirianthial said. "But you are correct. We are not far removed from the first settlers who landed here."

"So what happened to the ships you used to get here?" Irine asked. "And why did you give up technology?"

"Ship," Hirianthial said. "It was a single ship, Irine. And it was a choice, to live more simply. Perhaps not well-considered, given the many uncertainties of interstellar colonization. But we were the first to leave Earth. We were not acquainted with the challenges. No one was."

Reese cleared her throat. "We could probably spend all night talking out the implications of this, but we have more important business." She caught Hirianthial's eyes. "One of your Queen's enemies decided to knock on our door, and she knows we're here now. If the Queen was counting on surprising people tomorrow we should probably warn her that's off."

"What? Here?" Hirianthial sat forward. "Who, do you know?"

"She didn't give us her name," Reese said.

Irine sniffed. "Actually, she ran screaming down the hall. The only reason we know anything about her is because one of the foxines on the *Earthrise* recognized the pin she was wearing when we described it."

Hirianthial glanced at Reese. "A centicore, electrum, on emerald."

"Is that what you call the lion with deer feet?" Reese said. "But yes. So . . . can you take me to see her?"

"Yes," he said. "There are things I must discuss with her myself." As he stood, he added to the crew, "I trust your questions will keep for another day?"

"As long as the answers will too," Kis'eh't said.

Hirianthial's smile was a good smile for him. It reminded Reese of better times on the *Earthrise*, before Kerayle. "They have waited hundreds of years already. I assure you, they aren't going anywhere." He turned to her. "Lady?"

She was lady again. She was beginning to wonder how he decided what to call her . . . and what 'lady' meant. Obviously it was a translation of something Eldritch, but what nuance was she missing by not knowing the language or the culture here? She brushed off her pants and got up. "Lead the way."

He did not, though, once he'd gently shut the door on the suite. Instead he flexed his fingers once on the handle—an arabesque of metal with what looked like ivory inlay—and looked at her, so grave. And beautiful, like the romance covers from her monthlies but better, because he was real. He looked like what he was: descendant of royalty, heir to all the graces and powers that humanity wasn't. And yet, his eyes . . . he was concerned.

"Theresa," he said. "This news . . . may I ask . . . how you find it?"

He really was worried. About her reaction! Startled, she said, "I find it believable, I guess."

"Believable," he repeated. "I suppose that is a more promising response than 'appalling.'"

"Maybe it's a little that too," Reese said. "But I can't say I'm surprised." At his look, she shook her head. "It's nothing personal. Not against you. I don't blame you, if that's what you're afraid of. It's just. . . ." She rubbed her arm. "First the Pelted abandon Earth, and they go off and make the Alliance of all things, and they become these amazing, fascinating people, so varied and fierce and wonderful. Now, you too? I'm not surprised because it feels like humans are destined to be everyone's backward cousin. But it hurts, because you're all so . . . so beautiful." She looked away, composed herself, then finished, "Anyway. So, no I'm not angry at you. But I still feel. . . ."

"Crushed," he murmured.

She grimaced. "That's a strong word. Let's just say . . . sad. I'm a little sad. For humanity. Because we're so awful that everyone wants to get away from us."

"Among us," Hirianthial said, quiet, "we would say that only strong seed could beget such powerful offspring."

She chuckled, tired. "Thanks. It doesn't help much, but thanks."

"Then I will say instead that humans are also beautiful," he said. "And you should not think so little of yourself, either."

Was he complimenting *her*? In particular? Her heart skipped. She smiled and said, "It does get hard to describe you people to one another. 'What did your visitor look like?' 'Oh, she was white with white hair.'"

Hirianthial laughed. "Yes, rather a failing in our kind."

"And speaking of visitors," Reese said, trailing off.

"Yes. This way, please."

As she followed him, she tried not to think of his kindness. She was not living in one of her stories. In the real world—worlds—poor fatherless girls from Mars didn't get the princes. She especially didn't want to ask herself if this particular poor girl wanted this particular prince. Blood in the soil.

Unsurprisingly, Hirianthial didn't need an invitation to get them seen by the Queen on a whim; if Reese ever needed proof of the family relation, it was there in the alacrity with which the guards passed them into the Queen's parlor. Liolesa had been sitting behind her great desk, but as they entered she rose, a query in her cocked brow. Strange how seeing her, Reese didn't think of how hard it was to describe an individual Eldritch. Liolesa Galare wrote her own description and none of it involved anything as superficial as her skin.

Hirianthial stepped back with a graceful gesture. "Captain Eddings?"

So he was going to let her tell the Queen? He hadn't had to. "Your Majesty—"

"Liolesa," the Queen interrupted.

"Lady Liolesa," Reese said firmly. "Your enemies appear to have found us out."

"Thaniet, I am guessing," Hirianthial offered. "She was missing from Surela's side at the court."

"Mmm," said the Queen. She came around her desk. "That should make for an interesting time tomorrow."

"That's it?" Reese asked, surprised. "No worry? No details? Nothing?" She paused and her eyes narrowed. "No, that doesn't make sense. You planned for this."

Liolesa chuckled. "Theresa. There are several hundred people now in residence in this palace. They cannot go outside without hardship given the weather, and so have no way to entertain themselves by walking in gardens or going for rides. They have no data tablets to absorb them. Books are few and precious, and re-read to the point of memorization. What do you suppose such people do, lacking distraction?"

Thinking of her crew, Reese said, "They talk."

"And make new things to talk about, yes," Liolesa said. "And those who bring news have quite the cachet. So no, I am not surprised. And yes, I was planning it."

"But why?" Reese asked.

"Because my enemies are conniving, and I need them to reveal their methods," Liolesa said. "So I intend to provoke them."

Reese looked up at her, heart pounding. Then said, "So if I told you I had been planning to show up tomorrow as a vassal instead of a retainer, would that help make your provocation more provocative?"

"Theresa Eddings!" Liolesa exclaimed, delighted. "This is your idea, I presume? And you are willing!"

"You are?" Hirianthial said, gone still in a way Reese associated with shock.

"I am." She lifted her chin. "If that's all right with you, of course."

"Oh, absolutely," Liolesa said, eyes sparkling. "I assume someone has told you of the difference, and since my cousin here is speechless it must have been someone else. Lady Araelis perhaps? Or Felith?"

"It was Felith," Reese said. "She told us something of what would be expected. It's just that . . . the way she explains it, there's no way for my crew to be protected unless I accept protection in their name—or you take them all separately as retainers—and it seems easier for me to take responsibility for them. I have before." She thought of Irine and smiled a little. "They're fine with it."

"So you are prepared to bring me something of value?" Liolesa asked.

"I figured I have horses. We'd already talked about that."

Liolesa's brows lifted. "So we had. But a vassal doesn't sell horses to her liege-lady, Theresa. A vassal breeds them for her."

The frisson that traveled her spine was heat and shock and hope and terror. "Is . . . that what it sounds like?"

"I don't know," Liolesa said, voice casual. "What did it sound like?"

"An offer," Reese answered.

The Queen smiled. "You have good ears."

Blood and freedom. Was this really happening to her? Was the Queen of the Eldritch—the Eldritch!—offering her . . . what?

Power? A title? The chance to stay in one place for long enough to breathe and build something?

. . . a home?

But she'd have to give up the *Earthrise*, and trading. And she had no idea if her crew would want to stay, and she'd become attached to them. It was hard to think of them leaving her here by herself. And Hirianthial . . . she glanced at him. But he had family here, and other duties. She couldn't expect him to stay with them if they did. Even wondering about that was presumptuous, wasn't it?

And would she want to stay on a world if she couldn't leave it for the Alliance? She hadn't just fled Mars. She'd gone out, to meet the Pelted and the aliens they'd gathered together. Her enterprise might be on the perpetual brink of financial disaster, but could she give up the exhilaration of knowing she could go anywhere?

"That's . . . not a decision I could make without think-ing about it," Reese said finally, trembling.

"Then by all means," the Queen replied, her voice gentler. "Go and think about it." A hint of mischief again. "You have all of an evening for it."

Reese couldn't help it; she laughed. "All of an entire evening! You're so generous."

"Consider it a warning of what it's like to work for me," Liolesa said, grinning.

Reese shook her head. "You people. You're even more everything than your press said."

"More everything?" the Queen asked.

"More exasperating, more beautiful, more impossi-ble, more interesting, more frustrating," Reese said. "You know. More everything." She paused, then said, glancing at Hirianthial, "More real."

"Now that is a fine compliment," the Queen said. "Go on, Captain Eddings. Consider your choice. Consult with your people."

"I will."

"Do you need help back?" Hirianthial asked.

His expression had returned to a typical Eldritch inscrutability. What was he thinking? She hoped he wasn't dismayed over the talk. "No, I can find my way back. Thank you."

"I will call on you tomorrow," he said. "To bring you to the presentation, if you wish."

She smiled. "I'd like that, thanks." She nodded to them both. "Good evening."

Once she was outside the room she wanted very much to hyperventilate . . . but the watchful guards kept her from falling apart. She hurried down the cavernous halls, her skin pebbling from the cold. If she did decide to move into some Eldritch town, the first thing she'd do would be to get Taylor Goodfix to install proper heating. She liked cold, but only when she could turn it off at will.

By the time she reached their suite she was almost running. It was Felith who opened the door and she burst through it, and thought nothing of the fact that everyone was gathered around one of the chairs by the fire.

"Ariisen, you wouldn't believe the offer I think I've gotten—"

They all looked up at her.

"This should be good," Sascha said to Kis'eh't.

Kis'eh't said, "Well, all the other not-quite-offers and not-really-contracts have made her dour and grumpy. We haven't seen one that's gotten her excited yet."

Reese mimed throwing something at them. Sascha lifted his arms to block. "Ow, ow, we'll stop!"

"What's the offer?" Irine asked, ears perked.

"I think the Queen wants us to stay," Reese said.

"Stay like 'hang around in her palace whenever we want' stay?" Irine asked. "Or stay like 'make a nest and have kits' stay?"

"I told her I was planning to present as a vassal," Reese said. "And she thought it was a good idea. She said she'll accept."

A very long pause.

"Does that mean what I think it means?" Kis'eh't said. "Given my understanding of feudal cultures . . ."

Everyone glanced at Felith, who said, stunned. "Did she truly say she would keep that troth?"

"Unless you can breed horses in outer space . . ." Reese said.

"Well!" Irine said. "I guess that means you have to wear the dress."

"The what?"

"The dress," Irine said, pointing at the chair.

Reese looked down at it and stopped thinking.

Irine grinned and said, "It even comes with a corset."

Tearing her eyes away, Reese said, "We can talk about the dress later. There are more important things to discuss first."

"Like . . ." Sascha folded his arms, waiting.

"Like deciding if you want to be tied down here if I stay," Reese replied. "Assuming, of course, I can stay."

"Wait, why wouldn't you want to stay? If you can, I mean?" Irine asked, ears sagging.

"Why would she?" Kis'eh't asked. "Not that it's not a nice world—maybe, the weather hasn't been all that pleasant and the people seem hit or miss, pardon me, Felithalet—but staying here would be mean settling somewhere she has no roots."

"There's Hirianthial," Irine said.

"Hirianthial isn't enough," Kis'eh't said. "How do we know he'd be around, anyway? Doesn't he have responsibilities here? And this place . . . it's got no culture. Not real culture, with more than one species. You'd have to give up all that—"

"But how much of that did we really see?" Sascha said. "It's hard to enjoy the wonders of the galaxy when you barely have two fin to rub together. No offense, Captain."

"None taken?" Reese said, bemused at their arguments.

"When we dock at a starbase we see quite a bit," Kis'eh't said.

"But that's the thing." Irine leaned toward them, earnest. "We can only *see* it. We can't be part of it. We can't make anything. We never have enough money for that, we only have enough to get by. If we stayed here, we could be here, really be *here*, be part of things."

"Assuming the Eldritch let us," Kis'eh't said, ears flattening. "Xenophobes, remember?"

Felith cleared her throat and said, "Not all of us, if you will permit me to say so. And those of us who are not would welcome you."

"Come on, Kis'eh't," Sascha said. "You like a challenge, don't you?"

Kis'eh't frowned, then glanced at Bryer. "What do you say?"

Bryer opened an eye, looked toward the window, mantled his feathers and sank back into them. "Good place for a garden. Can fly here."

The words rang in Reese's heart like a bell.

Kis'eh't smiled and shook her head. "The Goddess does say we should not shy from creation, even when making is difficult."

"There, see? It's settled. Even Allacazam seems happy with the sun here," Sascha said. "So we're with you, Boss. What next?"

"Next," Reese said, "we think about offerings."

The door shut on Reese, and the room seemed far emptier for it than her presence alone should have warranted.

"Now there goes a woman I shall be proud to take into the family," Liolesa said with relish. She grinned at Hirianthial. "I had thought she would be a good investment when I bought her ship back from her creditors, but I had no idea how high the dividends would be."

"She is remarkable," Hirianthial said, folding his hands behind his back. He tilted his head. "You truly mean to make her a vassal?"

"If she accedes?" Liolesa huffed. "I had always planned to open the world to some number of aliens and have spent some small time in the cultivation of likely prospects. To have found one who cleaves to our ways as readily as she appears to, who *wants* to be here . . . I would be a fool not to."

"She swore to the Veil, you know," he said, quiet.

"Did she now?"

"And her people with her," Hirianthial said. "On the Galare unicorn."

"Did she!" Liolesa laughed. "And I am guessing you explained the ramifications of such a promise, and they made it anyway?"

Hirianthial looked away, eyes closing. "I told them about the Tams and Lesandurel, yes."

"And now you will have your own multigenerational household," Liolesa said, going to the fire.

"Me!" He suppressed his revulsion with difficulty. "They swore on your seal, not mine."

"But it is you they fell in love with, cousin, no mistake." She looked up at him as she sank onto a chair and sighed. "Hiran. Sit, please. You make my joints ache standing thus so rigidly."

"They do not—" He stopped because he could not continue, could not lie. He knew how much they cared for him.

"They do, and well you know it."

"They'll die," he said, low.

She was quiet a moment. Then she said, "So did Laiselin, and she should have lived fifteen hundred years."

God and Lady, how that could still hurt. "Then you know why I must not."

"Must not what? Must not care?" She shook her head. "It's too late for that. You do already, and so do they. All that remains is to decide what you will do about it."

"As if there is something to be done!" he said. "Lia, in less than a hundred years they'll all be dead!"

"So?" she said.

"So?" He stared at her, could not believe the settled

pool of her aura. "You would have me enter into something, knowing the loss I court?"

"Why not?" she said. "I have."

The truth of it shone through her calm like sun through water, a dazzling radiance.

"You have . . . what?" he asked, carefully.

"I have loved a human," she said, her hands folded on her lap. "And in the fullness of time he died."

"You . . . did what?" he said, stunned. "When? I have been your fast companion all your life—" He stopped. "No. Not when you were newly heir."

"And went off-world on behalf of our aunt?" she said. "Yes, that was when it happened. And then I stole away whenever I could, and said I was—"

"In the convent!" Hirianthial exclaimed. "God and Lady, Lia! I guarded the doors to Saint Wilthelmissa all those times!"

"And every time you did, I was far, far from there," she said, her eyes grave. "I couldn't bring you, Hiran. How could I? I was going to an assignation that would have seen me twice disgraced."

Now at last he sought the chair she'd asked him to use. Sagging into it, he rested a hand on his knee and leaned toward her. "You visited that convent for a good two hundred years."

"Of course I did," Liolesa said. "I had to give people a chance to discover me there, did I want the story to hold."

He had always known his cousin for a rebel. Not without forethought—she broke only rules that failed to fit in with her plans for the world and her rule—but this was not in her character. If her tryst had been discovered she would have been set aside: for consorting with humans, and for having risked the possibility of begetting a bastard, for it could be done, with humans.

"Who was he?" he asked, quiet.

She smiled. "A geneticist, if you will believe. Not someone I was formally to consult when Maraesa sent me to renegotiate the treaty terms with the Alliance . . . but Fassiana had been having trouble conceiving, do you recall? And she begged me to bring her some hope from the Alliance. And when I met him . . ." She trailed off, eyes distant and aura warm and intimate as candle-glow. "He was young, of course, and so was I. And he was passionate about his work, about helping those who wanted children." She pulled herself from the past with a sigh. "It was not inevitable. But all my life I had turned every moment and every act toward my goals for us as a species, Hiran. Pieter was something I did for myself."

"And this you did, knowing you would outlive him by some fifteen hundred years?" he asked.

"That I did not even knowing if I would ever see him again," she said. "And oh, yes. I gave myself to it whole-heartedly, and for a time I knew a very selfish sort of happiness. Even when he grew old . . ." Her smile somehow held her heartbreak, and the peace she'd made with it. "I watched him die and even then the only thing I regretted was that it was over. Not that I had done it." She looked up at him. "Do you understand the distinction?"

"I do," he said, low. "But I am not like you, cousin."

"Aren't you?" she said. She lifted her hand. "No, don't answer that. Not yet, anyway. Tell me instead your impressions of the court opening. I assume that was your reason for coming."

"Your enemies are far too pleased with themselves," he said. "And they are poised for something. If I hadn't learned that Thaniet only just discovered the presence of Reese and her people, I would have wondered if they'd already known."

She said, "Or perhaps there is something else they have been waiting on, and it is near fruition."

Liolesa's abilities were modest; she needed touch to sense feelings, like most Eldritch. But she had one talent he had never heard of in any other person: the ability to sense patterns around her, sometimes so acutely they bordered on precognition. He glanced at her sharply. "You feel something?"

"I would not be pushing if I did not," she said. "But it's less that I feel something about what they know, cousin. What I feel . . ." She searched for words, eyes gone distant. When they grew focused again, he liked not at all the smog that suffused her aura. "What I feel is that if I don't catalyze something now, we might not survive." She shook her head. "We can't afford to wait, so pray they react to the provocation tomorrow."

"God and Lady, Lia," he said softly.

"Chin up, cousin," she said. "If we get past this, our world will be the least of our worries." She glanced at the windows. "Something is moving out there and we are only the smallest part of it. But we are a part, and we shall have a role to play."

The instances in which her talent surfaced were rare, and he had always found her uncanny during them. What he had not expected was to be able to now sense it: less a color and more a powerful taste, a smell, a reaching that washed over his skin and past it, seeking. His skin prickled.

"Is there anything I might do?" he asked when the tide rushed back into her and left her tired and frustrated.

"There is, at that. When we come out the other side of this, assuming we are in any condition to enjoy it . . . play for me."

He had not played music since Laiselin's death. But set against the magnitude of what lay before them, it seemed a small gift to promise. He rose and bowed his head, one hand spread on his chest. "I will see to my calluses."

That made her smile, which pleased him. On his way back to his borrowed room, he reflected on how swiftly it had begun to matter to him, that he could make his cousin smile. Araelis's suggestion remained ludicrous, but his affection for Liolesa was real. Even when she was exasperating him by sending him to tag along after a human woman like a child in leading strings, as if attendance on a woman might cure him of his grief.

It manifestly had not. And yet he found himself remembering Reese's skeptical looks at the strangest moments, and the occasional softening of her eyes that made him wonder at what she would be like were she not in a state of perpetual agitation.

Did she really want to live here? Where was Liolesa thinking of putting her? Here in the capital? How would that even work?

He was distracted by the question when he entered his room and stopped rather abruptly at the sight of the woman sitting on the stool by his cot.

"So you really are staying here. I could scarcely credit the rumor but everyone insisted it was so, that you had returned but eschewed a place with your House despite carrying the swords." Surela rose, twitching her skirts as if to rid them of dirt. "Though it is a bit mean, don't you think? There is such a thing as too much humility, particularly for a man of your estate, Lord Hirianthial."

"Lady, I am not set up to receive guests," he said. "Indeed, you should not be here without a chaperone—"

"Oh so?" she said. "Shall I worry about a rumor of the two of us alone together? Would you wed me to save my reputation, if it was bruited about that you had ruined me?"

His skin stippled. "I assure you, Lady, I have no

intention of setting a hand on you."

"Are you sure?" she asked, smiling. "I wouldn't be disappointed if you did. Your pretty little Butterfly seemed so happy with you . . . that implies something about your ability to please a woman."

Hearing her call Laiselin by her song-name made him flex his hands where they rested clasped behind his back. "Is there something I might do for you?"

"You turned down Jisiensire's hospitality, so I had hopes that perhaps you were at liberty to seek new association," Surela said. "And I might have found some way to entice you to consider the notion. I know you don't like me, Hirianthial, but there would have been compensations. But now I hear there might be another reason you're pretending to a cot in the priest's quarters. Tell me it's not true—that you are consorting with a mortal woman."

"I beg your pardon?" Hirianthial said, startled, for she had shaded the word 'consorting' in the language's crimson mode, which left its carnal meaning without doubt.

"Consorting," she said again, advancing on him. "With a human. I know Liolesa's keeping her in the palace. And you've been with her."

"I pledge you, lady," Hirianthial said dryly, "if I have been consorting with a human woman in the manner you are intimating, I would be as shocked as you to learn it."

"So you deny it."

"Denial presumes guilt," Hirianthial said. "Shall I confess to a sin I have not committed?"

"At least you still think of it as a sin," Surela said. "In public, anyway." She stopped before him. "I would have welcomed you at my side before I knew you preferred the company of mortals to that of people. I am almost grateful to Liolesa for exposing this facet of your character to me."

"I am entirely grateful if it has at last disabused you of

the notion that I might have ever accepted your suit," he said. "And it is said 'the Queen,' not 'Liolesa'—by you, Lady."

She smiled without humor. "Good night, Lord Hirianthial."

He shut the door on her without returning the well-wishes and sat on the cot more abruptly than he'd planned as he realized just how close he'd come to disaster. God and Lady! The cheek of the woman, coming here alone and threatening to corral him into an unwanted union with a false accusation! He would be shaking with the chill of the adrenaline aftermath if he weren't so distracted by the thought of how Reese would have reacted to Surela's assumptions. Indignation, certainly. He smiled. Ah, but she would have ripped a strip off Surela's hide for saying such things. He would have liked to see it.

"This is not underwear," Reese growled. "This is a torture device."

"This is a necessary part of a lady's wardrobe," Felith said, at work behind Reese's back. Whatever she was doing involved the hissing sound of laces pulling through metal rings and constant tugging and tightening.

Irine, watching from the floor with her cheek in one palm, said, "Is this the kind that needs a set of ribs removed?"

"Don't even joke about that," Reese said. Then, concerned, "Wait, is it?"

"Of course not, Lady. Surgery is too dangerous to risk for vanity."

"They might not need it. For all we know they have fewer ribs than humans," Kis'eh't said. "Starting from a human template doesn't mean they didn't tinker with things like that."

Irine wrinkled her nose. "Who would tinker with genetics just to make it easier to get into a corset?"

"Same people who thought junking all their technology when they got here was a good idea?" the Glaseah replied, dry.

"All right, you two, that's enough," Reese said—wheezed. It was getting hard to breathe. "Felith, is it supposed to be that tight?"

"It should be tighter yet. It's wise to go in stages, however." Felith leaned back. "Breathe up and down, Lady. Not in and out."

"What the hell does that mean?"

"I think that thing's going to make her even more short-tempered than she usually is," Kis'eh't observed.

"That should be okay," Irine said. "She needs to be feisty, she's got a hall full of bigots and racists to face."

Reese covered her face. "Can we not make me nervous?"

"You will do excellently," Felith said unexpectedly. Surprised, Reese looked over her shoulder, and the Eldritch met her eyes. "You will, Lady. You do not seem the sort to quail in the face of the contempt of others."

"That's Reese," Kis'eh't agreed. "The worser the odds, the harder she plays."

"She's stubborn," Irine said with more pride than Reese would have thought the comment merited. It made her flush.

"Would that more of us had such virtues," Felith said. "Perhaps we would not be in our current contretemps." She leaned back. "There. How do you feel, Lady?"

"Like I'm going to faint," Reese said, pressing her hand against her stomach. It resisted, so she knocked on it. "Blood, are you sure this is lingerie? It's more like armor. Also, it's digging into my hips, is that normal?"

"It is neither lingerie nor armor," Felith said firmly. "It is an undergarment, and the best fit I could procure without more time. You are shorter in the torso than we are, so some pinching is inevitable until we have one made to your measure."

"You have got to be kidding me," Reese muttered. "I need one of these permanently?"

"It's an *undergarment*."

"It's a bother, and I'm not going to wear one anymore than is strictly necessary," Reese said. Or tried, anyway. It was more of a wheeze, given how little air she had. "So, I'm announced, and I go to the throne, about two-thirds of the way, and then I stop and curtsey—"

"That's right."

"And I hold it until she calls me up," Reese said. She paused. "That sounds uncomfortable. What do men do?"

"Men bow and keep their heads down," Felith said.

"That's better," Reese said. "I'll do that. So she calls me—"

"You cannot bow like a man!" Felith exclaimed, scandalized. "You are a woman!"

"I'm a woman who will probably fall down if she has to hold a curtsey for longer than a second," Reese said.

"Can you even bow with that thing on?" Kis'eh't said.

Reese tried it, regretted the dizzy head it gave her. "Yes, from the hips. Ouch."

"Do it more slowly," Kis'eh't said.

"Slowly, got it." Reese turned back to Felith. "And then the dialogue starts—what? Felith? I'm not actually an Eldritch, remember? I'm already breaking a million customs by existing on this world, adding one more isn't going to make much of a difference."

Felith sighed. "And then the dialogue begins, and you answer as you have been coached. And then you bring forth the gifts."

"Are you sure we shouldn't go with you?" Irine asked. "We can carry the gifts for you. It will look more impressive, right?"

Reese didn't understand the source of her discomfort, but it was a powerful one. "It would, but . . . I think one alien's bad enough. Adding more of them seems like it would be pressing our luck."

Irine and Kis'eh't glanced at Felith, who said, "That is a fair point, I am afraid. Let the shock settle from the first event, and then the Queen will no doubt have your entourage formally introduced later in a more intimate court function, one more likely to be peopled with your allies." She stepped back and studied Reese. "I will leave you to warm the fabric while I bring the seamstresses."

"The what?" Reese asked.

"The seamstresses. The dress will have to be altered to suit you, Lady."

Reese sighed. "I bet that'll take all morning."

"Yes," Felith said. "But you will only have to stand for part of it. The rest of the time we will spend preparing. And by that I mean grooming you." She eyed Reese. "I presume you understand what I mean by that."

Thinking ruefully of her romance novels, Reese said, "I have a few ideas, yes."

"Good," Felith said, and excused herself.

"You could at least take Allacazam," Irine said. "Call him a pillow, or an exotic animal or something. You should have some moral support, Reese. These aren't nice people you're going to be walking into the middle of."

"If Hirianthial's right, only half of them aren't nice people," Reese said. "The other half will be happy to see me." She sat, wincing as the corset gouged her bones. Trying for a deep breath failed, so she settled for a long, shallow one. "It's only a few hours, and then it will be done and we'll be able to move on from here to whatever it is that's next for us." Before she could think better of it, she reached for their hands and took them. "Thanks for sticking it out with me."

Irine hugged her, and Kis'eh't squeezed her hand.

"While I'm gone, make sure Allacazam eats, all right?"

"We will," Kis'eh't promised, and rose. "And now I'll leave you two to the primping process. I'll go talk to Malia about sending down those extra gifts for the presentation." She brushed off her forelegs. "I wish Pads could scoop you up from where you were. It would be much easier to go up to the *Earthrise* and get my sari myself than it's going to be describing where it is to Malia."

"Can you Pad a Pad someplace you don't have one?" Irine wondered.

"I thought the Fleet people did that when they came over after the pirates," Reese said, frowning. "But my memory of that situation's bad."

"If they did I bet it's some special Fleet model the rest of us can't get," Kis'eh't said. "I'm off. Maybe I can find some little jeweled box to put the cinnamon in."

Irine set a hand on Reese's arm once the Glaseah had gone. "It's going to be all right, you know."

Reese set her hand on Irine's and petted the soft gold and black fur. "You think so?"

"You remember back on Harat-Sharii when you told us we were leaving early?"

"And you said you knew you weren't coming back because it was your destiny, and Sascha's," Reese said. She looked up. "You think this is it?"

"I don't know," Irine said. "But taking on a closed world in need of renovation sure sounds like an epic undertaking to me." She smiled. "Besides, even if the rest of the world doesn't have marble stairwells carved with pretty girls and boys and lacy chandeliers, it still seems like a nice place to make a nest."

Reese stared at her. "It's cold."

"You said yourself back when we were trying to decide where to go for our vacation that cold makes you want to cuddle under blankets and drink hot chocolate and tell stories," Irine said. "I could see doing that with my kits." She grinned. "Besides, we're going to have heaters, remember?"

"When you put it that way . . ." Reese imagined it and smiled. "I think it would be nice to be Aunt Reese to a passel of Harat-Shar."

Irine laughed. "You wouldn't have said that a year ago!"

"A year ago I wasn't who I am today," Reese said. She breathed out carefully, feeling the bones of the corset flex. It was easy to blame it for her dizziness and pounding heart, but she knew better. She had always been so good at denying her own feelings, but her crew's affection had worn her down, and the past year had almost entirely shattered her barriers against that intimacy. Now she could see the shape of her heart's desire, and she wanted very much to look away before all the details were filled in and left her with no chance at all of turning back. "And I'm a little afraid of who I'm going to end up being."

Irine lifted a hand and paused . . . then set it carefully on Reese's cheek, curving soft fingers into her braids. "It's going to be all right. We'll be here to help you."

Reese closed her eyes and shuddered. "All right. All right. Thank you."

Irine hugged her, and this time Reese rested against the tigraine.

Urise was not in the library the following morning, and though Hirianthial waited half an hour for him, he did not arrive. Concerned, he returned to the priest quarters in the palace to ask after him, only to be told that Urise had resumed living in the Cathedral dormitories after retiring as palace priest and that he would have to seek the priest there.

He drew on the fur-lined cloak and gloves and left in search of his teacher. The Cathedral was walking distance from Ontine, but he wanted to waste no time and the weather, if he was any judge, was finally working itself toward either another cold rain or the first moist snow of the season. He had a horse brought around and rode, hooves clattering on the stone road, out beneath the gates and the louring gray sky. The wet and bitter wind drove him before it, all the way to the spires of Ontine Cathedral, its buttresses a grimy shade against a sky white with diffuse clouds. The gloom cast deep shadows over the stained glass windows, leaving only glints to suggest their magnificence, blood ruby, darkwater sapphire, a flash of lion's gold.

He could have married in this cathedral, by right of blood and Queen's favor. But he'd chosen instead the more intimate family chapel at Jisiensire's country seat. Dismounting now before the marble steps that rose higher than he was tall, he thought it strange that Urise should choose to live here when he seemed more akin to that atmosphere than to the overwhelming elegance of a cathedral large enough to seat the entirety of the capital during the high holy days.

One did not enter the cathedral proper on a casual errand. He went to the side entrance and was greeted there by a novice in the robes of the God, the arm devoted to ordinary services. The youth took his message and left him to wait in the narrow foyer. He sat on one of the benches that lined it and thought ruefully that it had probably been left bare of cushion to discourage petitioners—or to mortify them.

The novice did not return. Instead a full priest in the dark carmine of the Lord—the arm given over to the mysteries—came to him with a tale that Urise had taken ill.

"Ill?" Hirianthial said, rising. "Please, show me to him. I am a doctor."

The priest's pause was almost imperceptible. "It is nothing a doctor need concern himself with. Merely a flux, it will pass."

"Flux in the elderly can be dangerous," Hirianthial said. "Please. Allow me to attend him. It will take only a moment."

"We appreciate your offer," the priest said. "But he should not be disturbed. He is resting."

"I won't wake him. If you'll allow me to return to the palace for my instruments? I will be back in half an hour."

Now at last he came to the moment he'd been expecting since the man arrived with the story. "The Church can take care of its own, thank you. When the Elder is once again receiving we will send for you."

Hirianthial said, "Of course. Tell him I asked after him, please."

"Lord Hirianthial. We shall."

They wouldn't, because Urise wasn't sick. The only question that remained was what exactly had happened to his mentor, and why. A blood-robed priest suggested his brother's involvement, if Liolesa's intelligence on the matter was correct: he had come home, someone had told Baniel, and Baniel had learned that he was meeting regularly with Urise. It would be very like Baniel to attempt to block those meetings, whether he knew their purpose or not.

But if he did. . . .

He could force his way into the cathedral and try to find Urise, but there were catacombs beneath the capital and the most extensive ones were here, beneath Ontine and its cathedral, near the edge of the sea cliff. He could

lose himself in that warren and never find a way out again
. . . and when he extended his senses in a hesitant probe, he
found the entire building impervious to his investigation.
How had they done that? And could he learn? He ran an
invisible hand over its surface, admiring the work despite
its frustrating his aims.

So he left. Pulled himself onto the dull mount he'd borrowed from the palace stables and sent it cantering back
to Ontine, where he dismounted stiff from the wet chill.
He returned to his borrowed room and sent for a bath to
begin his preparations for the second day of court.

He had just finished dressing when a curt knock
announced a guest several seconds before that guest
slipped in, and there was Belinor, looking pale and breathless. "My lord, forgive me but they have taken the Elder!"

Hirianthial reached for his sword belt. "Tell me."

"When I woke up this morning he was already gone,
and they tried to tell me he'd taken ill but refused to allow
me to attend him. That was the first warning because what
is a novice for but to care for his tutor? So I left, and snuck
back in later to see if I could hear something, and they've
taken him, they took him to the viewing chambers!" At
Hirianthial's blank look, he said, "They use those for the
interrogation of mind-mages!"

"And there have been so many of those?" he
asked, startled.

Belinor scowled. "Of course not. They only take people
there they say are mind-mages, and then use that as an
excuse to kill them."

"Do you know the way?" Hirianthial asked.

"Yes!"

"Then I follow."

The palace catacombs could be accessed from the
chapel storeroom, and it was there Belinor led him; true

to his claims, he was fleet-footed, and it didn't take long for them to find themselves in the maze. No one knew what had hollowed the corridors out of the cliffside, but they'd been in use since the first Queen of the Eldritch had set down from the ship, and there were signs still of occupancy even in the most desolate corners. And always, in every nook, one heard the occasional whistle of a high, thin wind, trammeled off the ocean.

Canny Belinor stopped him at intervals; when Hirianthial realized he was listening for people, he began to extend his senses to help. In this way, they moved toward the edge of the cliff until at last they reached their hall.

It was guarded, naturally.

"There," Belinor whispered after they'd drawn back. "He'll be in one of those chambers. We have to get him out!"

It would have been impolite to reach for the priest's mind, but Hirianthial could at least grasp toward a sense of his presence, and that he found too easily: Urise was conscious and in pain.

His eyes narrowed.

Belinor, having crept toward the corner again, brought from beneath his robes a belt-knife. Before he could have himself killed, Hirianthial said, "Stay you, prithee."

"We can't leave him here!"

"No," Hirianthial said. "We can't. And we will not." He rested his back to the wall and drew in a long slow breath. On the exhale, he let his consciousness seep outward, gather all the glows of other minds. He cupped the first and began to dim it, trembling with the delicacy of it, until it went from aware to unconscious. In the corridor, amid the whisper of the wind on the floor, he heard someone fall.

He slid to the ground and began again. There were only six people to attend to, and fortunately four of them were in separate rooms. The fifth and sixth he had to do at the same time, and he was not altogether sure he would be capable. The consequences if he failed and snuffed one permanently—

Two final thumps in the hall. He breathed out. "Go."

Belinor darted past him, the wind of his passage pulling at the lace at Hirianthial's throat. It was damp; he would have to change before court if he wanted to be presentable.

He did not mark the time, only his exhaustion, how cold the stone was beneath him, how his joints throbbed, as if the effort had exacerbated the ache that had begun to dog them in the past few decades. But Belinor returned with Urise hobbling alongside him, and Hirianthial rose. He didn't have to look at the priest to feel the extent of his injuries.

"Back to my room," he said, anger clipping the words.

It took more time to return but they did, and Belinor laid his master gently on Hirianthial's cot. The medical tools he'd brought from the *Earthrise* were no replacement for a true Medplex, but they were far and away more than any Eldritch would hope to see in a lifetime on the homeworld. Hirianthial put them to use. He was washing his hands when Urise opened his eyes.

"Sa," Hirianthial said, bringing his fingers to the priest's mouth without touching them. "Rest. You need not speak."

"No," Urise said, hoarse. "I am afraid I must, my son."

"Then if you must, use your inner voice and spare your body the effort. I grant you permission."

Urise's mental chuckle sounded dusty. *Very well, my son. I will not argue with a doctor.*

"Good," Hirianthial said, and began stripping his sweat-stained coat. "What is it then that is so urgent?"

Your brother knows why you have come to me.

Hirianthial paused. More slowly, he resumed unbuttoning his blouse. "My brother, who is charged with the removal of excess talents."

Just so.

Belinor handed him a damp cloth, and he began using it to towel himself off, absently, his mind elsewhere.

"What is the usual procedure? Do you know?" he asked at last.

For what? The disposal? I imagine it involves disappearing the guilty. The process is not witnessed. If it were, no one would permit it, no matter the memory of Corel.

"Then we don't know what he'll do next," Hirianthial murmured. He frowned. What was Baniel planning?

"My lord," Belinor said, "you will be late for court if you do not dress faster."

"Is it so close to the hour already?" He looked toward his time candle and started. "God and Lady."

"Let me help you," Belinor said. "I have some experience with it."

"Please," Hirianthial said, and endured the feather-soft brushes of the youth's mind that came with his fingers on the buttons: pale impressions of worry and anger and worry again. When Belinor reached for the brush, he held out a hand. "Not that." As he settled with it, he said, "Run now to the White Swords. Tell Olthemiel or Beronaeth that I am entrusting your master to their care. Make sure he's guarded while I'm gone."

"Yes, Lord!" Belinor exclaimed, and flashed from the room.

Is that necessary? Urise asked. *They are quit of all use of me.*

"I don't know that they are," Hirianthial said. "So I will assume that they are not." He went to a knee beside the priest in the cot and rested a long hand on its edge. "For what they did to you, I am deeply sorry, Elder."

It was not your fault, Urise said and huffed, an audible

one through the throat. *In older days I would have seen him coming and I certainly wouldn't have let him find out about you. But your brother is very good with shields and better at going into minds.* He looked at Hirianthial. *He's very strong. Don't underestimate him.*

"I won't," Hirianthial promised.

Belinor skidded back in. "They're coming, and you will be late!"

"I go," Hirianthial said. "But I will return."

I'll be here, Urise said, closing his eyes. *Don't fear on that count.*

He ran then, because Belinor was right; he was late. Not for the court, for he had discharged the formalities on the first day, and could now come and go to the remaining sessions at his leisure. But he had not wanted Reese to be without escort to her presentation. She knew so few people, and would perceive herself to be with so few allies. To deprive her of a friendly face . . . he couldn't countenance it. Not only that, but now he had the additional worry of what his brother planned to do with his new knowledge. Hirianthial couldn't imagine him choosing a confrontation before the court, but he had been wrong about Baniel before.

He reached the stairs, took them two at a time, and paused on the second floor long enough to catch his breath and straighten his clothes before striding down the hall for her suite. He must present the proper semblance of composure, so as not to exacerbate her anxieties. She would need him.

Irine opened the door at his knock. "Oh, good, you came!" She beamed, ears perked. "And you look so handsome!"

"I am glad I am on time," he said. "Where is—"

But she was there, by the fireplace, talking with Sascha

while Felith straightened a few folds here and there on the skirting of a dark blue gown . . . and she looked beautiful because it suited her: suited her carriage, her unapologetic forthrightness, the neatness of her figure, compact but strong. Her aura was like a cloak to mantle the richness of her clothes, sparkling with excitement and pleasure, and if there was a tremor of nervousness in it, it served only to make the colors shimmer.

He was painfully struck by the thought that she might not need him after all. She could walk into that hall and take on every contemptuous courtier in it, and all their disdain would only make her more determined to follow through on her course.

And then she saw him, and the glitter of her aura erupted over a bright coral color warm as flesh and soft as skin, and he nearly backed away at his reaction to it. Instead, he managed, "Lady. You look truly lovely."

Reese resisted the urge to look down, make sure she hadn't missed any tiny button or fold. She'd assumed he'd realize she was planning to go in a dress, but from the look on his face—as obvious as any she'd ever seen on him—he hadn't. She hoped he didn't think she was trying to mimic the culture, or give offense or . . . or . . .

And then he spoke, and she exhaled. Painfully, since her ribs hated her for the corset. "Oh, I'm so glad you're not upset."

Behind Hirianthial, Irine put her face in her hand.

"Upset!" He said, and drew closer. "No, Lady. Not at all."

"And now," Reese said, hesitant, "I put out the wand, like this?" She glanced at Felith, who nodded one of those almost imperceptible Eldritch nods. "And that lets you touch it to greet me. Right?"

He rested two fingers on the wand, a jeweled thing in

bronze that Felith had lent her. "If I am a good acquaintance. If I am a stranger, I use the haft of my knife."

"And if you're a friend?" Sascha said from behind Reese.

"If I am a friend . . ." He trailed off, asking with his eyes. She nodded, trying not to look as nervous as she was. "Then you permit me to rest my hand on yours, thus."

The touch of his gloved fingers on her wrist made her heart race. It was because he was beautiful, like something out of a story in his fine dark coat and swords . . . just like a faerie king, who stole away some mortal woman to live outside of time with him beneath a hollow hill. Except the women in those stories always suffered, and the faeries lived forever without them. She wondered what in all hell she was doing, having palpitations at the touch of someone who would never—he was so far beyond her. This was not one of her stories. She was not a princess. Gowns did not make poor human girls from Mars into royalty.

"And I bow over it, if I feel inclined to do you honor," Hirianthial finished, and put action to words. His hair slid over his shoulder, and there, exposed, was the dangle the crew had made for him. It was his only ornament, gleaming rose and steel and glass.

Faerie king or not, he was still their friend. He might never be more than that, but at the very least . . . they had touched him. How many in the Alliance could say such a thing? Understanding that, she could breathe again. Well, as much as the corset permitted.

"And then," Sascha said from behind her, "You go, because you'll be late."

"Right," Reese said. "The bag—thank you, Kis'eh't." She looked in it: tablet, apple, vial. "All right, I've got everything. Hirianthial? Where do we go?"

"This way," he said, and led her out as the crew wished her well. She hated closing the door on their faces, and the silence in the hall felt oppressive, made her far too aware of how exposed she felt in the fragile gown, armored corset or not. She followed Hirianthial and struggled to master her emotions, and was so busy with that she almost didn't notice him pausing in the stairwell.

"You sure it's not presumptuous?" she asked, to have something to say.

But he sounded confused at the question. "I beg your pardon?"

"Dressing like one of you," she said.

"I was just noting that you are not entirely so, are you?" he said as he resumed his descent.

"Oh, you mean the boots?" Reese grimaced. "I have to pull this thing up to keep from tripping on it going down the steps. You weren't supposed to see those."

He flashed her a sudden, surprising smile over his shoulder, so candid it made her heart flutter. "I'm glad I did." Before she could ask, he finished, "No doubt some will find your very presence presumptuous. Your manner of dress will only serve as punctuation to that sentence. The rest of us will find it quite appropriate." They gained the ground floor and swept through one of the echoingly empty halls, and the further they went the more a vague buzzing sound began to fill it. "Do not fear, Lady. You will acquit yourself magnificently."

The buzz was conversation. Her skin contracted to gooseflesh. How many people were in the hall to make that much noise? "I will?"

"I have faith," he said, and paused at the door, edging it open and leaning toward the crack to listen.

"Am I late?" she asked, hushed.

"Not at all," he murmured. "We have a few minutes." He faced her and extended his hands to her.

Shocked, she stared at him, then glanced up at him.

"You're not serious?"

He lifted his brows, awarded her one of his faint smiles.

So she set her palms on his, felt him curl his fingers around her entire hand—she hadn't realized how much longer his hands were than hers. "Reese," he said, gentle. "Thank you for doing this."

"W-what?" she said. "Thank *me*? Why?"

"You have chosen to throw your lot in with my people's," he said. "It was not necessary. But I believe you can do a great deal of good here."

"Me," she repeated, her mouth dry.

"You," he agreed.

"Stubborn, pig-headed, cactus-prickly, constantly underfunded, not-so-great at succeeding me," Reese said, just to make sure he knew who he was complimenting.

"You," he said. "Courageous, faithful, generous, practical, persevering-despite-the-odds you." He paused, made a play at looking thoughtful. "But stubborn, I will give you that."

The comment made her laugh; like the dangle in his hair, it made him real, and that made the rest of the litany . . . true. To him, anyway. Her resolve stiffened and she squared her shoulders. "Well if you think so, then I can hardly back down, can I?"

"I have not known you to do so yet," he said.

Did he squeeze her hands before he dropped them? She thought he did. But then he was opening the door on a trumpet fanfare and there in front of her was a glittering hall to shame all her imaginings, and in it hundreds of pale-faced faeries wearing their riches like glamours out of stories.

Human steel had always trumped faerie magic. Reese set her face and marched in.

She wasn't sure what she was expecting: whispers,

maybe? But for the first half of the walk, she couldn't hear anything over the brass announcing her, and on the last half, the silence in the hall was so absolute she could hear her own blood pulsing in her ears. Once, she thought, there was a rustle, someone's gown or coat shifting, but that was it. She didn't allow herself to look right or left. Forward, that was it. Forward, where Liolesa was waiting for her with an expression Reese thought was encouraging; the Queen's face was smooth as a mask, but her eyes were warm, almost mischievous.

If the Queen could take this in the proper spirit, she could too. Reese stopped at the right distance—she hoped—and bowed, since even Felith had agreed that a curtsey that would reveal her very common boots was out of the question. As her heart raced, she waited for permission to straighten and wondered what everyone around her was thinking. A willowy, light-skinned human might have briefly passed for an Eldritch maiden, maybe. But Reese was neither pale nor tall nor skinny. She couldn't imagine how long it had been since the average Eldritch had seen someone like her in person.

"Rise, Captain Eddings."

She did, lifting her head.

"Why have you requested this audience?"

A hiss ran through the crowd: people's clothes moving, their gasps or whispered exclamations. The presentation of retainers began with Liolesa introducing her. Only ladies and lords requesting acknowledgement as vassals were asked their business.

That they were conducting a ritual as old as Eldritch Settlement in Universal was only the beginning of the upset.

"I come to offer suit to you, as the seal-holder for House Galare and sovereign over all Eldritch," Reese answered.

Now the gasps were audible, and the murmur of

conversation began, punctuated by impatient hushes.

Liolesa was enjoying herself, if Reese was any judge. "And what would you bring, did I accept this suit?"

Her hands were shaking, but she managed the velvet bag Felith had hung from a jeweled belt at her waist and brought the first thing out without dropping it. She held up the apple first for Liolesa, then showed it to everyone around her. "I offer foods from far-off lands, luxuries and treasures for the palate. I would make your orchards rich and your larders full with the fruits of our labors." Because bringing them in cargo holds counted, she assumed.

"We are intrigued," Liolesa said. "Is that the extent of your wealth?"

"No, Lady," Reese said. She withdrew the vial and opened it. "I also bring exotic spices. Cinnamon, nutmeg, feldhar, grains of paradise, and many others, to add to food, incense and perfume."

"May we smell?" Liolesa asked.

"Please," Reese said, and handed the vial to a page, who brought it to the throne. Liolesa made much of smelling it, eyes closing.

"We are pleased," she said. "Is that the extent of your wealth?"

Now for the final gift. Reese drew in a breath and brought out her data tablet, which Bryer had spent most of the night prying apart to make it capable of the demonstration she'd been planning. She started to bend down, discovered she couldn't around the corset, and wobbled a little as she went to a knee instead to set it on the ground. Then she tapped it and stepped back.

Even she was impressed with how the solidigraphic stallion seemed to leap from the ground. While the jury-rigging her Phoenix engineer had done to enable her ancient tablet to offer solidigraphic projections didn't include smells or heat like something powered by a gem grid could have, it was capable of a life-size solidigraph, one so convincing all the Eldritch lining the carpet to the Queen backpedaled, and several cried out. The projection snorted and pawed the stone ground, then settled, tail whisking around its legs.

"My Lady, if you agree, I will bring you horses, and use them to improve the breed strength of your herds."

The sigh that went through the hall then . . . that was a good sound. Reese decided to see if she could compound it by walking to the projection and resting a hand on its neck, and it worked. These people had no defense against technology; this was magic to them.

"This is a promise of horses to come?" Liolesa asked as the crowd murmured and moved, with people in the back struggling for a chance to see.

"They will look like this one," Reese said. "I also have access to swift coursers, powerful farm horses, destriers to carry a knight into battle . . . even ponies for children."

That sigh was avarice. She didn't even have to look at the people staring at her to feel it. No matter what they thought of her, they definitely wanted the horses.

"Food, spices, and horses," Liolesa said. "Is that the extent of your wealth, Lady Eddings?"

Lady Eddings! The words lanced through her, shocking as pain, and in the wake of them she felt clean and bright and present. The hall seemed larger, more brilliant; the moment dearer and more important, as if she stood at a tipping point.

"No, lady," Reese said. "I also bring the gifts of the out-world. Heat in winter, and cold in summer. Roofs that don't leak or fall. Roads in good repair." She drew in a deep breath and spoke louder, over the growing murmurs around her. "Books for everyone to read, not just the wealthy. People to tend your orchards, fix your cities, and map your world. I will not bring you more than you wish, in respect for your customs—I am not here to remake you in the Alliance's image. But within the parameters you set, Lady, if you make me your vassal . . . I will help you change your world."

A heartbeat pause, of shock, of waiting. Liolesa's eyes were fierce and glad and just a little dangerous.

"Lady Eddings—I accept."

In a book, the hall would have erupted into tumult. This one didn't. The stillness stretched and stretched, so painfully that Reese thought her nerves would break before it did. Liolesa let it extend, and at last said, "Come forth and accept the gift of your liege-lady."

Felith had mentioned this part, that Liolesa would give her a present to formalize the new relationship. A token, usually: a medallion, like the one the Queen had already given her, or a wand to symbolize her new status. Reese picked up the data tablet and put it away, then approached the throne to receive it with her hands, as she was now allowed, expecting a pin or some other piece of jewelry.

Liolesa gave her a scroll.

"Your Majesty?" Reese asked, low.

"Open it," Liolesa said, loud enough for the people around them to hear.

She stepped back and picked the knot free, then unrolled the parchment. It was . . . a map. Staring at the atlas with Kis'eh't allowed her to place it as a part of the northern coast. "My Lady?"

"A vassal who will bring us the fruit of her orchards and the progeny of her pastures needs a place to site them," Liolesa said. "For your liege gift, I deed you with the lands once held by House Firilith, in the north." The shock in the room this time came with exclamations, and even without knowing the language Reese could tell they were outraged.

She couldn't blame them; she was shaking. But the Queen had not finished. "Hear now the first commandment of your Queen, Lady Eddings. You are to repair to Firilith no later than the end of winter, to the estate of Rose Point, where you are to establish the new House of Laisrathera, of which you will be seal-bearer. There are Eldritch living there yet in need of a lady; introduce yourself to them and begin at once your duties as land-holder and caretaker. Your vassal gifts will be due to me at this time next year . . . and I expect at least one horse. Or two."

Could she speak? Her voice broke on the first word, but she got the rest out. "Perhaps Her Majesty would be more content with five or six. Or . . ." Yes, this might be a good idea, "if it pleases her, perhaps House Laisrathera will make a gift of one each of its first horses to each of the Houses who owe her allegiance."

"That is a generous gift," Liolesa said. "Are you certain of it?"

"I am." And she was. Half these people probably wanted to murder her, but she could at least set their greed at war with their prejudices; it might give her all of half a year to work before they came after her with their pitchforks.

"Then I am agreed," Liolesa said. "We welcome the newest addition to the peerage." She stepped down off her throne, and the rest of the gathering dissolved into mingling as if cued.

Reese remained where she was because she wasn't sure if her knees would hold her if she tried to walk. The Queen joined her, bending toward her to murmur, "You like my gift?"

"Are you sure it was a wise gift?" Reese asked.

"I don't know," Liolesa said, eyes sparkling. "Was it?"

"Your Majesty—"

"My Lady will do in public."

"My Lady," Reese said, trying to keep her voice low. "Isn't this giving your enemies a little too much provocation?"

"Theresa, Theresa." The Queen shook her head, the minute motion of an Eldritch. "You yourself offered to become a vassal. What did you think that entailed?" She grinned. "Chin up, my own. You can't do any worse at the duty than some of the people here."

Reese stared after the woman as she swanned away, trailing her aura of complete confidence behind her. Blood and soil, what she most needed now was a dose of reality and . . . here it came. She carefully didn't look up at Hirianthial as she said beneath her breath, "Tell me the Queen didn't just make me a noble landowner."

"And if she did?"

That he sounded pleased, amused, gentle . . . if he hadn't, she might have fled. But he approved. How could he approve? After all these months of telling them nothing of himself, of his people, to go from that to being fine with her living here? Raising horses here! She didn't even know one end of a horse from the other!

"Hirianthial, I . . . I can't do this."

"Can't you?" he said.

"I'm not one of you!"

"Do you have to be?"

She looked down at the map rolled in her hand.

"Laisrathera," he added. "It means 'earthrise.'"

Reese choked on her nervous laugh, pressed a hand to her mouth.

"And here is my newest sister!" Araelis said, gliding toward her and offering her wand. Reese fumbled for hers, gave up and touched it lightly with her fingertips. "Welcome to the peerage, sister."

"Uh, thanks," Reese said.

"You seem surprised," Araelis said, grinning. "Don't tell

me the Queen dropped this on you without warning?"

"It's more like . . . maybe I didn't understand the implications of what I was agreeing to," Reese said, rueful.

"Most of life is like that, I've found. And I've lived a long time." Araelis motioned with her wand. "Go on, cousin. My new kin-sister and I should speak about being a seal-holder for the Queen."

"I remind you I was a seal-holder before you," Hirianthial said.

"Yes, but you're a man, and while you're around I must constrain myself to polite speech," Araelis said. "You can have her back when I'm done. Look, Liolesa is lonely. Go be a former White Sword for her."

"Araelis—"

Araelis lifted her brows.

Hirianthial sighed and touched his palm to his chest, bowing to Reese. "Lady. Don't hesitate to seek me if you require me."

"Sure," Reese said, bewildered. "Of course."

And then he was gone . . . to the Queen's side, she noticed, where he seemed to fit as if socketed into the space at her right and slightly behind. They bent together to talk, and she noticed for the first time how close they allowed themselves to stand, even in public. She frowned and turned to Araelis. "What was that about?"

"Which part?" Araelis asked. She followed Reese's glance and said, "Ah. I had told you they were cousins?"

"Yes, but all of you seem related," Reese said, irritated. "I knew they were close, but . . . 'lonely'? Really? The Queen doesn't strike me as the type."

"Of course not," Araelis said, dismissive. "But they suit one another well. It would neatly solve a very many problems if they were to wed, not the least of which is the lack of an heir."

"I thought there was an heir?" Reese said. "At least, Felith mentioned serving one?"

"And you observe that Felith is now serving you," Araelis replied. "That would be because the current heir has been ruined by the Chatcaava. Her spirit is broken. She is too nervous now to sit a throne."

Reese stared at her, aghast. "You're telling me that she ended up in the empire?"

"As a slave, and nearly died of it," Araelis said, sober now. "She is at a convent, being guarded by the Chancellor—you have not met him yet, but you will—and there she will likely remain for the balance of her life." The woman looked toward the two. "They're of an age and have a long history together. He's guarded her life for several centuries as her White Sword captain. They're even fond of one another, and that is not something anyone can guarantee in a marriage. Traditionally we do not permit the wedding of cousins, but the Alliance can solve any genetic errors that might afflict the child they conceive." She sighed. "I have put the matter to them both, and of course it hasn't mattered until now because Hirianthial had no plans to come home. But now that he has . . ."

They did look good together. She forced herself to look away. "So. You said you might have advice for a new land-holder? Why don't you lay it on me?"

"Ah, I'd be delighted. Come, let's find something to drink. You'll have wine?"

"I will now," Reese said.

"You gave her Corel's demesne," Hirianthial murmured.

"I thought it an appropriate deed for the woman who brought me the first mind-mage since Corel," Liolesa replied, her voice so low he almost missed it.

He eyed her. The flow of the crowd had carried them to

a far corner where they were not likely to be overheard—
though watched, always that. By habit he kept his expression schooled and she was a master of it when it suited her,
and it did now.

"Do you disagree?" she said.

Did he? Reese's shock had been as intense as a lightning strike, so much so that he could still feel the waves
of it off her though the hall divided them. And beneath
the shock, something so painful he'd almost failed to recognize it for the joy she had not allowed herself to experience yet. Later, he knew, when it was real to her, when she
beheld the ruins of Rose Point and grasped that it was hers
to keep, the joy would surface, and with it excitement. For
so long, she'd done everything possible with what little she
had. To finally be freed of the constraints that had bound
her so long? To have all that she'd never dared allowed
herself to believe she might? The hard work of restoring it
wouldn't frighten her; it would simply make it more hers
when it was clean and bright again.

"No," he said. "I know she will do everything you
expect of her. But cousin . . . the hatred and the outrage
here, now, in this hall is overwhelming. And yet they have
said nothing."

"I know," Liolesa said, quiet. "I was expecting someone
to object long before I gave her the grant. Once I had . . ."

"They are waiting for something," Hirianthial said.

"Yes." Her eyes lost their focus briefly. "And it's so close.
But it hasn't come together yet." She looked up at him,
sharply. "What?"

"Asaniefa no doubt knew about Captain Eddings,
thanks to Thaniet," Hirianthial said. "My brother, I learned
this morning . . . knows about me."

"That you're here?" She frowned. "No. He has found
out why? How?"

"From Urise," Hirianthial said. "But neither of us knows what he will do with the knowledge."

Liolesa snorted. "Then you're a fool, cousin. He seeks your downfall. What else?"

"That is the question, isn't it? What else?" Hirianthial frowned, watching the crowd mingle, so different from an Alliance gathering with everyone standing so far apart. "I can't believe he would be motivated solely by revenge. It was not revenge alone that drove him to engineer our parents' death."

"He enjoyed seeing them die, is what you suggest."

"I think he enjoyed watching himself arrange for their deaths, and seeing it come to fruition just as he planned," Hirianthial said, feeling the words as he spoke them, tasting them for truth. They were bitter, but right.

"No doubt he is fast at work on it now, then," Liolesa said. "Have you told your Captain Eddings?"

"I fear Araelis has told her everything." He grimaced at the flash of a grin she allowed herself before the mask slipped back in place. "Yes, I know. But I suppose in this case it has been useful, Araelis and her feeling that she should be in everyone's business. She saved me the trouble of explaining a great deal."

"You should tell her—Theresa, that is—that Baniel knows your purpose, though," Liolesa said. "Your brother is many things, but stupid is not one of them. He'll assume you arrived with her, and that will make him . . . curious."

The thought made his skin run cold beneath the layers of silk and velvet. "I will find her directly."

"Good," Liolesa said. "And keep your step light. I feel the skein tightening."

"Always," he said. "God and Lady willing, though, we will be quit of this mess soon enough."

"And you can go show the Lady her new home, ah?"

Her tone had been casual, but that in itself spoke eloquently of her feelings on the matter. "If you are intimating something, cousin—"

"All I am intimating," she said, "is that you might enjoy being the one to witness her happiness when she sees it for the first time. After all the adventures the two of you have survived together, I thought you were owed that moment."

He could let it pass, so he did. "It would be a fine thing to see."

"You'll have to tell me all about it," she said. "I would love to be there myself, but I am hoping you'll be leaving for it long before I am free of this winter court."

"We shall see," he said, and went in search of Captain Eddings—now Lady Eddings in truth.

Araelis was exhausting. It wasn't that Reese didn't appreciate the mountain of advice, but she could barely hear it over the sound of her own head exploding. She was painfully aware of the looks she was receiving from far too many of the people around her, and while Eldritch stood a lot farther away from one another than normal people, there was no mistaking she was being avoided. Araelis introduced her to the few people who didn't seem to hate her, but their solicitous welcomes only made the seething outrage around her more obvious.

She didn't care that they hated her. Ma Eddings could have given every person in this room lessons in cutting looks. What bothered her was that she couldn't imagine their hatred not having repercussions, and she very much didn't want anything to disturb the fragile sense of hope she was struggling to protect. To lose what she'd been given before she could even believe she'd been given it . . . !

What she wanted most was her crew and Hirianthial and a private room where she could hyperventilate in peace, and maybe cry on a furry shoulder the way the tremor in her shoulders suggested she really wanted to. Barring that, she'd take Hirianthial right now, to keep her company among all these strangers. Knowing him he could feel her distress—couldn't he? He always had before—and was probably coming for her soon. She disengaged from Araelis and all her supporters and tried to find a quiet corner where she could sit on a cushioned bench and wait. There had to be one in a hall this size. She started walking, trying to stay out of the way of people who wanted an excuse to glare at her.

The wall she'd been heading for was not a wall at all, she discovered, but a curtain. She paused at it, wondering just how big the bleeding place was, when she heard him.

"Here, Lady."

Her relief was so vast she almost didn't feel the eagerness beneath it, running fast as a current. To keep from looking at that too closely, she stepped through the curtain. "Finally! I didn't know how long it would take to find you in this place. I had no idea how big it was." She paused at the view, wide-eyed. "Oh."

He didn't say anything; that was like him, to efface himself when there was something worth seeing. And the curtains had parted on an extension of the hall, a gallery partially built out over the still gray lake, and on its banks a powdering of snow that led to a wood out of a fairy tale, dark and knotted with shadows. Reese stepped to the balcony. "Oh . . . it's so beautiful. Is it okay to say that?"

When he didn't answer, she turned and froze at the sight. "You're not Hirianthial."

"No," the man said, and now that she was paying attention his voice was not an exact match, his baritone a little thinner in timbre. As he stepped into the light, she found that described the rest of him as well: very like Hirianthial, but just a little thinner, sharper, unfinished. He was also standing a lot closer to her than an Eldritch should. "No, that I most certainly am not. And it appears he hasn't told you about me."

"No," Reese said. "So maybe you could start with your name."

"I am Baniel, once Sarel Jisiensire," the man said with a smile, leaning down close enough so she could see the one thing about him that was very different: his eyes. His eyes were green as poison, and cold. "And that is all you need know of me, save this." His hands seized her waist and heaved her over the balcony, and the only thing that stopped her from screaming was that he came with her. The ground hit her far too hard and she scrabbled to rise first and failed; he had one hand on her mouth and the other holding her hands behind her. She tried to stamp on his foot and didn't connect; tried squirming and that didn't trouble him. The twins would have bitten him, so she tried that, but he just shook her by the head until the world spun.

She struggled when he started dragging her around the lake, but he seemed unfazed by her efforts. Was this how Hirianthial had felt all the times he had needed rescue? Reese decided she hated being on the other end. A brother! All the information Araelis had dumped on her with such glee, and yet she hadn't thought it important to mention that Hirianthial had a brother? An evil brother, apparently! And Hirianthial probably thought Araelis had said some-thing—blood and freedom! She'd as much told him so in the library!

But apparently this brother thought gagging her would be enough to keep her quiet. Little did he know. She cleared her thoughts of everything, of the smell of wet soil and snow, of the taste of Baniel's leather glove, of the bruises developing along her side where she'd struck the ground and the gouges the boning of the corset had opened in her skin along its edge. And then she screamed in her mind, where no one could hear her . . . except her Eldritch doctor.

The sound cut through the noise in his head, scattering his sense of every aura in the room but hers. Hirianthial excused himself from the conversation he'd been enduring with one of the neutral Houses and began walking. Not running—he didn't want to call attention to himself—but his pace quickened despite his best intentions. The only thing that kept him calm was that her scream had been less panic and more outrage. What had upset her? For Reese to call for him . . . it had to be something significant.

Again the yell, and the anger was more clearly developed, so much so that he heard a thought riding it: *I can't believe he thinks this will work*

The 'he' was a powerful flavor, the source of the outrage, and it felt like betrayal and indignation . . .

. . . and then he saw green eyes through hers, disorienting, powerfully so, like the afterimage of the sun in blinking eyes.

His hand flew to his sword and he dove through the curtain leading to the gallery, scanned the room—no one—lunged for the balcony and looked over it.

God and Lady . . . !

Baniel had left a trail plain as daylight through the snow, where Reese had been struggling. Squinting, he peered toward the forest's edge and spotted them approaching it. Where were the guards? And what did his brother think to accomplish, one man alone kidnapping a woman? Did he think to drag her into the woods to murder her there, then let the falling snow cover the evidence of their passage?

He had spared Baniel's life once, and he'd been wrong

to do it. It was time to correct his error.

Hirianthial went over the edge of the balcony and landed on his feet, ignoring the pain that lanced from his knees, unwelcome reminders that he was no longer the White Sword who'd been able to follow the indefatigable heir everywhere. He unknotted the cords on the sword as he ran the trail, his own rage mounting, redoubling, until it was hard to see. There was a word for men like his brother. *Gaienele.* Ruiner.

He was close enough to hear Reese's mind, a rushing river of anger that flowed into his until it overwhelmed him. The wrench of her arms where they were pinned behind her, he could feel in his own shoulders and elbows. The taste of leather in her mouth fouled his. He drew the sword and charged the last few yards in silence. When Baniel turned to him, it was too late to stay him—

—which is when the arrow struck him in the chest, just below the collarbone, with enough force to stagger him. Another followed, laming him. He fell to a knee, stunned.

Baniel bent toward him but didn't step closer, nor loose Reese whose angry chant had narrowed to a single screech: *he used me it was a trap*

Of course it was. Hirianthial lifted his head, struggling for breath. He felt for the wound at his chest, explored the edges. His sword arm was going numb, which suggested the arrow head had pierced the brachial plexus. The cervico-axillary canal was just under the clavicle . . .

His sword arm. Had it been an accident?

"I wasn't sure it would work," Baniel said, as if resuming a conversation. "Surela told me about her, of course, but you can't trust a woman to think clearly about another woman and the man she wants. I assumed you would at least feel something for her, but not enough to be quite so stupid." He paused. "Or was it me you had such strong feelings about?"

Hirianthial glared up through his hair, fighting the growing weakness. The blood spilling between his fingers was hotter than his skin.

"Well, it doesn't matter now," Baniel said.

Let him think so. Let him think the sword arm mattered. His strength was draining with every pulse of his heart, but he still had more than enough energy to deal with his brother and whatever archer he'd hired. He spread his awareness out, seeking . . . and froze.

"Ah, you've found them," Baniel said, smiling. "Good luck with that, brother." He shoved Reese in front of him and forced her to start walking as men armed with swords seeped out of the woods: two, four, seven . . .

It made no sense. Baniel was fond of elaborate plans. This one felt too simple. To arrange his death so easily and leave him in the snow?

The first men rushed him. He reached for the power and met them, and kept killing until they bore him down.

Reese wrenched herself as hard as she could, trying to break the man's grip on her. When she got out of this— when she and Hirianthial got out of this—she was taking self-defense lessons. And lifting weights. And buying a real weapon . . .

If she could just get to her boot!

Oh, God, Hirianthial! That arrow in his chest . . . was it low enough to hit his heart? Was he dying back there? She tried to look over her shoulder, then threw herself that way when she saw the number of people sprinting toward him. Freedom, he couldn't survive that! She had to help him!

Baniel shoved her forward again, but he had to use both hands to do it. With her mouth free, she howled for help. Screamed until her throat felt raw in the cold.

Again and again, cursing him halfway through it, writh-
ing for her boot and the dagger burning to be used. He
fumbled her arms and she lunged for the hilt, fouling it on
the way out from under her skirts and half-falling against
him before she squirmed around and stabbed him as hard
as she could. Blade met meat, ground against something,
sank until the crossguards struck his clothes.

"Take that, bastard," she snarled.

. . . and he . . . he *smiled* at her. With a heave he pushed
her away and she stumbled, falling onto the damp ground.
What the hell? She glanced toward the balcony and saw
people crowding there. The guards that had been myste-
riously absent for this mess were running toward them
with swords drawn. She looked at Baniel again and saw
he'd assumed a dramatic pose, bent over one knee with his
hand pressing at the wound, streaked with blood brighter
than his robes. When the guards reached him, he said,
"Thank the Lord and Goddess you've come. My brother
. . . my brother and his mortal pet intended to kill me, and
when my allies came to my aid, he revealed the depths of
his depravity. He is a mind-mage! See for yourself, he killed
them all with his mind alone! Like Corel, out of legend!"

They all looked toward Hirianthial, who had fallen in a
circle of the slain, a radius of dead that extended just as the
one on Kerayle had. One of the guards made a sign over
the edges of his chest.

"No, wait!" she cried. "That's not how it happened!"

They were ignoring her to help Baniel up. She pushed
herself to her feet and ran toward them. "No, he's wrong!
It was a trap! He did it!"

The sword pointed at her throat stopped her. The man
holding it snarled something at her she couldn't understand, which made her realize Baniel had made his accusation in Universal. She stared at him, aghast.

Baniel's expression remained the picture of wronged innocence as he spoke. "The lieutenant says he will not strike you, being that you are female if not a proper woman, but if you continue advancing he will have no regrets running you through."

She tightened her hands into fists but said nothing and let the guards motion her to begin walking. Behind her she could hear them talking over the bodies left by Hirianthial's attack, then the shuffling of boots on the ground. The first grunts of effort made her sneak a look past her shoulder; they were picking Hirianthial up and bringing him with them. Did that mean he was still alive? She sucked in a breath. The thought of him dead was unbearable. After all they'd been through, to be cut down here? Like this? With swords and arrows!

If she could just get him away from them, she could take him someplace with real medicine. If he wasn't already dead. If she could get away. If, if, if.

Reese lowered her head to hide her expression and gritted her teeth. She was not going to let these people win. And Hirianthial was not dead. She'd know it.

The guards marched her into the palace by way of a stair that led back into the gallery—apparently the more civilized way to descend from it onto the palace grounds—and from there to the central hall, where the silence fell with such speed it felt artificial. Liolesa was near her throne, conversing with Araelis, and she was the last to stop talking. She made it seem a choice that she paused to pay attention to the people bleeding on her blue carpet, and when the guards set Hirianthial down on the floor none too gently, she glanced at him without any change of expression at all . . . save her eyes. Her eyes had gone cold. Reese found herself thinking, ridiculously, that here finally was a look that her mother couldn't best.

To the guard in the lead, Liolesa said sharply in Universal, "What goes on in my hall?"

The guard began to speak and Liolesa cut him off. Reese had never heard her sound so curt: there was a power in it that stiffened everyone around her. "Speak in the language I use."

"Your cousin assaulted a man of the Church," the guard said, in accented Universal this time—dammit, had he understood her out there and pretended otherwise?—" who was only trying to save his soul. Father Baniel drew his brother aside when he heard of his sinful powers, and for that he has been repaid with treachery."

Reese began to object but Liolesa's eyes met hers, so swiftly Reese almost missed it. That look stopped the words in her mouth. Why? Why did Liolesa want her to be quiet in response to these lies? When it was obvious the guard had been coached? And not on the way to the palace . . . this man had to have been Baniel's from before. No doubt that's why the guards had been missing in the first place.

"What sin is this?" a woman said, pushing her way forward. She wore green, and the medallion hanging from her neck was the same hooved lion that Hirianthial had warned her belonged to the Queen's chief enemies. She was using Universal too . . . why? Maybe she didn't want that cutting tone aimed at her when she was busy trying to make a point.

The guard said, "Hirianthial Sarel Jisiensire is a mind-mage. You need only look over the balcony to see the wages of his sin. He is Corel come again, and for that he must be slain!"

The hall erupted into hissing whispers and discussion.

"So you mean to say that the Queen's cousin is a mind-mage?" the new woman said, her voice carrying.

"He is," the guard said. "I swear to it, and the evidence is there."

"Surely she didn't know," the woman said, eyes wide in a shock even Reese could tell was feigned. "The Queen cannot countenance such a thing. It would endanger everything, everyone. Our own history tells us of the dangers of the mind-mages."

"But she did know," Baniel said, still bent and bleeding and looking far too noble in his suffering. "She did. She sent the palace's own former chaplain to tutor him."

Now there were no whispers, only silence. Liolesa's boredom fell through it like a stone. "You are suggesting I was having my cousin trained to serve as my pet killer?"

"With a mind-mage at her side," Baniel said to the congregation, "who could stand against her? You see already how far she is willing to go. She has given land—land on our own planet—to a mortal and a *human*! Why would she do this, did she not think she could quell objection?"

Araelis stepped forth. "You can't seriously be suggesting something so ridiculous. Why would the Queen need someone to enforce her will? She's the Queen. She already has power for life . . . and an entire cadre of dedicated soldiers willing to kill for her. You want to tell me you are more afraid of a single man than you are of the entire complement of Swords?"

"I think the evidence speaks for itself," Baniel told her, chin high. He dripped blood on the floor, bright drops against white stone, something he had to be holding his robes close to manage.

"We cannot allow this to stand," the other woman said. She lifted her arms. "Those of us who disagree with the Queen's foreign policy, who have always disagreed with it, have never been allowed to speak our minds . . . or when we do, we are dismissed. But Liolesa Galare will see us ruined! Do we really want mortals overrunning our world? Do we want to mingle our blood with that of our lessers? And now this!" She turned to look at Hirianthial's crumpled body. "A mind-mage? She brought a mind-mage into our midst? Knowingly?" She turned to Liolesa. "I think it's time for me to speak the thought in everyone's mind." She drew in a breath and said, loudly, "It is time for the Galare dynasty to end!"

At the edges of the gathering, all the White Swords drew their weapons.

Mildly, Liolesa said, "And how do you propose to affect this end, Surela?"

A rustle from the gathering as all around them, Eldritch men freed their hands to reveal Alliance palmers. The sight of them was like being shot. Liolesa's enemies had modern weapons—how? The people who claimed to be against foreign influence?

It was chance that made Reese glance at Baniel in time to catch the sight of his heavy-lidded satisfaction.

"Oh, Surela," Liolesa said, shaking her head. "Really? Do you really want to begin it this way?"

"I'm sorry," Surela said. "But it has to be this way." She smiled. "But you'll find me a merciful Queen, far more than you were. Regrettably we must give the mind-mage to the Church. He is their lawful prey, and we must respect the customs that have kept us safe. But you need not die. We hear your heir is on retreat on the Isle of Songs. That seems a fitting place for you to live the rest of your days. Guards, take her away . . . and treat her well, as befits a woman of noble birth." She looked around the hall and spotted Reese. "And let her take her loyal pet with her." Her smile became more poisonous. "She'll only live a fraction of her mistress's years, but that's how it goes with pets." She turned her back on them and advanced to the throne, stepping up to the dais and settling on it. "And now," she said, "we will dispense with this language and speak the tongue of people."

The guard was the first to yell something in acclamation. Reese assumed it was 'Long live Queen Surela.' Her eyes remained on Hirianthial's body, splayed unconscious on the ground. How long ago had it been, that time she'd imagined him sprawled this way? Blood-streaked and laid low? It hurt her so badly, and enraged her so deeply, that the feelings canceled one another out and left her hollowed out and vibrating. When they dragged her away, she let them, didn't even see the walls of the palace as they passed, didn't even think until they dumped her in a room.

She also didn't see her crew until Kis'eh't and Sascha hugged her tightly, Allacazam pressed between her and Sascha's arm, and then the smell of fur focused her and she started crying. She didn't even know why. Anger? Terror?

"Boss, Boss, it's us. What's going on? They marched us here, no explanations. . . ."

Behind Reese, Liolesa said, "There is an attempt at a coup, I'm afraid."

Reese said the important thing, "They shot Hirianthial full of arrows. He's not dead yet, but he's going to die if we don't get him out of here."

"Then we'll just have to get out of here," Sascha said.

Reese lifted her head, rubbed her eyes. And frowned. "Where's Irine?"

"Somewhere," Sascha said, handing her Allacazam. At her look, he said, "We didn't know what was going on. We thought it would be best if one of us was loose. She's got Malia's telegem. If you've still got your tablet . . ."

Dressing for the presentation—she'd done that years ago, hadn't she? Reese checked in the pouch at her waist, found the tablet. She breathed out and handed it to Sascha.

"Thank the Angels," he said. "I don't think they knew what the telegem was, or they would have taken it for sure." He glanced at the Queen. "A coup, huh."

"Yes," Liolesa said, and as she came closer Reese's assumption that she was calm shattered. The waves off the Queen were too elemental to be called wrath. It was like standing next to an armed nuclear warhead.

Earth still used those. The Alliance had given them up as barbaric. Reese felt a sudden kinship with these people. Maybe they were both barbarians, but they were family, and she could get behind a good family fight. Blood knew she'd had enough practice. She petted Allacazam to steady her hands, and to feel the soothing wave of his support.

"I knew it was coming," Liolesa said. "And I wanted to spark it on my own schedule, not theirs. But they have made a tremendous mistake. A tremendous mistake."

Sascha glanced at Reese, who said, "Somehow they have palmers."

"Wait, the xenophobes have palmers?" Kis'eh't said. "Who did they get them from?"

"And why are they willing to use them?" Sascha asked, perplexed. "I thought they were against all things Alliance."

"That's it, isn't it," Reese said to Liolesa. "They used them first, so now you can too."

"You understand the laws of nature well," Liolesa said, and something about that sounded fairy-tale fell, dire in its symbolism. "One of them has ties to the out-world. Since they can't be official ties without my knowing about them, they must be to the underworld."

"Oh, blood," Reese said beneath her breath. She looked up at Liolesa. "The Chatcaava. Hirianthial has been chasing slavers who've been stealing your people. What if the reason the dragons can find them at all . . ."

"Is that they're being betrayed?" Liolesa said mildly,

and yet her incandescent rage made everyone else flinch. "Yes, the pattern had crossed my mind."

Bryer joined them from the corner of the room, feathers fluffing and then settling. "Time to go."

Reese sucked in a breath and nodded. To Liolesa she said, "Is there a place my ship can set down?"

"No," Liolesa said. "But if we can reach the library, we can use my Pad."

"Your Pad!" Reese said. And then, remembering, "Oh, the dais, right? That's why it was so springy. It's under the carpet."

"Just so." Liolesa frowned. "But you act as if you are sure we can leave. There will be armed men standing outside the door and they will have modern weapons."

"That's why Bryer's going first," Reese said. She tapped her temple. "Right around here is the only place they can hit him with a palmer if they want to hurt him. Otherwise his feathers do some magical thing that makes him impervious to it."

"Ah so," Liolesa said, glancing at Bryer with lifted brows. "You have a crew of many talents, Theresa."

"Most of which I didn't even know about until I started running all over the Alliance trying to keep Hirianthial out of the hands of slavers," Reese said, wry.

"So we break out of here, run for the Pad and take the Queen up to the *Earthrise*," Sascha said. "What about Hirianthial?"

"We're going to have to find him and get him to the library somehow," Reese said. "Talk to Malia, tell her we're coming, all right? And find out where Irine is."

"On it," Sascha said, and withdrew to a corner with the tablet.

Reese turned to Liolesa. "Our priority is getting you out of here. But once you're gone, we're not leaving without

Hirianthial. He'll die without real medical treatment."

"If they keep him here," Kis'eh't said quietly.

They both looked at her.

"You said yourself that our enemy has ties to the underworld," Kis'eh't said. "If it's the same person who's been giving away the location of the Eldritch to the Chatcaava, then it's the same people who've been chasing Hirianthial all this time. Someone gave those people real weapons, Reese. I'm betting they'll be dropping by to pick up Hirianthial too. They've wanted him for a long time now."

"They're going to keep wanting him, because they're not getting him," Reese said. She glanced at Liolesa. "Speaking of which . . . how the hell does Hirianthial have a brother who could do this and no one tells me?"

"No one told you?" she said, a hiccup in her rage. "But Hirianthial said Araelis had told you everything?"

. . . and she had set that trap herself by telling him they didn't have to discuss everything Araelis had told her. Reese sighed. "Apparently not everything."

"Your Majesty?" Sascha said. "Malia wants to talk to you." He handed the tablet over. After the Queen had backed into the corner to consult with the Tam-illee, he said to Reese, "Boss? What in all the battlehells is going on?"

"We want to hear the whole thing," Kis'eh't said.

"We might not have time for the whole thing," Reese said.

"The condensed version, then." Sascha's ears flattened.

She tried to suck in a breath and discovered she was shaking. Allacazam gave her the sound of ocean waters and she calmed her breathing until it matched their rhythm. "Hirianthial has brother who apparently hates him, and lured him into a trap by dragging me away and then having him attacked with so many people he had to use his esper abilities to stop them. That's apparently enough to get you killed here. The Queen's enemies said that Liolesa was planning on using him as a threat to force them to bow to her demands, which include making mortals land-holders." She swallowed. "Like me."

"Like . . . you?" Kis'eh't said carefully.

"I . . . ah . . . if we survive this, I apparently have a castle."

Their silence was as absolute as the ones she'd endured in the hall, but it was friendlier, and it ended more quickly. Sascha set a hand on her shoulder and said, "Boss, if there's a castle waiting for us on the other side of this, hells yes, you're surviving it. And so are we."

"A castle sounds great to me," Kis'eh't said. "As long as we can have heated floor tiles installed."

Bryer ruffled his feathers. "A sky is good."

Even Allacazam seemed to smile, something that felt like the memory of sunlight on her shoulders, except it wasn't her memory, and it wasn't the Flitzbe's. That sense of strength, of the smell of wildflowers she didn't recognize, and the sun-warmed spice of grasses . . . that was an Eldritch memory.

She put a hand to her face. She didn't want her last sight of Hirianthial to have been him crumpled on the floor in the hall, surrounded by his enemies.

Kis'eh't's hand on her elbow roused her. "Hey," the Glaseah said, quiet. "It's going to be okay. We're going to get him out of this."

"Thanks," she said.

Holding the tablet, Liolesa joined them. "We need to go soon, before my allies do something regrettable."

"Like attempt to break you out?" Reese said. "Speaking of that, what about your Swords? Are they going to do something about this coup?"

"They shouldn't," Liolesa said. "They had instructions on how to handle similar situations. I have to assume they aren't going to allow themselves to be massacred pitting their swords against energy weapons. I did not choose them to be stupid. This free agent of yours . . . she may be able to help us. The priests should know where Hirianthial has been taken. If she can get to the chapel . . . ? But she must be careful; Asaniefa's quartered on that side of Ontine."

"She can handle it," Sascha said. "Can you give her directions?"

"Of course."

Reese listened, trying to quell her anxiety. She hated the thought of her crew pent up in here with her, but she hated that Irine was out alone even more. Her nervousness must have shown, because Sascha said, "It'll be fine, Boss. My sister might not be much good in a fight, but sneaking around?" He grinned. "Remind us to tell you about how we scared our father into a clinic once."

"I will," Reese said. "When this is over." She looked at them all. "Are we ready? Do we know what we're doing?"

"From here to the library with the Queen," Sascha said. "And from there to where Irine tells us." He glanced at Kis'eh't. "You coming or going up?"

"Going up," Kis'eh't said. "If Hirianthial's as badly hurt as we think he is, I need to get the lab ready to act like a clinic. I'll take Allacazam too . . . we don't want him in a fight where he might get lost or hurt."

Reese nodded. She looked at Liolesa. "Are you ready?"

"I am," Liolesa said. "And Theresa—thank you. I expected you to prove your worth to me easily, but not quite this soon."

Reese flushed. Cleared her throat and moved out of the way. "Bryer, you're up."

Bryer looked at Kis'eh't, who nodded. "Ready? Go!"

Together the two of them rushed the door. Kis'eh't's

bulk ripped it open; Bryer's feathers flared as he leaped over her. The squeak of palmers firing, the thump of bodies striking the ground, and it was over. Sascha grabbed both the fallen guards' palmers and passed one to Reese. "Fire it, all right?"

"Don't worry," she said, though she was queasy. "I will." She hugged Allacazam against her side and ran behind them, wishing she wasn't in the damned dress and the twice-damned corset. How Liolesa was keeping up with them without any signs of distress she couldn't imagine.

They ran into more guards halfway to the library, and it worried Reese that they seemed to know how to use their weapons. Bryer's invulnerability was the only thing that kept them from being trapped in the hall.

"Hells," Sascha said as he stripped those guards too. "They've been training with these things."

"For how long?" Kis'eh't said, ears flattened.

"We'll discuss it later," Reese said. "Let's hide these people. . . . help me with this."

Together they dragged the guards into an adjacent room and shut the door, then hurried down the corridors.

No one was guarding the library.

"Why?" Reese asked as they shut the door behind them. "Why wouldn't they put guards everywhere?"

"My partisans are not likely to come here," Liolesa said. "They are allowing my allies to assume we're being held in our respective suites. Most of the guards will be there, at my office, at your rooms. And the only people who know this Pad is here are me and the Tam-illee who brought it in-system. Why would they guard a library?" She strode to the raised floor and crouched, flipping the carpet up to expose the Pad. She entered the coordinates, watched the lights go from red to amber to the blue of a full tunnel. "What's the danger in a room full of books?"

Reese shook her head. "Go up now, please. The sooner you're safe, the better."

"Follow me soon," Liolesa said, and walked over the Pad.

Kis'eh't went to her, held out her hands. Reese swallowed and squeezed Allacazam against her chest, then handed him over, hushing him with promises she prayed she'd be able to keep. Hadn't she told Hirianthial that sometimes people in power weren't allowed to keep their promises? She didn't want to be finding out this soon.

"You'll be fine," Kis'eh't repeated, clasping her arm.

"I have to be," Reese said. "Get that clinic ready."

Kis'eh't nodded and ran over the Pad, Allacazam held tightly in her arms. The moment she vanished, Reese flipped the carpet back over it and shuddered. "Okay. Three down. Now let's find our man."

Hirianthial strove for consciousness and touched it, barely, clung to it, to the stink of blood and the shriek of abused nerves, and there he would have remained but he was touched by a cold hand and the sensation that built then—

Curiosity first, anticipation heady as a kiss. And it crested abruptly into an epiphany that rolled through his body like the shudder of thunder, a knowing so intimate and so eager he spilled it in tears, for he could not contain it; it was a rising, a piercing moment of glory that shattered him. Did God know everyone thus? Did He discover them thus? He had never felt anything like it, and it overcame him. He lost his grip on the world and fell into the memory of it, into gladness at having known it and grief that it had been so fleeting.

When he woke the second time, it was into the firm grip of more pain than he'd felt in his life, and he had lived over six centuries. He froze, almost didn't breathe for fear of inciting it. What had they done to him? He barely remembered the fight, and then briefly being aware of Ontine's carpets. Had they done enough to him to make him hurt this much?

There were people talking in the room. Low murmurs, but one of them was Baniel. The other he didn't recognize.

It took him several sentences to realize they were speaking Universal.

". . . on their way."

"Very good. You had what you wanted of him?"

"Yesssss."

"And it was good, I see." A smile in Baniel's voice, sardonic. "You will forgive me my envy."

A huff. "Make him ready."

"Of course."

The door squeaked as it scraped on stone: he was in the catacombs, then, from the sound and the wet chill in the air, close and sour with mold.

Robes hissed on the floor. A stool dragged across the ground, creaked beneath the weight that settled on it.

Hirianthial reached toward that presence and lost the world for pain. When he swam back to consciousness, he found a foot pressing on his wrist, which was how he knew it had been broken. His eyes watered.

"You may try to slay me if you wish, but you'll find your previous exertions have strained you," Baniel said. "You may wish to leave off, if you want to have a last, touching conversation with your estranged brother before we are forever parted."

"Is . . ." He licked his lips and forced the words out. "Is that a promise?"

Baniel's smile was in his words again. "Oh, indubitably. We are both ready to be quit of one another, I think."

"And you will kill me," Hirianthial said.

"Don't be dull," Baniel said. "Killing you would be too easy. No, brother, I intend you to live a long full life . . . far, far away from anything or anyone you care about."

"If you leave me alive . . . I will kill you, Baniel. It may take the rest of my life, but I will kill you."

"Perhaps," Baniel said. "But not before I'm done destroying everything you think worth living for. I've already made a good start. Shall I prove it to you? Let me." He leaned forward, fingers lighting on Hirianthial's head, teasing through the strands of hair. The touch reminded him powerfully of the Rekesh, but reaching for the power made his eyes swim and the world bleed white.

When he could focus again, his brother had all his hair in one hand. He tugged, lightly. "A man should have locks as long as his years, yes? Proof that he is a man, and heir to all that men may have: power, wealth, a wife, a place in society." A sharp jerk and the strands swung back to brush his face, their shorn edges barely touching his throat. "I took your parents. Now I have made you a pariah among our people: Corel come again, they are calling you. Your wife you thoughtfully took care of yourself. But I am not done." Baniel reached forth, found the dangle and jingled it, the bell singing thin and small in the dank room. "When I have finished with your little mortal friends, I'll have someone cut this off for me. It won't be long."

Hirianthial stared at the coil of white strands in front of him. The chill on the back of his neck was foreign, sucked him straight back to his earliest memories before he'd been allowed to wear an adult's length.

"Goodbye, brother," Baniel said. Another of those smiles. "And good luck—with the dragons."

It was as if he'd been struck fresh with another arrow. His eyes flashed open. "No—"

"Oh yes," Baniel said. "Oh yes." Chuckling, he shut the

door, snuffing the light in the room. Hirianthial dug his fingers into the rock floor but couldn't push himself up. He had to escape. Had to warn the others, the Queen . . . if his brother could hand him over to the Chatcaava, what else had he arranged? But he couldn't rise. Couldn't reach out for any mind without incurring a pain so intense he could barely keep from vomiting. He made the effort anyway and lost his awareness of time in the attempts, until at last his cheek struck the ground and he couldn't lift it again.

Of all the captivities he'd endured, this one was the most galling. To be handed over to slavers by a man he should have killed decades ago. . . .

He would either escape, or go to confinement. Either way he would live, and in life there was hope that he might come back and finish the execution he should have committed when the blood was fresh and the memories cruel as wounds. He had lived to regret leaving Baniel alive. He would return the favor.

Sneaking through an Eldritch palace while dodging guards and random passersby was an experience Reese never wanted to repeat, especially not while caged in a corset and struggling to handle very noisy skirts. But somehow they made it across the length of Ontine and into a far more modest wing of the palace, where the ceilings didn't loom high enough to give her agoraphobia and the furniture wasn't too expensive to sit on. They'd barely gained that hallway when they were stopped by several very aggressive men dressed in white.

"No, no, they're ours!" said a familiar voice, and Irine pushed past them to throw herself into Reese's arms. "You're safe!"

"What, no hugs for me?" Sascha said.

Irine snagged him with her other arm and squeezed

them into a single embrace. "Hugs for everyone," she said. "Come on, in here." She pulled them into the room. "The angels decided to smile on us today. Reese, this is Elder Urise and his acolyte, Belinor."

The thin old man swaddled in the cot met her eyes and then smiled, and the brilliant warmth of it almost made her miss the bruising on his face and what she could see of his neck. "At last. Here is the source of the good lord's distractions."

Before Reese could decide how to respond to that, Irine shook her gently. "They know where he's being held. And they can get us there."

"But we have to go with you," the youth standing at the cot said, his Universal an accented staccato.

"Plus, we have men with swords!" Irine added.

Reese glanced over her shoulder at the two Eldritch at the door. "You are Liolesa's bodyguards?"

"You have the right of it, if not the nuance," one of them replied, and his accent was far cleaner.

"What's the nuance?" she asked.

"We are bodyguards who have trained to work together as soldiers, and we are fifty in number."

"Oh!" Reese said. "Well. That's a lot of nuance."

Sascha snorted.

"Anyway, yes, you can come with us, and if you turn out to be our enemies and you're lying to us about all this, I'll kill you myself before I die," Reese said, and was surprised to discover she meant it. "But time's wasting. Can we get moving? Before they kill Hirianthial?" She glanced at Irine. "I assume Sascha told you about the Pad, and you told them?"

"I didn't have to."

"We are the Queen's Swords," one of the armed Eldritch said. "We know her contingency plans. And we have had some training with foreign weapons, if you have them."

"Hand out the candy," Reese said, and let Sascha handle it as Irine grasped her arm. "What? What's left?"

"One thing before we go," Irine said. She grabbed a bag from the floor and thrust it into Reese's arms. "There's an empty room next to this. Let's get you changed."

"Do we really have time for this?" Reese asked, though she desperately wanted the answer to be 'yes.'

"You'll slow us down and make too much noise like this," Irine said, turning her to face the door and giving her a push. "Come on, let's get it done."

Reese had wondered how they were going to 'get it done' quickly. Irine answered that by taking a knife to the laces and cutting her out of her costume. She stared at the puddle of satin at her feet and struggled with a sense of dismay and foreboding.

"It's just clothes," Irine said. "If you're going to get upset about anything, get upset about your empty boot."

"My empty—" She stopped, remembering the dagger Baniel had used to lend credibility to his story. The weapon she'd promised Hirianthial she'd treat better than her first, and now she'd left both of them behind! She scowled. "That bastard. Next time I won't miss with it."

"That's the spirit."

Reese pulled on her pants, her shirt and belt, transferred her data tablet to the inside pocket of her vest before shrugging it on. Her hand glided over the medallion with its rampant unicorn; she paused, turned it over to trace the tiny figure on the back, sword and flowers entwined. There was no doubt in her about any of this. Ordinarily she would have found that strange, but maybe she'd grown inured to shocking twists of fate during the initial pirate-slaver adventure. Rescuing the Eldritch from disaster seemed like an appropriate encore. They wouldn't know what hit them, if she had any say in the matter, and there was no question that she would.

Reese tucked the medallion under her shirt. "Let's find Hirianthial and get out of here."

"There's at least one good thing about all this," Irine said as she led Reese out.

"What's that?"

"This time we don't have to worry about a cargo rotting out on us."

It took Reese a moment to make sense of that and then she surprised herself with a laugh. "It's too bad. We could have used the bombs."

Of course the Eldritch had dungeons. The youth guiding them through it had objected to the word—he insisted on calling them catacombs—but it was a dank maze lit by torches where evil Eldritch kept prisoners; as far as Reese was concerned, that made the place a dungeon. It was large enough not to be crawling with guards, which she'd been expecting, and for that she gave thanks. The men they brought were equal to the ones they ran into. Olthemiel was the name the first had given her, and the other was Beronaeth, and they were as grim a pair as she'd seen; their faces reminded her of Hirianthial's when he'd been talking about chasing down pirates and slavers.

They were so adept at handling the guards that it worried her when they stopped at a junction. Olthemiel withdrew, joining them a few feet back.

"What's wrong?" Reese whispered.

His eyes were somber. "We face priests now."

"What does that mean?"

"They may be able to sense us coming," Belinor said. The young priest held his robes closer against the chill. "Or they may be able to warn others by sounding an alarm with their minds."

To him, Olthemiel said, "You know what we must do."

"They would have killed my master, who is a good man, and one of their own. Why should we have more mercy than them?"

"Does this mean you're planning to kill them?" Sascha asked. "In an ambush?"

"Does that trouble you?"

"Hell no," Reese said. "Go for it." Olthemiel looked at her sharply, and that was enough evidence of surprise for her to say, "I think it's pretty obvious who the bad guys are. I'm not going to shed any tears about people who want to arm the Queen's enemies with guns they got from pirates."

He studied her a moment longer, brows up. Then inclined his head and went to join his man at the edge of the corridor.

Sascha whispered, "Sure you're all right, Boss?"

"Yes," Reese said, but reached for his hand anyway. She closed her eyes, listening to her heart race, fighting nausea. Would they ever attack? Would they be found? Would they end up in cells of their own? They'd found a way out of the first one they'd gotten thrown into, but she didn't want to push her luck. Besides, somehow she doubted the little trick she'd tried on Inu-Case would fool any Eldritch.

The barest scrape of boot heel against ground and her guards were gone. A moment later, she heard the scuffle and the bodies as they hit the floor. Sascha pulled her to her feet and they darted around the corner, Bryer and Irine at her heels and Belinor taking the rear.

"Here," Olthemiel said, hauling on a heavy door at the end of the corridor.

Reese dropped Sascha's hand and ran. She was too frightened to walk: if he was dead she had to face it now, before she lost her nerve. And the first sight of him, spilled on the ground, almost choked her breath out of her. She fell to her knees beside him and put her hand on his shoulder and hell with the Eldritch touch thing, she had to know—

—his skin was warm. That was good, right?

"Hirianthial," she whispered. "Please, please don't be dead." She bent down, trying to see his face. "Oh please, don't be dead."

He didn't answer and she let her head slowly fall until her brow rested on his hair. Under the blood stench, he still smelled like expensive cologne. It made her chest shudder, which is how she knew she was trying not to cry. To distract herself, she petted the silken hair . . . and discovered that most of it was missing.

Was it her indignation that woke him? He must have felt it surge in her, an outrage out of proportion to the triviality of the offense. But he opened his eyes, just enough to see her.

And then he spoke, rusted baritone gravel. "It will. Grow back. Lady."

"It was so beautiful," she said, tears leaking, drop by heated drop. "And they cut it!"

His chuckle was so rough it hurt her throat to hear it. But he had laughed—how was that possible?

"Can you be carried?" Reese asked. "We have to get you out of here, but will you bleed to death if we lift you?"

"They . . . have stabilized me. Or I would have died much earlier. That is . . . my guess."

"Your guess!"

He closed his eyes, concentrating. "Better a death . . . in the arms of friends. Than to stay here."

Her heart contracted so hard she thought she'd pulled a muscle in her chest. Her fingers fell off the shorn hair, touching the edge of the dangle . . . was it her imagination, or did he tense and then relax? She hoped all he felt through her fingertips was her concern, her grief at the sight of him this way, and her absolute resolution to save him. That and . . . everything else, all the things she could no longer hide. Her head slowly fell until it rested against her wrist and she whispered, "Oh, Hirianthial. We have got to stop with you ending up places like this." She managed a watery smile. "Prison cells aren't really your speed."

"Noted . . . for the future."

"I hope so," she answered, hushed, trying to hide her tears. She pulled her hands back to keep from discomfiting him and waved Bryer inside.

"Reese," Hirianthial said, as the Phoenix bent toward him. Bryer paused so she could lean toward him . . . but whatever he'd been planning to say was lost with the consciousness that drained from him, taking the animation from his face, the glow, the warmth. Bryer shook his feathers and gathered the Eldritch from the ground.

"Oh, blood, be careful—"

"Know what I do," Bryer said. And then, with more of an effort, "Trust me."

She'd never heard the Phoenix say anything like it, and was so shocked she could only watch as they left the cell. Then she shook herself and hurried after, wiping her face. The guards were conferring with Bryer, which gave her time to rub her nose and put herself back together again, and once she had she found the twins watching her with expressions she couldn't quite place. Not sad, and not proud, and not gentle, but all of those things?

"So," Sascha said, quiet. "You finally know."

She looked toward the body in Bryer's arms, saw the slack face with its too-short hair and over the neck the dangle now absurdly long without the mane to give it context. Swallowing, she met their eyes and said, "Yeah. Yeah, I know."

"Are you going to say something?" Irine said.

Reese shook her head. She lifted her hands to stop them from saying the inevitable. "He knows. He knows, and he hasn't said or done anything. I mean, how could he not know? He can read my mind. Has read it." She drew in a shaky breath. "I'm centuries too young for him, can't marry him, can't have his children and I'll be dead in the blink of one of his eyes. I won't force the issue. How could I?"

"But if he wanted it . . . ?" Irine asked, cautious.

Reese looked down. In the face of Hirianthial's injuries, she could no more deny her feelings than she could stop breathing, stop leaking tears. "I'd say yes." Up now, at their eyes. "Oh, I'd say yes."

Sascha stepped forward, clasped her arm. "Then let's get this business taken care of."

She covered his hand with hers and followed the guards.

Returning to the library, even with two casualties, was a lot easier with Belinor and the Swords to show them the back ways through the servants' halls. Even with Urise tottering on his acolyte's arm, they made good time. At Olthemiel's signal they emerged into the palace proper, pouring into the hall outside the library. There was no one in the hall: nothing between them and freedom. Berona-eth reached for the library door

. . . which opened for him . . .

. . . on the woman who'd run screaming from Reese upstairs, the one who'd told everyone about them.

Thaniet stopped abruptly, startled, and then her eyes flew to Bryer and the burden in his arms. She squeaked at the sight of Hirianthial, hand flying to her mouth. Reese almost forgave her the whole spying business when she saw the woman's dismay. Almost.

Olthemiel drew his sword.

"Are you going to kill her?" Sascha asked sharply.

"In front of two priests!" Irine added, though Urise was barely conscious.

"She is Asaniefa's woman," the Sword captain said. "She must be dealt with either way."

"Oh, oh, I won't tell Surela!" Thaniet exclaimed, going gray at the sight of the naked blade. She looked to Reese and said, rushing the words so fast they almost tripped on her accent, "I didn't know. I didn't know it would come to this."

"You have got to be kidding us," Sascha said, ears flicking back and teeth showing.

Reese remembered all the times she'd steadfastly refused to think something through because she hadn't wanted to face the repercussions. "No . . . I believe her." To Thaniet, she said, "But you're a risk we can't take. I'm sorry."

Thaniet gasped in.

"We could take her with us?" Irine said. "Maybe?"

"So she can sabotage the ship?" Sascha's ears were still flat.

"She doesn't know enough to sabotage anything," Reese said.

Bryer sighed and shifted Hirianthial in his arms. In a motion faster than Reese could track, his arm flashed out, smashed against the woman's head, and resettled Hirianthial in its crook. Thaniet dropped like a stone.

"You didn't—"

Beronaeth was already tying her hands behind her back and dragging her into a nearby room.

"She'll live," Olthemiel said. "Go, now. We'll guard."

"You won't come with us?" Reese asked.

"Someone must stay, take the Pad so it can't be used by the Queen's enemies," Olthemiel said. More quietly,

"We have our orders, Lady. We go into the countryside to await her direction, protect her assets. Go now, and delay no longer."

"Right," Reese said. "Everyone through."

The Pad was still on standby when Reese flipped the carpet up to check on it. She brought it to full power, watched the lights well as the tunnel stabilized. When it chimed she said, "Bryer, go!"

Bryer jogged across the Pad. The twins followed. The young novice hesitated, then re-shouldered his master's arm and the two of them tottered over it together. Reese brought up the rear, and the last thing she saw was Beronaeth bending to the Pad . . . and then she was home, amid the familiar smells and sounds of the *Earthrise*. Bryer was gone already, no doubt on his way to Kis'eh't and the lab/clinic. But the twins were waiting for her, with Malia and a blonde Tam-illee woman—Taylor Goodfix, Reese assumed—and next to them—

"Your Majesty—"

"Liolesa."

"Liolesa," Reese said, and sighed. "Now what?"

"Now what" was actually not an easy question to answer. They met in the mess hall to discuss it over one of Kis'eh't's apple pies: not fresh, but leftovers from the trip in. It reheated well, but Reese had no appetite and pushed it away in favor of the coffee. Blood, but she'd missed coffee.

"So the next step is for you to call for help from the Alliance, right?" Reese said. "You can do that, you're an allied power."

"That's correct," Liolesa said. Like Hirianthial had always seemed to be, she was completely at ease in the *Earthrise's* humble mess . . . but that didn't make it feel any less surreal to Reese, to have an Eldritch Queen sitting on one of her battered chairs, her pale beige satin overflowing it with pearl-encrusted folds.

"Fleet's stretched thin if my sources are right," Malia said. "My Lady, there may not be much they can do for us."

"Even one ship will be enough," Taylor said. "It doesn't even have to be very big. Or they can just ship us weapons. We'll do the rest."

Malia nodded. "Bring the family in. Nine generations of us have been waiting for this moment, my Lady. You need only say the word."

"And I may call on them yet," Liolesa said. "But let me see what my ally might do for me first."

"So we head back, is that it?" Reese said.

The door opened for Kis'eh't, who padded in and said, "Did I hear someone say something about leaving? Because Hirianthial needs a real Medplex as soon as possible."

"He's not—" Reese half-rose.

"He's stable," Kis'eh't said. "Not because of us, mind you. Someone did a job on him before we did. Someone with modern medical equipment." She glanced at Reese. "You know what that implies."

"That we were right about someone on the world selling him to someone off it?" Reese said. She sank back into her chair and rubbed her eyes. "Fine. So the decision is pretty easy, right? We zip away, grab help, come home."

"Can you do that?" Irine asked Liolesa. "I mean . . . you're the Queen. Can you just leave your planet like this? Wouldn't that be . . . I don't know." She glanced at her brother, who said, "Abdication in favor of the rebelling government."

"My chancellor remains on-world with my heir, whom I have not yet formally set aside," Liolesa said. "Neither of them have yet been slain or taken prisoner by the usurpers. So long as they remain on the world and at large,

Surela cannot make her claim to the Alliance. Particularly not with me there first, asking their aid."

"Sounds like a plan," Sascha said. "When should we—"

The intercom sounded, the triple-buzz of an emergency. Reese jumped from the chair and struck the button. "Yes?"

"Pirate has arrived. Am moving now."

Sascha hissed. "Battlehells. Tell him I'm on my way up!"

"Hide us somewhere!" Reese said, but the Harat-Shar was already gone. Taylor was quick on his heels.

Irine grabbed her tail, eyes wide. Reese leaned over and touched her shoulder. "We didn't come this far to end up slavebait at the end, all right? Go help Sascha. Kis'eh't—"

The Glaseah was already jogging out the door. "I'll go keep the vigil. Malia? Can you help? Have you had first aid training?"

"I'm with you," Malia said.

The room, emptied of everyone but herself, still didn't seem large enough to contain an Eldritch Queen. Particularly not this one, who reacted to the crisis by calmly sipping her coffee and setting the cup with deliberate precision on its chipped saucer.

"You're not worried?" Reese asked.

Liolesa said, "Not about what you are, no. They're not here for us. So long as your men get us out of the way before they notice us, they won't have cause to seek us." She looked up without lifting her face, and even shielded by her lashes, her eyes burned. "Over a thousand years, Theresa. Over a thousand years since our Settlement and we have remained hidden all this time. Our world isn't even in your navigational database. All these years, and now our secret has been revealed . . . by a traitor, to our enemies. There is a pirate heading for my world." She inhaled, like a dragon about to stream fire. "Yes, I am worried. About how far I'll go to destroy everyone and everything that has endangered my people."

Reese remembered to swallow, though her mouth had gone dry. She offered, "That . . . sounds . . . like a good thing to me."

"Does it?" Liolesa asked, glancing at her sharply. And then she chuckled, though the sound was bitter. "We shall see if you still think so ere the ending."

"I don't think I'll change my mind," Reese said. "I have a temper myself. A little one."

Liolesa snorted. "Then we are well-matched." She paused as the humming under the deck-plates changed. "We are moving?"

Reese tapped the intercom again. "Hey, bridge."

Irine answered. "They're still at the edge of the system, so we're getting out of the way before their sensors can pick us up. Malia says her people don't have a ship in-system that can do anything about them, and unless they head for the moon, the permanent base can't help either." A pause, then dry, "They have a base on the moon, by the way."

Malia's voice now: "It's debatable whether the moon-base could take on this thing anyway. It's half weapons. The other half's engines. Our outpost is an outpost; it's got room for ten people and only six people sleep there at a time."

"If the pirate's half engines and half weapons, where do they keep the crew?" Reese asked.

"I'm guessing in EVA suits strapped to the outside."

Reese smiled despite herself. "So they're definitely heading for the world?"

"Straight for it," Irine reported.

Reese looked now at the Queen. "They're going to meet the person who summoned them."

"Yes," Liolesa said, watching her now.

"And you . . . you have to go," Reese said. "Not only that, but you have to take my ship, because it's the only one here now." She turned to the intercom. "Right? Malia, you Tam-illee don't have one of your courier ships here right now, or due soon?"

"No," Malia said, sounding pained.

Reese looked at Liolesa. "The *Earthrise* is it. Your only ride out."

"Yes." Quieter now.

Reese swallowed. "Someone should stay behind. Find out what's going on."

From the intercom, Irine said, "Reese!"

Ignoring her, Reese asked the Queen, the Queen to whom she had just sworn an oath: "Yes?"

"I will not make you do this, Theresa," Liolesa said. "But if you were to remain and give our allies a flag to rally to, coordinate their efforts . . ."

She was crazy to even be considering this, and yet she was. To let someone else take her ship, bring Hirianthial to the help he needed . . .

That it upset her more that she wouldn't be there to make sure he'd be all right no longer surprised her, but it did make it very clear how much had changed. She could say a temporary goodbye to her ship. To trust other people with Hirianthial's safety had become far more difficult.

"I lost the deed," she said suddenly, because it hurt, because she was feeling her way through the responsi-bilities she'd accepted only a few hours ago and they felt too real to be so new. She'd been reading novels of epic romance for all her adult life, but she'd thought she was clear on the difference between fantasy and reality. So why did all this ring through her like a bell, rise in her like song? "It's somewhere in the gallery of your ballroom. If Hirianthial's brother didn't rip it up while I wasn't paying attention."

"The deed can be duplicated," Liolesa said. "And it is only a piece of paper. The property is yours, Reese. You and your own have paid for it already in blood. And make no mistake, you will pay for it with more, ere the end."

Again, like a song, like the distant sight of banners . . .like blood in the soil. She shivered, swallowed and forced herself to composure. When she was sure she could talk without her voice cracking, she said, "I'd need a few telegems."

"You'll have them."

"And I could really use a Pad . . ."

"If you coordinate with the Swords, they might be able to bring mine free of the library and on to you," Liolesa said.

Reese frowned, thoughtful. "And some of your Tam-illee? We need more people who understand the technology."

Malia's voice now, through the speaker: "We'll all volunteer. There are only seven of us in-system, but we're yours."

"And I'll come too," Irine said.

"Irine, Sascha can't stay with us," Reese said. "The *Earthrise* has to take Hirianthial to a doctor and he's the best pilot we've got."

"I know," Irine said. "And I'll miss him. But he'll be back. And he'll get Hirianthial there faster than anyone else."

"And in one piece," Sascha promised, his voice thinned by his distance from the pick-up.

Reese rested her brow against the wall beside the intercom. The cold metal stuck to the sweat on her skin; she could taste the salt when she licked her lips. It all came down to one thing: had she meant it when she'd said she would help? Had she really been willing to commit to a world full of far too beautiful, far too perfect, irritating, elitist, xenophobic princes and princesses?

No, that wasn't the question, was it.

Was she willing to stay, even if Hirianthial didn't?

. . . if he died?

The thought pierced her, stole her breath. He could die. Right now. On the way out of here. Hundreds and hundreds of years older than her, with centuries yet to live and he could die and leave her without his frustratingly beautiful accent, the distracting and infuriating way his hair never seemed to need care, the precision and grace of his movements, the terrifying understanding of how much he knew—about her, about life, about everything—that she would never have time to learn.

And it could all be snuffed out in the next few hours.

She could outlive him.

"Nothing is certain, is it," she murmured.

"Not in this life, no," Liolesa said.

Reese shuddered and forced herself upright. Squared her shoulders, staring at the smudge she'd left on the bulkhead. She wiped it with her sleeve and turned to Liolesa. "I'm still your woman, Liolesa."

Liolesa rose and joined her by the intercom. "It takes a rare heart to make the choice you are making now, Theresa."

"Yeah, well . . . my family always told me I was a misfit." Reese lifted her chin. "Tell me what you need me to do while you're gone. We'll get it done."

"This world won't know what hit it," Irine said through the intercom.

"You know it, fuzzy."

INTERLUDE

The body standing at the window fascinated Baniel. It was a perfect mimicry of an Eldritch: the skin was right, even to the glow gathered from the reflections of the sun off the snow. The height, the build. The clothes hung on it correctly. Even the hair fell a proper length for a nobleman, nearly to the waist in a long sheet. But the face, when it turned in profile, revealed eyes like drops of water, colorless, subject to the alien shape of their pupil . . . just a little too oval for the species the Chatcaavan was duplicating.

It was a good copy. The imperfection was jarring.

"So these abilities." The alien studied his long-fingered hands, flexed them. "You will educate me in them?"

"Such education is a matter of more than a few hours," Baniel said. "Is your ship not approaching orbit now?"

"It is. But I am considering a change of plans."

"How so?" Baniel asked, growing very still.

"I think I might stay."

Baniel studied the alien. "Is that so."

"I do not yet have a planetary fiefdom," the Chatcaavan said. "I like this world. I think I shall keep it."

"And the people?" Baniel asked.

"Oh. . . ." The Chatcaavan waved a hand. "To be sold, or used. I will bring enough people to keep them cowed. While they last, anyway. I have heard your kind are fragile and die easily."

"Won't your superior be displeased? I thought your purpose was to bring back word of the location of the world to him."

"My superior wants Eldritch captives," the alien said. "I shall deliver them, beginning with the one who supplied me with this . . . very enticing . . . shape. But I doubt he will much care that I am claiming the world for my own given how far it is from the empire. We'd have to cross the Alliance to reach it, which makes it far too distant to be easily managed without an overseer. Someone to breed the stock." He lifted one brow and smiled, and that smile looked alien on his face: his eyes remained a reptilian blank despite the creases around his mouth.

"So . . . you will take control of the world, use the people to breed slaves, and kill those who object?" Baniel said.

"That would be the plan."

"Excellent," Baniel replied. "We will have all the leisure required to educate you in the use of your new talents." He smiled. "I think you'll find the body you stole very . . . very . . . useful."

Their eyes met, and despite the alien intelligence in the one, they were very similar. It made the interruption of the moment jarring. Baniel turned toward the messenger, the words of reproach ready on his lips.

"My Lord!" the youth said, gasping. "The prisoner is gone!"

"Pardon me?" Baniel said.

"Gone," he said. "And all his guards dead behind him! They say the Queen has escaped as well, and her mortal pets with her!"

The Chatcaavan hissed behind him, but Baniel held up a hand. "Thank you," he said to the youth. "Go on, then. I will have instructions for everyone shortly."

The boy trembled, but withdrew with alacrity, glad perhaps not to be punished. Baniel turned to his guest.

"You have lost the prize," the alien said.

"A mere setback," Baniel replied. "Indeed, this might be even better than we planned."

"Ah?" The Chatcaavan lifted an Eldritch brow. "How so?"

Baniel smiled. "The Queen will return—she must—to

reclaim her world. And my brother will come with her, for he has me to deal with. Knowing that . . ."

"Ah." The alien smiled thinly, and already it was a better smile, a more natural one . . . or perhaps the predatory glitter in his eyes was merely a call back to his true form's face. "Yessss."

LAISRATHERA
Book Three of
Her Instruments

COMING IN SPRING 2014

The Queen of the Eldritch has offered Reese Eddings a life out of a fairy tale, one beyond the imagination of a poor girl from Mars who'd expected to spend her life eking out a living with a rattletrap merchant vessel. Unfortunately, the day she reached out to accept Liolesa's offer, Hirianthial's enemies betrayed him—and his entire planet—to a race of sociopathic shapeshifters with dreams of conquest. Now the only thing between Reese and a castle of her very own is a maniacal alien despot, his native quisling and all the Eldritch dead-set on preventing the incursion of aliens at any cost, including the ousting of their current usurper, who happens to be an alien himself . . .

Reese, Hirianthial and the crew of the *Earthrise* have been battling these pirates since Hirianthial's capture inspired their fateful meeting, but to beat them Reese will have to own the power she's always denied herself, and Hirianthial must make his peace with the bloody past and his uncertain future.

The stakes have never been higher, and this last time will count for all. The final battlefield awaits.

ABOUT THE AUTHOR

Daughter of two Cuban political exiles, M.C.A. Hogarth was born a foreigner in the American melting pot and has had a fascination for the gaps in cultures and the bridges that span them ever since. She has been many things— web database architect, product manager, technical writer and massage therapist—but is currently a full-time parent, artist, writer and anthropologist to aliens, both human and otherwise. She is the author of over fifty titles in the genres of science fiction, fantasy, humor and romance.

The Her Instruments Trilogy is only one of the many stories set in the Paradox Pelted universe. For more information, visit the "Where Do I Start?" page on the author's website.

mcahogarth.org
www.twitter.com/mcahogarth